APR 1 0 2017

ELK GROVE VILLAGE PUBLIC LIBRARY

3 1250 01176 5629

W9-AHT-583

DISCARDED BY
ELK GROVE VILLAGE PUBLIC LIBRARY

DISCARDED BY
ELK GROVE VILLAGE PUBLIC LIBRARY

ELK GROVE VILLAGE PUBLIC LIBRARY
1001 WELLINGTON AVE.
ELK GROVE VILLAGE, IL 60007
(847) 439-0447

THE FALLEN

ALSO BY TARN RICHARDSON

The Hunted
The Damned
The Risen (forthcoming)

THE FALLEN

TARN RICHARDSON

The Overlook Press
New York, NY

First published in hardcover in the United States in 2017 by
The Overlook Press, Peter Mayer Publishers, Inc.

141 Wooster Street
New York, NY 10012
www.overlookpress.com
For bulk and special sales please contact sales@overlookny.com,
or write us at the above address.

© 2016 by Tarn Richardson

All rights reserved. No part of this publication
may be reproduced, stored in a retrieval system, or
transmitted, in any form or by any means, electronic,
mechanical, photocopying, recording or otherwise,
without the prior permission of the publisher.

Cataloging-in-Publication Data is available from the Library of Congress

Manufactured in the United States of America
Typeset by Charlotte Tate

ISBN: 978-1-4683-1437-3 (US)

1 3 5 7 9 10 8 6 4 2

DEDICATION

For Maurice East,
Tacit's right-hand man, and mine too.

In memory of Anthony John Maddocks
1944–2015

"Let not the dead live, let not the giants rise again."

Isaiah 26:14

PROLOGUE

"Whoever knew men could bleed so much?"

The Priest's knees trembled as he took a step forward from the assembly of clerics into a landscape of nightmares. A hand caught and steadied the ailing figure, holding him firm until his nausea had passed.

Everywhere was covered in blood. In the cloying, churned earth, dashed across the rocks, gathered in curdled puddles from the heat of the day. Over the carpet of bodies piled on the cold ground.

"Is this really a vision of our dream?" the Priest asked, as a taller cleric, bearded and dressed in a black satin robe inlaid with carefully laced fabrics and glistening jewels, pushed past him to stand ahead of the gathered congregation. Slowly he surveyed the ruined, blasted battlements, where a mighty fortress had stood only a short time before.

"No," he said, beside a shattered column of rubble, once a vast support for the Turkish southern defences. He turned his head to look at the Priests who had accompanied him to this hellish place. "This is no dream. It is a nightmare. One that will soon embrace the entire world."

All in their party fell quiet, the only sounds those of the battlefield being cleared by those who had survived. The sounds of suffering and disorder polluted the silence, the moans of the wounded and the dying, the shrill whinny of horses trying helplessly to rise from the dirt onto shattered limbs, the panicked shouts of Russian officers attempting to regain control of their broken troops and urgently strengthen defences at the hard-fought site.

The clinging stench of smoke, the stink of gunpowder and butchery drifted across the battlefield, ravaging senses, choking throats. All life had been torn from the land with the weight of the conflict, leaving everything black and grey and crimson, everything smashed, turned to stones and wooden splinters. Every inch of the landscape had been burnt and charred, as if a great fire had been unleashed on the Turkish defences that had guarded the place and consumed almost all within it. Blackened craters littered the ground, filled with contorted bodies, twisted and torn, soldiers blown apart and lying where they had come to rest, so that they looked as if they were emerging from the fetid earth, clawing their way into the light.

For those not blasted away into bloodied hunks of meat, their bodies had taken on a drawn pallid hue, slaughtered and left to ripen under the infernal sun. Blood still dripped from the open wounds, nostrils and mouths of those caught by shrapnel, rifle bullets or the bayonet's charge. In places, Russians and Turks lay side by side, some in an embrace as if holding onto each other in a final death pact.

One of the Priests cleared his throat. "General Skobelev has taken the southern fortresses. He will hold them –"

"– until the Turks return," answered the great bearded Priest, his skin as white as the dead about him, "and in greater numbers too. We must work quickly." He peered back across the dusky landscape to the valley on the far side from where they had first entered the battlefield, towards the bleached white tent pavilion nestled on the grey granite hillside.

"They are watching," spoke the cleric who had come to close to fainting. "Czar Alexander and the Grand Duke."

"Of course they are watching us," replied the High Priest, casting his black glittering robe wide. "We promised them a miracle. Let us not leave them disappointed."

He went forward, his eyes fixed on the corpse-ridden floor over which they walked, as if searching for a specific spot, a certain location upon which to draw down his spell.

"The enemy might come back at any time!" called one of the party, his eyes trained to the far horizon.

"They will return," replied the Priest, "but not yet. Not till our work is done. It was so decreed. Here!" He commanded with a finger thrust towards the shattered ground, close to where a lone tree still stood, so much of it blasted away that only its twisted trunk and a solitary branch remained. Blood dripped from its bark, as if it were bleeding. "Set down the items here."

At once the Priests scurried forward and laid out the elaborate relics with well-trained efficiency and speed. A large silken black cloth was unrolled and set out on the churned ground, over which they laid a length of white ribbon and black candles, as thick as a man's wrist, set as the points of a star.

The moon, still drenched in the blood-red of sunset, had risen so that it sat like a dull orb in the heavens, weakly illuminating the spot where the Priests worked. Barely a breeze now graced the place the High Priest had chosen, as if nature itself had fallen silent to acknowledge the dark powers gathering.

A shard of crimson moonlight shone through the remaining tangle of twigs of the single branch, catching the folds of the Priest's dark cloak and making the gemstones sparkle like watchful eyes. He stepped back to the black cloth and regarded the assembly of objects laid before him. It seemed to please him and he smiled, turning his head heavenward, studying something within the stars. Around him the Priests had formed a circle, every eye trained on him alone.

"Will it be enough?" someone whispered.

"We have followed the ritual. Mirrored the sins. We have done all that was required of us."

"Twenty thousand lives?" another said. "Surely that is ample?"

"For them is anything enough?"

The bejewelled Priest drew himself up to his full height, his eyes staring hard into the fiery sunset. He drew a staff from his cloak, the head of which had been whittled into the image of a horned ram. At once lightning began to flicker in the heavens, and he turned his head to admire it. Thunder rumbled from the deep valleys leading down towards the Black Sea far in the east. A storm was growing. All eyes turned to scour the heavens for signs as to their coming, evidence that a link had been made. Crows, drawn by the summoning magicks and activity, had gathered in great numbers around the jagged stones and blasted trees, croaking and yammering angrily.

"For too long they have lain chained deep within the Abyss," the bearded Priest began, his voice deep, like the rumbling thunder. "They are blind to all but darkness and fire eternal, unable to feel anything but their jailers' wicked instruments of torture upon their calloused hides. But they have heard our every word, and they hear our words now! We call out to them, beseech them to prepare, for the time of their returning is nigh."

Lightning flashes streaked across the black heavens, the dark sky slashed open by forked barbs of slivery blue.

"They who would sacrifice all and nothing for their master, they who would fight and die, and yet can never be destroyed, for his majesty and his safe returning and reign, for they are as old as the foundations of time itself and created in the very fires of when time too was made."

He threw his arms wide as if crucified on an invisible cross, his left hand still clutching firm to the staff.

"Deadened eyes. Torn bloodied skin. Branded tongues burnt from toothless mouths. These are signs pleasing to our Lord. He has seen the sacrifices we have made for him here on this plain, ensuring the nourishing life-blood of the fallen has seeped down into the bowels of his domain. For too long this world has been full of light and life. A new age is coming, foretold by many, an age of apocalypse and ruin for those who choose not to believe, not to follow, not to give themselves entirely to his darkness and might."

At once, the storm seemed to dissipate and everything fell deathly still. He let his arms drop to his side. "Bring the final offering!" he called in a clear ringing voice. The crowds parted and a haggard beaten man was dragged out. He was bound by his torn wrists, but still wrestled as best he could between the two heavily muscled Priests who bundled him forward into the circle.

"Does he carry the marks of those who went before?" the bearded figure asked, as the man was thrown to his knees on the sodden bloody earth. "Of those who walked the earth as giants long ago, whose veins beat with the blood of Satan? The Nephelim?"

"He does," answered one of the Priests flanking the prisoner, reaching down and pulling up his bound hands so that the High Priest could see them clearly in the light of the pale moon. On both hands the man possessed six fingers.

The bearded Priest nodded approvingly. "We have soaked the lands with the pure blood of the innocents," he announced, drawing his arms once again wide. "Into this let us spill Satan's blood, the blood that courses within his descendant's veins before me."

A pair of ornate knives flashed from the Priest's belt and he held them high above his robed head. The grips were lined with finger holes, six of them on each dagger. A bolt of white light clashed with the glowing red dusk in the west.

"Please!" pleaded the bound man on his knees, weeping and spluttering, pressed down into the earth by the weighty hand of one of the guarding Priests. "Please! Let me go! I don't know what you mean! I'm a good man! A farmer! I know nothing of Satan!" Through tears he looked up desperately at the circle of Priests around him. "You're Catholics, like me. I recognise some of you. From local Mass. Whatever is the matter with you?"

The High Priest sneered, as if the man's words were blasphemy. "Gag him!" he commanded. "Let his tongue not tarnish this moment or erode the incantations of the spell."

At once a rag was produced and pushed roughly into the man's mouth.

"Abaddon, Prince of Darkness, Lord of the Abyss," the Priest called to the heavens, the veins in his neck protruding at the force of his voice. "I summon thee and thy six princes forth from your chains of Hell! Cross over the Abyss! Ascend, and make manifest yourselves within our mortal world and with our mortal semblance. For *he* is to return soon and *he* must be protected. We are willing servants but unable to provide him the succour and protection he requires as he prepares to ascend once more to his throne. Only thou, and thy lieutenants, can offer him the solace of the shield and the mace. Share with us thy thoughts and make known to me thy will, for thou art our guardians, and we are thy foot soldiers."

Abruptly the candles flickered as one and were extinguished by a phantom breeze.

"The flames have gone out!" someone exclaimed.

"There are new lights!" a voice cried from the opposite side of the watching circle. "Coming from within the star upon the cloth!" Tiny pinpricks of light, red and yellow spheres of flame and sparkling emeralds of fire had begun to manifest within the space above the pentagram marked out on the black background, turning and swirling as if stirred by unseen hands.

"They are gathering!" another voice called. "They are come!"

"It is them! They are coming across! They are coming!"

The dark High Priest stood unwavering, his eyes dazzled by the fire show he had summoned.

"With these blades we commit this final sacrifice." He spoke the words like an oath, before turning to stare at the gagged man. "Your fate has been decided by the blood which courses in your veins, that of the descendants from the city of Gath, those of the Nephelim, those of Lord Satan. Through your ancestry, your role is prophesied." The man shook his head and hung it low, sobbing into the choking cloth in his mouth.

"Let the blood of this sacrifice, given willingly by one of your descendants, merge with that of the others fallen in this place," the High Priest began, "be as a lifeblood to their returning. We have praised you in the three sins, we have given you this mass sacrifice to provide succour for your thirsty tongues. Now we ask you to come across the great divide and be amongst us, to act as his defenders, his lieutenants, and guide us all for when he returns."

With this, the man's hands were cut free and the daggers presented for him to take. He hesitated, and heavy hands took hold of him roughly round the neck, forcing him towards the ornate blades. The weeping man grasped the hilts weakly, his six fingers slipping into the six assigned holes, and looked to his left and right, considering his chances of fleeing. But, as if those who guarded him read his thoughts, heavy hands grabbed his shoulders and pulled up his wrists so that the knife blades were held tight to his throat.

"You have a choice," the High Priest revealed, and the man immediately looked up through his tears, "whether to live a thousand lifetimes within the deepest prisons of hell, your soul condemned to the damnation of the head jailer's whip, or" – his eyes narrowed on the prisoner – "to cut your own throat."

The bearded Priest looked down at the gagged man, his eyes boring into him, commanding him to act. The man could feel the pristine edge of the knives against his neck, the sting as they marked his skin. Once again he looked to either side, where all around the Priests were gathering closer to witness this final act. He knew there could be no chance of fleeing now, no way out of his predicament. For the last few weeks he had been held by these Priests, snatched from Mass at his local church three weeks ago and kept locked in a horse-drawn carriage as they had crossed mountains and borders to reach this place, wherever this place was. At first they had spoken kindly to him, fed and watered him. Assured him through the bars of the carriage door that he had nothing to fear. But now he knew what their intentions were. Death could be his only escape. He was a God-fearing man, but he feared the Devil even more. The thought of a thousand lifetimes within the confines of hell tormented him. He wept and remembered how painless the deaths of his goats seemed when his own butchering blade was drawn firmly across their necks.

The knives flashed one more time and then dripped with dark crimson as he toppled forward onto the blades, his severed neck bubbling with the last of his escaping breath. A cry of rejoicing went up from the crowd.

"We have bathed the lands with the blood of our enemies and drenched the spot through which they will emerge with *his* blood. Come now! Return and delay no longer!"

The dark Priest's words had barely reached the ears of the congregation when a sudden explosion of heat and flame erupted from the middle of the ring of figures, engulfing everyone in foul choking sulphurous smoke and knocking them all to the ground. About the blasted trees and crumbled foundations of the broken fortress, crows leapt from foot to foot before suddenly tumbling and falling like stones to the floor, struck instantly dead.

As the sulphur clouds lifted and the flames died, the High Priest staggered wearily to his feet, the left side of his face blistered and smoking from where he had been struck by the explosion of flame. He stared hard at the spot out of which he had expected the demons to appear, his body slumped in failed resignation.

"Damnation," he growled, like a curse.

"Where are they?" someone asked, looking about the scorched earth. Fireflies of light fizzed and flared in the circle, spiralling above the dead body of the six-fingered sacrifice, climbing higher with every passing second. "Have they come through?"

"Have they come amongst us?" another voice asked.

"I see nothing! There is nothing!"

"No," growled the High Priest, his dark eyes fixed on the lifeless body slumped across the now scorched ribbon. "The sacrifice was not enough. Twenty thousand fallen on this battlefield. It has proved to be not enough to raise them from the Abyss. But something has come through."

"How do you know? How can you tell?"

A sudden chill wind gathered among the stunned audience, tugging at their robes and gowns, crackling and spinning the last of the lights like flying embers from a dying fire. But as quickly as the wind rose, it fell away and at once the deathly calm of the battlefield returned.

"Can you not feel it?" muttered the High Priest, his burnt face impassioned. "A change has come. Something has come through. Something beneath which the wheels of oblivion shall turn."

From a ramshackle wooden house on the rocky ridge, the agonised screams of a woman shattered the quiet of the Tatra Mountain night.

"Push, Zofia!" implored the giant of a man between her feet. "Push! Our child, he is almost through!"

The mother-to-be bit hard into her bottom lip and pushed with all the strength her body could muster. At once she felt the child slip out of her and with it the pain.

"It's a boy!" cried the huge man, cradling the bloodied child within his huge hands. "It's a boy, Zofia! It's a boy!"

"My darling," Zofia wept, reaching out to take the child from him and bundling the tiny infant to her breast. "He is beautiful!"

"He is like his mother!"

"He is strong, like his father Eryk!" Zofia shot back, tears of joy and love in her eyes. "Whatever shall we call him?"

"He is a rare and beautiful thing, precious like a bloodstone," said Eryk, placing a hand upon his son's head. "Poldek! We will call him Poldek, after the gemstone he embodies. Poldek Tacit, born of compassion and generosity!"

PART ONE

"And they may come to their senses and escape from the snare of the Devil, having been held captive by him to do his will."
2 Timothy 2:26

ONE

The Inquisitor knew he was going to die. He had known from the moment they found him. Those who pursued him, he knew how thorough they were. How they could never give up. After all, he had been taught by them. He was one of them. They had shared the same faith. Now those who pursued him were dark imitations of their once proud selves, from the corruption of their minds to the hard looks they wore.

The Darkest Hand. Its reach had grown long.

Inquisitor Cincenzo knew they would catch him and they would kill him, after which they would remove every memory of him, every scrap of evidence about him from the face of the earth.

Root and branch. That had always been the Inquisition's way. They never left anything to chance. And since the Darkest Hand had infiltrated that most devout and secret of organisations within the Catholic Church, Cincenzo knew they had grown strong enough to stop at nothing to ensure that their plans went unchallenged.

He'd thrown himself from the top-floor window of the safe house two heartbeats after they had smashed their way in, catching the lower edge of the apartment terrace beneath in a shower of glass and dropping the remaining ten feet to the street below. There had been more of them waiting for him there, just as he'd expected.

He caught the Inquisitor closest to him in the throat, the man going down choking, his palms tight to his ruptured larynx. A cloaked figure flashed to his right and promptly buckled as Cincenzo delivered an almighty kick between his legs. A punch was thrown from behind and Cincenzo parried it, tearing at his assailant's eyes, raking his face. The point of a staff was hurled out of nowhere and the Inquisitor caught it and thrust it back, battering the attacker in the mouth, breaking teeth. Moments later, a grenade was in his own hand and the alley rocked with light and smoke, blinding eyes and shattering senses, disorienting all caught within its blast.

In the melée of confusion and noise, Cincenzo seized the opportunity and fled, his head down, his arms pumping, sprinting hard into the city, running with every ounce of strength he possessed. He spun out of the swirl of smoke in the alleyway into the red-grey lamp-lit streets of Rome, his Inquisitor's robe rippling in his slipstream. And as he ran, he thought about the events that had led him to become who he was, an enemy, to be murdered by those he once called allies, with whom he had worked and prayed and killed.

It had begun with the rumours months ago, the private murmurings in the inquisitional hall at the end of assignments, the talk of a darkness growing at the heart of the Vatican. At first Cincenzo ignored his fears, knowing it would be wrong to question. It was simply his duty to do as he was instructed and turn his eyes from things which troubled or concerned him. He was young and naive, only recently promoted to full inquisitional status. He put his doubts down to the rigours of the job, the horrors that he witnessed on a daily basis. The suspicions he now carried with him at all times, the questions without answers, the doubts without resolution, he buried as deep within him as he buried his blades in the bodies of his enemies.

Cincenzo had known that to talk to other Inquisitors of his growing unease would have brought down unwelcome questions from those who ruled the Inquisition. They never took kindly to the news that one of their own was having concerns. Concerns, questions, they were meant to have been crushed out of you by your master during your training years, not carried forward into adulthood when you became an Inquisitor.

But for the man now pursued through the night-time streets of Rome, the questions which troubled him, the rumours which confronted him, had never been explained as an acolyte. So instead he did what he knew would bring him damnation anyway. He went looking for answers.

Cincenzo had never expected to find them, or at least not answers that would satisfy him. But he had found something during his digging, and what he'd found had terrified him more than any of the doubts that had occupied his troubled mind.

He careered through the streets of the capital, sweeping into wide courtyards full of people and laughter, plunging into narrow empty alleyways which smelt of rot and stale water, going where his instincts led him, just running, never looking back, sweat stinging his eyes, the warm spiced Roman dusk air filling his nose, clawing at his lungs. His legs felt leaden and dead, but still he ran, never stopping, never resting, still fighting as he'd always been taught to do. A war without end.

He had to get word to them, to tell them what he had learnt, to warn those few who, like him, had also sensed the darkness and banded together in secret to face it. To warn them that history was repeating itself, only this time their attempt could not fail.

That the Darkest Hand had already secured a death grip upon the world.

The young Inquisitor threw himself into the long Via dei Pettinari and, for the first time since he had taken flight, hesitated, drawing to a retching, coughing halt, cursing and wondering if he should turn round and take another route. Behind him he heard the closing rap of feet on the cobbled streets and the decision was made for him. He flung himself on, the tread of his boots biting hard on the flagstones, his eyes firm on the way ahead.

Thirty paces in and he dared to hope. It seemed that no one lay in wait for him within that narrow way, the only sound he could hear beside his own snatched breathing being that of his pursuers' boots pounding behind him. Cincenzo could detect the tightness of breath in their throats, the coarse mutter of exhaustion on their tongues. And, for a moment, he knew he was outrunning them, they were failing, foundering, falling behind with every stride.

Belief stirred like prayer within him and a new strength returned. Doorways and shop fronts flashed by as he hurled himself out of the narrow street and into Lungotevere dei Tebaldi beyond, not stopping for an instant as he powered across it to Ponte Sisto bridge. His feet barely touching the grey cobbles as he ran, he flew up the bridge, then drew to a sudden stop.

A man, long presumed dead, stood at the apex of the bridge waiting for him. The hooded figure smiled and dropped his hand to the holster on his thigh, revealing the black enamelled grip of a revolver hanging there.

Behind Cincenzo, the shadowy figures charged from the grimy dark of Via dei Pettinari and formed a ragged line along the bridge, barring any chance of escape. The only way on was now through the man with the revolver, and the exhausted Inquisitor knew there would be little chance of managing that.

"So," the man at the top of the bridge spoke, withdrawing the revolver casually and shaking his head. His accent suggested he was Italian, but any joy and light within the language had long been crushed out of it. He clicked his tongue against his teeth and took a step forward. "You really have caused no end of trouble. What is the first rule of the Inquisition?"

The question was asked as a mocking jest and Cincenzo hesitated, looking back at the line of his brethren slowly closing in on him and then once more to the hooded man with the revolver. "Never question the faith," he replied, as one who had been instructed all his life.

The man nodded. "Never question the faith. And yet, what have you done at every turn?" He took another step closer. "I'll tell you what you have done. You've been … troublesome."

"You're not part of the faith!" Cincenzo spat back, edging slowly to the side of the bridge and considering a drop into the dark waters below. "I know what you are! I know everything."

The hooded man shook his head, his eyes narrowing to slits. "Everything, do you?"

And Cincenzo chuckled, a joyless final laugh. "I know what you're planning. What was done before. How it failed. What you hope to achieve this time."

Cincenzo looked down into the flowing Tiber below. A thirty-foot drop. The fall wouldn't kill him. The difficulty would be dropping over the side before he was shot. "You will not succeed," he told the hooded man, with something approaching victory in his tone. "You may be legion, but our numbers are growing too. Your presence is black, but behold, there is a dawn coming, and with it all evidence of your existence will be expunged." He peered back at the bridge's edge, surreptitiously creeping ever closer.

"And you talk too much," the man growled. He lifted the revolver and fired. The side of the Inquisitor's head tore open and he was thrown backwards, somersaulting over the edge of the stone bridge into the river below with a tumultuous splash. The man peered into the waters below. "And who ever said it failed the first time?"

On the path beside the river below, two figures in an embrace looked up through the murk of dusk in shock.

TWO

ROME. ITALY.

The heady scent of rose escorted the Priest and Nun as they walked beside the Tiber. By chance, their hands brushed together and Sister Isabella looked across at the man, still dressed in his black cassock, and smiled, tugging absently at the folds of her own gown, revealing a little more skin of her neckline. They stopped and turned to look at each other. She could hear the dry swallow of the man's throat in the warm quiet of the evening, and pressed home her advantage, fluttering her dark eyelashes while playing with the red rings of hair that hung on her shoulder.

The Priest's eyes widened and he swallowed again, clamping and unclamping his hands together, fighting with his private demons. A small red tongue ran across his lips before he swallowed yet again, looking away to the river like a doomed man waiting to be thrown in, perhaps thinking he could cast himself in and have his sins washed away. Salvation, he knew, lay away from here, away from the allure of this woman, but he recognised the salvation of a sweeter kind stood next to him. He looked back at her and started to speak, but stopped, rubbing his sweating hands on his cassock, his eyes once more on the river.

He remembered the words of St Augustine, feeling like Adam caught within the Garden of Eden. But here, in the shadow of the Ponte Sisto bridge, he looked at Isabella and found himself ensnared by an even greater temptation.

"Father Morritez," Isabella soothed, running her hand over her right breast so that the nipple hardened through her blouse, "do I not fascinate you? Do I not intrigue and tantalise?"

"You do," he muttered, trembling slightly. His hands shook and he knotted them in front of himself. "You do."

Isabella smiled softly and raised her delicately sculpted chin to reveal the soft pale white of her neck, the hint of pink on her chest.

"Mercy me, you do," Morritez mumbled, reaching forward and taking her fingers gently with a sweaty hand, no longer able to resist touching her. "You do," he repeated, squeezing her hand. "I have seen you often, in the corridors, in the squares about the city. You're a thing of beauty, surely in God's own image? I've never looked on anything so lovely."

The Sister's eyes widened and she levelled them at the man. "You blasphemous hound, Father Morritez!" she teased gently. "A woman in God's own image?" She tutted quietly and placed a hand over his, encouraging him to move closer. He did, with no more resistance.

"Forgive me!" he muttered, as much to his Lord as to Isabella, before leaning forward to kiss her. He was only a few inches away when a gunshot cracked from the bridge above them and a body tumbled from it, falling into the river. It hit the Tiber with a splash, and before the waves reached the river's edge Isabella was at the quayside steps leading down to the water.

"Giovanni!" she cried to the shadows beyond where Father Morritez stood, both terrified and bemused. Another Priest was already hurrying out from the hideout where he had been crouched, watching and waiting for the Father's indiscretion to be drawn out by the Sister. A sash of vivid blues and greens, colours of the Chaste, was tied round his middle. Isabella was in the cool water and wading towards the body floating past, when she ordered him to seize the errant Priest.

"What are you doing, Isabella?" Giovanni cried, one hand clutched firm to the flummoxed Father's arm, his other held out to her beseechingly. But instantly his eyes were drawn back to the bridge and the figures hurrying down the stone steps alongside it. "Isabella!" Giovanni called, but a shot rang out and he went down with a grunt.

Father Morritez leapt and recoiled in horror, dropping to his haunches, his hands held tight to his ears like a soldier manning an artillery post. A second shot caught him in the back of the neck and he slumped twitching to the flagstones of the walkway beside Giovanni, blood pouring from the wound.

Isabella dived beneath the dark waters, grabbing hold of the body from the bridge as she went. The side of the man's face had been blasted open, his wide staring eyes tracing a route upwards towards the stars. Bullets zipped and fizzed through the water around her as she kicked for the far bank. Isabella knew this was no Sicilian mafia. They were drilled, armed, indiscriminate. The mafia was many things, but it wasn't so conspicuous or so brazen in its operations.

As she reached the far side of the river bank, she was suddenly aware that the man's lips were moving, mouthing silent words. Amazingly he still clung onto life.

"What is it?" cried Isabella to the man, as another hail of bullets rippled the waters around her. She clasped him tightly, the brooch at the front of his robe coming away in her hand. "What are you trying to say?"

Breathlessly the man mouthed the same word over and over. A name. And with a final effort, a sound was pushed behind the breath.

"Tacit," Inquisitor Cincenzo said, the life slowly draining from him. "Tacit. Tacit."

Stunned, Isabella let go of the dead man, his body sinking fast beneath the surface of the river as another shower of bullets clattered about her. She stretched for the cold stone of the far bank and held onto it like a lost lover. Her feet touched the riverbed and she sprang onto the bank, rolling over and over the cobbles as more rounds sprayed around her, drawing sparks as they struck the stones.

She sank into the shadows of the far side of the walkway and lay still for a moment, trying to steady her nerves and collect her shattered thoughts on what she had stumbled into, what the Inquisitor had said with his final dying breath.

Tacit!

She could hear the armed men coming, dashing back across the bridge in her direction. She knew what they were. Inquisitors. The way they moved, the way they had acted without mercy. But even Inquisitors had limits. The Inquisition was a secret organisation, always acting under deathly silence and secrecy. She could not understand why they were here in Rome and gunning down their own kind in an open and seemingly unprovoked attack.

She leapt to her feet and ran, her sodden clothes clinging tight to her body. She wrenched her cape from her shoulders and flung it aside, moving more easily without its constricting embrace.

Behind her the pack of Inquisitors charged, their heavy footsteps slapping on the riverside path, weapons jostling in holsters. Cincenzo's killer, the man long believed dead, stopped and let them run on. Something else had caught his eye. He picked up Isabella's cape from where it had fallen, lifting it to his nose and smelling it. A smile came to his lips, as if he could recognise the sweet scent of the Sister and with it a memory long forgotten.

THREE

TOULOUSE INQUISITIONAL PRISON. TOULOUSE. FRANCE.

Tacit turned slowly on his hard bed in the cold and dark of his cell, the heavy chain on his leg clanking as it fell to the stone floor, the iron ring on his ankle cutting cruelly into the already torn skin. If it troubled the Inquisitor he made no sign, drawing a hand under his head to offer a little respite from the firm cold board which formed the bed beneath him. Sleep wasn't hard to find in that cell, not after long hours under the torturer's hand, but there was no comfort and a well-muscled arm would have to suffice as a pillow, as it had for the nine months Tacit had been held in that dreadful place.

The days of his imprisonment had crawled, as if time itself had been stretched by the monotony and torment of his confined life. His old life as one of the Catholic Church's greatest Inquisitors, dispatching monsters dreamt of only in your worst nightmares, now seemed a distant memory. The terror and fire of daily conflict had become a slowly cooling ember in the dark recesses of his mind. But despite all that had tarnished within him since his arrest and imprisonment, he could still recall with needle-like clarity the events that had led him to be bound in chains in the very deepest part of the prison: the treachery of Cardinal Poré; the fiendish but flawed plan to unleash terror within Notre Dame; the wolf pelt.

The case which had led to his incarceration had started innocuously enough, just another brutal killing of a Catholic Priest, this time Father Andreas in Arras Cathedral. With Sister Isabella at his side, sent to test his faith and see if he had fallen from his faith's vows, Tacit had quickly focused his enquiries regarding the murder on a local woman named Sandrine Prideux. Even though she managed to elude him herself, she was not able to keep the plot from him, devised by traitors within the Catholic faith and Hombre Lobo, werewolves, on the western front. A wolf pelt, taken from Sandrine's wolf father, had been sneaked into the coven of traitorous Cardinals by Cardinal Poré, part of a plot to unleash carnage at the Mass for Peace in Notre Dame in an attempt to bring an end to the world war and grant revenge to the wolves after centuries of persecution and torment. They were the Catholic Church's darkest secret, excommunicated for daring to defy the Church and cursed forever to walk as men during the day while transforming into wolves at night.

In a world fuelled by hate, at the end it was a love Tacit thought he never could feel again, this time for Isabella, which brought salvation for him and saved Isabella. Making sure she was out of harm's way, Tacit had bounded alone into the Mass for Peace and blasted Cardinal Monteria from the pulpit just moments before he had slipped the stinking wolf's pelt over his head and transformed into a bloodthirsty werewolf. Tacit wondered if he could have done anything differently to save himself, to avoid arrest. He had been over it in his mind time and time again, particularly when conditions within the prison were particularly bad. To have done so would have meant never being able to voice his true feelings for Isabella. Every time he asked himself the question, the same answer came back to him. No, he would have changed nothing.

Tacit sighed heavily, a shiver running down his spine. During the biting cold of that first winter, when the dungeon had grown so bitter that the walls froze and fingers and toes went dead to the touch, he had for a little while questioned if even he would survive it. But there was now the hint of summer in the air, a subtle warming of the cell. Not that Tacit could see it. There were no windows in his deeply buried chamber, but the ice on the walls had begun to thaw, the glistening stalactites dripping from the ceiling onto him and the piss-covered floor below. Tacit imagined the sun's warm tendrils reaching across and embracing the land, ripening the crops long dormant during the winter months. And he remembered another time, a happy time, when he worked the lands of Mila's farm, long ago, when life had seemed less dark, less troubled.

With this thought his mind turned back to Isabella, as it so often did in the darkest moments of his imprisonment, the soft feel of her skin on his fingertips, the light fragrance of her scent, her radiant beauty filling his mind. A tonic. A light in the blackness that had surrounded him since the death of Mila, his first love. A relief from his now intolerable life.

Despite the cold and dark, the memory of her could still easily be retrieved, like a hidden drawer within his mind to which he forever held the key. He thought of Isabella, of what she might be doing at this very moment, of whether her life had changed since the Mass for Peace, the event after which everything had changed for Tacit. A warmth blossomed within him and with it he dared to wonder if she still thought of him, or if he had now become nothing more than a vague memory, withered and shrunken. A weight grew in his chest, a feeling both aching and foreign, and he took hold of it and crushed it out of him with anger and spite.

Almost immediately something took the dying emotion's place within him, a pervading darkness, a shrieking, mocking thing, dripping with wickedness and alarm. This ancient evil, full of rage and remorse, attacked his mind when he was vulnerable, when he was in the darkest and most hated of places.

He sat up, his hand clutched to his head, embraced by a shroud of fear. He hated the voices and the messages they brought, but they had come to him all his life and he had learnt to find strange comfort at times in their baleful cries and grim confessions. As if through their guttural sounds, hope could be gleaned. He opened his eyes and found there were tears in them, and relief that he was still where he was, in that charnel house of torture and death. Better there than in the hellish nightmares of his mind. For he knew it was hell whence these visions came, and to which they were trying to drag him.

A mouse scurried from its hole in the corner of the room and dared to explore the ground beneath the cell's operating chair, where most of the heinous tools of torture had been played upon him. The tiny creature settled back onto its hind legs and looked up at the imposing blood-red wood of the seat, black-grey chains and manacles hanging lifeless from it, smelling of gore and sweat. The mouse caught the stench of horror ingrained within it and turned to run, darting for its hole and safety from the odious thing.

Tacit turned his eyes back to the ceiling and wondered again about the world beyond the thick walls of the place. He never knew if it was night or day, but he knew it would not be long until he heard the heavy clang of the iron gate and the sound of many heavy eager feet on the cold damp stone passageway outside his cell. Every day they visited him, the torturers of the prison, to try to break him. But his body was still resolute, his mind strong, strong enough to withstand the agonies set upon him by the torturer's hand. At least for now. How long could he hold out against their murderous tools, against the clinging dark, against the maddening sounds from the prison? Against the memories of Isabella and the ghost of their brief embrace, a memento of a life lost forever, save when it returned to taunt him in his darkest nightmares. And how long could he last against the demonic voices within him, the ones he had always heard, the ones who had always compelled him to react, as they were now, compelling him to rise and act and do?

FOUR

The Vatican. Vatican City.

"Poldek Tacit!" called Cardinal Bishop Adansoni above the growing throng of dissenters and cries of derision from the Holy See. "Poldek Tacit! Surely it is not my belief alone that he should never have been imprisoned?"

The circle of rallying Cardinals rocked and gestured manically within the inquisitional hall, a heavy scent of incense and teak oil on the air. "What are you suggesting, Cardinal Bishop Adansoni?" asked the newly appointed Cardinal Secretary of State Casado, the one supposedly in charge of keeping order within the inquisitional chamber and the protesting voices of the gathered Holy See in check. "That he should be released?"

"He murdered Cardinal Bishop Monteria!" seethed Cardinal Bishop Korek. Sitting next to the Secretary he scowled at the elderly Cardinal who, despite his years, still possessed the fire of youth behind his bushy eyebrows.

"We have since dropped Monteria's full title," countered Adansoni. "After all, the man intended to commit mass murder at the Mass for Peace in Paris." Adansoni pressed home his point with a thrust of his finger. "And he would have done so if it wasn't for Inquisitor Tacit."

"This is about who Inquisitor Tacit is, isn't it, Cardinal Bishop Adansoni?" asked Korek shrewdly, his eyes fierce on the man. "The boy plucked from his dead mother? The one the prophecy spoke of?" Adansoni made a noise of derision himself now, as if the old man's words were a pointless diversion, but Korek continued, ignoring him. "The one who will come from the East? The preordained one? That he'll be found abandoned on high and will be rescued from the clutches of death. That he'll display incredible skills of hand and eye. That he'll master languages. That victory will be his brand and emanate from him. That death will follow in his wake." Korek skewered the greying Adansoni with a piercing glare. "The boy that you found, Cardinal Bishop Adansoni. You feel he is too important to be imprisoned within an inquisitional cell, don't you?"

"I was simply Father Adansoni when I found him," countered the Cardinal, his tone softening in an attempt to defuse the rising tensions. "And while I might have been the one who found him, I never claimed he possessed any great qualities."

"Other than those of an Inquisitor?" said Casado.

"Of those significant skills I think we are all in agreement," said Adansoni, nodding to his old friend and then addressing the wider room for support. He paused, and looked back at Korek. "But in answer to your question, Cardinal Bishop Korek, no this is not about whether Inquisitor Tacit is too important to be chained to the wall of a cell for the remainder of his days or not. No! This is about doing what is right." The clamour of the inquisitional hall rose on this admission, but Adansoni managed to regain control over the throng. "To imprison Inquisitor Tacit for the crime of saving the Catholic faith simply cannot be right," he announced, when the room had fallen silent.

"Much like Monteria, I think we have since dropped Tacit's title?" spat the snakelike Bishop Basquez, who had somehow managed to obtain a place among the elected Cardinals in the inquisitional meeting hall this late evening. His narrowed eyes glowered at Adansoni. "Regardless of what you might think, Poldek Tacit is a murderer. Pure and simple. If we allow him to walk free from the Inquisitional Prison in Toulouse, what message would we be sending to all our other enemies within the Church who wish to do us harm?"

"Whoever said that Tacit was our enemy?" replied Adansoni. As he spoke, he saw the indefatigable figure of Father Strettavario among the crowd at the rear of the chamber, watching proceedings with his usual measured contemplation. Adansoni allowed his eyes to return slowly back to the Bishop as Basquez turned on the congregation for their assistance, his eyes now as wide as his arms were spread.

"Not our enemy?" laughed Basquez, with cold humour and feigned surprise. "Have you not forgotten our concerns as to his previous behaviour, the reason why the Holy See first suggested he be assessed in Arras? Something they were clearly right to do. The man is out of control. Possessed."

Now Adansoni glowered. "Possession is a strong word, Bishop."

"And so I do not use it lightly," Basquez retorted.

Adansoni shook his head. "Surely when you talk of possession, you talk of those whom Tacit processed in their thousands, those who truly are possessed with the spirit of the Devil?"

"Like those who trouble our city currently?" said Casado across the noise of the hall. He shut his eyes, bowing his head with the weight of worry, of responsibility. "It seems there are more episodes of demonic possession than ever before within Rome. Every day the number of new cases increases threefold. And not just within Rome. Across the world, signs of the Devil can be witnessed every day. A plague of locusts in Palestine. A famine in Lebanon. Strange warnings within the heavens. Statues which bleed. Rivers running red. The Inquisition can barely keep up."

"More reason why we need men like Tacit among us," replied Adansoni, his finger raised. "I say again, he is not our enemy. The Devil is our enemy."

"Not our enemy?" said Korek, rejoining the debate. "Need I remind the Holy See of Father Desrochers' broken wrist courtesy of Poldek Tacit in Paris shortly before the Mass for Peace? Or of Bishop Gagne's broken nose in Arras when Tacit was ransacking Cardinal Poré's private residence? Or of Monteria's murder?"

"And why must you keep referring back to the 'murder', as you so call it, Cardinal Bishop Korek?" retorted Adansoni, his nostrils flaring. "Tacit saved our Church that day. As I have said before, and said many times, surely he should be rewarded, not imprisoned for what he did?"

"The day we reward those who murder within our faith," the Cardinal replied coldly from the other end of the room, "is the day we should call for the Catholic faith to be brought to an end."

"Then perhaps we should end our faith right this moment," said Adansoni, going to sit in his chair, defeated. Casado called out to him before he could do so.

"Why say such a thing, Javier?"

"Murder in the name of our faith?" replied Adansoni, turning his eyes from his old friend back over to Strettavario. "The Inquisition. Remember the Inquisition, and what it is they do on a daily basis in the name of our faith."

FIVE

ROME. ITALY.

As she fled, all Isabella could taste was fear. Night had fallen across the city with alarming speed, plunging it into an almost instant purple darkness.

She sprinted along the river bank and up the stone staircase at the far end, onto the bridge above, her breath snatched, every twenty paces looking back over her shoulder to see if they were still on her tail. And as she ran, Tacit's name echoed over and over in her ears, though whether as a tribute or a warning she did not know.

Isabella knew she had one advantage over her pursuers, small though it was. She knew the capital well. Her Chaste assignments within the city, coaxing errant hands and snatched kisses from wayward Priests, had taken her to the more unfrequented areas of the city, the dark streets, the paths rarely travelled. She would lead her pursuers into the labyrinthine parts of Rome, the twisting confusion of side-streets, courtyards and alleyways, which could confound and bind the unwary. She would try to lose them there.

There was no question who was chasing her. She had recognised them from the moment she'd laid eyes on them through the grey dusk, their black uniforms, their ruthless demeanour, the way they acted without hesitation or doubt. But still she could find no explanation as to why, in the open heart of Rome, the Inquisitors had behaved so brazenly? Even the Inquisition had rules. Even it didn't gun down Priests and agents of the Chaste without good reason. What had the man who had toppled mortally wounded from the bridge done that was dreadful enough to demand his public execution? Why was his dying word the name of the man Isabella loved? And why did witnessing the shooting bring its own death sentence?

Isabella's light fleet feet barely made a sound as she sprang across the Via dell' Olmetto and plunged into the darkness of the street beyond. She was no longer cold from the river. Instead, she was chilled with fear. She had not felt like this since Arras, when Tacit …

As she ducked right down a side-alley, a handgun exploded behind her and a piece of masonry burst from the wall beside where she was running. She ducked beneath it, her hair sprayed with masonry and dust, unable to contain the cry of alarm from her throat, and turned into the alley immediately on her left, crouching low as she went.

There was a six-foot wall in front of her and she threw herself over the top of it, taking a moment to look back before she dropped down the other side. Four men. Robed. Hooded. Dark-featured.

Isabella raced up the alleyway into which she had dropped, climbing broad cobbled steps lined with slate. It was cold and dark, every shadow suggesting another Inquisitor lying in wait to reach out for her. She sprinted along it with reckless speed, taking the steps three at a time, her lungs burning, pleading for her to stop. But to do so would be the death of her. She knew that much.

There was a ladder to her right and she leapt onto the third rung and climbed, reaching the top moments before the Inquisitors reached its base. Two men went after her, bounding up the rusted iron rungs, the ladder groaning under their weight, the remaining Inquisitors taking another route, hoping to head her off at the far side of the building.

Across the roof tops Isabella ran, her arms held wide as if on a high wire, hoping not to lose her balance and plunge to the dark streets below. She reached the far side of the building, where, faced with a seven-foot gap between her and the building opposite, she took her chance, clearing it and landing on the other side. But her momentum carried her forward and she rolled onto the tiles beyond. At once she felt the roof sag and buckle beneath her. Seconds later, the aged rafters gave way, the tiles cracking and splintering in a circle around her, before plummeting Isabella downwards, down into the room below.

The air filled with clouds of choking masonry and plaster, clinging to her nostrils and choking her throat. She shook the dust from her hair and stars from her eyes, gathering herself gingerly to her feet. Through the hole above an Inquisitor appeared, levelling a revolver at her. She spun aside as the round buffeted the floor, and hurled herself through an open doorway.

There was a window at the far end of the corridor into which she had run, and she burst through it, not caring where it led, whether there was a dramatic drop beyond it or not, just desperate to get away from her pursuer. She thrust forward, her eyes closed, her arms held out in front of her, glass and wood splintering in every direction. She tumbled out onto a sloping roof and rolled and slithered down it, her hands and clothing ripped by the shattered window, coming to a halt at the edge of the eaves. An eight-foot drop onto the street below greeted her and she threw herself into space, sinking onto her haunches to cushion the fall. She was powdered white with plaster dust, as if she had risen from the dead.

And she was also aware of eyes on her. An Inquisitor towered over the ashen woman, smiling a wicked broken smile as he pointed his gun at her skull.

SIX

BERLIN. GERMANY.

Something loathsome howled in the dark of the bedchamber, a voice more like a dog's than the young child's it should have been. The guttural noises were coarse and profane, an abuse to the ears, and there were words woven within the noises, indistinct and masked. And the words were as putrid as the stench from the tiny person strapped to the bed.

"It's a child," muttered the Priest to the exhausted Inquisitor waiting in the shadows outside the bedchamber, wiping the beads of sweat from his lined brow. "No more than eight years old. An only child."

If the Inquisitor felt any sympathy for the little one, he did not show it. "Eight? For how long has she been like this?"

"He. And this is the third day."

"When were you first alerted that something was wrong?" The Inquisitor's tone was pressing.

"At first the smell. We thought something had climbed under the floorboards beneath the bed and died. We took some up but ..."

"You found nothing?"

The Priest nodded and looked back to the open door as the howling changed to yelps, like those of jackal around a kill. "We thought it prudent to send for the Inquisition after the second day, when the child's condition worsened." He looked across at the Inquisitor, into his searching eyes. "Rages. Profanity. Bleeding from orifices." He swallowed, his throat dry, and ran his tongue across his chapped lips. "We bound him to the bed after the first day, to protect him and the others within the dormitory, and isolated him after the second."

The Inquisitor's fingers curled into a gloved fist. "You should have sent for the Inquisition on the very first day. Not left this child to the torment of the beast within him."

"I heard you were overstretched. I didn't want to bother you."

"We are stretched, but we would have come."

A long high-pitched shrieking cry wound out of the room, suddenly stifled, after which a longer stream of profanity tore from the child's lips.

"Good Lord," muttered the Priest, his hand clamped firmly to his mouth. "Saints preserve us."

"I suspect they won't," replied the tall man next to him, moving half a step to his right to allow him a view into the bedroom. He saw it then, the possessed child, a mottled and twisted shape, blackened and sickly green as if the plague had taken him, strapped firm to the bedposts by greying bonds tensed tight against every corner of the bed. The fourth victim he had visited this very week.

"I have been told that this is the third occurrence of possession just today within the city," muttered the Priest. "Can it be true?"

"I am not at liberty to say. Leave me to do my job."

The Inquisitor moved towards the open door, but the Priest caught hold of his wrist.

"There were seven last week. I know. Priests talk."

The Inquisitor turned briefly to look at him, saying nothing, his eyes searching the dark places of the terrified Priest's face.

"I fear this is the start of something," trembled the Priest, "with so many possessions within the city, something is coming. He is gathering his strength to return."

The Inquisitor looked back to the open door. Instantly the child's eyes latched malevolently onto him, as if the mention of the Devil had drawn his evil gaze. It pierced the Inquisitor with a glare, its blue oily maw turning upwards into a dripping toothless grin.

"The Holy See," said the Inquisitor. "They know, and they are doing all they can to help." Without another word the Inquisitor strode quickly into the room, his case clutched firmly in his hand. Seconds later invisible forces slammed the door of the bedchamber shut behind him.

SEVEN

ROME. ITALY.

"You should never have run," the Inquisitor grinned, pointing his gun at Isabella. She could see his left ear was missing, torn fragments all that remained from a previous mission. "It would have been easier if you hadn't."

"Easier for whom?" asked Isabella, watching his finger whiten against the trigger. She shut her eyes and turned away grimacing, waiting for impact.

The mechanism turned over and jammed. Isabella heard it and, like a flash, lashed out with her foot, knocking the Inquisitor off balance. He swore and ejected the snagged round, slamming the chamber shut, moments before Isabella struck him as hard as she could on the leg with a lump of discarded wood. The revolver fired wide as the Inquisitor's tibia snapped under the blow and he went down with a pained cry, his free hand clutched to his shattered limb.

Isabella sprang to her feet and kicked out again, booting him hard in the side of the head, feeling the force of her blow run the length of her leg and gather like a jolt in her thigh. The Inquisitor went over with a groan, rolling onto his front and lying still, the gun spinning out of his hand. She snatched it from the ground and turned the very instant two more Inquisitors dropped into the street from the roof above her. She fired twice, killing both instantly before they had a chance to level their own weapons at her.

Staring aghast at the lifeless bodies lying before her, Isabella let her gun hand drop slowly to her side. She'd murdered two people. She'd killed them with such ease and without a moment's thought.

What have I done? What have I become?

Darkness swept into her mind, spinning every sense into a bewildering whirling frenzy; unconsciousness beckoned her. The revolver trembled against her thigh before slipping from her fingers and clacking onto the flagstone floor.

A noise from somewhere nearby, the approaching footsteps of more Inquisitors, snapped her out of her malaise and she turned away, her hand to her mouth, smelling cordite on her fingers, stepping over the bodies and back out onto a main street, reaching a flight of stairs down from where she had emerged.

At the bottom an Inquisitor came at her from the right and she ducked under his lunging arms, sprinting away. The man cursed, overbalanced and staggered after her. She turned right and darted into another cramped and cobbled street, but stumbled over an unseen hole in the floor and went down in a heap, gashing her elbows and knees. A shadow loomed and she rolled over onto her back, her bloodied knees raised, staring up at the Inquisitor. He shook his head and scowled, pointing the barrel of the gun at her chest.

"You're dead," he growled.

But then another voice, English, spoke from the darkness.

"Heads up!" it chirped, and the Inquisitor looked up just in time to see the butt of a rifle pummel hard into his face. He groaned and slumped backwards onto the ground, blood gathering fast around his right eye. The Englishman looked down at her and offered a hand, smiling.

"Sister Isabella," said Henry, turning his hand palm up in an invitation for her to take it. "It's been a while."

EIGHT

TOULOUSE INQUISITIONAL PRISON. TOULOUSE. FRANCE.

A wicked chuckle of laughter came from outside the cell door, and Tacit turned as a large heavy key was inserted into the lock. A crowd had gathered to watch proceedings. They often liked to watch, the wardens and guards at the prison. Tacit, the great Inquisitor, the murderer of Cardinals, fallen. He always drew a crowd.

Tacit moved himself onto his side and sat up as the door to his cell was unlocked. He swung his legs over the edge of his bed and leaned his weight onto them, his elbows on his knees. When he had first arrived at the prison, he had fought the guards every day for three weeks in an attempt to avoid the torture sessions. In doing so, he'd wounded thirteen of them, seven seriously, so much so that they'd never walk again. But more guards came, eventually overwhelming him, the cudgels falling with more venom each time he fought back. And he knew he was only putting off the inevitable, that the torture sessions would never be halted. For the first time in his life, Tacit learnt that it was easier to go to one's fate than resist it, a lesson he never believed he would, or could, learn.

The door was shoved open and a line of familiar figures staggered in, drunk on their power and a desire to witness pain. At their head was a man Tacit had long known, the knots of torn skin and flesh in his face a constant reminder of that fateful day, years ago, when the witch had broken free of Tacit's hold and exacted her revenge on the head torturer of Toulouse Prison. Over the weeks and months Tacit had come to despise the man more than he had ever believed possible.

"So, our fallen Inquisitor awakes," Salamanca spat, his eyes burning wild with anticipation. "Ready for his correction!"

Laughter and the scuffling of bodies vying for a prized position from which to watch the torture followed, leering wretched faces staring at him like a baying crowd of savages. Salamanca turned and nodded, and three men went forward, ropes and shackles in their hands. Although Tacit made no effort to fight them, they still approached him with caution, knowing the violence and the strength of which the man was capable.

"So obedient," Salamanca mocked, watching Tacit being bound, his mouth contorting with cold humour. "Like a whipped dog. How have the mighty fallen," he hissed, as Tacit was led to the chair and thrust into it, cuffs and chains locked to hold him tightly in place. "So telling that even one like Tacit can have the fight and the spirit beaten from him."

"You've not beaten me yet, Salamanca," warned Tacit, his hard eyes unmoving on the torturer.

"Perhaps not. But we have time. There is no rush. You are going nowhere. We have ways of making people show emotion. Of making people plead. Even people like you, Poldek Tacit. And believe me, you are proving to be the most pleasurable upon which to operate."

The torturer's hand rose to his own torn face, his fingertips tracing the deep grooves and fissures the witch had dug across his cheeks. Not a day had passed without Salamanca remembering the moment when Tacit had failed in his duties and allowed the witch to attack him with her terrible claws. Every incision, every twist of the blade, every scalding touch upon Tacit's skin had inched Salamanca closer towards something resembling revenge. And yet, to the torturer's mind, there was still a huge price to be imposed upon the Inquisitor before his debt would be paid in full. He knew it would be many years before that moment was reached.

"Sitting comfortably?" he asked lightly, turning to the wall and preparing himself for his work. He set down the wooden box of tools he had brought with him, cutting implements, drills, a selection of bladed instruments for delving deep into the flesh to find the most choice and fragile points of pain.

"You'll no doubt be pleased to know that I have orders," announced Salamanca, "orders from the Vatican, to perform these trials upon you. It seems you have caught the eyes of some within the Holy See, some who have come to fear you, resent you, admire you, for what you are, what you represent, what you could be." He lifted a scalpel from the box and tested its edge with his thumb. "Of course, it's an honour to act for people so highly regarded within the Church, to know we're remembered down here in Toulouse, not forgotten about by the Vatican. What miracles we can do, what results we can achieve, given the right opportunities." He turned his sickly leer to Tacit. "And you, Poldek Tacit, you will be the most rewarding of subjects."

Tacit strained momentarily against the chains and manacles, his natural urge to fight against a threat impossible to subdue. But the bonds held him fast and the jeers of the watching audience made him realise attempts to fight were pointless. He knew he had to conserve his energy, focus his mind from the searing pain that was to come. He felt and smelt hot iron and turned his eyes to Salamanca, inches from his face; a smoking brand was in the torturer's hand.

"You're a tough one, Tacit," he said, licking his thin cracked lips. "I'll give you that. But you need to understand that no one cares about you. You're all alone in here, with no one but me. And because of that, you'll break. Everyone breaks eventually." He smiled as he lifted the flaming poker and thrust it hard onto Tacit's exposed skin.

NINE

Rome. Italy.

Isabella winced as she leant on Henry's shoulder and hobbled to the door of the black Fiat 70 automobile he had parked nearby. There were tears in her eyes and the taste of dust and iron in her mouth from where she had bitten her tongue and drawn blood during the chase. Henry reached ahead of her and opened the door to the vehicle, helping her to drop inside. She sighed and sank back into the leather seat, relieved to have the weight taken from her twisted ankle and feel some comfort at her back. She closed her eyes and took slow and measured breaths, trying to collect her racing thoughts.

Henry shut the door, furtively checking the dark street as he circled the vehicle and cranked the starting handle to fire the engine. Two swift turns shuddered the car into life and, with a final look both ways, he climbed into the driver's seat, placing his 1912 Mauser rifle in the back.

Isabella shivered, realising then how cold she was. Exhaustion flooded into her like a tide. "What are you doing here?" she asked Henry, as if waking from deep sleep, her unfocused eyes narrowing.

"Not now," Henry replied, guiding the rattling car away from the curb and beyond the pale luminescence from a gas light above. "Let's talk when we're away from here."

She sat back in the chair resigned, drawing her sodden clothes around her in an attempt to warm her frozen bones. She closed her eyes in another attempt to slow her whirling mind.

"Are you cold?" asked Henry.

"A little."

"Here." He reached into the back of the Fiat and took out a blanket, pushing it onto Isabella's lap. She accepted it willingly and drew it over her shoulders, feeling warmth from it at once. He looked back across at her briefly, before returning his eyes to the dark of the road ahead. "Are you hurt?"

Isabella shook her head, causing dust to slip from the damp tendrils of her curls, and lowered her forehead into a shaking hand, before reaching down towards her calf with her other hand. "Only my ankle. But it's all right." She drew breath firmly. "Inquisitors," she muttered, disbelievingly. "I killed them. Two of them." There was bitter emotion tangled in her words. Resentment and grit.

"Better them than you," replied Henry, steering the car from the bright lights of the main street into a narrower lane, checking behind him as they slipped from view into the embracing shadows of the side-street.

"Where are we going?" she asked.

"Somewhere safe. For a while, I hope."

Isabella looked across at him, captured intermittently in faint incandescent light as they slipped past gas- and candlelight from shuttered houses and street lanterns. She thought he looked far older than when they had last met nearly a year ago. Aged.

He turned onto the main thoroughfare through the city, finding top gear and with it the car's cruising speed. Isabella peered into the pockets of light and passing crowds of the city as they flew past. She was aware she was trembling and pulled the blanket tighter around her, her fingers clutching the edge of the fabric and nursing the soft fibres. Its touch reminded her of home and cold winters in northern Spain. She lost hold of the memory and realised she was still clutching the brooch taken from the dead man in the river tight in her aching fingers. She opened them to reveal the green locket embedded in dull silver. An Inquisitor's broach. She was aware of Henry's eyes on it and snapped her fingers back tight, as if it were a treasure she wished not to share for the moment.

"Your name," she asked, drawing the blanket tighter around her. "I've forgotten your name."

"Henry," he replied. "Henry Frost. Lieutenant Henry Frost, though I dropped the title a long time ago."

"Fampoux," she replied, as if the name held a special place in her heart. "I saw you, in Fampoux."

Henry nodded, a little ruefully.

"What are you doing in Rome? What's changed since to bring you here, Henry?"

The young officer looked across at her, his face grave. "Everything," he said.

With that a gunshot sounded and the windscreen between them cracked, the glass punctured by a single bullet hole. Instinctively, both Henry and Isabella ducked, Henry dragging the wheel, and with it the car, sharply right into a road alongside, thrusting his foot firm to the floor. Behind him, two black sedans turned and roared after them, four Inquisitors in the leading car, three in the one behind. Henry checked over his shoulder and threw the car into third gear, feeling the engine whine a little higher in tone.

Pedestrians, taking in the last of the city's night air, scuttled from Henry's path as he flew past, only to stand open-mouthed as the two chasing Ford Ts plunged after them. Rome flashed by as Henry tore down a side-street and up the other side, crunching second gear and spraying loose rubble from the road.

At the top of the climb he took a right, the tyres screeching hard on the tarmac, cutting in front of an oncoming Maxwell Roadster. He turned left, feeling the rear of the car spin out and wrestling hard to claw back control, overtaking a horse-drawn cart in front of him on the inside and finding a lower gear to get some more traction beneath his tyres.

A sudden explosion erupted from the left-hand side of the cab and Henry ducked beneath the steering wheel, staring into Isabella's seat. He half expected to see the shuddering bleeding proof that she'd been hit, but instead she was leaning from the window, training the Mauser rifle she had taken from the rear seat at the pursuing cars for a second shot.

"Isabella!" he cried, ploughing left into a narrow street strung with washing lines. They cut through, dragging wires and sheets behind them as they drove, Henry slipping down to first gear and turning hard right back onto the main road out of the city. "Do you know how to fire that thing?"

She recalled her young years shooting rabbits in the fields at the back of her father's home, before death had claimed him and the Church her. She prayed the rifle she now held was no different to the Vetterli rifle she used back then.

"Just drive!" she shouted back, and Henry cranked second gear and checked over his shoulder once again. The cars behind were thirty feet away, quilts and pieces of clothing spinning into the night's black air in their wake.

Twenty feet and gaining.

Now fifteen.

Isabella released the magazine and checked the rounds inside. Three left. She thrust the metal canister home and leaned back out of the window, raising the rifle to her eye and pulling the trigger. The first round ricocheted harmlessly off the leading Ford's front axle, the second taking the rear left tyre, the third the front right. The car ground to a sudden halt and twisted. A sickening crunch sounded from the base of the car and it seemed to split in two somewhere beneath the carriage, the Ford standing immobile in the middle of the road.

"More rounds?" she shot back at Henry, holding out her open hand to him.

"No more left," he replied, veering left and then right to avoid a stranded pedestrian in the road. He turned the wheel left in his sweaty palms and roared onto another road, the remaining sedan screeching in hot pursuit. He jostled in his pocket. "Here," he said, handing her a service revolver. "Take this."

She snatched it from him and leant back out of the window, her fingers clasped around the grip. She closed an eye and fired, twice. The sedan's windscreen cracked and the Inquisitor driving took evasive action, jigging left and mounting the pavement, ploughing through tables and chairs, sending them spinning and careering into the late night air, diners scrambling for safety.

More shooting sounded, now from Henry's right, and his side window shattered into a million sparkling fragments, showering his face and clothes with needle-like splinters. Another black car roared up after the gunfire, battering the right side of Henry's Fiat, almost throwing Isabella from her window. At once he braked, grinding the Fiat to a sudden devastating stop, which threw the Inquisitor's Ford way ahead of the Fiat and Isabella into the windscreen of their car. She groaned and crumpled to the footwell, the revolver dropping from her hand. Henry found first gear and turned off the main route, the sedans further up the road stopping and trying to manoeuvre themselves around and give chase. The trick had bought Henry and Isabella a few extra seconds, but not enough. Gunshots flashed from the running boards of the following cars and the back of the Fiat bristled with revolver and rifle-fire.

Henry steered left, plunging into a long promenade of shops, halfway along which stood a fountain gushing water onto shimmering black marble figurines clambering from a pool. He took his foot off the accelerator and peered over his shoulder, feeling the car slow to a lope.

"What are you doing?" cried Isabella, her side groaning as she spoke.

The Inquisitors' cars roared up behind, the leading one pulling out of the slipstream to sit alongside. At the very moment it drew level, Henry floored the Fiat and steered hard into it, connecting with the front left wheel guard of the Ford. It plunged right and ploughed into the water fountain, mounting the pool's stone wall, its undercarriage hooking itself firm to the figurines, the vehicle instantly grinding to a stop. The Inquisitors on the running board were thrown clear, arms and legs flapping helplessly, as they rose and then fell through the plate glass window of the shop opposite, vanishing into the black beyond, glass obliterated behind them.

Henry allowed himself a brief smile before more gunshots peppered the carriage, winging him in the left arm. He cried out, his hand clasped to the wound, as Isabella reached across to him.

"Keep down!" he shouted, turning from the promenade into another side-road before flooring the vehicle. The Ford rallied and Isabella did too, climbing from the footwell, the revolver back in her hand. She looked and fired off a round. The headlights of the chasing car dazzled her. She turned around to the road ahead, letting the lights in her eyes pass, preparing herself for the next shot.

Suddenly, from in front of them, there was a flash of grey, an immense figure vaulting their car in a single leap and flying towards the Ford behind. Isabella gasped and turned to look, but Henry had already steered off the road.

She heard the screeching of brakes followed by the sudden scream of metal and the shattering of glass. Whatever had leapt their vehicle had ploughed straight into the car behind. As darkness swept back into the car and the road rolled beneath their wheels, Isabella was sure she could hear the pleading cries of men, a solitary gunshot and the long harrowing cry of a wolf.

TEN

Rome. Italy.

The Fiat rattled on its hard tyres as Henry inched forward over the glistening cobbles. In the chaos of the chase Isabella had lost her bearings but suspected she was in one of the poorer districts of the city. Rats ran ahead of them, their scattering matted bodies and grey-pink tails illuminated by the car's sickly light. Water could be heard dripping from broken guttering onto slimy green slabs below, a mouldy clinging smell in the alleyway.

Without warning, Henry drew the car to a shuddering halt and pulled hard on the handbrake with a grating crank. The vehicle shook their bones for a moment before falling silent and still. Only then did he hang his head, his hands loosening on the steering wheel, exhaling slowly, his eyes lightly closed, his eyelids twitching like a man trying to chase a nightmare from his dreams. It was evident that his night's exertions had taken a toll. Cold sweat had beaded on his forehead, his shirt was drenched with perspiration and his hair was matted in untidy darkened clumps.

He returned his right hand to the bloody tear on his left biceps and clamped hard upon it, grimacing. Isabella looked across at him. "Are you all right?"

He nodded, saying nothing.

"What was that thing?" Isabella asked, fearing she already knew the answer. Henry remained silent, his eyes still shut, his right hand clamped to his crimson weeping wound. She took his silence as her answer and made to open her door, but without warning Henry reached across and took her wrist, drawing her back. His hand was slick with blood and it slipped on her skin. He grasped at her again, this time more firmly, only now fixing her with a warning gaze. "Wait." He reached into the depths of his pocket, while all the time pulling her hand towards him. He turned her palm upwards and dropped a locket into it. "Wear this," he said.

Isabella regarded the necklace, a round pendant on a fine silver chain.

"Francis of Assisi," she muttered, lifting the necklace to allow the metal locket to drop and hang free. She inspected the item before her eyes, recognising at once the reverend bearded figure of the Saint.

"The tamer of wolves," Henry added darkly, and instantly Isabella's fears were realised. Their eyes met and Henry held Isabella's stare for a moment, before snatching the rifle from her lap and climbing out of the car. "Come on," he said, his voice quiet but his tone grave. "Let's get inside. It's safer in there than out in the open. Especially at night."

Henry stood at the shuttered window of the end of the ground-floor terrace apartment and stared out onto the quiet street beyond, checking both ends of it and then back again. The rifle was still clutched in his hands, and only when he was finally sure they were alone did he let go of it, setting it down against the wall of the darkened room. It smelt dank and old, the walls mottled with age and decay, the once white plaster withered to grey and moss green.

Isabella pulled the blanket tighter across her shoulders and wondered how it was she had found herself catapulted into this nightmare world of darkness and terror. She watched Henry light a candle, set it down on a small wooden table and pull out a chair, gesturing for her to sit. He then walked across to a cupboard on the far side of the room, out of which he produced a bottle and glasses.

"Are we safe here?" she asked, taking a seat.

"For now," replied Henry. "Do you want a drink?" His tone was forced and assured, rather than hospitable.

"I want answers," Isabella replied. The candle's flickering light caught on the circle of silver now hanging at her throat. "What are you doing in Rome?"

"I could ask you the same thing," he replied, uncorking the bottle and pouring a stream of golden liquid into two of the three glasses. "Skulking in the depths of the city." Isabella knew for whom the third glass was set and thought again about what it was she had seen flash past them as they had been pursued throughout the city. "What have you done to attract their attention, I wonder?"

Isabella hesitated. "Their attention?" she replied. "Who are they? I know they are Inquisitors, but there was something different about them, something desperate." She suddenly seemed to appreciate the accusation that had been thrown at her. "But what I did to attract their attention? I was doing nothing!" Henry shook his head and scowled, taking up his glass and necking half of the liquid in a single go, showing teeth and tight lips as the spirit burnt the back of his throat.

"Don't play games," he retorted. "We're too far down the road for that. We know. Almost everything. A lot more than you, I suspect. So put your little act of innocence aside and answer me this. What were you doing to attract so much attention at Sisto Bridge?"

He raised the remains of his drink to his lips and Isabella studied him carefully, noticing how his hand shook. She knew then that his performance was exactly that. An act, and that he was as scared as she was. And his Italian was clumsy, forced. Isabella dropped into English, to make it easier for him.

"I don't know what I've done," Isabella replied, reaching forward and lightly picking up her own glass. She remained leaning forward, her elbows on the edge of the table, the drink nursed in her hands. "I just happened to be there, at Ponte Sisto."

"What were you doing at the bridge?" asked Henry, his tone as jaundiced as the candlelight. "Did you see who shot the Priest?"

She placed the brooch she had snatched from the Inquisitor on the table between them. "You mean who shot the Inquisitor?" Isabella corrected, and Henry smiled for the first time. Instantly she felt more relaxed and sat back, stretching out her long legs beneath the table and feeling the tightness in her muscles groan.

"So what were you doing there?" he asked again, gathering strips of cloth from the side and laying them on the table. He took off his beige shirt, bloodied and torn near the shoulder, in order to bind his wound. A vest covered his compact chest. The muscles in his arms and beneath the vest were tight knots.

Isabella remembered Giovanni and crumpled a little with emotion at the question. "Walking," she said softly, as if it was an effort to think back, finding all her memories confused. "I was walking. With another Priest."

The words seemed like therapy as they came out, and she did nothing to stop them. She no longer cared for secrecy, not now, not with this man who already seemed to know so much, even though her admission would cost her more than her profession.

"I work for the Chaste. We are a secret organisation within the Catholic Church. We test the faith of wayward Priests, or Priests we suspect of failing in their vows of chastity. I was trying to tempt an indiscretion from him, the Priest who was with me at the time. We'd stopped just beneath the shadow of the bridge. He was about to kiss me when a gun fired and a body dropped into the river from the bridge. Before I knew what I was doing, I was wading into the river to try to reach him. To try to save him. It was that which saved me. The next minute, the Inquisition, or whoever they are, they were shooting. Giovanni was hit and went down, as did the Priest. I grabbed hold of the body which had fallen and dived beneath the water, reaching the far side of the riverbank."

"He was dead?" asked Henry. "When you reached him?"

"He was," lied Isabella.

"He said nothing?"

She recalled Tacit's name.

"Were you hoping he would?" But Henry had fallen silent. "They chased me, chased me across the city, until you found me."

She looked up at him, her face now filled with the cold emotion of anger and defiance. Henry studied her carefully before he pursed his lips, nodding his head, as if what she had said made sense. He pulled out a chair and sat, beginning to tie the strips of cloth to his arm to bind his wound. If it pained him, he showed no sign.

"You were lucky," he muttered. "You don't know what you've stumbled into."

"I know the Inquisition. I know what they're capable of." Isabella's eyes turned to the Inquisitor's brooch on the table, the emerald stone glinting in the weak amber candlelight. "I just want answers."

"So let's see if we can find them," called the rich alluring voice of a woman from behind her. Isabella knew who it was before she turned to look.

"Sandrine Prideux," she said.

A tall dark-haired woman rested causally against the side of the open doorway, patting her face with a towel as if she had just returned from bathing, a loose shirt hanging from her shoulders, buttoned only to her breast line.

"Sister Isabella," replied Sandrine, her eyes flashing. "I am surprised to see you again."

"And I you. It would seem then that 'Peace and Revenge' never came to be?"

Sandrine's lips curled, her features hardening. She dropped the towel into the crook of her elbow and crossed her arms. "Perhaps not Peace," she replied, her eyes glowering.

Isabella smiled thinly, weighing the comment in her mind. She recalled the ruin of Fampoux, the resolute defiance of Sandrine as she and Henry prepared to leave that town for the final time.

"I should kill you," Sandrine continued, stepping lightly into the room, drawn towards Henry. She stroked a hand up his back and spread her fingers through his hair, pulling herself towards his face for a brief kiss. Her hand closed about Henry's bound arm in a sign of concern, but he shook his head in assurance. Isabella used the opportunity to check her proximity to an exit, before her eyes met Sandrine's again. "You know that, don't you? I should kill you for what you did in Paris."

"And why should you do that?" Isabella asked, as Sandrine took up the liquor and poured herself a large measure. She set the bottle down hard, so that the impact of it shook the table, and snatched up the glass, holding it up to the edge of her chin, observing the Sister as if formulating the words to reply to her retort.

"You, and the Priest. The Inquisitor. The one they call Tacit." She hissed the name with contempt. "You ruined everything. At the Mass for Peace. You killed the Cardinal Bishop Monteria."

Isabella had long laid awake at night after the events in the French capital and the Mass for Peace, imagining what might have happened had Cardinal Bishop Monteria not been stopped from donning the wolf pelt and transforming before the massed congregation at Notre Dame. Passion fuelled her words as she replied. "That Cardinal Bishop was about to commit mass murder within Notre Dame!"

"That Cardinal Bishop was helping us to strike back at our enemies! All our combined enemies! We had planned everything for months. Me. Cardinal Bishop Monteria. Cardinal Poré. My father." A shadow seemed to draw across her face like a veil, sorrow replacing her anger. "We were willing to risk everything, even our lives, for a chance to avenge what had been done to my people for centuries, to repay the curses cast upon us, to give those who had spun those corrupt incantations a moment to stop and reflect on the wickedness of their actions. To throw open the windows to this wickedness for all to see."

"By killing so many innocent people as well! Is that what you wanted? To kill all those innocent people who were attending the Mass in order to show the errors of our Catholic faith's past? The diplomats? The royal families? The innocent civilians? All slaughtered for revenge?"

Sandrine's teeth were bared. "And this war doesn't slaughter enough innocents as it is?" She took a step towards Isabella, her fists clenched and raised, but she caught sight of the pendant at the Sister's throat and paused, drawing back a step and seeming to shrink and calm. "Peace! That is what we sought primarily. A chance to end this infernal war. A chance to make mankind realise that there were more terrible things within the world for them to face together rather than their own kind, their neighbours, their foreign cousins, those separated by race or religion. Peace and revenge! Peace for the world, and revenge for our people. And you took both away."

At once Isabella's defiance shrunk. "It never would have worked," she said, but her words came falteringly. She knew that she and Tacit had saved a thousand lives at Notre Dame, but by doing so, had they perhaps ensured the continuation of the war? Not a day had gone by when the thought had not troubled her. She watched Sandrine take a deep pull on her drink, before she said, "I never realised."

"Realised what?"

"That you were one of them."

A cold smile drew itself across Sandrine's face, one of resignation and pain. "We are all one. We are family drawn together by blood."

"And yet you can walk abroad freely, as any normal person, not tethered by Hombre Lobo's curse of daylight or the moon? I don't understand."

"There's much you don't understand, and never will."

"So educate me."

"Why? Why should I? What have you to offer me?" Sandrine's fingers were splayed like claws. "Why should I not kill you now?"

"Because I can help you."

Sandrine laughed, a bitter cruel laugh which froze Isabella's blood. "If you could help, why would you wish to?"

"Because I cannot go back, not now, not back to the Chaste, not to my Church. Not after what has happened. They will kill me, the Inquisitors. I have nothing. I am not safe anymore." The realisation of her predicament grew as she spoke, and caught as a moan in her throat.

"It feels terrifying, doesn't it?" asked Sandrine. "Being all alone?"

Isabella nodded and let her head drop. She could feel the slow creep of fear draw over her. Sandrine tutted, drawing Isabella to look at her again.

"Imagine how my people have felt, for a thousand years. Terrified. Alone."

"Who was he?"

"Who?"

"The man on the bridge who was killed. Why was he so important? At least tell me that."

"He was one of us. We watched out for each other. We worked together."

"He was an Inquisitor! Why are you working with someone at the Inquisition? I thought they were your enemy?" Isabella said, forcing a laugh, but the fierce look which was returned crushed the chuckle to silence.

"You come here, a stupid Sister from the Vatican, who believes all that is important in life is to test the chastity of those who have taken the vow of celibacy."

"I don't believe that. Not for a moment."

"Good, because revenge, it no longer matters. Everything has now changed."

Isabella's voice was now gravely serious. "Henry, he said something similar to me earlier. But he never told what had changed."

"Then I will." Sandrine took a deep breath, as if summoning the will to speak. "There's a darkness, which has descended. Light has been extinguished. A hand is clawing across the world, and we know to whom it belongs, a hand which must be stopped, regardless of the cost, of allegiances and beliefs." She heard the dry swallow of Isabella's throat.

"How do you know this?"

"Our allies. Our spies. Rumour and investigation. We never rest. In 1877 something was unleashed on the world. What it was, we don't know, but that year the crops failed in many countries of the world, the animals simply died in the fields by their millions. Parts of the world came close to famine. India was almost destroyed by one."

"And you think to blame this on some higher power?" Isabella questioned. But Sandrine continued regardless.

"Some devilry had crawled into the cities and towns from somewhere, somehow. Demonic possessions paralysed whole communities with panic and fear. Monstrous children, the mirror of demons, were born in their thousands within the populations. The rivers ran red with blood. Wolves live in the shadows but we hear things, we have our sources, and we felt the evil that had come to the world."

"And why does something which happened nearly forty years ago matter now?"

"Because it's happening again. We can feel that something stirring. This Inquisitor who was murdered, our contact within the Vatican and the Inquisition, we think he found some clue. Something big. He had found something we needed, something we could have used to fight back. He was coming to tell us."

"I thought you only care for your people?"

"Not any more. For this fight concerns every man, woman and child throughout the world. We must find what it was our man had discovered. If we do not, then all will be engulfed in the shadow of war."

Isabella sat back. "I know what he had found." The words came out of her like a torrent. She was aware that Henry had been drawn out of the shadows to hear and that Sandrine was bending closer towards her.

"What had he found?" asked Henry urgently.

"A name."

"Whose name?"

"I suppose the name of the person who can help us. The only one who can."

"And who is that?"

"Tacit," said Isabella, turning from Sandrine to Henry and then back again. "Inquisitor Poldek Tacit."

ELEVEN

ROME. ITALY.

A choral melody was rising up from somewhere in the depths of Trastevere Monastery, angelic voices lifting the gloom of the corridor within which Cardinal Bishop Adansoni stood. His shoes creaked on the uneven floorboards of the passageway, and he winced and tried to place them where they would make less noise, as if ashamed to disturb the choir's pristine sounds.

The door to the Sister's residence was plain and black, made of a single panel of wood that sat awkwardly under the twisted lintel in the slanting wall. Adansoni raised his fist and knocked. Almost without delay, he was asked to come in.

Sister Malpighi was sitting in a chair looking out of the window, her hunched back turned to the door so she could not see who had come in.

"Cardinal Bishop Adansoni," she said, only then looking over her right shoulder and smiling. She was ancient and withered, but there was a sharp light in her eyes that suggested great intellect and energy.

"Sister Malpighi," replied Adansoni, bowing and waiting to be beckoned into the room. "I apologise for my rude and unexpected interruption."

"Cardinal Bishop Adansoni, it was neither rude nor unexpected," she replied, the light gathering in her warm features. "Will you take a little refreshment?" She poured a stream of water from a long fluted china jug into a glass on the table beside her and moved it so that Adansoni would be able to reach it easily when he sat. "Of course, I know why you're here."

"Of course," replied Adansoni, smiling and setting himself down slowly. "I forgot." Sister Malpighi had long been well regarded by the Holy See and Inquisition for her powers of insight and premonition. Her skills had served the Vatican in times of concern and difficulty. There were others like her in the employ of the Vatican, people blessed with the power to predict the future and advise on it, but none had ever been as accurate or as long serving as the Sister who now watched Adansoni closely.

"Troubling times," she mused, pursing her thin lips.

"They are," nodded Adansoni, taking the goblet and sipping at its contents. The water was lukewarm and stale, as if it had stood in the jug for some time.

"I find myself sitting here so often now, Cardinal Bishop Adansoni," she revealed, peering out of her window over Rome, "looking to the city beyond, the city I love, my mind drawn to lands far away, places I have never visited or seen, other than in my imagination, or in books, and wondering, thinking what horrors must be taking seed right now within those terrible places of the western and eastern fronts. What terrors must be entwining man?" Sister Malpighi blinked, and Adansoni saw there were tears in her eyes. "The lamb of God is being murdered, the blood run out of him."

"Whatever do you mean?"

"In the Caucasus, there will be a massacre, a genocide of a whole people, two million Armenians killed, driven out into the desert to die by the Turkish authorities."

The old Cardinal swallowed. "When will that happen?" he asked gravely.

"It is happening now. At this very moment. As a prelude to *his* returning."

Adansoni shook his head in shock and turned his attention to the small window looking out over the capital. "It seems as if the war is polluting all the towns and cities of the world already. As if *he* has already returned."

"He is not returned yet, Cardinal Bishop Adansoni," the Sister announced. She lifted an eyebrow pointedly. "But he will return. That is certain. It will not be long. When the forces of Britain and Germany meet on the plains of the Somme, when a whole generation is wiped from existence within one morning, from out of their bloodshed and sacrifice he will be born."

"What about the others, those who come before him?" asked Adansoni without ceremony, his left hand tightening into a fist. "The ones who will protect him?"

"Why do they concern you, Cardinal Bishop Adansoni?" asked Sister Malpighi, a light in her eyes, the hint of suspicion on her lips.

"Does the coming of the Seven Princes of Hell not concern everyone?"

The Sister took a breath, a leathery stilted gasp, as if breathing was difficult. "It is unclear. There are forces, uncertainties, things which are still to be revealed. The waters of time are muddied and there is a breeze which blows over the top of them. But if you mean is there still time to stop them from returning, my answer to you, Cardinal Bishop Adansoni, is yes."

TWELVE

The Italian Front. The Soča River. Northwest Slovenia.

The Italian Third Army had been held in the clearing for days, just down from where the mountainside began the slow long climb to the Karst Plateau of the Carso. Pine forests surrounded them for miles in every direction, the scent of the sap rich in the heady air. It was hot, too hot for the soldiers' heavy uniforms, infrequent solace provided only when the sun slipped behind the occasional cloud. The choke of coal smoke was in the air, the endless bark of Sergeants' commands echoing down the mountain towards where valleys ran with the dazzlingly clear cold water of the Soča River.

The trudge of a hundred thousand pairs of boots sounded like a beating snare drum, the maddening noise echoing up and around the steep rocky valleys and sheer cliffs. White limestone shone with vivid light from the mountain, its glare so bright that the soldiers at times squinted to see. Units marched aimlessly in long snaking grey lines up and then back down the surrounding paths and tracks, or put their backs into lugging provisions and supplies to the depots of the camp.

As a break to the monotony of camp life, a new contingent of soldiers had recently arrived and were being processed and broken out into their allotted units. They looked too young and lost among the sea of men who had arrived earlier and already experienced some of what the mountainside and the elements could throw at them.

With them, a group of Priests, black-cassocked, peaked birettas balanced on slick foreheads, had followed at the rear, all five of them flanking a solitary young Private, as if in some way he was special, ordained. As soon as they arrived in the camp, it was clear that they intended to direct this new intake themselves, gesticulating and leading the nervous band of young men towards a particular unit of soldiers who watched the new influx arrive with interest.

The Italian Sergeant Major, standing at the top of the track up which they marched, didn't try to mask his disagreement at the small entourage of Priests seemingly doing his own job for him. He rubbed his hands down the front of his coat, filthy from his work, and looked from the starched collars of the Priests' necks to their road-weary features. He tried to measure the greeting he should give the clergymen and the end opted for, "What's your jurisdiction here then, Fathers?"

The leading Priest scowled and sized the solider up disdainfully.

Immediately the Sergeant knew there was something different about these Priests, all of them sombre, hollow-eyed, cheerless. Worn, as if they had travelled far and hard to reach this place under great difficulties.

"Long way off the beaten path, aren't we?" the Sergeant Major enquired, addressing the leading Priest, and then wondering nervously for a moment if word of his own little foray into the local town with a couple of his men whoring and drinking before the big push east had found its way back to the officer's mess and drawn Priests to investigate.

"Long time on the road as well," the Priest replied joylessly, his stubble the same jet-black as his eyes, and the Sergeant wondered what calling could had driven the Priests to have agreed to visit this ungodly place.

Hard men. That was the Sergeant's immediate impression of them, men not to be crossed. Men who would stop at nothing to answer their God's goals, no matter what the cost. Equally though, he supposed no harm could come of having Priests uttering prayers behind their backs as they climbed into the heights of the Italian-Slovenian border with the weight of the Austro-Hungarian army against them.

When the Sergeant Major had been first told of the plan, to drive east into the impenetrable heights of the Carso towards Monte San Michele, he had erupted with uncustomary derision, knowing that it would be madness. These northeastern border mountains, which now surrounded the Third Italian Army, were long known to provide Italy with both a shield against invaders and a wall to check their own ambitions of expansion. He knew any assault up them would be carnage.

"This one," the Priest said, indicating the youngest soldier they flanked. "He is to go with that unit." The Priest pointed towards a group of soldiers who had risen as one when the new recruits had arrived. He took the Private by the arm and urged him towards his new platoon.

"I beg your pardon?" asked the Sergeant, stepping into the Priest's line of sight. "I'm the one who decides who joins which unit."

"Not this time," replied the Priest, producing a piece of paper from the depths of his robe and pushing it into the Sergeant's hand. The soldier's eyes caught sight of the signature and at once he blanched and nodded.

"Very well" he said, stepping back. "And are you intending to stay?" The Sergeant's tone had changed instantly to one of subservience.

The question seemed to surprise the Priest. "Of course! We intend to ascend the Carso with them! Our prayers, we hope, will be heard and answered for swift victory."

"Well, all seems to be in order," muttered the Sergeant, handing back the paperwork, having looked no further than the signature upon it. After all, that was all he needed to make him realise this was not an appointment he should question.

"Good," nodded the Priest, taking the sheet from him. "I thought it would, with orders from Commander-in-chief Cadorna himself. Make sure the soldier remains with that unit. Do not let him leave it, not under any direction." The Sergeant nodded. "You will not want Cadorna to know his own orders have not been followed to the letter, will you? Now," he went on, looking over the massed ranks of infantry spread out across the stunted grass of the scorched mountainside, the endless, unmoving lines resembling bodies laid out in an open air morgue, "Where can we find lodgings? We need nothing extravagant. A little privacy will suffice."

The Sergeant pointed weakly to an officer's tent on the side of the ridge, standing empty as it had done for the last few days, ever since it had been erected. He supposed that would suit their needs. Few officers had risked coming into the front line from the lower valleys, even though the enemy was still miles away, high up in the crevices and ravines of the Carso, waiting for the Third Army itself to come to them.

"But sir," the Sergeant Major added quickly, his confidence still dented by the image of his unflinching and ruthless Commander-in-chief's signature, "surely you'll be more comfortable lodging further down the valley, won't you? Your type, begging your pardon, they are all encamped down there," he said, waving with his arm. "All the officers are posted away from the infantry. Surely you'd be happier among them?" The Sergeant was suddenly sure he no longer wanted the Priest and his fellow chaplains to stay in his camp. A harrowing sense of tragedy reflected in the darks of their eyes, the deep frown lines around their drawn and unyielding features. Malice lingered like a presence about them, as if death was their past and would be their future. He noticed the way the Priest he was addressing wouldn't make eye contact with him, that his gaze constantly strained to the high summits to the east as if they held a great fascination. And the Sergeant was glad that he hadn't looked into the Priest's eyes. He was sure that, had he done so, he would have seen something that would have haunted him for many years to come

The Priest raised his hand to silence him. "No," he said. "Where you indicate is fine," and he walked on, the chaplains falling into line behind him, taking their boxes of paraphernalia and swollen packs of provisions with them for the long march to the summit.

THIRTEEN

THE ITALIAN FRONT. THE SOČA RIVER. NORTHWEST SLOVENIA.

The group of soldiers gathered around the young Private, personally delivered by the Priests, and inspected him as if he were some gift given to the unit.

"What's your name, son?" the Corporal within the group asked at length. He had an open, swarthy face, from which emerald green eyes sparkled.

"Private Gilda. Private Pablo Gilda," said the young soldier. Next to the weathered appearance of the Corporal, burnt by sun and wind, the young Private looked like a child.

"Delivered to us by God?" said one of the soldiers in the group, mockingly. Pablo looked confused and the Corporal added, "The Priests. A personal entourage?"

"They're Priests from my local church."

"Are they now?" replied the Corporal, pursing his lips and considering the comment with suspicion. Pablo noticed that the Corporal's eyes kept dropping to look down at his hands, and surreptitiously the young man hid them behind his back. The Corporal clapped suddenly and his face broadened into a smile. "Anyway, Private Gilda, we are forgetting our manners. Welcome! Hope you brought your climbing boots?"

Pablo looked about his person anxiously. By now the Sergeant Major had crossed the ravaged dry limestone ground and joined the circle of soldiers. "Leave him alone, Corporal Abelli," the Sergeant warned. "You'll do well to ignore this idiot," he went on to say to Pablo.

"Catholic Priests," offered Abelli, taking out a large unlit round-bellied pipe and sticking it into the corner of his mouth. "Delivering our recruits now." He shook his head, and searched in a pocket for a match. "Looks like we're being honoured by the presence of the almighty, Sergeant Major? An army from God?" There was a trace of cynicism in his voice.

"Got to wonder why they suggested this poor sod goes with you, Corporal Abelli," said the Sergeant, looking Pablo up and down disdainfully.

"They obviously know class when they see it?" another of the soldiers replied, chuckling.

The Sergeant Major ignored the comment and scowled at Pablo. "You sure you're able to carry all that gear up a mountain," he asked doubtfully, looking at the Private's meagre frame.

Pablo nodded. "I've done my training. Six months."

One of the soldiers whistled and another laughed.

"Try six weeks in the Carso," said one of them.

The Sergeant Major told him to shut up. "You're in no position to lecture, Private," he told the soldier. "You've not even seen any action yet." He turned back to Pablo. "So, the Priests, they must care about you if they delivered you here personally."

Pablo shrugged. "I suppose so. They were my Priests, at the church in Udine."

"Family in Udine, are they?" asked the Sergeant, and Pablo's face darkened and he shook his head, looking at his boots.

"No, I don't have any family," he answered bluntly.

"Everyone has family," replied Corporal Abelli.

"Not me," said Pablo, and there was heat now in his face.

"Well, we're your family now," said the Sergeant, cooling the situation.

"Poor bloody sod," said one of the Privates, and laughter followed among his peers.

"Hey!" the Sergeant replied, raising a chubby finger in his direction, "the army cares about all of its soldiers."

"If they cared about us," growled a Private from across the path, "they wouldn't have sent us to this godforsaken place in the first place! Less than two months since Italy entered the war and already men are dying by the thousands in these mountains."

The Sergeant Major rounded on him. "Some soldier you are, Sarem!" This is war, Private! Death is caught up with it. You should know that! It's why you wear your uniform."

"Well some crazy war this is!" replied Sarem. "What are we even fighting for? You tell me that!"

"To do our bit."

"Well I cannot see any sense in it. There's nothing but rock and stone for two hundred miles over my back. No good will come of it. There is nothing to be gained from striking against the Austro-Hungarians here."

The Sergeant laughed. "Private Sarem! I never knew you were so gifted in the art of warfare planning? If I'd known, I'd have asked for you to have been transferred to the military camp in Santa Maria Capua Vetere!"

The newly arrived Private anxiously cleared his throat and the Sergeant turned back to hear him speak. "The Treaty of London," he said. All eyes studied Pablo and his skin flushed crimson.

"There you go, Sarem," replied the Sergeant, looking over into the adjoining unit. "The Treaty of London. You're clearly wasted among these fools, Private Gilda. Why'd they bring you here anyway?" he asked Pablo.

"The Priests brought me," replied Pablo. "Just told me it was time for me to do my duty and I did what I was told to do."

The Sergeant tapped him on the shoulder. "You carry on like that, Private Gilda," he said, winking and turning to leave, "and you'll be just fine."

"Don't worry about Private Gilda," Corporal Abelli said to the Sergeant, "We'll take good care of him."

"What about this Treaty of London?" asked Lazzari, another soldier of the platoon, seemingly intrigued. "I never heard of any Treaty."

"This war, it is a chance to take territories along our border long desired," replied Pablo, as if reciting from a book.

"Well that's one reason for it," said Abelli, and Pablo followed the line of the soldier's stare to the valley sweeping beyond them. "How do you know so much then, Gilda? You schooled?"

Pablo reddened even more deeply and shrugged, wishing he hadn't been so quick to speak. "Only by the Priests. They've looked after me for much of my life. And from the newspapers."

The Corporal laughed, and some of the men around him laughed too.

"You'll never find anything of value in those papers, son," the Corporal warned. "Lies and propaganda. They won't tell you anything of worth. Not anything of what this land really represents. Of what really resides within them."

"And what is that?" asked Pablo.

"Horrors."

"Do you mean the enemy?"

"I do. But which enemy?"

"I don't understand."

"But I thought you read the papers?" Pablo shook his head and the Corporal leaned towards him. "You a god-fearing man, Private?"

"Isn't everyone?"

"There is a legend that the Devil resides within the Carso, that it is his domain, that the limestone mountain is his iron flesh, that the turquoise Soča river which courses through the valley his cold blood, that the very highest peaks are his throne where he resides."

The Corporal had returned his gaze once more to the very top of the Carso mountains where Pablo knew he and the rest of the Third Italian Army would soon be headed. He shivered and was no longer aware of the low murmur of conversation from the rest of the army, the rhythmic clank of a hammer on an anvil, the occasional hoarse shout of laughter from somewhere within the camp.

Instead, he ran his eyes back along the high ridge of mountains above them where he knew the massed ranks of the Austro-Hungarian Fifth Army lay entrenched in narrow crevices and passages waiting for the Italians to begin their push east.

Its height brought a weight to Pablo's chest when he looked up, but the Corporal seemed to peer at it fondly. "Nothing can live here and prosper, save for unspeakable things which crawl out of their caves and lairs on a night, scavenging for the unweary, the foolish."

"What things?" asked Pablo urgently.

But the Corporal either couldn't or wouldn't say. "Nothing can hope to gain favour from this barren land," he said instead. He had produced a steel cup from his belt pocket and filled it with coffee from the smoking pot over the fire, setting it to his thick ruby lips. The coffee looked hellishly black and as strong as death. There were flies on its onyx surface but he either didn't see or didn't care. The sun beat down on the back of his ruddy neck, a rivulet of sweat running from his broad hairline down the side of his face. He swiped the trickle away absently, before turning his attention back to the young soldier. He shook his head and muttered something which sounded like a curse to Pablo.

"This wasteland, it is a place of blood and death and suffering. We go to it to face our ending, however that might come to be, and face our true enemy within it. It is a cursed place, cast away by God as a execration for allowing the Devil to find shelter and refuge within it. 'Let this be a kingdom of stone,' God spoke, 'where men labour to survive.' And so we shall."

"Survive?" asked Pablo, feeling his heart beat in this throat, knowing the Corporal with whom he had been placed was clearly troubled.

The soldier looked at him and shook his head. "No, we shall not survive," he replied, turning to look at the Sergeant who had blanched at his words, transfixed by their barren nature. "But we shall labour," he said. "Greatly." Corporal Abelli's attention fell to Pablo's hands. Pablo noticed and immediately scrunched them into fists in an attempt again to hide them from him. But not quickly enough. "Your hands," asked his Corporal.

"What about them?"

"Let me see them."

Pablo hesitated for a moment before holding them out. All his life he had been tormented because of them, shamed by his parents, taunted by those he knew and strangers alike for his oddity while growing up in the foothills of Udine. Eventually, turned out at the age of twelve by those he loved, he had been taken in by the Church, who had cared for him and, on his eighteenth birthday, had encouraged him to join the army. A life fit for a man such as him, according to their wisdom. Six months later, Italy had entered the war and drawn Pablo in with it.

"Six fingers," said the Corporal, looking between the outstretched hands, "on each hand."

"Go on then," retorted Pablo, taking them back and hiding them from view in his armpits, "say something."

"Like what," shrugged the Corporal. "Congratulate you that you're descended from Saph and Rapha of Gath, and the giant Goliath? If so, seems to me you've come to the right place," he said, his face brightening.

"I don't understand?" asked Pablo, fearing a trick. "What do you mean by that? Of Goliath and Gath?"

"What is the matter with you?" asked the Corporal. "I thought you were the wise one? Have you never studied your Old Testament?"

"Of course."

"You're a liar," the Corporal laughed. "Ishbi-Benob. Saph. Lahmi and his brother Goliath. They were all descendants of Gath, the Nephelim, born of Satan's blood, great warriors and wielders of six fingers on each hand."

"I never knew!" replied Pablo, holding his hands up in front of him, as if regarding a gift he had unknowingly carried with him all his life.

"So it would seem," said Abelli, clapping him on the back. "You're just the person we've been waiting for, Private, a great warrior, come to claim back his domain."

FOURTEEN

Toulouse Inquisitional Prison. Toulouse. France.

Tacit was breathing hard now. The nails driven firmly through his hands into the wood of the chair had done the trick, made him break sweat, his chest tighten, his heart pump. He looked up through his brows, his wild bloodshot eyes set firm on his torturer, and spat at him wordlessly, hissing and seething like a demon.

Salamanca smiled proudly and drew another nail from his tray of implements, the gaggle of jailers and miscreants of the prison guard hooting with laughter and excitement. This had exceeded their expectations. They never expected Salamanca to have reached for the nails so soon with this prisoner. The torturer held the spike up in the light, admiring the six inches of matt grey iron as a connoisseur might a glass of fine wine. He turned his eyes onto his unyielding victim and his face hardened.

"What are you resisting for?" he asked, unable to hide his disappointment that the Inquisitor had still refused to break despite all Salamanca had done to him. The torturer had never known a subject like Tacit. They always broke with the nails. After everything which had gone before, the blades, the hot irons, the tearing of the fingernails, the raking of the skin, nails hammered hard and firm into the arms and hands always broke even the most determined of resisters. It was why they nailed victims up onto crosses during crucifixions. The practice had long been stopped but here, deep within the Inquisitional Prison, a few liked to keep at least some aspects of the past alive.

"You will break eventually," he warned Tacit, taking the nail and setting it hard into the skin of the Inquisitor's right forearm. He raised the hammer high above his head and behind him the audience clapped their hands in expectation. "You may as well do it sooner rather than later. Trust me, it'll make it easier, if you break now."

"Who for?" growled Tacit, his lower lip hanging slack in his mouth, a stalactite of spit dripping from it. "You, or me?"

Salamanca allowed himself a brief chuckle, but inside his anger raged.

"Oh, you're a brave one, Tacit. Brave, but deluded. It doesn't bother me to see you resist, to see you hold out like you're trying to do. I've seen other men, better men, braver men than you do much the same, but all go the same way in the end. It's the application of pain which I like. It gives one such a sense of … superiority. But you'd know all about that, wouldn't you, Inquisitor?"

"Unchain me and we'll see what superiority you really have," warned Tacit, tensing against his bonds and the nails which held him firm to his chair.

A voice, shrill and deceitful, caught suddenly in Tacit's ear, speaking of baleful actions and power, words only he could hear. Tacit fought harder against the chains in a vain attempt to silence the demonic sounds.

"Such strength!" mocked the torturer, watching Tacit struggle, lowering the hammer and standing back, crossing his arms. He'd made a note in his book for his contact at the Holy See, as instructed. The person there had wanted to know everything about Tacit's behaviour and his reaction to the different techniques Salamanca was so skilled in applying. Whether he reacted differently to fire or the knife's edge, if the torture of the mind affected him as much as the torture of the flesh, if ever it seemed that a particular method significantly influenced the reaction of the prisoner.

If Salamanca ever felt the presence of the Devil in the room through his actions. They had been quite insistent.

"Such bravado! Such determination! Pathetic!" he hissed, and snatched Tacit tight by the throat, thrusting him hard into the chair, his face held close to the Inquisitor's. "You playing the part of the strong man? Hah! You're nothing! Nothing but a fool and a joke. You've already shown your weakness once, Inquisitor, to the whole Catholic world at the Mass for Peace. You might think you're important, that you're better than everyone else, that you can act as you please, above the doctrine, above the faith. But you've not fooled me. Do you honestly think you're somehow more special than everyone else? You're no more special than the shit on my shoe. In fact, you're worse. Special? Pah! How can someone who does exactly as his masters decree be special? A lackey more like, a lackey around the finger of the Pope and everyone else in the Holy See."

Salamanca allowed a wicked chuckle to escape his lungs and then scowled, squeezing hard onto Tacit's throat, making the veins protrude from the Inquisitor's skull. "Pissed on by everyone you know, that's what you are. Your masters, your colleagues, your acquaintances. How sad that they see you as nothing more than a bucket to piss in. I would say friends, but you don't have any, do you? Never let anyone close enough to you, did you?

"Although there was one, wasn't there? What was his name? Georgi, wasn't it? Georgi Akeldama? Was that him? Your friend from those very first days? Those innocent days as an acolyte, before you became a fully-fledged Inquisitor. Died, didn't he? Vanished, apparently. Consumed by the Inquisition and the fires of their hate, so the rumour goes. Oh yes," said Salamanca, recognising the surprise in Tacit's face, "we know. We know everything."

"Except what happened to him," Tacit retorted, with grim pleasure at the flaw in his torturer's taunt.

Salamanca stood back and slowly unbuttoned the fly to his trousers. The throng of guards and jailers behind him hissed and threw insults at the chained prisoner for they knew what was about to take place.

"What are you resisting for, Tacit?" Salamanca asked, reaching for his cock and dragging it out, a diseased putrid-looking thing in his hand. Long had it been used as a weapon upon the witches and depraved brought into the prison. Often it stung Salamanca with agony and leaked a thick diseased sludge from its end whenever he tried to use it, a sure sign, in his mind, that he had drawn the poison out of the afflicted when he used it against them. It was a weight and a pain he was willing to bear, for his faith. "What are you resisting for, piss bucket?" he spat, forcing a stream of urine out of the tip of it and onto Tacit. The Inquisitor moaned when the spray touched him, but the bonds and nails held him tight. "Don't tell me you're holding out for some hope?" mocked Salamanca, the stream of glistening yellow piss curving onto Tacit's soaked clothes. "For somebody to come and rescue you? To call for your release?" He stopped urinating and corrected himself, secretly pleased to find the act pained him less than usual. "You forget, you have no friends anymore, no one who cares about you. They're all dead."

He laughed and stepped forward, picking up the hammer and nail and setting it back to the skin of Tacit's forearm, the hammer held high. "It's just you and me now for the remainder of your days, at least until I've decided I've had enough of you. So come on," he growled, his eyes growing wide, "entertain me while you can!" He brought the hammer down hard on the head of the nail.

And the private voice returned, more loathsome than ever, crying guttural curses. And deeper still, lights began to flicker and burn red within Tacit.

FIFTEEN

The Vatican. Vatican City.

Father Strettavario watched Bishop Basquez slip from the Vatican Library and moved across the Belvedere Courtyard to meet him where the shadows of the Apostolic Library were erased by the sun.

"Bishop Basquez," the Father greeted him, standing square and firm. It was a stance never intended to intimidate or impress. Strettavario had always been squat and thick-set, ever since puberty had failed much to give him height, only widen his shoulders. He had always had the appearance of a man who could handle himself, should the teachings of God fail him.

"Father Strettavario," replied the Bishop, making no effort to mask his displeasure at seeing the ginger-haired Priest approach. "What can I do for you?"

"A little tense this morning, aren't we?" asked Strettavario, enjoying the opportunity to mock the wily Bishop.

"Considering the times in which we live, I feel it prudent to be tense," replied Basquez, his eyes narrowing with distain. "Inquisitors being killed within the streets of Rome. Demonic possessions enslaving a nation. A world war enflaming a continent. A war now come to Italy's borders. And yet you face it with your pitiful wit, no doubt some attempt to form humour at my expense?"

Strettavario snatched hold of Basquez's sleeve and drew him close, the old Father's strength alarming the ambitious young Bishop as he tried vainly to pull his arm free.

"Don't try to warn me about when and how to be prudent, Bishop Basquez," growled Strettavario menacingly. "I've lived years longer than you, in situations far more grave than you'd ever dare to face, rubbed shoulders with folk who'd turn your hair white and your heart to pallid rubber. So don't you dare lecture me about the dangers we face!"

The Father's grip on Basquez's cotton sleeve loosened a little and the Bishop pulled it clear, the crimson flush of emotion slowly fading from his neck.

"I am busy," Basquez announced, workmanlike, choosing not to look in the pale eyes of the Priest. "It is not in my nature to squander what little time we've been given by God in talking of inconsequential issues or sharing lectures. I must go and attend to my duties."

"Then you won't mind me accompanying you for a little way, will you?" asked Strettavario, falling in alongside the Bishop as he strode from the courtyard. He saw the Bishop scowl and allowed himself a smile.

"I know what you're up to," said the Father.

"And what is that?" replied Basquez, passing under the archway at the far end of the walled square and into the stone cloisters which ran to the main complex of St Peter's Bascilica buildings.

"Tacit."

"What about him?"

"What you're doing to him in Toulouse Prison."

"And why should it concern you, Father Strettavario, what punishments we are inflicting upon the fallen and corrupt within one of our inquisitional prisons?"

"I have known Tacit for a long time. Longer than most. You don't know what you're dealing with."

"And that is why we are experimenting with him. To find out if what they say about him is true, if there is more to him than meets the eye."

"So that is what this is then? An experiment?"

"Among other things, yes," replied Basquez swiftly.

"Who's bidding are you acting upon?" asked Strettavario, the question bringing the Bishop to a halt. "Who are you working for?"

They had plunged from the cloisters into a covered wooden walkway along which hung portraits of long dead Fathers. Strettavario wondered if one day after his death his painting would be hung in public or left to moulder in one of the lower chambers of the Vatican.

"Unfortunately some actions of the Holy See, and those behind them, need to remain secret." Basquez smiled, and made to leave, but drew back. "Perhaps like others you too share a certain fondness for this Tacit?" he said, resting a mocking hand of false concern on Strettavario's wrist. "Think of past Saints and the sacrifices they have made in order to ensure the improvement and continuation of our faith. Think of Tacit's fate as being similar to theirs. Their sacrifice to benefit us all. That way I'm sure you'll find it more palatable. Not nearly so unfair, nor so unjust. This war, Strettavario," said Basquez, looking down on the squat Father like an officer on one of his juniors, "this suicide of Europe as Pope Benedict calls it, it demands that we must all make sacrifices in order to overcome. And make unpleasant choices in order to persevere. That is what we are doing."

But Strettavario shook his head and drew his lips into a tight knot of thought. "You misunderstand. It's just a warning for you, Basquez," said the Father, his pale eyes hardening once more, "that what you're doing doesn't blow up in your face and come visiting you sometime, in the middle of the night."

SIXTEEN

The Vatican. Vatican City.

The ghost of electricity crackled through the dead air around Vatican City. Those still awake could feel it, in their hair, at the tips of their fingers, could smell the charged metallic odour of the atmosphere that always comes just before a storm. Working servants threw open shuttered windows to peer at the growing storm and then drew them back on seeing the sky, while Priests holding private midnight services crossed themselves and muttered liturgies on silent tongues.

Along the top of St Peter's Basilica, recently arrived crows squawked angrily from the statues of Christ and Saint John the Baptist as the Inquisitor, dressed all in black but for the notch of white at his neck, stepped out across the slowly emptying square far below. He marched swiftly and with purpose towards the red granite obelisk standing tall in the very centre of the darkened square and the solitary figure hunched on one of the benches facing it. The Inquisitor strode with his head down, his body hurrying with every stride, as if the message he was bringing could not afford to be delayed further.

Behind him crows savagely harried doves from their roosts around the clay-tiled roofs, while above dramatic clouds gathered in the pitch-black sky, flecked with reds and purples.

Without a word, the Inquisitor chose a place next to the hooded figure and drew the corners of his cape about him to offer a little more protection against the gathering cool of midnight. For several moments the pair sat in silence, their eyes drawn to the obelisk as if in silent communion.

"Are the wheels in motion?" the hooded figure began, his tone grave and solemn. The Inquisitor didn't look across at him, but instead kept his eyes firmly on the summit of the needle of stone, the tip almost lost in the black of night. "The Priests," he replied in a hushed tone. "They have reached the foothills of the Carso. The descendant of Gath is with them and has been delivered safely into the hands of the unit. All is in hand."

"Excellent. This war, this carefully orchestrated conflict, it is a testament to what we have become, how far our power has spread, how much control we can command. Already most of Europe is in flames. The English, French and Germans have ground themselves into an impasse on the western front. The same can be said on the eastern front, the Russians pouring themselves into the fire of the German and Austro-Hungarian cannons for little gain. Now a third front has been opened, a third side to close the triangle and to lock in the horrors, the killing. The magicks."

He smirked grimly with an anticipation he could barely contain. "Three fronts to mirror the three cardinal sins of man. Three cardinal sins to wake them from their chained slumber. A fertile ground drenched ready to accept them."

He exhaled and shook his head, pushing back his hood to reveal his weathered, hard features. His muscular jaw was square and shadowed with dark growth of several days. "It seems like a lifetime for us to have finally reached this moment. For me I suppose it has been a lifetime."

The man looked down into his lap, as if touched by sudden emotion at recalling his past. "I died for them, you know," he said, rubbing his calloused hands gently over each other, "when the time came, when the call was made to leave the faith and join them. I pretended I had been defeated. Murdered. It has been a weight I have carried ever since, the pretence that I was weak, so weak that I would die in the line of duty."

He looked and stared across the square, any sorrow now replaced with rage. "It is the Catholic faith that is weak!" he spat. "What power do they wield that can possibly compete with that of the lord of darkness? When I served in the Inquisition, every day brought news of yet more deaths of our fellow Inquisitors until only Poldek Tacit and I remained from the year of our intake. I knew then that they were failed by a faith which could not face its enemies with any hope of victory. Only one could assure me of dominance. He has shown and given me so much."

"Georgi, the signs of their returning are already everywhere," spoke the Priest. "Visions of their legacy manifest within the cities and the towns all across the region. Across the world! Talk of possessions and devilish occurrences. The Inquisition is barely able to cope. Those of us who have seen the light, we are doing all we can to propagate the fear and fan the flames of hell's brood."

Georgi nodded. "Good. This time things will proceed as planned. There can be no chance of failure. Not this time. We have invested so much, sacrificed all in their name."

"The rituals of the sins?" asked the Priest.

"I will begin them at once."

The Priest smiled, as if satisfied. "Sister Isabella," he said, after a long pause, his eyes still not leaving the pillar of rock, as if he spoke more to himself than to Georgi beside him. He noticed that the man did not move, save for the lines around his eyes which seemed to deepen, as if the name was known to him. "She killed three Inquisitors."

Georgi unfolded his arms, knotting his fingers together in his lap and looking down at them with quiet resignation. "The woman has spirit. And a talent few of us realised when she was first chosen to accompany Poldek Tacit in Arras. It was a surprise to me when I discovered she had witnessed Cincenzo's execution."

"And you're sure it was her?"

"The cloak I retrieved, discarded at Sisto Bridge. It was hers. I could smell her scent upon it. Someone helped her escape."

Almost at once, lightning appeared to flash in the heart of the gathering clouds and a rumble of thunder rolled across the city moments later.

"Who?"

"We don't know. We never got a look at them. We can only suppose it was one of the group to which Inquisitor Cincenzo was affiliated."

"They are proving to be troublesome."

"We will continue to hunt them. They will not affect your work."

"They had better not. Our masters would be displeased if anything were to derail what has so far been achieved. Have you identified your targets?"

Georgi threw a barbed look in the Priest's direction. "Of course I have! I have prepared long for this moment. My training has been endless, the application of my study unyielding. I know what I must do and against whom. The one with the power of 'sight' and the one with the power of the 'flesh' shall commence the ritual. Just make sure I am allowed to work unmolested."

"We shall."

He looked across at the Priest. "Sister Isabella. She will play her part yet, for ours, and his, gain. It is time now to complete the work and prepare the world to welcome their return. When the third and final act must be done, I will hunt Isabella down and ensure that Tacit does what has long been required of him."

PART TWO

"Children, it is the last hour, and as you have heard that Antichrist is coming, so now many Antichrists have come. Therefore we know that it is the last hour."

1 John 2:18

SEVENTEEN

Monsignor Benigni had never in his life expected to be involved in a murder case.

He knew he shouldn't be here. The usual business of the Sodalitium Pianum was to weed out attempts to modernise the timeless fundamental values of the Catholic faith, a far cry from dangerous inquisitional work. But no matter the task, Benigni knew that if the work brought him closer to God, then he would be happy. After all, he was a devoutly God-fearing man. Anything he could do to gain favour from his Lord would be comforting to him.

When he had established the Sodalitium Pianum in 1907, he had done so to help root out and censor the teaching and distribution of condemned doctrine within the faith, to stamp out the threat of modernist thinking within the sound traditional values of the Church.

However, he had accepted the request by the Holy See to investigate the murder without hesitation. The Inquisition, more adept and experienced at handling such a case, was stretched, its ranks overwhelmed and strained by recent events within the city and further afield. The Devil's grip upon the earth seemed to be tightening, and Monsignor Benigni knew that his work here might perhaps not only help in some small way to loosen his scaly-taloned hold, but would undoubtedly win him greater admiration and respect from many within the upper echelons of power. And, with this admiration, Benigni knew he would be enabled to further expand the remit of the Sodalitium Pianum's work.

Monsignor was a simple, earnest man, but he had big plans for his own secret organisation.

An overweight bear-like figure, dressed in stern starched black save for the square of white at his neck, he stood at the apex of the bridge and looked down into the Tiber. They'd found Inquisitor Cincenzo's body nearly a mile down river from here, snagged on rocks where the river bed rose and the waters ran quicker. He'd been shot, clean through the head. Death would have been instantaneous.

Benigni turned his notes in his short stumpy fingers and pushed his glasses back up his nose, absently humming a tune he had recently heard. It was a waltz by an American arranger called Frederic Knight Logan, a most offensive tune, and Benigni forcibly caught hold of himself and shook his head to remove the song, dragging a hand across his forehead to mop his sweating brow. Clearly he needed rest. He seemed overworked and weak, susceptible he supposed to the Devil's temptations.

Refocusing his mind on his case notes, he considered what he knew. The round which had been used was a .455 and had come from a Webley revolver, standard issue for Inquisitors. Inquisitor Cincenzo, the individual who had been killed, was young, eager, had achieved good grades during his acolyte years and showed a penchant for learning, perhaps too much. Perhaps it was that which got him into trouble eventually, speaking to the wrong people, asking too many of the wrong questions?

Benigni looked back across the bridge and the marks in the dirt where the pack had surrounded Cincenzo and hemmed him in. The grip marks proved they were regulation inquisitional boots. Everything pointed to an internal killing.

Everything except the sulphur.

There was a smell of sulphur which seemed to linger around the spot where Cincenzo had been shot. That was hard to explain.

"Monsignor Benigni!" called one his team of the Sodalitium Pianum, approaching with urgency.

"What is it?"

"Something we have found scrawled on Inquisitor Cincenzo's wall in his residence."

"Oh? And what would that be?"

"Simply three words. Eyes. Flesh. Life."

"Whatever does that mean?" Benigni mumbled, more to himself than his fellow Priest.

"I have no idea. He'd scrawled it on his wall beside his bed, along with a name. Tacit."

"Poldek Tacit?" muttered Benigni, adding Tacit's name to the three words in his notes. "Why should Cincenzo ever name him?"

EIGHTEEN

ROME. ITALY.

"I'm surprised," said Isabella, pulling her still damp clinging clothes away from her skin, "you dealing with Inquisitors? The soldiers of the Catholic Church? I thought the Church was your enemy?"

"Have you listened to nothing we've said?" Sandrine shouted, propelling herself forward to lean over Isabella. Her reaction was so extreme that Isabella, thinking the woman was about to lash out at her, cowered away in fear. "Everything has changed. Old feuds have ended, concessions have been made. They've had to be, especially now in these dark days. This Inquisitor? He was an ally."

"And how many of you are there?"

"Not enough," Sandrine sighed, turning away. "The Darkest Hand, they have corrupted too many minds, enslaved too many hearts. Where there is fear in a person, there is an open harbour within which to moor the seeds of hate and darkness. And we are even fewer now." She looked across at Henry, who nodded.

"There were four other Inquisitors who had joined us but we lost contact with them three days ago," he said.

"Where?"

"In the city. There were rumours of demons in south Rome. They went to investigate and sent a message, something about a seer."

"A seer? Who's that?"

"We don't know. And they've not been heard from since."

"But we are a start," insisted Sandrine, her jaw squared by her gritted teeth. "A beginning. Soldiers, Priests, Inquisitors. We are all fighting for the same reasons against the same enemy."

"For many months now we've infiltrated the Vatican," said Henry. "Found allies."

"We've had to," said Sandrine, anticipating Isabella's next question. "For it is there that the Darkest Hand first took root, perhaps even before 1877. We have learnt that much. From that black seed it has spread far, throughout the faith, enslaving many within the Inquisition and the Priesthood, slithered into industry, politics, royalty, the military, wherever there is the opportunity to gain favour and an initiative against others presumed to be weaker. The lure of the Devil is strong. And we must work together to fight him."

"And who exactly are you?" Isabella asked.

"We are what comes after the Mass for Peace," said Sandrine.

"The Mass for Peace failed."

"And that is why we exist today. This world war, we think it is part of their plan, the precursor to his returning, the preparing of a land fit for one of his wickedness and ruin, for when he returns."

"And who is he?" asked Isabella, but she feared she already knew his name.

Sandrine's voice had fallen to a low murmur. "The Antichrist."

Isabella hesitated, attempting to speak, but the words failed her. She shook her head, letting out her breath, looking between the pair of them disbelievingly, their hard glares burning into her.

"I … I don't believe you," she said.

"Don't, or can't?" asked Henry.

"Both! The Antichrist? Just because events are mirroring what happened in 1877, that doesn't mean anything." She could feel her face flush with shock. "It doesn't mean *he* is involved!"

"The famine? The possessions? The demonic births?" said Sandrine, raising an eyebrow.

"Do you think he has returned already?"

"No. He is biding his time, waiting for his moment to grasp power and drag the world into an apocalypse from which it might never recover. But he cannot do that yet. Not until all is ready for him."

"But I still don't understand!" exclaimed Isabella. "How do you know it is him? I have seen the wickedness of man with my own eyes, what he is capable of. It does not mean that the Devil guides his hands or his actions."

"You talk of evil," replied Sandrine. "You cannot begin to imagine the depths of its corruption."

"I don't know what you mean."

"I wouldn't expect you to, not unless you had witnessed it first hand, and even then you would doubt what you had witnessed. This evil is hidden deep, buried within the very roots of the Vatican, and now commands the highest echelons of power through persuasion, fear and black magicks. This is why we cannot trust anyone else to fight it. The Holy See, the Inquisition, the governments of the world, they are all polluted by the Darkest Hand's influence."

Isabella held up her hands. "Stop!" she said. "Stop! Look, I am sorry. I am tired and I am cold and this brandy is too strong. You're telling that great swathes of people have sided with the Devil? That it originates from within the Vatican? That they are attempting to see his return to the world?" She looked across to Henry, hoping to see some sense from him, but the young officer showed no emotion. Isabella looked back at Sandrine. "I will not believe it, not for a moment!"

"And that is why they are allowed to grow, fester like a disease in a wound. For long we have investigated. They are preparing his domain. But he will only return when the world is truly ready, and his lieutenants are in place, the seven princes of hell."

Isabella shivered and drew the blanket tighter about her. It seemed as if the temperature within the room had dropped at the mention of such things.

"What plans they have, we do not know. But they must be stopped. You saw what they did to Inquisitor Cincenzo. What they tried to do to you. They'll stop at nothing, nothing to achieve their goals. They're wicked, black beyond words."

"How? How did you come to be here, in Rome? To travel all this way?"

"Wolves talk," replied Sandrine darkly, and Isabella looked at her confused. "After Fampoux, Henry and I went south, both to escape what was intended to happen at the Mass for Peace and to escape the madness of the war." She looked across at Henry and for the first time Isabella saw her smile, a sad determined smile full of love and admiration for the man seated at the table.

"At Lyon we felt we'd gone far enough away," continued Henry, picking up the story. "The house we found we rented from the farmer. It was decrepit and small, an old animal shelter, barely big enough for the pair of us, but the farmer seemed happy for us take it and turn it into a home before it fell to stones in the ground."

Sandrine stepped back to the table, leaning over it, her knuckles white to the wood. "After we settled in the South of France, it was not long until I caught the rumour of clans close to Lyon. I would visit them, cautiously at first, but I garnered their trust over long months and eventually they welcomed me into their burrows. They appreciated the company of others from outside their community who did not balk at the sight and smell of them. They learnt of my past, and I learnt of theirs, and of what they had heard from deep beneath the roots of the Vatican."

"What had they heard?"

"That the darkness was returning once again. Wolves talk long in their lairs. It is all they have during the hours of sunlight, they talk, and they tunnel and they dig deep and far. And during that time, they caught word that there were dark forces at work within the fabric of Rome. Something rotten growing deep in the heart of the Vatican, something which had been on earth before, and was now returning again. This war all around you, this is a sign that the age of darkness is coming. Indeed, some say, the age has already arrived."

"And how had they come to learn this? They cannot leave their lairs by daylight, and when they do at night, they are rent of all sanity."

"Because those who have since become our spies told them."

Sandrine drained her glass and cleared her throat.

Henry leant forward into the light from the candle and rested his hand on Isabella's in an attempt to lessen the horror etched into her face. "We are not alone," he assured her. "There are others who fight with us, both outside and inside the Church."

"Wolves?" asked Isabella incredulously. "Hombre Lobo? Do they fight for you as well?"

"Those that will," nodded Henry. "And Inquisitors too."

"Enemies, now allies?"

"Of sorts," said Sandrine.

"One being Inquisitor Cincenzo."

"Precisely."

"He was working with us, at least until he was found out and killed."

"Tacit," said Sandrine.

"What about him?" asked Isabella, suddenly protective at hearing his name mentioned in such a dark conversation.

"You said Inquisitor Cincenzo said his name as he died. Why?"

Isabella shrugged, overwhelmed by the question and the confusion of her mind. "I don't know. I don't know anything. Only that I know Tacit, what he is capable of."

"I know too," growled Sandrine. "The ruination of our plans in Paris was because of him."

"And I was to blame too," countered Isabella, feeling a strength renew within her, "and yet you are talking to me, telling me all you know."

"So the question is," Henry mused, picking up the Inquisitor's brooch from the table and turning it in his fingers, "just what was it about Tacit that was so important to Cincenzo that he spoke his name before he died?"

Isabella hesitated, feeling her stomach lurch. "We need to break him out."

"Why?"

"You said you needed help. Perhaps Tacit is the one who can? Maybe he's the only one who can?"

"Where is he now?"

"In Toulouse Inquisitional Prison."

"Impossible," replied Henry, shaking his head.

"Why?"

"We have no one there on the inside who can help us."

But Isabella paused, putting her hand to her lips. "Perhaps the one who can help us is not at the prison."

Sandrine sat on the table's edge, leaning a well-toned arm on her raised knee. Candlelight caught once more in her olive-skinned face, turning her features demonic and sly, but her tone was calm. "What do you mean?"

"You talk about us being not many, just a few," the Sister said, taking up the bottle and refilling her glass. She raised the strong liquor to her lips. "Perhaps then we need someone else to join us. Someone to even up the odds."

"Can we trust this person?" asked Henry, turning briefly to look at Sandrine doubtfully.

"Probably not, no," replied Isabella. "But there's no one better connected I know of who can help. And he cares for Tacit. Maybe he's the only other person left in the world who does."

NINETEEN

Paris. France.

The white sheets of the bed were spattered red with blood, as the woman arched her back screaming, pushing against the infant in her belly.

"Maria!" cried her husband, clutching her hand tight so his own turned white.

"She is fine!" exclaimed the old nurse, shooing him from the bedside in order to examine her from the foot of it. "She is giving birth. That is all. We women have done so for a hundred thousand years. And we shall continue to do for another hundred thousand, if the Lord preserves," she continued, peering across to the Priest in the shadows of the room and then up at the crucifix nailed to the wall above the bed.

"He shall, and he will," replied the Priest assuredly, his hand to his heart, and the nurse smiled back, before wiping the sweat from her brow with her sleeve and refocusing her attention on delivering the child.

"Now go and get some more hot water, Duilio!" she said. "And towels!" she called after him, as he fled from his wife's screams to the kitchen beyond, where he had already stoked a roaring fire in the hearth at the centre of the room. He found that the pan on top of the grille over the fire had boiled dry and at once refilled it from the jug on the side, the water sizzling and steaming into his face as it touched the scorching metal.

Without a moment's hesitation, he ran back to the room, pushing past the Priest and grasping his wife's hand again.

"It is a miracle," Duilio said, tears growing in his eyes as he looked down at her struggle. "For years my wife and I, we tried for a child. And for years our Father did not answer our prayers. And then, when we felt that our time was over and that I would never have an heir, he rewards us!"

Maria's screams gathered to a crescendo and both Duilio and the Priest gathered round to the nurse as she called, "The baby! The baby is coming! I can see its head!"

"Push, Maria! Push!" urged Duilio, her hand back in his, his eyes fixed on the nurse's studious face between her knees. "Let us see our child with our own eyes!"

Suddenly the old nurse's face changed, turning from wonderment to horror.

"What is it?" asked Duilio urgently, as Maria's screams faded and the nurse's took over to shake the foundations of the tiny house. "What's wrong?"

"What is it?" Maria now asked weakly, feeling no more pain but instead seeing the concern on her husband's face.

"What is wrong?" Duilio asked again, but the nurse didn't answer, instead throwing herself away from the bed, the backs of her bloodied hands to her face, covering her eyes from the thing she had pulled from the woman.

As if by a hook, Duilio was dragged to look and now he cried out to see the thing on the bed, his hands clutched tight to the sides of his head, tearing wildly at his hair.

"What's wrong?" wept Maria, but Duilio never heard her, his ears filled with his own screams.

The infant resembled a grotesque demon, a thing found in fairy tales, rather than a human child: clawed hands, teeth sharpened to points, cat's eyes flashing wildly in its head, hooves where its feet should have been, a barbed tail lying bloodied and limp between its buttocks. Slick with gore, it stared up at its father and skewered him with a hateful glare.

The air was full of his and the nurse's shrieking, joined with the beseeching chants of the Priest, fighting against the baleful curses of the devilish thing writhing pathetically on the bed.

At once Duilio lurched forward, grasping hold of it, taking it by the ankles as it bit and scratched at his hand. Without thought, he ran to the flames of the kitchen fire and cast the demented thing into the middle of them, his head buried in his hands, weeping uncontrollably, as the flames burnt the creature's mottled flesh and the venomous cries from its foul craw faded to silence.

TWENTY

THE VATICAN. ROME.

For a moment Father Strettavario thought it was snowing in July when he caught sight of flakes of grey falling outside his residence window. He peered through the glass, his pale eyes shining with wonder, before he realised that something was burning in the city beyond the Vatican's walls. The air was full of ashes, rising up on hot thermals from a plume of flailing smoke within Rome and cascading down like a snowstorm upon the Vatican. He opened the window and leaned out. The faint smell of smouldering hay and wood mixed with the spiced scent of incense and lavender coming up from the Vatican's streets produced an intoxicating mix.

The old Priest rested for a while at the window, the billowing smoke and ashes reminding him of heretics burning in the Riga many decades ago, the stench of burning flesh, the flash of heat, the snatched cries moments before the flames consumed the victims' bodies and breath and condemned souls. The memories brought the hint of a quiet satisfaction to his wrinkled paunchy face. He'd led a hard life, a dedicated life, doing one's best, all one was able to do. Yet now, in the twilight of his years, something he'd never felt before, something he'd never expected to find within him, had begun to take seed. Doubt. Doubt about his work, his life, his faith.

Things had changed, within him and also about him. The change had come recently and had come fast, over the last few months. It seemed to Strettavario that the rhetoric of some things within the Church had changed, proclamations hardened, ambitions broadened, intentions darkened. Doors to meetings once held open were now closed. Information shared among the parties was now covert and distributed only to closed groups. No longer was the talk of containment and tolerance. Talk was now of cleansing and preparing. Of torturing fallen Inquisitors and lapsed Priests, rather than trying to redeem them. Of disposing of broken things, rather than trying to fix them.

Why attitudes had hardened and fears had begun to manifest within the Vatican, Strettavario could only guess. But after hearing the news that the Eagle Fountain in the grounds of the Vatican was running red with blood, he feared he had more than an inkling of what was to come.

The squat old Priest looked up into the heavens, watching the ashes fall on the city below. He imagined each to be a spirit, spinning and turning like the souls of the departed, darting and falling among the rooftops and ridged towers of the Vatican's skyline. He watched as many as he was able, as if it were a game, his eyes trying to focus on each passing ash as it fell to the ground below. And then he felt the hard point of a blunt object nestle between his ribs and he froze, staring straight ahead and watching no more ashes fall.

He'd been around and handled enough firearms in his time to know the make of many weapons by the touch of barrel alone. His mind teemed with a thousand possible suspects, names and motives as to who might have ambushed him in his residence. Was this to be his end, a bullet in his back as, like a child, he'd watched the ashes fly? He wondered if he was too old to deflect the weapon and his attacker too naive to fire before he moved. He knew the names of living Inquisitors who could escape from such a predicament, if the gun was pressed to their ribs, but he knew that he himself was too old and too slow to try.

"If you want me dead, shoot me and throw me out of the window," he said, quite calmly, as if advising his assailant as to the best next move. "The impact from the fall should crush the wound and hide the bullet."

"Why would I want you dead, Father Strettavario?" replied a voice in stilted Italian, and Henry eased the gun from the Priest's back, his finger remaining tight to the trigger in case the Priest tried anything foolish.

"Why indeed?" Strettavario replied, allowing a little air back into his lungs. He turned slowly to face his assailant, his hands raised to show he was helpless. But having turned to face his opponent, the old Priest now knew he possessed enough in his limited fighting capability to disarm and incapacitate the young man who had dared to break into his private quarters. He smiled and his pulse slowed. "And what can I do for you, Englishman?" he asked, in English, detecting Henry's accent. "A long way from home, aren't we?" Strettavario's eyes dropped to the curvature of Henry's chin, the indentation and muscular build of his neck, his broad shoulders, his tanned complexion, and suspected at once British infantry. "Or the western front? I thought Britain and Italy fought on the same side?"

"We do," replied Henry, a wry smile on his face, "but Vatican City remains neutral."

"Apparently," replied the Father.

"And Sister Isabella requires your assistance."

The Priest's face hardened at the mention of her name. He laughed, a cold controlled laugh. "And how does someone like you, an English deserter, come to know of Sister Isabella?"

"It doesn't matter how. Not at the moment. Sister Isabella has told me you're just the man we require."

"And why would she suggest that?" Strettavario said, his milk-white eyes intent on the soldier.

Henry shrugged and considered lowering the gun. It seemed to him that there was something rather pathetic about the old man, the stooped curvature of his back, his eyes which seemed half-blind. He played the grip of the revolver gently in his hand and said, "She said you were well connected, that you could be of use getting a message to someone?"

"Pigeons pass on messages," replied the Father, a smile turning up the edges of his mouth. "Use one of them."

"Pigeons can't get to where we wish to reach."

"Perhaps you've been misinformed about my capabilities."

Henry shook his head gently. "From what I've been told, I think not."

Strettavario's hands began to drop to his side and at once Henry stepped back out of reach of a lunge should the old man be foolish enough to try anything.

"You do surprise me," said Strettavario, knotting his hands together. "Sister Isabella?" He chuckled, shaking his head gently, and Henry saw how the folds of skin beneath his chin wobbled. "The last I heard she was engaged by the Chaste with a multitude of Priests willing to pass on any messages she requested. Indeed, most would do anything to help that woman, it would seem?"

"Not this time. She needs your help," said Henry.

"What do you mean, help? I am an old Priest. There is little that I can do." He opened his hands and Henry saw that they were calloused and thick, hands which had seen action. He gave the Priest a look of suspicion.

"From what I have been told, I do not think you either too old or unable. This is important, Father Strettavario." He gripped the revolver tightly. "It involves Tacit."

Strettavario seemed to cool. "Tacit?"

Henry nodded. "We need him back."

The old Priest's eyes turned heavenward and he chuckled more freely this time, a quiet laugh into the rafters of the chamber. "Back?" He laughed again, revealing a face that must once have been handsome. "Why on earth would you want Tacit back, or believe that he would choose to return, or is in any way able to?"

"Things have changed."

At once Strettavario thought again of the Eagle Fountain.

"I am not disposed to going away with strange men," he said, "especially those who hold me up at gunpoint and tell me they are intending, with my assistance no less, to break convicted murderers out of prison. You need to do more to convince me."

"You care for him."

The old Father hesitated, dropping his head to his chest, loose skin hanging in folds beneath his chin. He imagined the instruments of torture being used on his Inquisitor friend at this moment in a cold cell buried deep beneath the earth.

"Who suggested I cared for him?" he asked.

"Sister Isabella, she said you believe in Tacit."

Strettavario shook his head. "My evidence at his trial helped condemn the man. Life imprisonment. No chance of release."

"You did only what was expected of you." Henry took a step forward and grasped the old Father gently by the arm. "We need him back. And only you can help."

But Strettavario shook his head. "I don't think you or Sister Isabella understand. It's inquisitional rules that when you go into Toulouse Inquisitional Prison, you only ever leave in a coffin."

"Then it's time to break the rules," said Henry, his fingers straining against the grip of his weapon. "Father Strettavario, we need him. And you're going to help us get him out."

TWENTY ONE

The Italian Front. The Soča River. Northwest Slovenia.

Pablo stopped and looked back down the way he had climbed. Below him the mountainside seemed to writhe with the sight of ten thousand grey-green infantrymen following in his wake, as if the Carso was a rotting hunk of meat on which maggots were feasting. It was a scene which both inspired and terrified him, the immensity and the power.

"We cannot lose this war!" he exclaimed, on seeing the vast numbers of soldiers of the Third Army, raising his rifle as a mountaineer might his pick on conquering a summit. A smile broke across his face for the first time in days.

"Take your fucking hands down, you fool!" shouted Corporal Abelli, reaching out and slapping the young Private's arms back to his sides. "You want to draw every fucking Hungarian sniper in your direction?"

"No. But look, sir!" Pablo said, giving the rocky crags a cursory glance for the enemy, before looking back down the mountainside, Private Lazzari beside him turning to look as well.

"What about it?" snapped the Corporal.

"We are so many!"

"And the Austro-Hungarians aren't?" called the Sergeant Major, stepping up and snorting, a sound Pablo had quickly come to despise since his time in the Carso. "Don't worry, we have more than our equal ahead of us."

The Sergeant pushed past him roughly, warning the three of them not to dawdle on the mountainside path. Fellow soldiers, who had stopped to listen to what the Corporal and their Sergeant had to say, turned and trudged after him with heavy feet. The young soldier watched them go, his enthusiasm and momentary joy trickling away.

"What have you got to be so unhappy about?" asked Corporal Abelli, sucking his teeth. Pablo shrugged and he patted him on the shoulder. "Come on Pablo! We go to do a great thing!" he said, and Pablo wasn't sure if he said it partly in jest. "Surely the Priests told you so? They wouldn't have brought you here if they didn't think it to be a good thing. An act ordained by the Lord!"

Abelli chuckled, his good humour returned, but Pablo shrugged once again. "They never gave me any choice. Always I've done as I've been commanded by the Priests."

"And I should think so!" replied Abelli. "After all, they've fed and watered you all your life!"

"How do you know that?" asked Pablo.

"Priests talk," Abelli deftly replied. "I wouldn't be doing my job if I didn't know where my men came from. I know that they took you in when you were just a young child, cast out by your family and friends for the shame of your deformities." The Corporal indicated Pablo's hands, and the young man blushed and drew them into tight balls. Now it was Abelli's turn to shrug. "As long as you can fight and know how to stay alive, that's all that matters to me. I don't care what you look like." He indicated Lazzari and said, "Look at that poor bastard next to you!"

Pablo laughed. "Do we have to go the entire way to the top?" he asked, peering up into the Carso.

"To the very top," the Corporal nodded, soldiers trudging up beside them. He lifted a finger to the summit far beyond. Pablo traced the line it made, up through the clouds to the heavens where he supposed the summit of the Carso lay, hidden in thick cotton white.

"And what lies at the top?" asked Pablo. "Why's it so important?"

But the Corporal shook his head. "If I told you, you wouldn't believe me!"

Pablo tucked his rifle over his shoulder and gripped it tightly with his six-fingered hands.

TWENTY TWO

ROME. ITALY.

Father Strettavario smelt liniment and sour brandy from the moment he stepped into the damp terraced house. And something else. The earthy musk of wet fur. He recognised the stink at once, and his immediate reaction had been to brace himself for an attack, to harden his limbs for the assault and to tune his mind away from the pain which he supposed would come when he found himself in a fight, even more so when he heard the door close behind him and lock.

But it was an attack which never came. Instead, a voice he recognised called his name; he relaxed and watched Isabella step out of the shadows towards him. "I apologise for the manner by which you've been brought here, Father Strettavario. We've had need for secrecy and haste."

"Then you should have not brought the automobile," replied the squat Priest, pulling his robes back around his shoulders in an attempt to present some semblance of respectability. He caught Isabella's curious look. "Whoever it was who pursued you the other night, the Inquisition will be aware, and they will be watchful." While his voice was quiet and restrained, it carried a presence of authority and control. "The Inquisition do not take kindly to people riding recklessly through Rome's city streets at night, killing Inquisitors. They will have spotted the Fiat. They will be on their way. You know that, don't you?"

Isabella looked across at Henry and he nodded. "This was only ever a temporary place to stay. We have somewhere else to go." His voice was assured, but she noticed that he immediately crossed to the shuttered windows to survey the street beyond.

"I trust the next place you have in mind is better than these poor lodgings," replied the old Priest, only now catching sight of Sandrine resting against the far wall.

His eyes narrowed on her as she stepped across the floorboards towards him. "Sandrine Prideux," he said, his lips gripped white.

"You know me?" Sandrine asked, tensing.

"Yes. Arras. Your little game. We never met, but your description precedes you. You caused us a lot of trouble."

"Sadly not enough," retorted Sandrine.

"Which thankfully failed. And now you are reduced to living like this?" Strettavario tutted, looking about the room disdainfully.

"Unfortunately we are not afforded the luxuries of those in the Vatican," she sneered. Then she caught sight of the Priest's eyes and hesitated, glancing over at Isabella. "I don't like the look of him. Are you sure we can we trust him?"

"Probably not," Isabella replied, "but he's all we have if we want Tacit back."

"This Tacit," said Sandrine, lifting her chin so she looked down even more on the stout Priest, "I've been told it's important we free him. Why? I don't understand, he's only a man ..."

Strettavario chuckled and felt something stir within him. "Only a man? I wouldn't call him that."

"Then what would you call him?"

"A force of nature." The Priest said the words quickly, as if he knew them without question to be true. "So, you want to break Tacit out of prison? Why would you want to do that? And why should I help you?"

"Because we'll kill you otherwise," warned Sandrine.

Strettavario chuckled. "That does not concern me. I have been threatened many times before, been told my life is at an end by many enemies. I have made my peace with God. Tell me, have you made your peace with him?"

Isabella stepped between them. "We want you to help us break him out because of what is coming."

"And what is that?"

Car lights from the street outside reached through the shutters and swept the length of the room.

"They're here!" cried Henry, clawing at his rifle.

"We can go out the back," said Sandrine. She stepped towards the darkness, Henry following without a word.

But Strettavario remained beside the chair, unmoving. "Tell me, Sister Isabella, what do you think is coming?"

"The Antichrist," she replied. "He is preparing the world for his return."

She expected Strettavario to mock the announcement, but instead he nodded, his eyes growing serious and dark. "I believe you."

"You do?" said Isabella, with a start. "How so?"

"The Eagle Fountain in the Vatican Gardens."

"What about it?

"It has begun to flow with blood."

"My Lord!"

"I have seen these signs rarely, but when I have previously, they've only meant one thing."

"What do the Holy See believe?" asked Isabella, the emotion drained from her words.

The pale-eyed Father chuckled weakly and shook his head. "The Holy See are paralysed with indecision and fear. They know what these signs mean, but choose to hope that they are wrong. When you see your enemy coming, sometimes it's easier to look the other way. So how do you propose we get Tacit out?" he asked, looking at the Sister. "No one has ever broken out of Toulouse Prison. No man can."

"That is why we found you," replied Isabella. "We hoped you would be able to help."

"We don't have time to discuss this here and now. We must leave!" Henry interrupted.

Strettavario paused, his hand to his chin, his eyes boring into Isabella, "He likes you." His gaze was fierce. Determined. "Tacit, he likes you."

"I wouldn't know," Isabella replied, too quickly.

"We don't have time for this!" ordered Henry from the open door. There were footsteps in the street outside the building.

"I think you're the only person he's ever felt anything for, since Mila was taken from him." Isabella looked away, but it was more to hide the emotion welling in her eyes. "I think you're the only person who can bring him back, give him back his spirit and a reason to live and fight."

More footsteps sounded in the alley outside, harsh voices intermingled among them.

"I don't understand," Isabella said, her hands held out towards the old Priest. "I don't understand. What I can do?"

A heavy blow on the bolted door behind them rattled its hinges and drew plumes of dust from the lintel. Strettavario stepped towards Isabella, his hands clawed and raised, as if about to throttle her. "Sister Isabella, it's very simple," he muttered, his face a murderous scowl, "I need you to die."

TWENTY THREE

Toulouse Inquisitional Prison. Toulouse. France.

Tacit's skin was slick with blood and sweat, his mind shattered by the torment of his suffering, delirious with pain and exhaustion. The cell sank and spun from his vision and momentarily he felt he was falling down into darkness, embraced by the raw talons of death. He thought then it was his time to die, alone in that cell, butchered and broken, no longer human but a piece of meat, hacked and desecrated for another's pleasure.

Why they were doing this to him, he did not know, only that someone hated him enough to unleash their most depraved of visions upon his body and then retreat when there was just enough left of him to survive, only to return the following day to continue the torture.

His body was spent. He knew that he had nothing more to give, no more strength to resist. Not now. Not after so much had been done to him. Not after last time. The thought of Isabella came into his mind and he smiled through the delirium of death's closing embrace. A fleeting image. A final moment of peace.

The door to the cell creaked open and Tacit looked up. He knew there was something different about this visit from Salamanca from the moment the head torturer first entered his cell, the way he looked at him with his head turned to one side, the way his eyes flashed, as if he had divined some inner secret about Tacit and was waiting for the most opportune moment to reveal it.

As if Salamanca possessed something which he knew would hurt the prisoner far more than any nail, blade or flaming brand could ever do.

Tacit watched him closely, his eyes heavy and his teeth bared, waiting as the usual mass of subordinates followed in Salamanca's wake into his cell. Somewhere inside him an ancient baleful voice shrieked. "What is it?" he hissed, tensing himself against the nails and the bonds which still held him, the chains cutting hard into his already torn skin, the iron spikes grinding against his bones. "What's so amusing, Salamanca?"

Salamanca smiled and leant back against the prison wall, his arms drawn about him. He crossed his ankles and chuckled, studying Tacit with calculating eyes. The pack of jailers and miscreants of the prison guard laughed with him, they too recognising the unfamiliar manner of their master this visit, intrigued by it. "You're a brave man, Tacit," Salamanca nodded, puckering his dry lips while he examined one of his dirt-encrusted nails in the sickly light, "I'll give you that. Strong. Unfeeling. Unyielding. Seemingly impervious to physical pain."

"What's that I detect, Salamanca?" replied Tacit, allowing himself the hint of a smile. "Envy?"

"How could I possibly be envious of you? Chained and unloved! Or maybe there is, was, someone?" Salamanca allowed the words to hang in the air before he followed them with a hoarse, withering chuckle. "Do you think there's someone out there waiting for you, outside these prison walls, someone who holds a torch for a monster like you?"

Tacit's eyes narrowed.

"I mean, we've all heard the rumours that Poldek Tacit, the heartless Inquisitor, had in fact a heart after all."

Tacit tested the bonds. "Let me out of here and I'll show you how much heart I have!"

Salamanca ignored him. "But those rumours, it seems they've grown, taken on a life of their own. Blossomed from rumour into what some believe is fact."

"And what is that?"

"Perish the thought that you'd let someone close enough to thaw your frozen heart!" And then Salamanca stood back and smirked. "Or did you?" he asked, at length.

Tacit stared hard. "What do you mean?" he growled, but there was the root of doubt growing within him, and with it the hellish voices of hate were growing too.

"Sister Isabella?"

At once Tacit held himself rigid. "What about her?" he seethed, his jaw set wide, his eyes fierce.

"She's dead, Tacit," Salamanca smiled, and his eyes flashed with triumph at seeing Tacit's face fall. "She's dead," he repeated laughing, seeing how his words were finally defeating the prisoner. "Dead! Dead!"

The blood drained from Tacit's face and his mouth crumpled open. Instantly, tears welled in his wide eyes, his pupils now pinpricks of black, every feature in his face frozen, as if time itself had stopped. Shrieks of derision and coarse laughter from the crowd of jailers shook the cell, and all along the cell block inmates wondered what terrible injustice had been done to the most feared and reviled of prisoners.

Inside Tacit's head, old memories danced and then burned in the terrible rage growing in his mind. Fragments of the past, of laughter, love, warmth, passion, of Isabella, of her touch, gathered like fiery brands of hope, almost too dazzling to behold, and then fell spinning into the torment of black which was overtaking every sense, every perception Tacit possessed. A darkness was creeping in from the edges of his consciousness, of his very being. A devilish cold clutched him, as if an angel of death had placed her icy talon into his heart. But Tacit knew who it was who had wounded his heart and his eyes were on him. The man in front of him, Salamanca, laughing and slapping at his knee, as the revelation bent the torturer double with hilarity.

Out of the darkness there came a cry, like that of a demon dragging itself from the very bowels of hell itself. And with it a strength even Tacit never knew he possessed, grew. At once Salamanca stopped laughing and with him the other jailers began to rush for the door. For the cry had become a roar and the roar was now a thunderclap. And with it the chains that held Tacit's left arm tight ripped clear, whipping in the air like bonds broken from a caged animal. The jailers were shrieking and falling back, scrambling for the door and fighting each other in their urge to get away.

Tacit tore his right arm from the bonds and then his legs. Down the length of the cell block bells of alarm began to sound, but Tacit never heard them. He wrenched his ankle from the chain which had held him firm to the wall for so long and powered after Salamanca, catching hold of him within four broad strides. The first blow broke the torturer's spine below his ribs. The second spun him flat out on the floor, his broken back against the piss-covered corridor down which he would walk no more. Tacit sprang on him, setting his entire weight on his chest.

"A name," he growled, his teeth gritted so firm in his jaw that they sounded as if they were cracking, his whole body shaking with fury. Lights seemed to gather and fork from the ends of his fingers. The voice within had become a wail. "You're going to give me the name of the person who killed Isabella. And then death will seem like a gift after what I'm going to do to you."

TWENTY FOUR

Toulouse Inquisitional Prison. Toulouse. France.

The prison hammered with noise and people, guards and gunfire. Tacit didn't know which way was out but he suspected up was as good as any, knowing he'd been buried deep within the prison, as deep as it went.

"Isabella!"

If Tacit screamed her name as he ran, he never knew that he was doing so, only that her name roared aloud in his skull. Over and over.

There were three guards at the end of his corridor, cowering as they watched him approach from behind their locked door. He knew them all. They'd witnessed him being tortured often enough. He took the door at a run and bundled into it, knocking it from its hinges. The men went down beneath it with a grunt and didn't move.

Tacit felt nothing but red rage coursing within him, a devouring anger to which he gave himself entirely, the voice, the screaming beseeching voice, urging him on. On.

There were stairs just ahead. He took them at a bound, four steps a stride, roaring up them as rifle-fire sprayed down onto him from above. Something bit hard into his shoulder, failing to break his pace. He bounded across the room and caught the man at the gun post firm in the throat, his fingers tightening so that they touched together through the flesh and skin of his neck. The warden went down gasping for air as Tacit gathered his rifle from the ground and checked the magazine. There were four rounds left. He put three through the heads of the next three guards he found in the corridor beyond and the fourth through the lock of the heavy metal door ahead, allowing him to plough through it and its shattered lock as if they weren't there.

The corridor into which he had run was too narrow to swing the rifle so now he used it as a spear. He caught one man wielding a knife in front of him in the eye and he went down without a sound. The rifle wedged firmly in his socket and Tacit left it there, falling on the next guard and gouging with his thumbs. The tips squeezed through the man's eyeballs and he continued thrusting with his great thumbs all the way in until he'd pushed through bone into something soft beyond, his thumbs buried up to his palms in the man's head.

Tears poured from Tacit's eyes, but these weren't cold embittered tears. They were scolding tormented tears of wrath. He thought of Father Strettavario and the anger boiled within him. All his life he'd expected the killing blow to be delivered to him by the conniving guarded Priest, never upon the person he …

He hesitated, unable to compose his thoughts, to grasp just what it was he felt for Isabella, above the anger and violence and the incessant voice, now she was gone. Another who had touched his life cut mercilessly from it.

Gunfire from a heavier calibre rifle battered the wall next to him. He ran towards it with the man he'd gouged still in his hands, held up as a shield, throwing him to one side at the last moment and dashing the gun emplacement and the guards over with his bare bloodied hands. The door in front of him was locked. He ripped it from its hinges and threw it over his shoulder, tumbling breathlessly into the guardroom beyond. Eight men fell on him with truncheons and knives. Within six seconds, they lay still.

Tacit caught the scent of the air, coming down from the way ahead, his lungs filling with fresh oxygen, the first he had tasted for too long. It was like a tonic. At once his limbs felt re-energised and empowered, his strength renewed. There were stone stairs going up, broad and more ornate than anything he had passed so far. He took them at speed, curving up and around the outside wall of the jail block to a mezzanine platform above, from where it was possible to look down on the cells below. As he reached the top floor, his eyes fell on the head jailer, a pistol clutched tight in his white shaking fingers, whimpering and weeping as he tried to keep the weapon straight.

"I'll shoot!" he warned, as Tacit strode towards him. "Damn it, I'll shoot!"

Tacit snatched the pistol from him and drove it hard, barrel first, into the top of the jailer's balding skull. It snapped through the man's pallid scalp and sunk cylinder and trigger deep. The warden's eyes rolled up into his head, and he fell backwards, grunting as his life passed out of him.

"I believe you," Tacit retorted, pausing for a moment to catch his breath, his head bowed, his chest heaving. He'd not worked so hard in a long time, the agony of his lungs and limbs testament to that. His eyes turned to the far end of the mezzanine and the door. There were more guards coming, a lot more judging by the encroaching noise. To his left was a window. The light beyond was almost blinding. Tacit squinted and looked out over the French countryside, the city of Toulouse a dark smudge on the horizon.

Outside! Freedom.

He looked down at his bloodied hands, his anger swelling again, and drew his fingers into tight bleeding balls. The clamour from the guards was growing by the second. Isabella's beauty came once again into his mind like a vision. He felt her, he smelt her, he heard her calling to him, telling him to go, to find those responsible for her death.

The window shattered as Tacit blasted through it. For a moment there was nothing, nothing but the sound of shattering glass and his heart beating hard in his ears. And then he began to fall, down to the tree line below. And as he fell, reaching out to the branches rushing up to meet him, he swore to himself that he would never stop, no matter how far the trail took him, until he found Strettavario and until Isabella's death was avenged.

TWENTY FIVE

PLEVEN. BULGARIA.

The Inquisitor placed the silver crucifix pendant tenderly to his lips in a moment of quiet contemplation, before strapping a nail-studded knuckle-duster onto his right hand and pulling a grey-black revolver from his left holster. The cool summer sun had fallen beyond the western range of hills and either side of him, in the murk of the dusk, men readied themselves for battle. All eighteen of them were filthy and drawn, weeks tracking the enemy exacting its toll. There was a reek of sweat and alcohol in the air, the quiet mutter of prayers broken only by the occasional jagged bark from an intoxicated tongue searching for words to inspire and galvanise.

The Inquisitor looked across at the man next to him, sharing his fox-hole, and placed a heavy hand on his shoulders. "The unit's spirit is up tonight, Inquisitor Kuhr, eh?" he said, his Nordic accent giving his words a generous warmth.

"After walking for so long, Bodil, what else do you expect?" Kuhr replied, his brown cape drawn over his head for warmth against the cold of the Bulgarian mountain tops. "We're not dogs to be chained. We are fighting men."

The young man nodded sagely. "Well, I think we're about to be let loose."

From somewhere along the line a low whistle was blown. The clawing trepidation Bodil had felt grow within him over the last few weeks, chasing the Slav enemy east towards the Black Sea, began to fix its hold upon him again. It wasn't a fear of what he was about to face. Battle itself did not cause him to waver. After all, killing was all he knew. Instead it was a fear of failing which so terrified, failing before his faith and his fellow Inquisitors. If he fell in battle, he hoped he would not be one of the first.

In the clear moonlight Bodil's eyes shone crystal blue, his cork-blackened face giving them an ethereal glow. He swallowed on the dryness of two days without sleep and fell silent again, the fingers of his right hand playing beneath the iron plate of the knuckleduster.

He looked up out of the shallow pit, sprinkled ash white with the sharp evening frost in that high inaccessible place, and watched the moon fall behind a cloud. In the valley from where they had come, ice-dusted firs shimmered in the silver moonlight. Every now and then something shuffled through them, cracking twigs and tumbling frost from the branches above. He closed his eyes and pressed the iron points of his weapon into his temple, muttering a silent prayer to his faith, reminding himself of his oath.

The low blow on the whistle sounded for a second time and the Inquisitors rose as one from their holes and went forward. Bodil had faced many battles over the four short years of service he had given to his faith, but he had never fought alongside others on a field of battle within an Inquisitional unit before. He was reminded of the words of his tutor who led them tonight and had drawn him to one side two days into the chase across Europe.

"Fight as if you are alone. Fight as if all the hordes of hell have been unleashed upon you. Fight to the last man and the last breath. Fight like the Inquisitor you are."

He took a deep breath and felt something shift in his guts. The Inquisitors made no more effort to hide themselves on that high ridge, standing tall and silhouetted against the crimson moon like statues, malice and spite seared into their faces. The time to skulk in the shadows had passed. Below them the Slav camp was quiet, save for the occasional snort of a horse, the vague mutter of chatter around the fire. Every man in the line felt invulnerable and ordained for this moment.

"For the Catholic Church!" someone cried.

"For the Inquisition!"

"For our freedoms!"

The Inquisitors flooded forward down the hillside like a dark torrent unleashed from a dam, curses on their tongues. By the time the Slavs reached for their weapons, the Inquisitors were on them.

Bodil effortlessly dislocated the jaw of a man reaching for his rifle, tearing skin as he drove through with his jagged knuckles. Seconds later he put a round from his revolver into the chest of another gathering an axe from the fireside. The dull thuds of metal on bone battered the quiet of the night into submission, bodies staggering blindly from their blasted wounds. Almost at once, Bodil found himself in the very middle of the battle, flailing fists and arms all around. He smelt sweat and excretion, every sense on fire. Like a drug it enlivened and drove him on. It reminded him of something. Fear. He uppercut a stumbling figure and stood down hard on the man's neck as he fell, setting the revolver to his forehead. He recounted the words of his tutor as he pulled the trigger, a splattering of congealed matter landing at his feet.

Deafened by the cacophony of noise, he clawed his way about the heart of the battle, his eyes now blind to anything but the torrent of blood and falling bodies in front of him, feeling nothing but a carnal desire to inflict total damage upon the enemy. He lifted his revolver and fired twice, two bodies crumpling to the ground in front of him. A third figure leapt from a ledge on his right and Bodil brought him down with a sickening blow in the windpipe, battering him senseless with the back of his hand, the side of the Slav's face breaking open under the savagery of the blows.

Broken and delirious with terror, the last remaining Slavs threw themselves to the floor, their hands held helplessly, hopelessly in front of faces as the final blows rained down upon them, pummelling all to bloody husks.

A cry went up from the heart of the carnage, a cry of celebration and rejoicing at the manner of the victory. Bloodied hands and rifle-butts were raised skywards, smoking firearms left to cool in holsters, as the last of the enemy were put down like dogs.

Laughter quickly joined the cries, bodies embracing, strong arms across backs. The Inquisitors' work was done, their losses mercifully small. They could return to the Vatican victorious, their heads held aloft, receiving adulation and thanks from their masters. Their laughter turned to raucous cheers of merrymaking and foolish bravado. Compliments were shared and narcotics broken open. Their mission had been a long one, taking them across three countries, evading warring units from both sides of the world war conflict. Now, at last, their own little war had come to an end in an orgy of violence, short-lived and fierce.

But then, from the tree line in the distance, a single howl rose like a spectre into the night. At once the Inquisitors froze and looked east, for they knew the only thing the sound could mean.

A second howl caught the tail of the first, closer now. The Inquisitors staggered forward through the mud and bodies towards the dreadful sounds, struck dumb by the wicked taunt of the howls.

A third howl sounded, away to their left, and the Inquisitors turned as one, their hands back on their weapons, but all knowing they were useless against such an enemy. A fourth howl followed, this time from the ridge behind them, and they turned and cried out at the silhouette of the vast feral form standing astride the rocks. The great wolf-like beast, its hide knotted and fetid against the moon, raised its snout to the sky and howled again, a menacing dreadful cry which chilled the blood of all in the valley below.

"Silver!" came a roar from the ranks of Inquisitors. They had never expected this, to meet their mortal foe on such a mission. They had been assured Hombre Lobo did not reside here, cleared out, so they'd been told, a decade ago in the Great Eastern Purge. Celebrations turned to cold dread and alarm. They were unprepared and unarmed.

More howls came, closer still from the field beyond, the shapes of running creatures moving fast over the broken ground towards them, dashing through the shimmer of frost-blanched fields.

The call for silver came again, but the Inquisitors knew the demand was as useless as the weapons they raised to defend themselves, shambling forward to form a defensive square around the camp they had just taken.

Within fifteen broad strides the wolves had cleared the hundred yards of brush land and were upon the Inquisitors. The grey-black of the beasts fell on the men like a wave driving against a castle wall, fangs and claws dashing against chain mail and gauntlets. The line toppled and the wolves bound forward to snap and tear at those beyond.

"Sweet God!" cried a young Inquisitor, drenched in the blood of both his Slav enemy and his fallen comrades. "Werewolves!" before one of the beasts bit clean through his chest.

Bodil gathered a flaming brand and thrust it into the eye of a leaping wolf. The giant creature went down shrieking in a tone too sharp and terrible for one of its monstrous size. He backed away, his eyes wild, caught firm in terror's grip. All about him wolves fed on his fallen comrades. His eyes fell on the body of Kuhr torn to bloody ribbons, like a butchered carcass at an abattoir.

He wept and thrust his torch aside, turning to run. This was no battle he could win. His only thought was to flee, to escape that savagery and hope to tell others of what he had seen, what he had witnessed. He ran, half stumbling, half falling over the bodies of the slain, slipping in the dirt and the blood, churned to a blackened paste which clung to boots and held him firm in that murderous earth. A wolf came out of the gloom from behind and dashed him hard across the earth, turning him over twice, so that he landed on his back, his ribs shattered, blood gushing into his lungs. He coughed painfully, torrents of crimson spouting from his mouth. As he sank down into the earth, the wolf climbed over him, its wide jaws bloodied and foul with the tattered remains of his comrades' flesh, chain mail rings and torn cloth hanging between its teeth.

In that moment all his senses seemed to rally. He heard for the first time the sounds from the battlefield, the final cries of the Inquisitors as they fell, the sound of feasting, the cracking of bones, the tearing of flesh and mail, the pitiful moan from a dying throat as the last breath left it.

Pinned to the ground, Bodil's fading eye caught movement over to his right and he managed to turn his head to stare at an approaching figure, walking upright on hind legs. It stopped a few feet away, and, with a vast taloned claw, pulled hard at its own neck. The fur and flesh peeled away and instantly the body seemed to wither and shrink. Almost at once, from where there had been an immense wolf, now stood the hunched figure of a man, dark greying hair closely cropped tight to his fleshless skull, dark sullen eyes like black pits, a look of disdain etched in his morbid skeletal features.

A passion grew once more in Bodil's heart, his spirit renewed on seeing this wicked trickery. "Who are you?" he whimpered, blood frothing at his mouth, torn lungs, tears of pity and rage burning his eyes. He knew of the rumours, but had never before witnessed with his own eyes men who donned pelts to take on the form of werewolves.

"Who are you?" Bodil cried again, his voice now breaking with exhaustion and defeat.

"Gerard-Maurice Poré," the dark-eyed man spat, a sneering malice catching in the corner of his mouth. "It's a name you can take to hell!" And the wolf still pinning the Inquisitor to the ground tore his head from his body in a single bite.

TWENTY SIX

The Vatican. Vatican City.

Monsignor Benigni descended the dark spiral staircase into the bowels of the Vatican, his hands clasped loosely together across his ample middle. He walked with his head bowed, his fat lips pursed, his perspiring fleshy face etched with thought.

He had come this way into the halls and vaults beneath the Vatican many times, always preferring the quiet and the isolation this route offered to the busier thoroughfares elsewhere in Vatican City, with their wide sweeping staircases and opulent marble corridors. In these lowly passages, where natural light never reached and the cold stone of the floor had been worn smooth with centuries of passing feet, there was little chance of meeting another coming the other way, less chance of questions being asked and private thoughts being interrupted.

There was a yawning black archway to the side of the spiral staircase, leading deeper still beneath the foundations of the Vatican. Only a select few, other than the librarians and scholars who worked within them, had ever gone beyond into those catacombs and silent halls, where the sum of all Catholic knowledge was assembled and stored.

The Vatican's libraries.

Without hesitation he plunged into the black, drawn deeper by flickering torchlight at the far end of the sloping corridor. Benigni reached the end of the narrow constricting passageway and turned right at the junction, walking with his right hand brushing against the brick wall, imagining the centuries of history scraping against his fingertips. The corridor descended, sloping down in a long arch, before arriving abruptly at a small room, book-lined and lit by lantern light, rows of narrow desks set out in uniform lines, studious Priests huddled behind each.

He ducked his head beneath the archway and slipped into another hall, its walls covered in papers and sheets of animal skin, maps of the world and strange illustrations from remote countries. He crossed the chamber, bowing to step through yet another archway. This time there was a flight of stairs leading immediately downwards from the exit, ready to catch the unwary, dropping into a tiny cell-like room that was empty save for a door in the opposite wall and a red-eyed, broad-skulled Priest sitting behind a tall narrow desk, his skin as white as alabaster.

"Monsignor Benigni," he said, his face impassive, but with a light coming into his eye. "We have not seen you for many months. What brings you back to us?"

Benigni spoke without hesitation. "The three cardinal sins."

The Priest paused, something resembling admiration playing at the corners on his mouth. "I see," he said. A frown began to form on his face, a worried look, as if the resonance of what the thick-set man had asked for had begun to sink in. He pushed himself away from his desk, swivelling on his chair and padding slowly away from it. "You had better come with me," he suggested, turning for a moment and watching the Monsignor follow him.

The Priest's lower lip had withered through years too long to remember to resemble a thin line of gristle, and his yellow teeth protruded prominently. In the dark of the vault, lit only by copper-coloured lanterns, he ran his finger across the spines of the books and bound sheets of papers lining the shelves to his right, counting quietly as he went.

There was a smell of ink and linseed in the corridor, a rich golden light emanating across it, as if the vast room beyond was a giant hall filled with treasure. And it was filled with a treasure, the sum of all man's knowledge stored in a single vast room.

The Great Library.

"Three sins?" the librarian Priest repeated, turning from the main thoroughfare of the hall into a narrow side avenue, lined with the broad ends of shelves. "And what brings Monsignor Benigni to look upon such a topic? I thought it was the policy of the Sodalitium Pianum to reserve their investigations to those of modern indiscretions, rather than those identified since the coming of Man?"

Benigni raised an eyebrow, his piggy black eyes flashing. "And I thought it was the policy of the Great Library and its servants to refrain from enquiring as to visitors' topics of interest?" he asked, his tone perfectly balanced between wit and warning. "And anyway, surely all indiscretions sprout from the three sins?"

The Priest bowed his head in submission. "Very well," he replied, before vanishing around the corner. Benigni took the opportunity to peer about himself and the hall in which he stood. The chamber was immense, a hundred feet tall, three hundred feet long, filled with innumerable broad wooden shelves reaching to the ceiling, serviced by tall ladders manoeuvred on giant wheels, running on metal tracks. The hall echoed with the quiet bustle of a thousand Priests, poring over the shelves, returning books piled on heavy carts or studiously turning over pages. He savoured the calm atmosphere, the smell of aged leather and paper, waiting patiently for the Priest's return. When he emerged he was carrying a great pile of books, up to his nose, over which he peered.

"This should help you with what you're looking for," muttered the Priest, handing the stack of tomes over to the Monsignor's outstretched hands. "There's a desk just over there," he said, pointing with a hand. Benigni nodded and turned towards it. "Just be warned," said the Priest, his eyes narrowing. "Some subjects have teeth. And what's more, some bite."

TWENTY SEVEN

THE VATICAN. VATICAN CITY.

Father Angelo Coronati bore his sermon notes like a gift he was bringing to a gathering, for that is exactly how he saw them, gifts for those who had come to hear him speak. He'd been told he had a keen skill with words, an ability to express clarity and resonance, to send his words rising and ringing among the congregation, to bring all who heard them solace and insight.

He slipped into the cool of the early morning Vatican air from a rear door of St Peter's Basilica, clutching his bundle of papers tight. He could hear the sound of distant choral music emanating from one of the churches in the city. For a moment he closed his eyes and bathed in its beauty, before making the ten steps across the grass of the Vatican lawn to the cobbled street in front of him, the winding road snaking its way through the gardens and between the chapels of the city. But Coronati did not need to follow it. The church of St Stephen of the Abyssinians, set back in the shadows of a towering fir, stood just across the road from where he approached. He cleared his throat and set his head low in a determined pose, his hard-soled shoes tapping against the stone cobbles.

He had led Mass in this particular church for nearly five years. He was proud to have done so, to lead a service to God in the oldest church in Vatican City. One could almost feel the years of faith and joy living within the building, like a heavenly embrace clothing all with its love and fervour.

In the shadow of the church's doorway, the white stone of its arch etched deep with the pattern of the Lamb and the Cross, Coronati raised a hand to the door and pushed, holding his sermon to his chest with a firm arm. Instantly he shivered against the brutal cold which greeted him from inside the thick-walled chapel, far colder than the cool of the dawn.

He drew the front doors wide, bustling beneath his robes in an attempt to tease some warmth into his chilled limbs. There was a candle-stand to the left of the entrance and he set down his sermon notes upon it, lighting a candle with shaking fingers, light radiating slowly into the room. Coronati couldn't help but feel that the air within the chapel seemed not only cold but oppressive too, as if the pitch of night had somehow remained inside the building. The joy so often keenly felt when stepping inside the building was no longer there.

The Priest picked up his sermon and walked deeper into the chapel, stopping to light more candles as he went. Slowly the church began to burgeon into life, the amber luminescence seeming to bring just a little more warmth to the building. But still Father Coronati shivered, the sermon tight to his chest. He reached the ambulatory and noticed how his breath ballooned in clouds before him, that his fingers ached with cold. It was a chill more reminiscent of a deeply buried prison cell than a place of worship.

He looked back to the church's open door eighty feet away, pale tendrils of dawn searching inside. Something troubled him, not just the sudden ice in the air. It was an unsettling sense of doubt. He wondered if he was ailing with a malady, the early signs of a fever perhaps? He placed his sermon on the lectern and put a hand to his forehead to feel for a temperature. An almost overwhelming sense of sorrow, agonising in its melancholy, suddenly took hold of him. He shuddered, clutching the edge of the stand for support, and felt the urge to weep, to cast aside all hope. A cry caught in his throat and he fought to keep hold of it in case it escaped as a moan. Such desolation and despair! He'd never felt anything like it before.

In final hope, he raised his heavy eyes to the fresco of Madonna and Child. After all, it always cheered his spirits to see it. But as he looked up he cried out, recoiling in horror. His hand reached out to the lectern to steady himself, but the shock of what he had seen was too terrible and he dragged it with him as he fell, casting the carefully ordered sheets of his sermon to the ground around him.

There was blood on the fresco, blood pouring from the eyes of the Madonna and her child, pouring from cruel wounds gouged deep into the paintings and the very stone of the church walls on which they had been painted.

TWENTY EIGHT

Rome. Italy.

The passageway was too narrow and low for Georgi to pass through without having to hunch, his head and shoulders stooped as if in subservience.

At times his arms brushed the wood-panelled walls of the tilting corridor, the nun leading him through the winding labyrinth of the Trastevere Monastery minuscule before him, ancient beyond years. It seemed, if anything, that the corridor might swallow her.

"It's most unusual to accept a Priest here, particularly at such an hour," she said, her voice thin and subdued.

"Apologies, Sister," growled Georgi, checking the doors they passed to gauge whether the particular Sister he had come to visit had close neighbours. "I would not usually trouble you, but the Holy See insisted I speak to Sister Malpighi with utmost urgency."

"Bad news from the Vatican?" asked the diminutive Sister, stopping before Malpighi's dark varnished door.

"Far worse than that, I fear," replied Georgi, earnestly.

She knew the Priest had come to the right place. Only Sister Malpighi had the true vision to advise and direct on pressing matters, which could not be resolved by debate alone. The Sister nodded, accepting the Priest's reply and knowing it prudent not to enquire further. Sister Malpighi would resolve the situation. She always did, whenever trouble arose and the Holy See sent one of their Priests to speak to her, even one like this man, someone Sister Maltese had never seen before. Malpighi's visions were rarely wrong. Sister Maltese tapped twice on the door and instantly a tiny voice called back.

"Sister Maltese. You and my visitor may come in."

Sister Maltese opened the door and stepped quietly inside, Georgi following her in, bowing beneath the door frame as he did so.

"My apologies, Sister Malpighi," said Georgi, his hand to his chest. "I have been sent from the Holy See to have words with you regarding something of terrific importance."

"Really?" replied the reverend Sister at the window tersely, her face growing more doubting with every passing moment. "Whatever is required, it does not demand Sister Maltese to be present. Sister Maltese, please leave."

She spoke with such force that Maltese's hand gripped at the collar of her shirt, aghast at Sister Malpighi's manner. She'd never heard the Sister talk in such a way before, always thinking of Sister Malpighi as a polite and measured person in all she said and did. Sister Maltese bowed her head in quiet acceptance and backed away. Georgi watched her and closed the door behind her when she had gone, holding it shut with his hand.

"There was no need for her to die as well," said Malpighi. "I know what you were thinking. You need only me."

"So it seems they were right," said Georgi, a ruthless smile crossing his face. "That you have the 'sight'."

"This does not end well for you, Georgi Akeldama, you who 'died' once to hide from your old masters in order to join with your new ones," said Malpighi, her voice firm and unrelenting. "You will die again, but this time permanently in the arms of the one you love."

"I think you're getting me confused with someone else, Sister," said Georgi. He locked the door with the key in the lock and stepped towards her. "So, tell me, then," he said, drawing out his knife from the folds of the robe. "What do I want from you?"

"My eyes," replied the Sister. "You've come to take my eyes."

TWENTY NINE

ROME. ITALY.

Something ageless and profane was on the wind tonight, something funereal and withering to anything it touched.

Soldiers on the western front drew their coats tight about them and supposed that autumn would soon be here. Soldiers on the eastern front called for extra rations of vodka and took out letters from home. Sailors on their ships, far out to sea, felt a wave of homesickness wash over them. Mothers, pressing photos of their sons to their breasts, stopped and gasped, feeling that something terrible had happened to their loved ones serving overseas, while infants in rooms above sobbed pitifully in their sleep.

Something wicked and eternal had been awoken, and exhaled a foul breath.

All across the world, Priests crossed themselves at the malice they sensed, Cardinals sat up and muttered silent prayers, Inquisitors paused in their deadly pursuits and stared out into the black heavens above for a moment, wondering what wickedness it was they had felt.

Candles flickered, cattle lowed, cats hissed, dogs sprang from baskets and barked at shadows.

Crows flocked towards the Vatican in huge numbers. Something undying shifted restlessly in its dark abyss.

THIRTY

The Vatican. Vatican City.

The city's sewer stank, as did Tacit's mood.

He drained the remaining inch of brandy from his bottle and began climbing the rusted iron rungs of the ladder. It hadn't taken him long to arrive at the capital after his escape, riding the train he had stowed aboard from Toulouse almost all the way to the Vatican. Throughout the journey he had played Salamanca's admission around and around in his mind, the revelation that Strettavario had murdered Isabella still inconceivable to him. Unfathomable.

And yet, for all that, Tacit knew exactly what the old Father was capable of, how dispassionate he could be, how he could act without question or mercy to ensure the orders of his Church were carried out.

How murder was not beyond him. When required, Strettavario could be as unyielding and cold as his pale staring eyes. There had always been something about the man Tacit had respected, admired even. Perhaps it was because he saw so much of himself in him?

But that was then. Now the old man was going to die. The journey to the Vatican had given time for Tacit's wrath to ripen and fester like a poison. Now, back in the capital, he felt ready to let the venom loose.

The ladder led up to a courtyard within Vatican City. Tacit emerged from the dark sewer hole and slunk back instantly as an Inquisitor took him by surprise, walking past at the very same moment. The pair stared blankly at each other, both startled. Tacit moved first, wordlessly breaking the man's neck in an instant and dropping him through the sewer hole.

Inquisitors patrolling the Vatican? At once Tacit knew something was not right.

He took the stairs at the far end of the colonnade at speed, heading towards Strettavario's apartment, and reached the third floor, breathing hard. A Priest met him coming the other way and Tacit knocked him on his back with a punch and dragged him unconscious into a side-room, shutting the door firmly behind him. There was no point in silencing the Priest permanently. The Church would know soon enough that Tacit had returned, once they found Strettavario's body. All he needed was a little silence for a while, enough time to exact his revenge on the traitor.

The apartment Tacit was seeking was at the far end of the corridor. As he ran he recalled the years Strettavario and he had spent together, past assignments on which the old Priest had trailed Tacit. It had seemed to the Inquisitor that the Priest was always just a few paces behind him, watching him, as if he didn't entirely trust him, as if always waiting for him to step over a line never supposed to be crossed. But now the old Father had stepped over a line himself and it would be he who regretted doing so.

The door to his apartment was locked and Tacit kicked it off its hinges and bounded inside. The room beyond was empty, as was the rest of the residence. Tacit spotted Strettavario's diary on his desk and leafed his way through it. Empty. There were no visits scheduled to take him out of the city, no assignments which needed his attention. Tacit knew he must still be in Rome.

There was dirt on the carpet, the tread marks close to the window. Not Priests' shoes. A soldier's boot. At once Tacit knew that Strettavario must have received a visitor, but this visit had not ended in a struggle. Strettavario had gone peacefully, willingly even, with the visitor and with enough presence of mind to lock the door behind him. Tacit lifted his eyes to the greying outline of Rome beyond. Somewhere within the city Strettavario and his accomplice were hiding.

Tacit strode from the room knowing he would find them. The question wasn't if. The question was merely when.

THIRTY ONE

The Italian Third Army was marching again. After two days being held down in the lower reaches of the Carso, burning under the scorching endless sun and growing despondent about home and loved ones, the order had been drawn up for the army to move.

An endless grey shabby line of stumbling sweaty soldiers snaked out from the lush green of the tree line below, climbing barren paths winding slowly and at times steeply up around the mountain side, always up, towards the grey and blinding white of the Carso's ridged peaks in the distance.

The Karst Plateau lay at its very summit, a broad flat terrain like a lunar landscape, but pricked with a single pinnacle of black rock on its western edge. An ungodly place, spurned by man and beast.

The perpetual summer sun bore down on the marching soldiers like a curse. Backs of necks burnt red, dry mouths hung open and tongues, caked thick with a skin of saliva, lolled from between split parched lips.

Up they marched falteringly, through gorges strewn with rubble and the detritus of a population which had fled before the Italian enemy had arrived, doing all they could to slow the invaders. Carts had been drawn across paths and their wheels broken to wedge them firm in the dust and rocks. Rolls of old wire fencing, once used to house poultry and keep out vermin, were strung across roads. Often the soldiers came across a ramshackle sea of garden implements, hoes, rakes, spades, all of which had been set in the cold unyielding earth as a flimsy wall, or thrown across the route with broken barrels and anything else that could help slow progress.

All too rarely for the soldiers' liking, they would cross stone bridges over rivers of turquoise, and fall out to fill bottles with fast flowing water that was ice cold from the mountain peaks and tasted like nectar in the clinging heat.

"Make sure you all drink," said the Sergeant Major to the soldiers lined up along the river bank, some of them up to their knees in the cold water. He watched Pablo fill his bottle. Satisfied, he went on, walking with his swagger stick tight to his right leg. Pablo watched him go, then found himself looking absently across the vista.

"The Priests," he said, taking a drink from his bottle, "they're just standing there staring at me. It's off-putting."

"You seeing things?" replied Private Lazzari, splashing himself with water from a scooped hand, before gathering up his gear from the bank.

Pablo knew he wasn't. They'd been watching him, like overcautious parents, ever since he had first come into the mountain with them. He snatched up his equipment and ran quickly into line.

"Always the first, eh?" muttered the Corporal, watching Pablo standing near the head of the column of men on the gravel road cutting a rough course across the mountainside. The Corporal set his hat squarely over his head and pushed it into place. "Careful. Don't you know that first in line means first over the top, the first to be shot. Cannon fodder." He chuckled to himself cynically and took a fat-bellied pipe from the depths of his jacket, which he shoved into the side of his mouth.

"We've not seen any of the enemy yet," replied Pablo, as the Sergeant called them forward. "Maybe they've all gone? Retreated? After all, if this place is as you suggest, it has no value."

"I never said that," cautioned the Corporal, smiling. "It has value, beyond measure. And no, the enemy has not left."

"How do you know?"

"Because it's been long prophesied."

"What has?"

"The battle. The battle to come. On top of the Carso."

As they climbed higher still they passed through towns, sad and decrepit, all of them empty, save for old people who couldn't or wouldn't leave. Slovenians, Hungarians, Italians, all eyed the vast line of soldiers with suspicion and a distant unflinching stare. Few soldiers dared to return their stares, as if to do so would curse and send them to damnation.

By midday on the third day of the climb, had they crossed the broad Isonzo river and reached the flooded plain's low lying areas beyond, where the sluices had been blown up by the Austro-Hungarian army to further slow any assault. After the initial burst of excitement of an army on the move, the slow torment of the constantly interrupted march into the Carso towards the enemy had worn away at hope with every tired step, so that it now hung by the finest of threads. It seemed to the soldiers that all they were doing was climbing over the unforgiving terrain or stopping to clear the path ahead.

"Does this route never end?" asked Pablo, stumbling among the stones of the scorched earth and struggling to regain his rhythm with those alongside him.

"We are walking in the valley of death," the Corporal called from behind. "It is a valley without end, save when *he* decides you have reached it."

"By *he* I suppose you don't mean God?"

"Look about you. Do you see God in all this desolation?"

Pablo didn't need to look. He'd seen enough of the Carso to know it was forsaken.

THIRTY TWO

PLEVEN. BULGARIA.

Poré sat some distance from the rest of the men, as he did every night, nestled close to his own fire, preferring his private company. Rowdy drunkenness enslaved the faction who followed him. They were intoxicated by the power they wielded in the wolf pelts Poré had given to them and by the strong liquor inside their bellies.

Poré had had many doubts in the days after the Mass for Peace, particularly doubts about those in his employ. He had encountered this bunch of drunken thieves and strays as he had wandered, broken and lost, within Paris, sharing with them at first nothing more than a desperate thirst for vengeance and the desire to thrust an eager blade deep into Catholic flesh. This had been enough at the beginning, when his plans for the Mass for Peace had been thrown into disarray. At the time he was grateful to find solace with others as desperate as he had been, people who shared a common hatred for that accursed religion.

From an inside pocket he took out the letter he had carried ever since leaving Paris, the letter which now drove him and had given him a reason to keep going. To keep fighting.

At the time, when Cardinal Monteria lay dead on the floor of Notre Dame at the Mass for Peace, Poré had thought he had failed in the task allotted to him, but that, he now knew, was a merely a cul-de-sac, a false hope. An impasse.

Now, with the letter in his hands and the revelations it presented, he understood.

The letter had never been meant for him. Poré had taken it from the mauled and partially devoured remains of a young Inquisitor whom had he slaughtered and fed upon in one of the quieter suburbs of Paris a month after the events at Notre Dame. Poré had told himself that he wasn't getting a taste for young Catholic flesh, but, as a wolf, he found their meat as sweet as any he tasted when a human.

Perhaps it was chance that Poré had happened upon the Inquisitor and the letter, but deep inside he supposed it was always meant to be. As he plucked the letter from the bloodied envelope, once he had fed, he supposed it contained general orders from the Inquisition, a broad suggestion as to what deed was expected of the Inquisitor.

It turned out that he was only partially correct.

Carrying the mark of the Vatican, the letter had outlined a most pressing and urgent case, one which required the Inquisitor, one of several it seemed, to act swiftly and precisely. According to the Bishop who had written the letter, one of the two knives of Gath, a relic from an earlier age last used in a satanic ritual years ago in the fields of Pleven, Bulgaria, had gone missing from where it had been kept safe under inquisitional guard within the Church of Saint Pierre de Montmartre. Its retrieval, so it seemed by the tone of the letter, was of the utmost importance to the Bishop and those he represented within the Church.

The mention of Satan, ratified by the Seal of the Vatican, had at once captured Poré's attention, impelling him to discover more about the little-known events in Bulgaria, events of which he had not been previously aware.

He'd followed what evidence he was able to gather in secret across Paris and then France, his path taking him away into the east, always under the pretence to those who followed and fought for him that he was hunting Catholics. But all the time Poré was hunting for something else: knowledge about just what had happened in Pleven on that fateful night. For he knew it was his destiny to find out. The call to do so had come from a higher power, many years ago, an event he recalled as if it had happened only yesterday.

He held the letter now, reading over the words, devouring them by the light of the fire, as he did most nights, before raising his eyes to the darkness beyond. Somewhere out there in the dark something fearful had taken place, something that was attempting to return again.

A drunken cry rose up out of the gloom from the valley below, a barking voice imploring Poré to join them at the bottle. He ignored the call and folded the sheet of paper, carefully placing it back in his inside pocket, holding his hand there for a moment. Tomorrow, he trusted, the long journey he had taken from Paris might reach an end after which … but beyond tomorrow he dared not think.

THIRTY THREE

The Vatican. Vatican City.

"Blasted crows!" Cardinal Korek cursed from the window of the chamber, his arched spine turned away from the gathered assembly of Cardinals and Bishops behind him. "They're making a terrible mess of the roofs and the square." His face was scrunched in disgust as he attempted to wave them away with a hand. There was dandruff on his shoulders, his skin a pallid grey like that of a dying man. "Where did they all come from? Blasted things!" He waved again, even more frantically.

"They might have come in from the shoreline," suggested Cardinal Adansoni, stepping closer, his hands hidden in the sleeves of his robe. "The storms of late must have forced them inland. I've noticed the same with the gulls."

"They're chasing the doves away!" said Korek, clapping his pale hairless hands, calling out to the birds in a futile attempt to scare them away.

"Undoubtedly," said Cardinal Secretary of State Casado from the heart of the room, his own face pale and drawn as if sleep had been at a premium lately, "but can we leave the crows for just a little while please, Cardinal Korek, and focus our attention on the more urgent matters of the hour?"

"Such as the Eagle Fountain bleeding?" asked the white-haired Cardinal Berberino, and Casado looked crestfallen at its mention.

"That, among other things," he replied.

Korek grumbled quietly, casting a final stare in the direction of the black oily birds, before returning to the gathering and looking to take a seat around the table set in the very centre of the room. This chamber was plain, by Vatican standards, and around it the other members of the meeting were waiting impatiently for proceedings to begin. Cardinals, Priests and all manner of other clergy were present. Casado prepared to speak, but the door to the chamber suddenly opened and through it lurched an imposing looking man, dressed all in white. Casado paused and looked up knowingly as a shudder reverberated around the room at the man's arrival, many turning away and busying themselves elsewhere so not to have to look at the menacing figure.

They knew him all instantly. Grand Inquisitor Düül, the head of the Inquisition.

Chilled sweat glistened on his dark skin, shimmering like mother of pearl under the pale lights of the chamber. The white folds of his garments, hanging from his weighty frame, gave him an eldritch glow, as if he were a ghost returned to bring retribution to all from beyond the grave.

Grand Inquisitor Düül had been a handsome man, at least until a blade had nearly split his face in two. He had lost an eye in the incident. Afterwards he claimed the wound helped him shoot faster with his revolver as he no longer needed to close one eye to aim.

Most Inquisitors wore only dark colours. It aided them when skulking in the shadows, avoiding being seen by an enemy until it was too late for their victim. But Düül wasn't like most Inquisitors. He liked to make sure he announced his arrival long before he thrust the death blow between the ribs of a victim. To put the fear of his reputation into them, before the fear of God followed. He'd worn white on the very day he was made a Grand Inquisitor. It was his little joke, suggesting that his soul was pure, his methods clean. Anyone who knew him knew he possessed the blackest of hearts and a history to match.

Adansoni did not look at him, instead following the still muttering Cardinal Bishop Korek to the table, joining him in the empty chair to Korek's left. His eyes caught the narrow glance of Bishop Basquez opposite and something twisted inside him. The Bishop's lips pressed into a thin leer before he turned his attention to the clamour of the meeting. Since Tacit's escape from Toulouse, it seemed to Adansoni that Basquez's demeanour had turned even more sour.

Cardinal Bishop Casado cleared his throat, a deeply resonant growl into which he seemed to pour all his frustration. "I hope none of you object, but I took the liberty of inviting Grand Inquisitor Düül to our gathering. Considering the concerning nature of recent events, I thought he should be fully informed, and we might be able to benefit from his superior knowledge." Düül swept the room with a fierce inquiring eye; Casado cleared his throat and made his main announcement. "You will no doubt all be aware that Poldek Tacit broke out of Toulouse Inquisitional Prison a week ago."

"Good heavens! I was not aware!" muttered Berberino, his hand slipping to his throat.

"How was Tacit allowed to escape?" Cardinal Korek demanded to know from the far side of the circle, his face seeming to flush at the news. "I thought that anyone confined to the prison never came out?"

"We don't know how he escaped," replied Casado, pinching his nose as he studied his notes. "We don't know what happened, other than it seems Tacit broke free of his cell and rampaged through the prison complex."

"The monster," muttered Korek, staring firmly down into his lap, his thin lips drawn back against his bared teeth. "What has the warden at the prison to say for himself?"

"The warden's dead," snarled Düül, his eye as cold as the blade in his belt.

"And Salamanca?"

Casado chewed the side of his mouth. "Salamanca cannot speak. He has no tongue."

"What happened to him?" asked Berberino, from the confusion of gasps accompanying this latest revelation.

The old Cardinal Bishop gripped the ridge of his nose and closed his eyes for a moment. "Whatever Tacit said to him, did to him, it made Salamanca chew off his own tongue."

Korek cursed and hung his head.

Düül smirked. "Poldek Tacit. He was always very good."

"Do you think he'll come looking for us?" asked Berberino.

"I doubt it, Cardinal," replied Adansoni, calming with the wave of a hand. "I am sure he escaped to find freedom, rather than come back to the Vatican looking for trouble and risk further incarceration."

Düül chuckled slowly, a sound like nails being drawn down a chalk board. "Don't be so sure, Cardinal Bishop," he said.

"You have news?"

"More than that. I have a sighting. Father Stradlov came face to face with the man in the residence quarter of Vatican City."

"Is Father Stradlov alright?" asked Adansoni.

"He'll live. As for Father Strettavario …"

"What about the Priest?" asked Berberino, his fingers turning white.

"Gone."

"Gone?" asked Basquez, the suggestion of pleasure pulling at his lips. "What do you mean, gone?"

"The door to Strettavario's residence was broken down. Tacit almost certainly came to visit him."

"How dreadful," squeaked Berberino.

Düül sneered at the sound the man had made. "Seems that Strettavario was lucky on this occasion. He wasn't home when Tacit came to call. If he was ever there."

"What does that mean?"

"There was no sign of a struggle. And we've not found his body. But a car was seen leaving the residence matching the very same one seen a week ago and pursued during the disturbances in the capital. The car was trailed to a property, but the residence was found to have been recently vacated."

Adansoni cleared his throat. "Have you any leads as to where Tacit might have gone to now?" he asked, attempting to draw the increasingly chaotic proceedings to order.

"Not yet," replied Düül, "but we have a heavy presence within the city. We already had a number here due to recent occurrences."

"By which you mean these demonic signs?" asked Basquez.

Düül did not reply directly, instead saying, "We've increased our numbers wherever possible."

Casado nodded. "Grand Inquisitor Düül is at the moment mobilising Inquisitors all across the city, and Monsignor Benigni has already begun to direct the Sodalitium Pianum, his team of investigators. If Tacit attempts anything else, he will be caught. Between the Inquisition and the Sodalitium Pianum we'll find him, one way or another."

"The Sodalitium Pianum?" asked Adansoni, raising a bushy eyebrow in surprise. "I thought their work was rooting out rumour and suspicion of modernity rather than getting involved with inquisitional work?"

"It is," said Casado, his reply measured, "but Monsignor Benigni has been working with the Inquisition closely in recent months."

"We've been forced to combine forces," said Düül dryly, his expression showing he was less than enamoured at the prospect. "Resources are … stretched." He clicked his tongue.

"So I heard," said Basquez guardedly. "I heard that Monsignor Benigni was seen reviewing the scene of Inquisitor Cincenzo's death?"

"It's no secret that the Sodalitium Pianum and the Inquisition have been trying to see if there is any truth behind these recent rumours," said Düül.

"And what rumours would those be?" Adansoni asked.

Casado coughed and straightened the front of his gown. "That End Times might upon us."

The air seemed at once heavy with unease. "Why say such a thing, Cardinal Bishop Casado?" asked Adansoni, aghast.

But Cardinal Berberino was less easily perturbed. "Inquisitors running amok through the streets of Rome? Gun battles within the city? Prisoners escaping Toulouse Prison? We were warned," he said, and Adansoni saw that his hands were shaking. "I know I am not alone in having witnessed countless exorcisms throughout the city of late, and the births of hideous things."

"It seems you are not alone, Cardinal Berberino," muttered another. "Every day brings new signs, new horrors. We were warned long ago. That dark times would return. That one would come out of the East and that a trail of destruction would be left in his wake. Which brings us back to the one we have long been concerned about. The one who has escaped. The one who is back in Rome. Tacit. He is dangerous."

"I agree," said Korek. "Tacit is a concern, if the prophecies are true."

Adansoni scowled and placed the tips of his fingers together. "I was never one for the prophecies," he riposted.

"If memory serves, it was you who suggested such a prophecy involving Tacit in the first place, Cardinal Bishop Adansoni?" retorted Korek.

"I was younger then. Hasty and more free to embrace the implausible. Perhaps arrogant too."

"You are saying you lied to the Holy See about Tacit then, Cardinal Bishop Adansoni?" asked Casado, sweat under his skull-cap drawing his thinning white hair into clumps. "When you first brought him to us as a young man?"

"We were all younger men," added Korek, grimacing. Adansoni smiled in acknowledgement before continuing to speak.

"I merely want to make it clear that when I first found Tacit and brought him to the Vatican, the excitement of the moment overtook me. I remembered the Pope's words, his suggestion that someone great would soon return, recalling the prophecies of the sages of old. I was full of excitement and youthful overenthusiasm, as you point out. I accept now that Tacit is just a man. Nothing more."

"I also heard that members of the Chaste were gunned down in cold blood at the Ponte Sisto?" said Berberino. "Along with Inquisitor Cincenzo?"

"Father Pellegrini was killed also, an innocent," muttered a Bishop from the far side of the circle of tables. Casado's and Korek's eyes met briefly before they swept the congregation.

"I heard too that Sister Isabella was somehow involved," continued Berberino, "that she was caught up in proceedings."

"Sister Isabella?" questioned Korek, amazed. "Weren't she and Tacit on assignment together? Peculiar if you ask me." He looked around the gathering before continuing. "Sister Isabella chased though the streets, while Tacit escapes from prison and returns to Rome? Sounds like the two might in some way be connected."

"I agree," said Berberino. "For isn't it true that they formed some sort of … fondness for one another during their last assignment?" He cast a sideways glance at Adansoni, but Adansoni shook his head once again.

"Sister Isabella is apparently dead," he said. "I have it on good authority."

"Whose authority?" asked Berberino.

"Members of the Inquisition. They appear to have heard a rumour that Father Strettavario apprehended the Sister and killed her himself as she tried to escape the city."

"Which is why Tacit returned to Strettavario's residence? To exact revenge?"

But Korek was unconvinced. "If that is true, where is her body?"

"Apparently she has already been buried."

"How convenient," said the ancient Cardinal.

Adansoni turned on him. "Why would the Inquisition lie?" he asked, glancing towards Düül for support.

"And why would Father Strettavario kill Sister Isabella?" Someone else called from the auditorium. "He is one our most trusted of Priests."

"Why would he, indeed?" croaked Bishop Basquez, playing with the frayed edge of his sleeve. "And where is Strettavario now?"

"Apparently he has left the city."

"So would I, if I knew Poldek Tacit was after me," said the Bishop.

"Do we know where he's gone? What's his next assignment?"

"We have no record of forthcoming assignments," replied a dark-skinned Cardinal with a voice deep as a pipe organ.

"So either Strettavario has fled, or Tacit has caught up with him?" Berberino persevered, tilting his head to one side like a snake considering a strike. "I suggest preparations for his funeral might be in order."

"What I find more mysterious," said a hooded-eyed Cardinal, "are these Inquisitors, the ones running amok in Rome."

"Often it is what Inquisitors do best," said Korek, looking across at the Grand Inquisitor in an attempt to show the man that he had his support.

"They need bringing under control," the Cardinal continued.

"Cardinal Bishop Gunderson," Düül replied. "I assure you, I do not like an Inquisition which is not under control. Anyone stepping out of line will be dealt with most efficiently."

"Well, someone seems to be trying to control them most efficiently in Bulgaria," said Basquez, his voice shrewd and languid.

"Oh?"

Basquez appeared to relish his role as bearer of news; his face brightened for the first time in the session. "A whole unit of Inquisitors, tracking Slavs through the mountains, wiped out."

"Good God!" cried Berberino, "By whom?"

"Hombre Lobo, led by Cardinal Poré."

A joint intake of breath seemed to draw the air from the room.

"Cardinal Poré?!" exclaimed Berberino. "I thought he died after the Mass for Peace?"

"No," replied Casado, shaking his head. "He was never found. We knew he fled from the city, but assumed he died during last year's harsh winter."

"Clearly not," croaked Korek. "What was Poré doing in Bulgaria? And how has he fallen in with werewolves? To my knowledge he was never excommunicated?"

"He must have found the pelt after the ceremony," said Adansoni.

"Wasn't it destroyed?" asked Korek, aghast.

"It would seem not," said the recorder at the session, checking his file. "It too was lost after the event, perhaps discarded by someone who didn't realise what it was. There was a lot of confusion after the event."

"Those Inquisitors," asked Casado. "Were they not prepared with silver?"

"It was not believed that werewolves dwelt in that part of the mountain range," growled Düül, disliking the growing accusatory feelings in the room towards him and his organisation.

"Send a squad to the area to deal with them," Casado shot back, emphasising his words with a flick of his fingers. "Deal with Poré."

"His head on a spit?" asked Basquez, a malevolent light in his eyes.

"If necessary, yes," said the Secretary of State, looking at the Grand Inquisitor.

"Despite our stretched numbers?" Düül asked. "Despite Tacit being back in the city?"

"It is important that Poré be done away with. He is a problem we can easily eliminate. Send a small but appropriately armed group to find him and silence him for good."

"Why do we seem always to be at war?" mused Berberino.

"And for the coming of war to our borders," Adansoni said, "it seems to me that this conflict, this suicide of Europe as our Pope describes it, is worthy of urgent discussion within the Holy See. We talk of End Times. Perhaps when our Pope spoke of them thirty years ago, when the vision came to him that time, he was right?"

"Austria-Hungary is many hundreds of miles away," Korek said, with a sideways glance. "We do not need to act, nor should we act, with the speed you seem to suggest is required, Cardinal Adansoni." The aged Cardinal's words were accompanied by a sudden gust of wind which blew in from the open window and caught the papers of the scribe close to him, showering them to the floor. "We should remain objective and neutral. It is not the Holy See's role to take sides within world conflict."

"But they are our neighbour," countered Adansoni, "and close enough to cause us concern."

"To act with too much haste, without a chance to consider what we might find ourselves involved in, would be unwise, Cardinal Adansoni. And we should be careful whose mast we nail our colours to."

Adansoni grimaced and forced a cold laugh from his lips. "Whose mast we nail our colours to?" He shook his head. "With all due respect, have you quite taken leave of your senses, Cardinal Korek? We are Italians. The Italians fighting on the border, they are our people."

"Speak for yourself," the aged Cardinal replied.

Adansoni looked away, now directing his comments to Casado. "I have heard that the Austro-Hungarians have tens of thousands of men on their borders. Perhaps hundreds of thousands. That they are well armed and trained. That the Italian army has nothing. A poorly dressed, poorly provisioned force, made up of conscripts, boys and old soldiers. How are they to take the Carso, so few in number, and so poorly prepared? If the war draws out into winter then they will be defeated by the cold, let alone the enemy."

"More reason to choose our sides carefully," replied Korek. "Adansoni," he croaked, his bright eyes defying his age, "I knew you were a tactician, but it seems you've missed your vocation in life? It seems you should have been a military man?" There was a lightness to the Cardinal's thin lips, something which resembled a smile.

"Cardinal Korek, as you know well within the Holy See," replied Adansoni, "it is wise to be prepared. After all, we fight our battles on many fronts."

THIRTY FOUR

The Italian Front. The Soča River. Northwest Slovenia.

By nightfall of the third day the Italian Third Army had reached the steepest part of the climb and fallen out into a makeshift camp. The chill night air stank with the reek of a thousand camp fires and the caustic bite of strong coffee boiling in pots. The rumble of voices, punctured by the melodic chirp of a mouth harp, crept like a prayer up the mountainside towards the Austro-Hungarians waiting for them, silently, in their defences above.

The Italian soldiers, seeking solace from the cruel cold night, slept under their capes on the hard rock, or dug into unyielding earth with mattocks and picks to fashion a trench. Blood and iodine hung in the air, bandaged hands cradled tin coffee mugs.

"What do you think of the Carso then?" asked the Corporal, smirking.

"It is a cruel master," replied Pablo, drawing his cape tighter about him. "But what is the matter with you? You seem to gain some kind of pleasure from seeing the rest of us suffer in our labours."

"Did I not say you would labour?"

"Heads up!" someone cried suddenly from the sea of seated grey figures, as the darkening horizon of rock away to the south bristled with shell-fire and burst into flame. A sound like thunder came and with it the splintering of falling rocks all around the encamped army, as if the sky was raining stones. The sound of thundering rocks was accompanied by the muffled cries of injured men hit by jagged scorching stones.

"I warned you," said the Corporal, moving to stand in front of Pablo, and the young Private thought for a moment that he might be trying to shield him. The falling stones ceased to rain down and all around them soldiers tended the injured or threw themselves down on the hard rock in an attempt to find rest. He corrected the woollen hat on his head and drew on his pipe so that the dull embers lit in his green eyes. "This mountain is the Devil's flesh. Hard like iron. Shells cannot penetrate it. They just shatter and splinter."

"You're great fun to have around," replied Pablo, putting his plate to one side and trudging away, his hands thrust deep into his pockets.

"Where are you going?" asked Abelli.

"Anywhere but here," said Pablo, hating the sound of his whining voice. But he felt the urge to get out of the camp and walk a little way down the mountainside, away from the panicked cries and the moans of the injured.

"Go with him," said Abelli, waving to Lazzari.

Pablo found a vague path, worn he supposed by mountain goats, and followed it for several minutes, going nowhere in particular. He was aware that Private Lazzari was following and felt a desire to turn and tell him that he wanted to be left alone. He stopped and Lazzari did too, a little way off. Pablo looked up into the cold night sky.

"What are you doing away from the camp?" came a voice Pablo recognised. He still jumped to hear it, before turning to look at one of the Priests.

"I just felt I needed some fresh air. Away from the camp."

"You have taken it," replied the Priest impassively. "Now go back to your fellow soldiers, Pablo Gilda. Private Lazzari will accompany you." Pablo started to object, but the Priest raised a hand to his shoulder and instantly he fell mute. It had always been the way things were done while he was growing up in the Church, any defiance beaten out of him, always subservient to their wishes. The touch of the Priest was cold, as it always was, and with it Pablo could detect the faint smell of sulphur that hung about the Priests, wherever they went.

THIRTY FIVE

Plezen. Bulgaria.

"What is this terrible place you've brought us to, Poré?" growled the outlaw beside the gaunt figure of the Cardinal as they looked up at the desolate ridge. "The sun is high above the horizon and yet it feels cold as winter, as if something happened here, something dreadful."

"Something dreadful did happen here," replied Poré, his cool eyes surveying the lands to the south. He drew his hands into the sleeves of his robe for warmth. "Many decades ago, a battle took place here. The siege of Pleven. Between the Russians and the Turks. Twenty-five thousand killed on this very ridge. They say the land ran with rivers of blood."

"Sounds like too many?" grunted the man, scratching at his hairy face. "Or too few."

"What are we supposed to be looking for?" another of Poré's clan called across the gap between hillocks.

"I don't know," Poré called back, doubt consuming his thoughts. Over the raised summit figures paced the grassy plain, their heads studying the ground. "I am hoping I will know when I see it." Limping heavily on his wounded leg, he walked awkwardly up the embankment for a better vantage point, climbing to where a line of stunted trees grew alongside another shallow ridge.

"You are not giving us much to go on, Poré!" the haggard man said, following after him, scouring the ground for he knew not what. He stopped and kicked over a rotting branch before walking on.

"I will know it when I see it!" Poré repeated, tired of the questions. It was all he had heard from them since they left Paris. Questions. Many times he had wondered if they were a fair exchange for the brutality and the lust for violence they brought with them.

French soldiers of the Boxer Rebellion in China, they had been sent to fight and die for the defence of the Catholic faith in Beijing. They had done what had been expected of them by their masters in that campaign, only to return to France and be ignored by those they had gone to defend. Homeless and destitute when Poré had found them on a Paris street close to Notre Dame, cast out by those they had served, the six of them had flocked to Poré's banner and the promise of striking back at the faith which had disowned them.

Attracted by his grim charisma and the promise of retribution and riches, they had followed the man across much of Europe, able to take whatever they wanted courtesy of pelts worn on their heads, divided into seven from a single large pelt Poré had produced, the largest of which Poré had kept for himself. Whatever witchcraft was bound up within the stinking pieces of fur, it gave the old soldiers powers unrivalled by any they came up against and bestowed on them a savagery and bloodlust that tantalised and entrapped them like a powerful narcotic.

Wearing the pelts, nothing could stand in their way, no prize was beyond their reach. And they fought for Poré, for when they donned the pelts they were filled with an unquenchable rage and wished only to kill and gorge themselves on their victims.

"You say you will know when you see it," muttered the man walking behind Poré in tired reply, "but what about the rest of us?" He put his filthy hands on his hips and turned a circle on the spot where he stood. "I see no rich pickings here. I see no Catholic churches to tear down, no Catholics to kill!"

Poré walked on, his eyes sweeping the ground like someone who had lost a treasured keepsake among the grass and stones. Suddenly he stopped, his eyes riveted to a spot just ahead of him. His heart beat faster in his chest as he slipped forward and sank, with some difficulty, to his knees. The earth here was burnt but the ground was quite cold and the ashes hard, as if many years had passed since they had been alight. The sharp musk of sulphur hung in the air.

"What is it?" asked the haggard soldier, walking up. "What have you found?"

Another had joined them, attracted by Poré's close scouring of the ground. "What is it? A fire?"

"Yes, but not a recent one. And no fire with which you will be familiar." Excitedly Poré placed his hand into the centre of the scorched ground and closed his eyes, as if feeling for a presence.

"What is that smell?" asked a third man, stepping up and wrinkling his nose, his long arms hanging beside his heavy thighs.

"Sulphur," replied Poré. And he knew then that he had found what he had been looking for. He dug hard into the baked burnt earth and lifted some of the solid ashes from the ground. They seemed like metal, as if the heat had been so intense that it had melted the rocks. He weighed the tarnished metal in his hand as if trying to divine arcane secrets from its mottled shape.

"This is it?" asked the haggard man, disappointed. "This is what we've been looking for? A cold fire?"

But Poré ignored him, staring out across the vista, trying to imagine the scene thirty-eight years ago, the carnage and ruin of the battlefield, the energy and violence of the ceremony.

"Poré!" another man called. "You're a fool! You've brought us all this way to look at an old camp?"

"I had to come," replied Poré, more to himself than to the brigands gathering around him, lost within his own maelstrom of thoughts.

He looked up, studying the greying heavens. Their shadows were growing long over the field, and Poré could feel that a remnant of the past still lay heavy over the hillside on which they perched, a cold and bitter blight no number of years of summer sun could erase. They had tried to raise something here, to bring something through from the Abyss.

All but one of the men in Poré's band began to turn and walk away.

"You owe it to the men to explain to them why you've brought us here, Poré," he said, and at once Poré leapt to his feet and stood a hair's breadth from the man, smelling his wretched breath.

"I need to explain nothing to you! Nor to anyone!" he hissed, rage bristling through him. He turned back to the cold fire and dug the toe of his boot through the ashes. "This is not the end. This is only the beginning. If the men are not willing to follow me, then let them go. I need strong men at my back, not those who lack conviction."

"They don't lack conviction, they just need to know where we are going."

"That I don't know," replied the old Priest, and he hung his head as if suddenly defeated. "I don't know." He dropped the ashes to the earth and brushed his hands clean. "But I must find out. I must do as I was bid. As I was commanded. Everything depends on it. Everything."

THIRTY SIX

THE VATICAN. VATICAN CITY.

The three small figures were almost hidden in the shadows of the church of St Stephen of the Abyssinians. The Cardinals stood in utter silence, their hands clutched firm about them, their faces drawn, trying to comprehend the desecration of the ancient fresco before them.

"The prophecy," croaked Cardinal Korek, his eyes never once leaving the bloodstained wall. "Are we to now accept that this sign proves that it is coming to pass?"

Cardinal Secretary of State Casado shook his head urgently. "This is just one event," he said, trying to sound more assured than his private thoughts suggested. "We cannot declare that *he* is returned because of this one incident."

"But with all the other signs?" countered Cardinal Bishop Adansoni. "The possessions? The birth deformities? The failed crops? The Eagle Fountain running red with blood? They come together to suggest this cannot be just a chance occurrence."

"There have been other such occurrences in the past, of statues which have bled, of frescos which have been defaced. None of them have suggested that –"

"Speak not his name," muttered Adansoni quickly. "Not in this holy place."

"I would not dare to defile this chapel of God by doing so, Cardinal Bishop Adansoni," said Casado. "Nor would I say this vandalism proves anything. Look," he exclaimed, going forward and raising his hand to the wall. He hesitated for a moment, as if summoning the will to continue, before placing his hand against the stonework and smearing the blood. "Look how the so called 'blood' wipes clean. If this were an act of his, then surely …" But his words faltered as the blood began to flow once more from the gouged holes in the stonework, as if oozing from deep within the fabric of the building. "Sweet mother of God," Casado cried, quickly retracting his hand and clenching it into a fist. He stepped backwards, uncurling his hand and looking at the blood smeared on his palm and fingers. "Sweet mother of God," he said again, his face ashen.

"It is the sign we have all been dreading," said Adansoni gravely, "the prophecy we've been watching for. It is the shadow of the first of the three acts after which they shall come through and after which he shall rise on high."

"This does not mean we are too late to stop the first act," Korek tried to reason. But Adansoni shook his head.

"For this sign to have come to pass, the first act must have already been performed."

"Where is the body though?" asked Casado, his face tense.

"No doubt we will find it, soon enough."

"The horror of it," muttered Korek, and for a moment both Casado and Adansoni thought the aged Cardinal Bishop might be crying. "Eyes, taken," and Korek looked back at the hollowed bleeding eyes of the fresco, the suggestion of a tremble in his hand as it touched his face. "Now I understand."

"We must doubt no more," said Casado. "We must accept it has begun." He uncurled his fingers and looked again at the blood trails on his hand, as if trying to divine a reading from them.

"And what part do you feel Tacit plays in all of this?" asked Korek. "The Pope's vision? Tacit's appearance? The prophecy which spoke of one like Tacit coming from the East? The fact he has returned to the city, at this very moment too? Do you think there is any truth in any of it?"

"Whether there is or not, we will not take any risks. When Poldek Tacit is found, we will kill him. Grand Inquisitor Düül understands his orders and knows what needs to be done. There is none other as good as Düül. Not even Tacit."

"And of the second ritual?" asked Adansoni.

"The lust of flesh?" asked Casado, and all three old men seemed to blanch at its naming. "Düül has been informed of this also. He has the men and he has the apparatus to stop it."

"Do you have faith that he can? He is gravely stretched, with all that is happening within the city and wider afield."

"As I said, he is the best we have."

"Really?" asked Adansoni, a devious light in his eye.

"Tacit is good, but he's reckless. He makes mistakes. And the moment he does, he's a dead man."

"We should never have simply imprisoned him after the Mass for Peace," muttered Korek. "It was a mistake. We should have killed Tacit, there and then."

Casado turned away from the fresco, making for the light of the grounds outside. "It is not a mistake we will make for a second time."

THIRTY SEVEN

ROME. ITALY.

"Are you sure he will come?" asked Henry, his thumbnail scratching a line on the table in the new safe house they had acquired.

"He'll come," nodded Strettavario, not bothering to look up, his nose buried in a black tome, spidery engraved writing across its front cover.

"How can you be so sure? The Inquisition have not managed to track us to this place. What makes you think Tacit will?"

"Not yet they haven't," replied Strettavario, raising a finger from the edge of the leather-bound tome. "And this is Tacit. He will want revenge. Revenge for what I've done to him. To Isabella. He'll stop at nothing. He will find us."

Henry remembered the size and manner of the man from when he had observed him in Fampoux and absently dropped his hand to the handle of his revolver, the other tightening around the body of the rifle in his lap. His stomach convulsed.

"And they won't help you when he arrives, if that's what you're thinking," said Strettavario. Henry saw the old Priest's face brighten with a knowing smile. "When he arrives, keep clear, or he'll kill you."

"You make him sound like some kind of elemental force."

"He is a force," replied Strettavario, only now looking up, weighing the comment on his lips. "Of sorts."

"How long have you known him?" asked Henry, taking a sip of his tea and making no effort to hide his disapproval at how the old Priest had made it.

"His entire life as an Inquisitor." Strettavario put down his book and gathered his own cup into his hand. Through the pale flickering light of candles on the table, Henry could see the steam twist before the old man's pallid eyes.

"Was he always … so fearsome?"

"No," the Priest said quickly. The question seemed to embolden him, capture a memory. "No, when he was younger he was a good man, too good for the Inquisition. But he was brilliant and strong and quick, the best of us. They took him and they made him one of them."

"Do all who join the Inquisition change?"

"Mankind's deeds know no depths and yet our souls can only sink so far before they are submerged within the domain of the Devil. He blackens hearts and corrupts minds. It takes a great man, greater even than Tacit, to withstand such a life and not find himself corrupted by it, not be left with its indelible mark. And there are few as great as Tacit."

"The war," said Henry, turning his cup between his thumb and fingers, "what little time I spent at the front line, I saw many terrible things, the depths to which man can fall to do his duty when commanded by those in authority. Or simply to try and live. It terrifies me to see what we are capable of but also the lengths our spirit will take us in order to survive. It gives me hope that one day this spirit will be put to good use by all, not used against mankind. I realised when I met Sandrine that really there is only love. Nothing else matters. It changed me. I knew I could not stay fighting an enemy that I did not know or feel anger and hatred towards. She helped me to see." Henry was aware of the Priest's cold empty eyes upon him. "What is it?"

"This woman you travel with."

"Sandrine."

"She is Hombre Lobo, the sworn enemy of the Church."

"She is my love."

"She is not to be trusted."

"She is my love," Henry repeated, the shadows around his eyes darkening.

"They are deceitful creatures, as they were before they were struck down by excommunication."

"But Sandrine was never excommunicated. She was born of wolf and woman."

"That I find hard to believe," muttered Strettavario.

"And that is the truth."

"Tacit, he will kill her. You know that, don't you?" The Priest's face seemed to harden.

Henry swallowed. "Then I will have to kill him first."

Instantly, Strettavario's demeanour softened and he chuckled and shook his head, so that the hanging skin beneath his chin wobbled. He took up his cup and sipped at it again. "I am sure you were a good soldier, Lieutenant Henry Frost, but you were never Poldek Tacit."

A sound on the brickwork of the narrow ledge outside caught their ears and they both froze. Henry's eyes flickered over Strettavario through the gloom and then back to the closed window.

"Did you hear that?" he asked, his voice tense.

Strettavario shushed him and slowly drew his chair back, preparing to stand. The sound, the creak of boots on stone, came again and Henry pushed back his own chair, stepping away into the dark of the room, his hands gripped tighter to his rifle, watching the window carefully.

"Perhaps it was the wind?" he asked, but in that moment the window shattered inwards and a vast figure hurled itself into the room, roaring like an unleashed beast. The rifle in Henry's hands exploded and then the man was upon him, wrenching the weapon free and breaking it in two with his hands. A giant fist came out of the black and Henry's head cracked backwards. He saw darkness and nothing else.

Tacit spun on Strettavario and turned the table over with a violent swipe, lurching towards him, his hands drawn into tight fists.

"Good evening, Poldek," Strettavario said calmly, moments before a blow to his guts bent him double and a hand grasped the back of his neck, lifting him, gasping for breath, from the floor.

Tacit growled, taking two steps forward into the shadows and thrusting the Priest hard into the wall. Strettavario felt his ribs shatter and blood spluttered into his throat. "Tonight you die."

"You're later than I expected," groaned the Priest with a pained smile, a shard of moonlight striking across his face, catching in his white eyes.

"Is that so?" Tacit retorted, pulling back a fist to crush Strettavario's face with a single punch.

"I thought Isabella meant more to you? I thought you would have got to her sooner?"

"Don't play games with me, Strettavario. You killed her and now you're going to die. But slowly, just as you deserve."

"Tacit!" came a woman's voice.

Tacit's fist froze, his head yanked in the direction from where his name had been called. His fingers loosened around Strettavario's collar and the old Priest dropped to the ground with a groan. Tacit turned like a man struck dumb towards the figure in the open doorway.

"What is this?" he hissed, his arms drawn tight to his body, his hands splayed wide, crouching low, suspecting a trick. He stood motionless in the dark of the place, his eyes fixed on the figure before him. "What is this?" he repeated, taking another step forward towards the woman. There were tears in his eyes and his hands were now held out beseechingly. "Is it you?" He spoke the words as if the vision was a ghost come to haunt him.

"It's me, Tacit," replied Isabella, her heart clutched tight inside her chest, her hands wrapped across it. "It's me."

PART THREE

"For everything in the world – the lust of the flesh, the lust of the eyes, and the pride of life – comes not from the Father but from the world."

1 John 2:16

THIRTY EIGHT

All night Pablo had been unable to sleep, kept awake by the sound of rifle-fire from the lip of the trench and the churning of his mind, ruminating on his predicament, the Priests, the consortium of soldiers to whom he had been handed. All his life it seemed he had been guarded, protected, advised and shadowed by the Priests, who did all they could to ensure he was drilled in the right rhetoric and schooling, but chiefly that no harm came to him.

It seemed to the young man that they had taken him into their fold, with something approaching reverence and adoration, from the very day he had been turned out of his family home, branded a freak, a blight upon the family name, for the deformity he bore. The Priests assured him it was a divine blessing to carry such imperfection, and lucky chance that they were in the northern Italian city of Udine on the very first day that the twelve-year-old Pablo wandered its streets homeless, weeping and loveless.

In the six years that followed they showed him nothing but kindness and protection, ensuring his every whim was catered for and his health carefully monitored.

Strange then, he thought, that they had been so quick to recommend him for the army, to thrust him into the front line when the call came. And yet even here it seemed as if he was still being protected, both by the Priests who followed in the shadow of the forward line and by the soldiers in the unit into which he had been placed.

He watched his six fingers in the pale silver moonlight, drawing his other arm up behind his head to try to find some comfort in the shallow trench. All his life he had cursed his deformity, but in many ways it had proved to be his security and his benediction. He had lost the love of his blood family but had gained another family, one built upon the foundations of faith, endeavour and Godly rhetoric.

A line of soldiers, picked out at random from the massed ranks, had been ordered to lie thirty feet apart along the length of the forward trench, a little way ahead of where Pablo and the others rested, and fire spasmodically into the blackness beyond.

"What are they shooting at?" Pablo had asked, dragging his blanket across his chest to fend off the biting chill of night.

"Ghosts," replied Private Lazzari. "What else do they hope to hit in this darkness?"

"They are keeping the Austro-Hungarians on their toes," answered Corporal Abelli, pulling on his pipe and sending a plume of smoke rising into the frigid night air. "Making them aware we're here."

"I think they know that already," said Pablo mournfully.

From somewhere behind him a chorus of field guns opened up and buffeted the black mountain beyond. Pablo imagined the shells breaking apart among the rocks, the limestone splitting open and spinning a thousand razor fragments of stone hundreds of metres into the dark of the enemy front line, every shard a lethal weapon.

He thought of mud and sand and wished he was not halfway up a mountain of brittle stone.

The echo of the brief artillery barrage faded, replaced by the bark of rifle-fire, making Pablo think of the depleted supply of rounds in his bullet pack for his Carcano carbine rifle. He looked over to the front line, muzzle flashes preceding each crack of the rifle like little fires being lit and then instantly extinguished. He knew that every shot fired into the darkness was one fewer in his own rifle.

THIRTY NINE

The Vatican. Vatican City.

Bloody water pooled in the basin before him. Georgi flicked his wet hands and reached for a towel, drying them on the rough cotton fabric, leaving a red residue. "Don't bother getting yourself clean," called a voice from the shadows of the room behind him.

Georgi spun round, his knife instantly in his hand.

"Oh, it's you," he said, putting the knife away and continuing to dry himself. "More work needed of me? The second ritual is not ready to be performed yet."

"Monsignor Benigni," the voice warned, the figure remaining resolutely hidden in the darkness at the edge of the chamber, as if the light from the room might burn him. "He has become … troublesome."

"Benigni knows nothing," replied Georgi.

"Benigni is looking for you. He's tenacious, resolute. Experienced."

"Surely Düül is the real threat?" asked Georgi, the name seeming to catch in his throat and his fingers tightening around the hilt of his knife.

"His time will come. You know that. For now, deal with Benigni. He will find you, eventually." The figure turned to go. "Make sure you find him first."

FORTY

The Vatican. Vatican City.

Monsignor Benigni felt a rivulet of sweat run down his spine and allowed himself a moment of pleasure from the sensation. It always pleased him when he perspired from the exertions of the day, or night, as it now was. It was proof he was working hard in his role to stamp out the offensive and the unwelcome within the Church. "Tears of God," he often described the sensation of feeling sweat on his body. "The Lord is weeping in blessing for me."

The chubby bear-like figure swept into the old quarters of Inquisitor Cincenzo, knowing it would be his final visit of the evening. Afterwards he would return to his office and, perhaps with a glass of wine to moisten his lips and enliven his mind, he would make the final marks upon the file he had compiled on the dead Inquisitor, before binding it shut with ribbon and retiring to his own quarters to rest.

He stood in the centre of the small chamber, the thin file fixed under his right arm, the fingers of his left hand tapping lightly upon its hazel cover. He scowled and looked about the room, searching for anything, any last clue which might complete his findings on the murdered Inquisitor. Not that he needed anything else for the moment. He understood. The three rituals. The lust of the eyes. The lust of the flesh. The pride of life. He had read about them within the Great Library, the three cardinal sins made real through rituals which, when committed in the correct manner and order, would summon great powers to a single point. Clearly Inquisitor Cincenzo had discovered that the rituals were being planned, although how exactly they would manifest themselves and how Inquisitor Cincenzo had managed to discover them, Monsignor Benigni did not know – yet.

But he knew he would find out. He always did. He prided himself on his tenacity, his ability to smell out corruption and wrongdoing. To ensure appropriate punishments were brought to bear on the guilty.

He gave the room a sweeping look – a dour and plain residence, just as he expected and appreciated. The home of a man on the road, very little in the way of furnishings, save for a single picture in a frame. Benigni stepped over towards it, surprised to have missed it on his previous visit to the apartment, and picked it up in his pudgy fingers. It was a grainy line drawing of a young woman, perhaps nineteen. On the back was a name, Katerina, a date three years before and a series of numbers written in two lines, one under the other. The bespectacled Priest frowned and looked back at the front of the picture, scrutinising the woman's face carefully. He didn't recognise her, not from the choirs or the nunnery within the Vatican or from Rome. And he suspected, from the way she was dressed and held herself, that the Church might not have been her first calling.

Without further hesitation, he removed the file from under his arm and unlaced the ties, slipping the photo inside, before turning on his heels and striding purposefully out of the room. It was clear Inquisitor Cincenzo had been careless. Had attracted the wrong kind of attention. They had countless witnesses claiming to have seen a group of men fitting the description of Inquisitors chasing him through Rome. The bullet pulled from Cincenzo's head pointed to Inquisitors being involved. The Inquisitors who had chased Cincenzo had obviously killed him, but were they trying to stop Cincenzo committing the three rituals or where they themselves somehow involved with those rituals? That was, for Monsignor Benigni, the most worrying part. He had often heard talk of the Devil among Inquisitors, of the Antichrist lingering on the edges of their society, waiting to entrap the feeble and the unwary. He wondered if that was what had happened here, that these wild young Inquisitors had reached too far out into the Abyss and become ensnared?

He sighed and decided the best thing would be to try to forget the case for the evening. Everything would make much more sense in the morning. It always did. He allowed himself a small smile at the prospect of a glass of good vintage wine and perhaps a little study of Psalm 96:

He will judge the world in righteousness and the peoples in his faithfulness.

Unknown to Benigni, a dark figure rose from the shadows of the corridor behind and followed him.

FORTY ONE

THE ITALIAN FRONT. THE SOČA RIVER. NORTHWEST SLOVENIA.

Close to dawn, the Italian field guns opened up. For hours the artillery flew so close that it seemed to Pablo that he could reach out and touch the shells, running his hands through the grubby slipstreams they left behind as they flew towards the Austro-Hungarian front line. The sun had just begun to rise above the high ridge of the Carso ahead of them, golden tendrils of light feeling hesitantly across the broken blasted terrain, moments before the onslaught began.

Medium-calibre guns opened up all along the rear line of the Italian Third Army, each blast a throaty bark compared to the bellowing roars of the larger calibre cannons and mortars used by the Austro-Hungarians that had savaged the Italian army so badly every night. The two armies had yet to meet upon the same field, but there was already a long stream of bloodied, blackened bodies being carried from the mountainside on stretchers and in carts courtesy of the barrages.

From the shallow trenches of the western face of the Carso, the Italian soldiers could now see the Austro-Hungarian front and wondered what value the blasted smoking ruin of clipped rock and stunted trees could possibly have for Italy to want to possess it so desperately.

Hour after hour rounds were fired by the Italian artillery teams, bristling the vista with smoke and noise, the shattered sounds echoing around the mountainside like fractured rumbles of thunder. Pablo watched the front until his eyes ached, then put down his rifle and rubbed his face with his hand. The initial charge of adrenaline with the first explosion of the field guns had now faded into a lingering feeling of sickness.

He was suddenly aware of the unit Sergeant's barked orders and set his felt hat on his head and listened. From the words he was able to snatch above the incessant roar of the light artillery and the noise of soldiers preparing themselves for battle, he understood that there would be a charge upon the enemy, the target something called 'Mount San Michele'. The word 'charge' brought a pain to his stomach and the malign sense of sickness seemed to heighten again. So much walking, so much climbing, and now Pablo knew that this was it. He looked up at where they had to go, a steep climb to a rocky ridge six hundred yards over hard limestone rock, the target heavily engulfed in smoke from the barrage.

Pablo looked to the front and swallowed, trying to harden his resolve. Terror raged within him. He shuddered and felt tears in his eyes. He sniffed at them and heard a Sergeant speak above the roar of the shells, telling them to do great things for their country.

"Don't worry," said Corporal Abelli. "We'll look after you." And then Pablo was aware that the shells had fallen silent, that whistles were blowing all along the Italian front line and soldiers were rising up and out of their shallow trenches and forward up the mountainside.

Almost immediately the air was full of noise and fire and smoke and flies, and Pablo's first thought was how quickly the bluebottles had settled in the heat, oblivious to the clamour and torment all around. To him there was nothing but a roaring in his ears, from the soldiers all around him, from the guns behind him, from the enemy ahead.

At first he and the other soldiers of his unit followed the rest of the Third Army into the flames of conflict, running forward over the broken terrain littered with smashed stones and blackened splintered tree trunks. "Savoy! Savoy!" was cried into the air, in respect for the royal family for whom the Third Army fought, while behind the soldiers, Staff Sergeants followed with revolvers pointed at their backs.

When no enemy at first fired back, Pablo thought, like the other soldiers, that the enemy had fled and climbed into the higher ranges of the Carso, perhaps even as far as the Karst Plateau itself, or been obliterated by the initial barrage. But when they reached the barbed wire, great winding walls of the wicked stuff dragged across the wide vista, their progress was checked. It was then, as they began to climb over it, that the enemy appeared, the enemy who they'd been assured by their superiors had been reduced to a few ragtag shocked units left behind.

The heavy clunk of machinegun posts started up and soldiers began to topple like pins. The enemy's front was now just two hundred yards beyond the wire, but the hail of bullets meant the only way forward was to crawl. If ever a head was lifted too far from the ground, it was turned instantly into a bloody shredded mass.

Pablo crawled, wincing every time his bare skin touched the scorching white rock. He felt his head was about to explode, such was the thundering noise all about him. His eyes were full of dust and dirt, kicked up from the boots of soldiers in front of him and the shells dropping all around him, so much so that he kept blinking the dirt from them and scooping nailfuls of filth from his lids with the edge of a finger.

Despite the roar of war, he was aware of laughing too and looked to his right to see Corporal Abelli crawling beside him, his woollen hat shredded by fire and the shattering of rocks. Pablo stared at him, disbelieving.

"Why are you laughing?" he shouted. "What is so funny?"

"The Devil's flesh!" the Corporal laughed back, tapping the stones. "Can you not feel the fires of hell beneath? We are getting closer! Closer to the end!"

A short way ahead of them a shell landed in a flash of red and yellow, the bare rock stripped from the mountainside, flinging brittle fragments of limestone into the crawling masses. Something bit into Pablo's skull and intense searing pain rippled across his forehead and down his back. His hair dampened almost immediately and he knew it wasn't sweat.

He rolled forward into the hole the shell had created and lay there, his ears ringing, the ground beneath him sinking away as if he was tumbling into it. Perhaps he was tumbling into hell, being drawn down into its fiery depths? Perhaps the Corporal was right? Perhaps this mountainside truly was the flesh of the Devil?

Everything seemed far off, but Pablo felt the ground beneath him and he fell no more. Instead he just lay there, broken, his body shattered. He wondered if he was dying, if this was what death felt like. Calm. Remote. And he was aware that the entire landscape was shaking, rumbling with the weight of shells falling onto it. It was as if the whole earth was moving, trembling in its death throes.

Pablo lay there, not knowing how long. He was aware that men were climbing over him, always going east. He turned with great effort and crawled onwards, up the mountain.

There were more bodies now to clamber over, but ahead there was shouting and more and more soldiers ahead of him were getting up and running the final few yards to the enemy's line, curses and cries in their throats. Pablo staggered to his feet and ran after them, bawling like the rest of the soldiers, the beast within him let loose. There was dust and smoke and wrestling bodies in the trench ahead of him, which looked like a tunnel to hell. He dropped into it and turned in time to see a Hungarian charge towards him. Instinct kicked in and he thrust out with his rifle, his eyes tightly shut. The rifle went heavy and the figure hung limp on the end of it. Pablo lowered it and the man slid off, dead, pierced clean through the heart. Pablo looked down into the dead man's wide staring eyes.

There were tears in his own eyes, and tears in the eyes of the man he had just killed.

FORTY TWO

ROME. ITALY.

"Is it you?" Tacit asked the woman before him, his mouth open, his chin jutting forward like a slab of stone.

"It's me," Isabella replied.

Something blazed inside him and he swallowed, fighting emotions which threatened to overwhelm him. "My God," he muttered, raising his fingers towards her face, to test she was who she claimed to be, not an apparition. "Isabella!" And then he stopped and his face went dark once more. He spun on the heel of his boot and glowered at the old Priest. "What the hell are you up to, Strettavario?"

But Isabella took his arm and turned him back to her, her free hand curling inside his calloused palm. The touch of her skin on his was like fire and Tacit wrenched away as if burnt. She held up her hands as a way of pacifying him and showing she would not touch him again. "I'm sorry," she spoke as a whisper. "I'm sorry. I'm sorry." She said the words over and over, her eyes burrowing into Tacit's, as if casting a spell. She could hear Tacit's breath calming, in and out, slowing and growing shallow. "Don't blame Father Strettavario." She took a step towards him and Tacit didn't move. "He only wanted to get you out of there."

"How did you know?" replied Tacit, still staring at Isabella, but the question was meant for the old man.

"That you would try to break out? Exact revenge?" Tacit nodded and turned his head to one side to hear the answer. "I know you, Tacit, perhaps better than you know yourself."

"I killed a lot of people in that place," Tacit growled, looking back at Isabella, something approaching regret bound up in his words.

"I heard," answered Strettavario.

"Why've you done this to me?" And for the first time Tacit resembled a man aware of his actions, sullen and cowed, not some beast driven by rage. "Why've you lied to me?"

"We need you," said Strettavario. "More than ever."

A black fire seemed to flicker once more on Tacit's features. "The man who put me away, the man whose evidence condemned me after the Mass for Peace and cast me into Toulouse Prison, the man who saw me bound and gagged and tortured for nine long months." He turned on the Father and took a step towards him, his powerful fingers splayed. "He now needs my help? I should kill you where you stand."

"Yes, you should," replied Strettavario. The Priest's top lip had beaded with sweat, but there was a hint of humour beneath it. "But you won't."

"And why's that?"

"Because then you'll never know why we had to get you out."

"I can live with regrets."

"But not with the consequences of not knowing."

Tacit hesitated. He could feel the pulse beating in his neck begin to slow, the madness of his rage lessen. He looked between the pair of them, trying to work out just what it was they knew and why it was so important to have brought him to them. Tacit worked his tongue around the rough contours of his mouth, finally looking away and setting his weight over the table, spreading his great palms across the wood.

"Does anyone have anything to drink?" he asked at length, his eyes settling on Henry and Sandrine sitting at the far end. He narrowed on them, as if only now realising their presence.

"Who are you?" he asked.

"Does it matter who we are?" spat Sandrine.

"The hell it does."

"It's not important, Tacit," called Isabella.

"The hell it isn't!" replied Tacit. He caught sight of the bottle of brandy on the sideboard and his hope flared. He powered across the room towards it, gathering it up as if claiming a great prize. It was uncorked and at his lips in a flash, the contents swirling. To Tacit it felt as if the memory of the months of torment was diminished with every fierce burning gulp of the harsh liquor.

"Something is coming, Tacit." At once he stopped drinking and took the bottle from his mouth. "Something terrible."

Waves of haziness flooded across his mind and his eyes rolled in his skull. The caress of the alcohol was like a soothing lullaby. Ambition and anticipation wavered and then slipped from within him. He shrugged and raised the bottle to take another swig.

"The Antichrist," said Strettavario, and at once Tacit froze. "He is returning, as was prophesied by our Pope thirty years ago."

Tacit scowled. "Rubbish."

"Strettavario is right," said Isabella, coming forward and gripping hold of Tacit's arm to make him look at her. "Remember what you said to me that time in Arras? About the way the demon looks at you? About the way it knows it is winning?"

Tacit studied Isabella's face for a moment, drinking in her beauty and feeling a weight rise once more inside him, a feeling stronger than the drunkenness pulsing about him. "How long?" asked Tacit, his hand gripping tighter to the bottle. His eyes flickered over to the old Priest who had now clambered into a chair beside the table to ease his pain. "How long have you known of the Antichrist's return?"

"Three months. Maybe four? Possessions. Signs of demons among the newborn. Other signs, not just across the country but across Europe. Across the world. People are seeing and feeling his return. The Eagle Fountain, it is running red with blood."

Tacit stopped mid-pull on the bottle and lowered his hard eyes onto the Priest. Strettavario continued.

"These signs, they have happened before. In 1877."

"The Russo-Turkish war," said Tacit without hesitation. "In Bulgaria. I know of it. It cost many lives."

"But perhaps not enough," countered Strettavario, "for his purposes. This war, it is the preparation of his domain for his return. We have chosen to ignore this possibility. But now, we cannot deny the darkness anymore."

"Where does the heart of this darkness reside?"

"It grows within the Vatican."

Tacit's eyes narrowed and something cold sliced through him. "How did you find out?"

"Inquisitor Cincenzo," announced Henry, nursing his bruised jaw with his fingers. "He was one of our spies, the one who confirmed the darkness to us. He too had suspected that something was wrong. Had seen the signs. He'd gone looking for answers and we think had found them. The last message we received was that he had found the 'location'."

"What location?"

"We don't know. He was intending to tell us that final evening, but they killed him before he was able to reach us. He paid with his life for what he discovered."

"Did you know Cincenzo?" asked Strettavario.

Tacit shook his head. If the name was known to him, he couldn't recall it. He turned the bottle in his fingers, his back resting against the sideboard.

"Well, he knew you," said Isabella. Tacit skewered her with a glare. "He mentioned you by name as he died."

Tacit stood quietly for a moment, trying to take in all he had been told, trying to make sense of it. "Why you?" he asked after a while, looking at the strangers at the end of the table dismissively. "Why did Inquisitor Cincenzo know and trust you?"

Sandrine hesitated and Tacit detected something treacherous about her.

"There's more to this than meets the eye," he said. "Outsiders, dealing with dead Inquisitors, announcing the return of the Antichrist? I don't like the smell of you. It reminds me of things I hunt in the dark places of the world."

"Used to hunt," Sandrine retorted, and Tacit fell silent, pursing his lips. "You're no longer an Inquisitor, Poldek Tacit. It seems to me you're as abandoned as the rest of us."

For a moment Tacit felt wrong-footed, snagged by the cruel truth of her words. What the woman had revealed was right. Everything he had known, it was gone. He was as exposed as the heretics he used to hunt. He looked across at Strettavario.

"Who else in the Vatican knows about this?"

"The Holy See suspect, but hope they are wrong. They are putting precautions in place, one of which is to stop you."

"Why me?"

"They think you are in some way bound up with everything."

Tacit rolled his eyes. "What about you?" he asked, indicating Henry and Sandrine. "Is this it? Just you two?"

Sandrine shook her head. "There are others, throughout the Vatican, who too have felt this darkness and fight with us."

"Do you know any of them, Strettavario?" Tacit asked the Priest.

The old man shook his head.

"That's a first for you." Tacit thrust the mouth of the bottle back between his lips. He needed the drink to help take in what he supposed he was hearing, what he had long feared but never dared to believe. Just like the Holy See.

"You always drink so much?" asked Sandrine, distain lifting the edge of her mouth.

"No," replied Tacit, feeling his tongue slur between his teeth. "Not when in prison."

"You got demons?"

"Don't we all?"

"Is that why you drink?"

"I don't like people prying into my personal business," growled Tacit, slamming the bottle down on the sideboard, his hand slipping to his hip and the holster which wasn't there. "Particularly people I don't know. People I don't trust."

Isabella stepped between them. "What do we do first?"

"We?" replied Tacit, shaking his head. "You're not going. It's not safe."

"Tacit, it's not safe anywhere!" said Isabella, her palms held out to him helplessly. She let them drop. "Not anymore."

The giant man considered the words. "All right," he said after a moment, weighing up his options. "We find out what this location is, where it might be. Only thing we can do is to break into Cincenzo's residence and see if there's anything there we can find which might help. It's not much. And they'll be expecting us."

"Does the word 'seer' mean anything to you?" asked Henry, thrusting his revolver into his belt, having checked the cylinder was full.

"Seer?" replied Tacit, the edge of his lip turned up. He sank his chin deeper into his hand. "I wonder if they mean Sister Malpighi?"

"Who's she?" asked Sandrine.

Strettavario chuckled. "An intolerable gossip within Trastevere Nunnery!"

"And someone often used by the Holy See for insight and visions of things still to come. How do you know about her?"

"Our contacts, they sent us this one word. 'Seer'. It was the last we heard from them. We haven't heard from them since."

"Must be her," replied Tacit, his hands turning to white fists. "That's settled. We go and see her."

"Can she be trusted?" Isabella asked.

"Sister Malpighi is many things, but she's not someone to be easily turned by the Devil. You two," spat Tacit, looking at Sandrine and Henry, "can you be trusted not to get into trouble if you come with us?"

"Just worry about looking after yourself, Inquisitor," retorted Sandrine, standing and gathering her belongings from the table.

"Good," said Isabella. "Are we going straight to see this Sister?"

"No," replied Tacit, "there's somewhere I need to go first. Something I need to do."

FORTY THREE

Pleven. Bulgaria.

The stars had come out and the nocturnal insects were biting by the time Poré and his clan returned to the nearby town they had left six hours before. The air smelt of warm grass and flowers, bleached under a hot, relentless sun, but there was something mixed with the light summer scents, something acrid. Smoke. And there were sounds too, faint, but growing louder with every step closer to Pleven. Gunfire.

"Whatever is going on?" asked one of the old soldiers under Poré's command, as they neared the town's outskirts and saw torchlight and horses ridden hard down the roads, men gathering in crowds to hear messengers speak.

"Perhaps war has come at last to this place?" replied the Priest roughly, stopping to rub a little life into his ruined thigh. "It seems that the conflict's flames have reached everywhere else. Why not Bulgaria?"

They walked on, catching snippets of fleeting words from passing groups of men, about Italy and mobilisation.

"Whatever can they mean?" asked another of Poré's men. "Italy mobilised months ago! Can it be that the news has arrived here only now?"

"News travels slower in the east," replied Poré. "But for the news of Italy's war to have arrived only now, I find that hard to believe."

They reached a main square, where pear and cherry trees lined the outer perimeter and a large crowd had gathered around a belvedere to hear a man speak. He was dressed in a suit, a pillbox hat on his head, and he was remonstrating with his hands, his commanding voice audible from the very edge of the enclosure. But despite his best efforts, the crowd was wild and unrestrained and a fight broke out among the throng of men, rucking left and then right, as the mass brawl threatened to engulf the entire square.

"What is going on?" asked Poré in stilted Bulgarian of a local man hurrying from the fracas to avoid being enveloped by the fighting.

"Have you not heard? Mobilisation!" He held his hands to his head. "They are saying that there will be mobilisation!"

"Who says?" called Poré, but the man had already turned and fled. Poré took hold of another, grasping him hard by the arm so he could less easily slip away. The man spun on him, expecting to throw a punch to protect himself, but on seeing the gaunt figure of Poré, stayed his fist.

"Let go of me!" he shouted, yanking his arm free.

"What is going on here? Who is mobilising?"

"Nobody yet. But it is just a matter of time."

"For what?"

"Till Bulgaria mobilises for war! Already they are saying that Tsar Ferdinand and Radoslavov are drawing up plans. That we will march on Serbia before autumn!"

"Why?" cried Poré, but this man too fled from the erupting chaos all around them before he answered. "For what reason?" Poré called after him.

"Because of Italy," answered another man, heavily bearded and red-faced, hurrying past.

"What of them?" asked Poré, hiding anything in his accent which might suggest he was from the west of Europe.

"The treacherous scum. They are marching on Austro-Hungary!" The man waved with his arm away towards the west.

"Where? Where are they marching to?"

"Apparently they have already crossed the Soča River. They are marching on the Carso! A great army, a hundred thousand strong! They dare to try to take those lands and with it the monastery of Sveta Gora! Mount San Michele! The Slovene national treasure!"

A cold sweat clamped around Poré as the man made fists in front of him.

"We will fight back," the man warned. "With these!" he said, lifting up his clenched hands. "With anything we can lay our hands upon. We will turn the earth red with their blood!"

He turned and sloped away as if drunk on his rage, and Poré and his men watched him go.

"And so now I know where it is I must go," he muttered to himself.

"Where must you go, Poré?" asked one of his clan. "Surely not to war as well?"

"The Carso," he replied, looking at them all. "It is the place decreed. The place to be bathed in blood. I must go to the Carso."

FORTY FOUR

THE VATICAN. VATICAN CITY.

Moonlight flooded the silent back stairs of the Vatican, casting everything silver-black. In the dead of night, Vatican City was as quiet as a morgue. Tacit descended the stone steps as quietly as possible, his ears alert to any sounds from the passageway behind and beyond. Isabella followed closely in his shadow, her hand to the wall. "I'm touched," she said in a hushed voice, masking a smile as they reached the bottom of the stair well and paused.

"By what?"

"That you came back. For me. Strettavario said you would."

"I thought you'd been killed," replied Tacit, peering into the dark of the room beyond.

"It's nice to know you care."

It seemed to Isabella that Tacit froze. "Of course I care." He waited for a moment, as if summoning the courage to speak. "I told you, that time in Paris."

"Why did you leave me, in that corridor? You shouldn't have. It was cruel."

Tacit looked beyond to where Sandrine and Henry stood, crouched tight to the wall of the passageway, aware they could hear every word that he and Isabella were saying. He leant in to her, drawing her close. "It wasn't your fight."

"It wasn't yours to fight alone."

"No!" hissed Tacit, turning from her. He crushed his hands into fists and looked back. "I couldn't stand it, to think of losing you. Of what they might have done to you had you come with me." He dropped his hands to her shoulders, appearing to diminish before her, no longer the giant man he was. "Look, I don't expect you to come with me. You can stay here, or return to the Chaste, tell them I took you hostage and that you escaped. Strettavario will look after you. I'm sorry. I shouldn't have brought you along."

But Isabella pulled her hands free and shook her head. "Don't patronise me, Tacit," she said. "You left me behind once before. You won't do it again. Promise me you won't do it again?"

"I can't do that," replied Tacit, shaking his head.

"Promise me," she pressed, facing up to him.

He relented, allowing her this one victory. "Okay, I promise." He bowed his head, as if making an oath, before looking up. "I won't let anything happen to you."

"This touching reunion is all very pleasant," called Sandrine, "but it's not achieving much."

Isabella ignored the comment and raised her hands to his face.

"God, Poldek," she muttered, her hands moving to the bound wounds on his forearms from the nails. She had bandaged them the best she was able from the provisions Henry had with him, but the Inquisitor still looked ravaged beyond hope from his injuries. "What did they do to you in that place?"

"It's not important," he replied, as she placed her hands on his face, smoothing the hair from his eyes. In the harsh light from the single lantern, Tacit looked grievous and daring, his face butchered and broken from his time in prison.

"Thank goodness they never touched your eyes." Tacit slipped from her grasp to peer back at the door again, as Sandrine called, "So what exactly are we doing here?"

Tacit said nothing, surveying the hall beyond. They'd picked the right time to come. The inquisitional hall was deserted. The rare time it was ever quiet was in the middle of the night, shortly before dawn. Witching hour. Inquisitors were either in bed, on assessment or dead. He hoped that, in a few minutes, he wouldn't be joining the deceased, four slugs of lead in his chest from an overenthusiastic Inquisitor on guard in the hall. He knew they would be hunting him even here. They wouldn't give up on their man that easily. The prospect teased his gut.

The moonlight had turned Isabella's hair an ashen rose in colour, her skin deathly white. She looked as if she had risen from the grave, deathly beautiful.

"I need to get my bag, my tools, my weapons," said Tacit. "Beyond this door is the inquisitional hall. It looks deserted but chances are it's not. If there are any Inquisitors inside, we've got a problem, but it's mine alone. No one's to follow me. Understand?"

"Fine with us," replied Sandrine, crossing her arms and leaning back against the wall. "I'm not getting myself killed for some old junk."

He looked back at Isabella, his tone even more commanding. "Stay here. If I'm not back in five minutes or the moment you hear shooting, leave."

He pushed the door wide and slipped silently through it into the black. Just beyond the entrance he dropped to his haunches and looked across the hall. Empty. Tacit breathed deeply and rose, bounding towards the glimmer of the open hatch at the far end, the light of the inquisitional stores emanating from within. As he powered across the room, Tacit recalled the first time he visited the hall with his master, Inquisitor Tocco, his young eyes wide and disbelieving. That memory, the thrill of seeing the vibrant secret world beneath the Vatican's polished and brilliant halls and corridors, would never leave him, the charge of adrenaline it left forever branded on his soul like a medal of honour.

Within five steps he heard footsteps and peered back, cursing.

"I told you to wait for me!" he hissed.

"And you came to me for help," retorted Isabella. "That means we stay together."

"And die together?"

"If so be it, yes." She allowed herself a vague smile and looked towards the green shimmering light of the open store a little way ahead of them, a rectangular hole carved out of the thick stone of the roots of the Vatican building. Tacit halted alongside it, Isabella next to him.

"Gaulterio!" he hissed, hoping that in the nine months since he had last visited the store, the old keeper who always kept the graveyard shift within the inquisitional hall was still there. They would never have got rid of him. He was too knowledgeable and respected for an unceremonious expulsion. Only death would have taken the old man from his post.

"Who's there?" came the croaked reply after a moment, a reticent caution to the voice.

"You know who it is," replied Tacit, still not showing his face.

"Poldek Tacit!" Gaulterio called urgently, but the fact he kept his voice a whisper gave Tacit hope he would not raise the alarm, at least not immediately. They had a history, the old storemaster and Tacit, a strong tie of admiration and respect. Gaulterio had always respected Tacit for the stories of heroic deeds he had heard of the Inquisitor, and Tacit admired Gaulterio for never asking him further details of his assignments, unlike many of the other gossip-hungry cubs who helped Gaulterio run the storeroom.

Tacit stepped out of the shadows into the light of the storeroom counter.

"Jesus, Mary and Joseph," the storeman muttered, his hand clutched to his throat, taking a step back. "They said you'd broken out."

"They were right."

"What the hell did they do to you?" the wizened old man asked, studying Tacit slowly, a look of shock and disbelief at the wounded, battered appearance of the Inquisitor.

"Bad things. But that's in the past."

"Are you back for your things?" Gaulterio asked, a light coming to his eyes. He tilted his head to look down the length of his roman nose.

"I am."

"They wanted to have it," said the old man, his lips trembling.

"Who wanted it?"

"The Holy See. They wanted to take it. Make sure it was locked up. Safe."

"Why?"

Gaulterio shrugged. "No idea. I suppose they thought you wouldn't be coming back for it any time soon." His face lightened and a mischievous smirk took root. "I gave them some old junk. Said it was yours. They didn't ask any questions and they took it and locked it away. Never knew other people's cast offs could ever be so valuable." Bird-like, the old man turned from the counter and stepped away, pausing and looking back briefly from the shadows, as if to assure himself that his eyes and ears were not deceiving him, shaking his head. "It's good to have you back, Tacit."

Tacit muttered something under his breath and shifted around to rest his bulk against the edge of the counter, crossing his arms.

"Nice to know you still have friends," said Isabella.

"We'll see," replied Tacit darkly. "I could do with a drink."

"You're not alone."

Isabella pushed a hand through the gap at Tacit's elbow and tightened it around the man's biceps, pleased and a little surprised that he didn't pull himself away from her. "God, I missed you," she muttered quietly, as if a private thought to herself.

"Not here," replied Tacit, and at once drew himself away. Their eyes met, so much said in their glances. Tears welled in her eyes. "I thought I'd never see you again." Tacit turned away as if he couldn't stand to hear the words, to see her pain, but she drew him back to look at her. "Why does everything always go so ill for you Tacit?" she asked. "You seem … forever doomed."

"There have been times," he said, turning his eyes to look at the flagstones of the floor, a hand to his broad chin, "there have been times when I've wondered."

"What?" Isabella asked, and she saw a light catch in the Inquisitor's eye.

He shrugged. "That something wasn't right, that someone within the Vatican was watching me. Wishing me ill." He thought back to Arras and the warning the pale-eyed Father Strettavario had given him in the bar that night, that 'they' were after him. "But maybe …" He let his words trail to silence and cursed himself for his lack of conviction. He had threads of possibilities, but only that, threads leading merely to tangled confused conclusions.

"They tortured me, but it seemed to me as if they were torturing to see."

"To see what, Tacit?"

"See what would happen. See if *they* came."

"What came?"

"The lights."

Isabella looked at him, crestfallen and confused. "I don't understand."

But Tacit shook his head and looked away. "Neither do I. But they've always been there, the lights. I don't know what they are, what they mean. I've never told anyone about them. But always they appear to me at times of weakness, or power, when I am troubled."

"What do they do?"

"They speak to me."

"And what do they say, Tacit?"

"Terrible things." He looked at her, and he could see the love and concern in her eyes. "I think they were trying to test me, whoever in the Vatican is studying me, hoping to awaken the lights through their torture. I think someone was seeing what it was I possessed."

"For what purpose?" asked Isabella.

But Tacit only shook his head.

A noise drew them back to the stores and to Gaulterio.

The old man wheeled a vast wooden case on coasters in front of him. He drew to a halt in front of the counter and pondered for a moment how he was going to lift it up. Tacit didn't give him too long to wonder, reaching forward and effortlessly dragging it onto the counter before him, the wood bowing beneath the weight. At once the lid was thrown open and Tacit was delving deep within it, pulling out all manner of items; weapons, tomes, holy symbols, felt stitched bags, glass implements and test tubes, herbs and fine powders encased in metal pots, placing them into the deep pockets of his coat. From the bottom he dragged his chain mail armour and held it up, examining it briefly in the pale light before handing it to Isabella.

"Here," he muttered, before raking the final depths of the chest for anything of use.

The craftsmanship and weight of the metal suit astounded Isabella, so light but as hard as steel.

"You didn't see me, Gaulterio, right?" he muttered over his shoulder, menace in both his eyes and voice.

The old man nodded and threw the lid of the box shut.

"And Gaulterio," the Inquisitor added, plunging his hands into his pockets and still finding room for them among everything else. "Thank you."

FORTY FIVE

The Vatican. Vatican City.

In the passageway just down from Inquisitor Cincenzo's residence, Monsignor Benigni stopped dead in his tracks and spun around to face the person following him, his back hard to the wall of the corridor.

"Who are you?" he shrieked, his hand thrust to his mouth. "What do you want?"

Georgi emerged out of the shadows and loomed over the trembling man.

"Georgi Akeldama?" Benigni exclaimed, his piggy eyes growing wide behind his spectacles. He recognised the man at once. He'd made it his business to recognise faces and put names to them, even names of people long dead.

"Monsignor Benigni," answered Georgi, shaking his head. "Always sticking your nose into matters where it's not appreciated. Did they never warn you of the dangers?"

"I am only doing what they asked of me," he muttered pitifully.

"Me too, Monsignor," replied Georgi. "Me too."

He raised his hands towards the cowering Priest.

"Don't take my eyes!" he cried. "Don't take my eyes!"

Georgi laughed. "Monsignor Benigni, you're not nearly important or gifted enough to have that honour bestowed upon you," he smiled, before taking another step towards him. "You're merely a nuisance."

FORTY SIX

The Italian Front. The Soča River. Northwest Slovenia.

It was cold and it had started to rain, the first rain any of the soldiers had felt in weeks. Pablo thought he would have celebrated feeling the droplets on his hair, on his back, but he was frozen by the biting chill of night. Scorching day was always followed by freezing night on the Carso.

Ahead of them a battle was raging, while behind them, the taken lands were covered with the churn and action of the Third Army making good their gains.

A hamlet burnt away to his right. He remembered it when they arrived beside it at dusk, four houses perched precariously on the edge of the mountainside, the occupants old, too old and frail to leave their homes or the hamlet. Now the four houses were aflame. Pablo didn't know what had happened to the old people, and didn't dare to ask.

Everyone and everything looked distorted and wicked in the reflected glow from the burning buildings. The call was made to move out, to move further up the mountainside, mugs clinking as they were stowed away into backpacks and fires sending up swirling burning ashes as they were kicked out.

As they fell into the line the rain seemed to lessen a little.

Small mercies, thought Pablo, as they began to march higher up the mountain through the dark into the heart of the battle.

Four hours later Pablo had slept, a black sleep without dreams. He wasn't sure how he'd managed to sleep in the middle of all that horror and murder, of the shouts and crying of the dying, of the torment of the shells still raining, though now with less frequency, along the trench the Italian army had won from the Austro-Hungarian defenders at such a terrible cost. But Pablo had slept, although in slumber he resembled just another corpse in the morgue the trench had become, a long shallow grave for the thousands massacred on this first of many assaults up the mountainside which would have to be made before they had reached their goal. The summit. The Karst Plateau.

The first thing he felt as he forced himself awake was someone trying to take his rifle. Instinct kicked in, months of training, and he gripped hard on to it and snatched it back. He knew he'd be shot if he lost his rifle. He knew that he could not be killed that way, shot for dereliction of duty. That would not be the way to go. Not after he had come so far.

The soldier cursed and drew back.

"Stop fucking lying down and playing dead like a coward!" the man barked, before moving on.

Pablo rose to his knees and found himself kneeling in the praying position. He lowered his head and spoke words from his favourite prayer, a moment of tranquillity and peace among all the hot anger and death.

He was suddenly aware of a Priest next to him, speaking directly in his ear.

"Do you know why are you here, Private?" the Priest asked, crouching down by his side.

"I am here to do my duty."

"Yes, but for whom?"

"For my King and Queen and my country."

But the Priest laughed.

"Why are the soldiers looking after me so carefully?" Pablo asked cautiously. "Why have they not let me go forward into battle yet?"

"We wish only to keep you safe. You and your six-fingered hands." The Priest reached forward with his own hand to help the young soldier up, but instantly Pablo drew himself away, crying out. For the Priest's long pallid hand had turned rotten and black, like that of a corpse long dead. "Whatever is the matter?" the Priest asked, as Pablo scrambled for his rifle and his footing. "Come on," he shouted, his face wild with emotion, "let's see your hands! Let us check they are still undamaged!"

Once again Pablo woke to the sound of gunfire and shells buffeting the ridge above where he lay, now realising it had been a nightmare, his eyes opening on the Corporal sitting opposite. Other soldiers were kneeling in a trench a little behind him, waiting to go over the top.

"Am I dead?" asked Pablo, the first words which came to his tongue. "Am I in hell?"

"What do you think?" asked the Corporal, taking the pipe from his ruddy lips and setting the short blade of a knife into the bowl.

"I don't know," replied Pablo, looking about himself at the bodies of dead Italians and Austro-Hungarians piled high either side of him.

Abelli stared hard at him. "We've won the forward trench of Mount San Michele."

"At what cost?" asked Pablo.

The Corporal laughed and passed the pipe between his hands. Pablo studied them carefully to ensure they did not change to the decaying horrors that had grabbed at him in his dream, before turning his attention to the elevation beyond, up which soldiers had begun to scurry.

"What lies at the top, Corporal Abelli?" asked Pablo.

"Why do you ask?"

"Why is it so important we take it? Surely there are more valuable targets which are worth all this sacrifice?"

"You're a shrewd young man," replied the Corporal, waggling a finger. He set the knuckle of it to his lips. "Most soldiers don't question. They just do."

"That doesn't make me shrewd. Just cautious. Maybe a coward? I just don't want to die."

"And you won't," Abelli assured him. "Not in battle."

FORTY SEVEN

THE VATICAN. VATICAN CITY.

Tacit and the others took the stairs at a jog and ducked into the corridor at the very top, once they knew it was clear. There was a ground-floor window halfway along it through which they had come half an hour earlier and they made for it, Tacit checking every passageway and doorway before they slipped past. Down here there were no lights save the moon's pale glow through the windows. Suddenly Tacit stopped dead in his tracks and dropped to his haunches, Isabella following his lead, Sandrine and Henry pausing three paces behind her.

"What is it?" she asked, placing a hand on his broad back.

"Shhh!" he answered, his head turned to the side, as if trying to make out a sound from beyond. He rose and scurried down a bisecting corridor, his body low, his fingers spread wide. He dropped again to his haunches twenty feet on and listened, his head craned to one side, senses honed. Five seconds later he moved on once more, further into the depths of the new passageway.

"What is the matter with the man?" exclaimed Henry, breathlessly. "That's not the way we're supposed to go!"

Isabella swore and scuttled after him, the chain mail still folded across the crook of her arm.

"Tacit!" she called under her breath, feeling concern beat in her chest. This was no time for heroics, no time to get side-tracked. For once she agreed with Henry and Sandrine. They had to get out, get to Sister Malpighi's quarters and see if she was able to shed any light on events, on the Darkest Hand, suggest a way forward. She knew the longer they dawdled, the greater the danger would be. Tacit moved forward again. Isabella cursed once more. She had always felt coming back to the Vatican was a mistake.

Tacit was looking down at something in the corridor in front of him. She joined him and felt the breath sucked out of her.

"Monsignor Benigni!" she hissed, looking at the figure lying prostrate on the floor of the passageway.

Tacit turned the dead man's head to the side, Benigni's blind eyes staring away into the black corners of the corridor.

"Broken neck," Tacit muttered darkly, his mouth turned up with grim admiration at the manner by which his death had been delivered. A swift blow. A strike from a professional. An Inquisitor. "He never would have felt a thing." He set the flat of his palm against the forehead of the leader of the Sodalitium Pianum. "Still warm. Only just killed. Missed it by minutes." Tacit looked up into the darkness beyond. "Which means his killer is still nearby. Never had a chance to hide the body."

"Come on," said Isabella, pulling at his arm to get him to rise, "let's get out of here. We need to go. Now."

"Do you know if Benigni still lived at his old residence?" Tacit asked, stepping after her, but with his eyes fixed to the dead body behind them. His mind had begun to turn, homing in on this new and, he supposed, important discovery. Isabella confirmed that he did, as they broke into a gentle run to reach Henry and Sandrine, following the pair of them to the open window.

In the moonlit doorway not far from where the body lay, a figure watched them leave, the hint of a smile touching his lips, as if remembering his old acquaintance.

Georgi mouthed the name "Poldek" and grinned.

FORTY EIGHT

PLEVEN. BULGARIA.

Poré took his few belongings from the cupboard and threw them into his bag.

"Whatever are you doing?" asked the man with whom he shared at the room at the boarding house. Poré had taken three rooms for his men in the low terraced building in Pleven for the duration of their stay, the sign in the window promising clean and cheap lodgings, as they had proved to be. It had felt good to sleep in a bed rather than trying to find comfort under the stars with one's back to the hard earth, but now Poré knew that it was time to return to the road. And with urgency.

"We are leaving. This evening. Pack your things. And tell the others."

"But what about tonight's meal? And you promised us beer!"

"Stay if you wish," replied Poré, walking around the man to reach a drawer, out of which he pulled the last of his clothes, stuffing them roughly into his backpack, "but I am not staying in Pleven any longer."

The man scowled. "What is the hurry?"

"Perhaps it is better that you remain ignorant. However, know this," said Poré, pointing at him with a long finger, "we leave, in twenty minutes."

"Not me," the man answered back, crossing his arms about him. "Not until I have a full belly and a full night's sleep. And I'm sure you will find a similar answer from the rest of the men."

"He will," called a voice from the open door to the room.

Poré's eyes narrowed on the man standing there.

"Then I will go alone." He threw the pack over his back and tightened the straps.

"What is the matter with you, Poré?" asked the man at the door. "When we first came away with you, you told us we were hunting Catholics, looking to make our fortunes through thieving and ambushing. A life on the road."

"And we go back to the road. Going west, for Slovenia."

"For what purpose?" the man demanded, stepping into the room. Others were at his back and followed him inside. "You bring us to Pleven, away in the east, to look for signs of old camps and cold fires, and now you are saying we next go to the Carso?"

"At least tell us why we should go with you?" another of the party asked.

The memory of noise and heat came to Poré, of a light so bright he had had to shield his eyes from it with his hands. He shook it from his mind and looked at the brigands beginning to surround him.

"If you are not coming with me, you will return the pelts I gave to you," he said, his face puckered up in anger.

"How so?" growled the man with whom he had shared the room, as more of the men appeared at the doorway and pressed their way inside, attracted by the noise.

"They were the bargain I made when you came with me," said Poré, aware that they had now surrounded him completely, a menacing gang. "Power, but only while you shared my path. If we part, you part with the pelts. That is what we agreed." Poré's face had turned red at the mutiny unfurling around him.

"What if we do not wish to give them up?" one of the men asked, measuring himself up against the gaunt man.

"I do not wish to fight you," replied Poré, his teeth gritted, his nostrils flared wide, "but I will if I have to."

The men laughed. "How will you do that, old man? We number six and you're only one!"

"The pelts," another hissed. "They are the least we deserve for what we have done for you."

"Least you deserve?" spat Poré. "When I found you, you were snivelling drunks, barely able to piss straight! I have given you hope, belief."

"You have given us power. Leave now if you must, but the pelts stay."

His temper flared and Poré lunged towards the man but, as he did so, the window to the room burst inwards and two robed figures swung into the room.

"Inquisitors!" cried Poré, dropping to his haunches and rolling away, as the first of the gunfire erupted. Two of the men were hit, thrown back and lying still on the floor of the room.

The door to the room was still open and Poré made a dash for it, grabbing his bag and hobbling low as yet more gunfire raked the wall. He reached the exit and threw himself through it, staring back at the confusion of dust and tumbling bodies to see two of his men shudder into wolf forms and leap at the swelling numbers of Inquisitors. The rest of his men had been too slow, splayed over the floor, their dead eyes staring blindly across the room.

Bloodcurdling howls accompanied the sounds of armed combat as Poré hobbled as fast as he was able down the connecting corridor to the door at the far end. He threw it open and fell out into the side alleyway. The air was torn open with howling, explosions and cries. More sustained gunfire followed and then silence descended like a shroud, the last crackle of shooting dissipating in Poré's ears.

"Are any of them Poré?" he heard one of the Inquisitors shout, and his blood ran cold.

So they knew he was alive. They knew he was here.

They were here for him, this unit sent to kill him. He didn't know why he was surprised. For months now he supposed they would have been hunting him, the fact he had escaped from Paris and survived now known to the Holy See and Inquisition after the trail of carnage he had left for them across Europe.

"I think he crawled this way!" one of them called. "Out of the room."

"The rat, he must have gone down here!"

Poré could hear footsteps in the corridor behind him. Urgently he looked both ways along the alleyway. There was a door opposite him and he tried it, relieved to find it unlocked. He vanished inside the moment the Inquisitors burst out into the alley behind him.

"You sure he came this way?" someone asked.

"Opposite," an Inquisitor replied, and Poré sensed the man was pointing to the door through which he had just gone. "He must have gone inside."

Beyond the door, Poré pulled the pelt from his bag and dragged it over his head.

"Come and get me," he muttered, as rage flowed down from his scalp and into his limbs. Everything turned red and silver and an insatiable hunger grasped him.

The handle of the door turned and the wolf exploded from the other side, decapitating the leading Inquisitor and removing the arm of the next in line.

"Shoot it!" one of them cried from behind a hail of silver bullets, as Poré leapt, clawing and slashing at everything that moved, snapping wildly with his vile, monstrous jaws.

FORTY NINE

ITALY. ROME.

Grand Inquisitor Düül heard the jostling of weapons in the passageway outside and stood in readiness as the Inquisitor bounded into the room.

"Tacit!" he said. The Inquisitor had sprinted all the way from Vatican City and was drenched in sweat, fighting hard to catch his breath.

"What about him?" replied Düül, his eyes narrowing, his pulse quickening.

"He's been spotted! In the Vatican. The inquisitional hall!"

"Take a unit!"

"A whole unit? Can we afford a whole unit?"

"This is Tacit we're talking about," said Düül. "We know what he's capable of. Seal off the building. Make sure he doesn't escape. Find him and bring him back here alive."

"Aren't you coming?"

Düül took his eighteen-inch scimitar from its sheath on his belt and ran his finger along its keen edge. "No," he said, drawing blood from his thumb, "I'll wait and apply final judgement to the man as he kneels before me."

FIFTY

THE ITALIAN FRONT. THE SOČA RIVER. NORTHWEST SLOVENIA.

It had not taken long for Pablo and the rest of his unit to become entrapped within the battle again, as if the war were a vortex pulling them forever towards its centre. Three hundred yards across the plain, a renewed onslaught came from the shallow ridge at the end of it, bristling the rock all about them with small calibre rocket-fire.

"I have no ammo left!" cried Pablo to a soldier beside him, as they trundled into a run and charged towards the waiting enemy. The air felt hot and drenched with smoke, the ground beneath rising higher over broken rocks, which tested the legs and lungs and made chests burn. "I have no ammo left!" he cried again, knowing he was as helpless as a child as he charged towards the enemy trench.

At the top of the ridge was a scene straight from the fiery depths of hell. Every yard of the landscape was scarred with shell holes, splintered stone and the detritus of war, broken weapons, wagons, guns, shell fragments. The ground was covered in a crimson sheen turning black under the sun, spilled blood from the soldiers, both those attacking and defending. Body parts had been thrown over the place, torn apart by the ferocity of the battle that had raged here.

Pablo's feet tangled in something and he went down with a cry onto the sharp rocks, cutting his hands and wrists deep, tearing the front of his uniform. His rifle scuttled from his grip and a voice barked behind him to pick it and himself up. He watched as a slim Sergeant careered past, and Pablo looked down to see that his boots had become snagged by telephone wires from a communication base. He picked himself out of the trap and staggered on, wiping his hands, slick with blood, on the front of his coat, seeing that Corporal Abelli was waiting for him, crouched in a shell hole, the bottom of which was filled with blood.

"I have no ammo left!" he cried pitifully to another soldier, reaching out to him with a clawing hand. "I have no ammo left!" He realised that he sounded pathetic and desperate and the soldier didn't turn to look at him. "Help me! I have nothing to fight with!" He shook him by the shoulder and the soldier toppled over onto him, dead, a great hole punched through his chest.

"You have your rifle," called the voice of his Corporal from over this shoulder, as Abelli dropped into the dip and took a moment to survey the enemy line ahead. "Use your rifle!" he commanded, as an order.

"But I have no ammo!" Pablo called back. Then he realised what the Corporal meant and felt like weeping. He knew he couldn't knock a man's brains out with the butt of his rifle. That would be just too barbaric. And he was only slight. Everyone else seemed so much bigger than him. Everyone except those lying dead on the stones, shrunken somehow by death. "I can't do it!" Pablo wept, sinking to his knees. "I can't beat a man to death."

"Of course you can," muttered Abelli, placing a hand on Pablo's shoulder. "You just need to remember to never fear death. Once you come to accept that it is the only certainty in life and that no one can evade it, everything is easier after that."

FIFTY ONE

The Vatican. Vatican City.

"We shouldn't be doing this," repeated Isabella, standing at Tacit's shoulder in the residential quarters of the Sodalitium Pianum, Sandrine and Henry three paces from them, watching the pair of them closely.

"Change of plan," said Tacit. "Strettavario said that Benigni was investigating Inquisitor Cincenzo's death on behalf of the Inquisition and the Holy See. If Benigni's been killed, perhaps he had discovered something, something someone didn't want him to know. It must be worth investigating. We'll go and visit Sister Malpighi later."

The door lock clicked open, and Tacit stowed the picks he had brought with him from the stores, pushing the door open.

"No one home?" asked Sandrine.

"Seems empty," the Inquisitor replied, stepping cautiously into Benigni's Vatican apartment, the others following. Isabella closed the door behind her. Even the silent click of the lock as it closed sounded to her like a gunshot in the quiet desolation of the place. "We shouldn't be here."

Tacit ignored her, stepping through the dark of the residence with more caution than Isabella realised he possessed. There was only moonlight by which to see, coming in through the shuttered windows like lines of silver. In the still air, dust could be seen floating through the slivers of light.

"I feel like a thief," Isabella continued, catching up with Tacit and reaching out to his arm. "It doesn't help to know that the Holy See might have found Benigni's body and be coming here next." Behind them, Sandrine and Henry were stalking through the other side of the apartment, looking blindly for anything which might be of use. "How do you do it, Tacit?" Isabella asked softly. "Two hours after you reappear in my life after nine months of being away, you've got me sneaking into the Vatican, chancing upon a dead body and then breaking into the victim's apartment." A ripple of excitement shivered through her at the words and she felt a lightness in her chest. After the long months of Chaste servitude, she quietly realised how much she was enjoying herself. She felt an urge to embrace Tacit's arm, to pull herself to him. She battled it into submission and uncurled her fingers. "I suppose I forgot how much fun it is with you around," she grinned.

Tacit remained silent, pacing slowly into the depths of the apartment. There was a desk in the room beyond and his eyes immediately caught sight of the file upon it, illuminated by the moonlight. He picked it up and thumbed his way through it, crossing to the shuttered window so that he could read the contents with greater ease. He flipped back to the front cover and inspected it closely, passing his fingertips lightly over the crest of the Sodalitium Pianum, the seal around which the binding could be tied and Benigni's precise hand spelling out the edition and volume numbers of the file next to it. Tacit was pleased to see the volume number was high. The Sodalitium Pianum could never be accused of being lazy when it came to matters of investigating members of the flock who had fallen from grace.

Tacit turned back to the contents contained within, picking his way through the pages more carefully for a second time, his face studious and unyielding. He recognised most of the names listed within it, storing the infidelities of the accused in his mind for possible use later. Theft, greed, the hint of lost faith, a suspicion of homosexuality. The findings within might prove useful one day, he supposed. He froze suddenly and remembered he was no longer an Inquisitor. It was no longer his role to investigate and pursue. The realisation stung him and he cursed, forcing his eyes back onto the file. Regardless, the pulse of intrigue beat hard and fast within him. He couldn't change the behaviour of a lifetime. He had to find out why Benigni and Inquisitor Cincenzo had been killed. Regardless of his place in the order of things, some questions needed answers. And he was certain the two events were linked.

"Anything?" Isabella asked, joining him at the window after looking briefly through Benigni's desk drawers.

He paused, his face taut with surprise and realisation at what he had unexpectedly found. He closed the file and ran his fingers down the length of the spine, feeling the thickness of it before opening it again, slowly picking his way back through the pages. He held it open and dragged his finger down the rough edge of the inside spine, then held the file flat against the silver of the moon's face. A light caught within Tacit's eye, his anticipation pricked at the discovery. Papers had been torn from the file. Now he knew why Monsignor Benigni had been killed. The leader of the Sodalitium Pianum had discovered something someone wanted kept secret.

The find was as tantalising as it was exasperating. Just what had been in the file to merit the Monsignor's death?

Isabella saw the look on Tacit's face. "What is it?"

"The reason Benigni was killed. Something he found. A file he had compiled."

"Is it there?"

"No. That's the point. It's been removed. Torn out."

"Let me see," said Isabella, and Tacit handed the file to her absently, his fingers stroking the bristle of his broad chin, his eyes on the moonlit Roman streets below. He wondered if Benigni would have compiled the file alone, or if he had done it with others. If so, then they would know the file's contents too but, equally, they would be in danger. Finding their names would be easy. Getting to them would be harder. And he knew he lacked the resources and the contacts to reach them.

Thwarted. He could feel frustration gather inside him.

"There's writing here," Isabella announced excitedly, turning the first page immediately after the missing file into the light of the moon and running her fingers gently across its surface.

"What sort of writing?"

Isabella moved a lock of scarlet hair out of her eye and looked back to the desk, hurrying over and gathering a pencil from the top of it. At once she started to scribble with its lead gently over the surface of the indented paper, making a mirror of words on the reverse.

"Where'd you learn this?" asked Tacit, impressed.

"No secret is secret in the Chaste," replied Isabella lightly, her tongue clenched firmly between her teeth. "There," she said, setting down the pencil and stepping back to the window. The reproduced numbers shone silver-grey in the moonlight.

48.881196.

13.561646

"What are they?" asked Isabella, looking up into Tacit's tired heavy face.

"File numbers?" he wondered aloud, snatching the paper from her and bringing it closer to his face to see. "Perhaps within a library? Whatever Benigni found, I suspect the answer lies with them."

Something in the shadows at the far end of the residence moved from where it had been hiding and swung a fist hard into Sandrine's unsuspecting temple. A black-clad Inquisitor. She went down with a grunt and didn't move. Instantly Henry moved towards the man.

"Bastard!" he roared, moments before another Inquisitor came at him from the side. A blow to his stomach took the wind from his chest and a second the light from his eyes.

More darkly dressed figures bundled into the room and Tacit leapt forward towards them without a moment's hesitation.

FIFTY TWO

The Vatican. Vatican City.

Tacit made the first move, kicking over the desk, his fists raised. The closest Inquisitor to him ducked, but was too slow and took a full blow to the side of his head, cartwheeling away and clattering into furniture. A second Inquisitor threw a punch and Tacit stepped aside, retaliating with his left and closing the Inquisitor's right eye permanently.

The remaining intruders backed away and Tacit's next swing flew wide, leaving the left side of his ribs exposed. One of the attackers used the opportunity to crack three of them with a sharp hard jab, making Tacit curse and stumble backwards, his hand slipping to his side. The man's face was obscured, but Tacit was sure he saw relief and a smile in his eyes.

Tacit lurched forward again, feigning a body clasp and then leading with his knee, a cheap shot, but effective, battering the man back against the wall. Tacit gave him no chance to recover, following with a quick one and two to the face, which rocked him on his heels and dropped him to his haunches. Arms reached around his neck from behind, attempting to throttle him. He threw the man over his shoulder, twisting his neck with a sickening crack as he hit the ground.

Another swung a baton and Tacit crouched beneath it with all the time in the world, coming up and battering the man once, twice, in the face. Tacit thought the man was down and out, but instantly he rolled aside and came up fighting, his hands moving like lightning. They hit with a ferocity and speed which shocked Tacit. Whoever this Inquisitor was, he could take the punches and deal them out.

Tacit took six hits before gauging the angle of attack, snatching the seventh blow in mid-air and twisting the arm at the elbow, making his attacker cry out in pain. Tacit turned the man and brought his own elbow down hard on his neck.

Good night, he thought as he delivered the blow.

Two more leaped onto his back, a third lashing out with his leg, catching Tacit firm in the groin and making him crumple to his knees. Instantly the low blow was followed by a second, a kick which landed beneath Tacit's chin and battered him backwards.

He rolled over onto the balls of his feet and crouched low, watching the men adopt similar poses. They were good, but it needed three of them to even up the odds with Tacit. He was exhausted now, nine months' imprisonment taking its toll on him. He considered ending it here and now, pulling out his Colt service revolver and blasting them away. But he knew that to do so would alert every other Inquisitor in the Vatican.

"Who sent you?" Tacit growled, stalking in a wide circle around them, looking for a way in through their defences, waiting for their next move. "Tell me! Who commands you?"

The lead figure shook his head, hunkered low, his firm unblinking eyes on Tacit throughout.

Tacit smiled cheerlessly and shot forward at a speed which surprised the leader. He feigned a roundhouse and uppercut the man, rocking him on his heels and then planting a blow firm in the middle of his face. Tacit heard and felt the teeth break and saw blood darken his chin. He could have left it there, knowing the fight had probably gone out of the intruder now, but Tacit reminded himself that he never liked to leave a job unfinished. He led with his left, catching the ailing opponent in the guts and turning him over on himself, using his right to break two of his ribs, then his left again, hitting him hard on the right of his face and crunching his head back the other way with his right.

Tacit was breathing hard now. Tight muscles and tighter breath. And he had given the other two remaining Inquisitors a chance to attack.

Just a hesitation, a fraction of a second was all it took.

One of them threw an uppercut which caught Tacit between his Adam's apple and his chin bone with the weight of a freight train, a blow he never would have missed nine months ago, never would have missed if he'd not been distracted. He staggered back, the room spinning. He clung on to the man until his senses began to return, fending off more blows. Now he was happier, fighting dirty, fighting close. He knew how to move, just where to hit. But so did both Inquisitors, just the right amount of force, not too much to end the contest but enough to make Tacit know he was in a proper fight.

Tacit caught the man he was grappling a beauty in the solar plexus, but the man was big enough to take it, returning the blow with interest to Tacit's kidney. He went down on one knee, crying out as his right side seized up from the hit. He rode the next blow, buying himself enough time to twist free and catch his breath. His breath! Tacit couldn't believe how much he was puffing and how little the men he faced were. Tacit came at the second of them and the man rolled away, Tacit catching the glint of an Inquisitor's brooch in the moonlight. He tried a haymaker, wild, desperate but devastating if it connected. The Inquisitor ducked and brought a heavy fist up onto Tacit's jawbone, as the Inquisitor behind him battered him back with a blow to the back of the neck. Darkness and cold came in from the edges.

This is it, thought Tacit, but from somewhere consciousness returned and the figure in front of him merged from two back to one. He thrust with his index and middle fingers, hard as nails, and drove them deep into the Inquisitor's eyes. The man cried out, his hands to his face, sinking blindly to his knees.

Now there was just one left, the Inquisitor behind him, but he was on Tacit before he had even had a chance to raise his fists. The Inquisitor was quick, quicker than Tacit, now he was so spent from the fight, and almost as big. Tacit felt a fourth rib crack and then break from two quick jabs to his chest, his right eye closed from a left hook. Everything was slowing down. Tacit was tired and rusty. And stupid. He should have used the Colt revolver. He should have ended it. Instead, he was going to die here. He'd been imprisoned for too long. It had been a mistake coming here. He should have fled, made a new life for himself. But then he would never have found out just who had killed the Inquisitor and if the Antichrist really had returned. And Isabella. There was Isabella. Isabella …

A figure came out of the dark and brought a broken chair leg down hard on his attacker's head. He stumbled and shuffled right, his left hook flying wild. Tacit took his chance. He got one in just under the ribs followed by a beauty in the splenius capitis, which slackened the man's entire left-hand side. He stumbled forward, his hands grasping out blindly. Tacit let him fall before turning to face his accomplice. Isabella. He bundled her into his arm, leaning on her for support.

"Thank you," he groaned.

"Are you all right, Tacit?" she asked, knowing he was not.

He nodded, surveying the room for any remaining Inquisitors. At the far end of the apartment he spotted Sandrine and Henry. He stumbled towards them and crouched down, Sandrine stirring as he checked her pulse.

"What's going on?" she asked, groggily.

"No time to explain," replied Isabella, as Tacit dragged Henry from the floor and threw him over his shoulder. "Are you okay to walk?"

Sandrine struggled to her feet, testing her senses, and nodded.

"Good," growled Tacit. "Let's get out of here. The Inquisition will send more once they know what's happened."

"Gaulterio?" asked Isabella. "Did he betray us?"

But Tacit shook his head. "We must have been spotted, triggered an alarm."

"I knew it was a mistake coming here," she said, following him into the passageway outside the room.

"No," replied Tacit. "Thank God we did. We've discovered something."

"And what's that?"

"Something someone clearly didn't want us to find."

FIFTY THREE

ROMALDKIRK. NORTH YORKSHIRE. ENGLAND.

The three children had run all the way from school to reach the farm, as quickly as their little legs could carry them. The instant the bell had rung in

the school hall, signalling the end of the day, they had torn from the building, their satchels thrown over shoulders or swinging from tightly clasped
fingers. They loved visiting the shepherdess and her flock, and had been
promised a special treat this day. For the lambs were to be brought down
from the hills in readiness for the farmers' market at the weekend and she
had told the children they could take one lamb away with them, to keep as
a gift, if their father allowed it. He had begrudgingly assented after catching
his wife's insistent eye.

"I could almost explode with excitement!" squealed Maisie, her ginger
plaits bouncing as she ran. "Where shall we keep it?"

"Father said in the garden would be fine," said her brother Ross. "As
long as we don't let it get under his feet."

"Or eat his carrots!" laughed Annabel, the youngest of the three siblings.

"We'll be ever so good at caring for it," insisted Ross. "And every summer we can make our own wool!"

"I'd like a black lamb," said Maisie.

"Come on! First one into the yard can choose!"

They ran out of the shadows of Phillis Wood, the girls behind Ross,
racing along the rutted stony path that cut between the two fields at the
bottom of the Simpsons' farm. Now that the grey stone farmhouse had
come into view, the children's excitement became greater with every stride.

"I can't hear anything," said Ross as they grew nearer, his pace slowing
a little to allow his sisters to catch up. "I'd have expected to hear baaing if
shepherdess Simpson had brought them down into the yard."

"Perhaps she hasn't managed to bring them down to the farm yet?"
asked Maisie, immediately disappointed.

"Perhaps she never intended to?" said Annabel. "Perhaps she was only
lying when she said she was going to bring the sheep down from the field?
She did seem awfully strange that day she first suggested it, as if she was out
to play tricks on us. Do you remember how she looked? As if she was teas-
ing us?" The little girl recalled how unkind the shepherdess had appeared at
moments during their visit and how she had scared her at times, an unnerving light in her old grey eyes.

"Mrs Simpson would never lie," retorted Ross. "Maybe the sheep are
just behaving themselves. Being good girls and boys and keeping quiet for
us?"

They ran along the back of the house, snatching peeks through the windows of the place and the courtyard beyond. They were sure they could see
the silhouette of the shepherdess in the yard among the flock, but didn't

pause to look more closely, instead dashing up the stone path at the side of the house and into the yard itself to see her with their own eyes.

The figure of the shepherdess, her stooped back to the children, hesitated and then turned to look at them, a violent slash of a smile on her face, splashed with blood. She was holding something. There was blood down her front, on her hands and all across the yard which was covered with the massacred white bodies of the lambs.

At once the children froze and Annabel and Maisie screamed, Ross breaking down in tears, his hands to his eyes.

"Whatever are you doing, Mrs Simpson?" he cried. "Whatever have you done?" His hands dropped a little and he stared at the bloody mess stretching to the far end of the yard.

The shepherd dropped the lifeless lamb in her arms onto the cobbled stones and took a step towards the three children

"The lamb of Christ lies down before him," she spoke, as if reciting a passage from a sermon.

"Before who, Mrs Simpson?" wept Ross, shaking his head in anger and confusion.

"Before the Antichrist!" she laughed lightly. "He is coming. And his power reaches around the world."

FIFTY FOUR

The Slovenian border.

Naked, bloodied and covered in dirt, Poré dropped to his knees and hung his head like a man defeated. But he wasn't, not quite yet. He had run for hours from Pleven into the west, wearing his pelt, still transformed into the form of a wolf, stopping not even once, not until he knew he was far away from the town and the Inquisitors hunting him. Not until he knew they would no longer be able to follow his scent.

As a wolf he was stronger, faster. He found the wound to his leg did not trouble him as it did when he was a man. But even a wolf had to rest occasionally.

Slowly he recovered his breath and looked west, into the dark ridge of night which clung to the rolling hills beyond. Slovenia and, beyond that, somewhere, Italy and the Carso.

He looked back down into the damp grey and white of the fur pelt, turning it over in his fingers. His thoughts turned to his travelling companions who were now dead, killed by those who had thwarted him in Paris. A feeling close to sorrow enveloped him and quite without warning he felt the sudden need to weep. He let the cries come, shuddering and weeping into the pelt, feeling so alone, so terribly alone. Privately he had been grateful to find solace in others as desperate as he had been, people who shared a common hatred for that accursed religion. They were scoundrels and thieves, all of them with a history of mischief and violence, but they had come away with him and trusted him, for a while at least.

He had dared to believe, from the moment when he had found the pelt of Frederick Prideux discarded and stinking in the rubbish behind Notre Dame that night after the Mass for Peace, that the Mass had merely been an essay in a greater story he was to write. He had begun to understand that the road he travelled was assigned to him by a greater power and that it was always going to be long and difficult.

But now everything was close to its end. He just hoped the end had not already come.

A sudden heat exploded on the back of his head, as if the sun was shining just for him. He peered into the glittering heavens above at the new day breaking, as if trying to discern a reading from the constellations.

Now there was a light, shining down. And with it came a voice, a voice he recognised from long ago when he was a young man, the sound ringing sweet in his ears, just as it had back then. He almost expected to see a host of angels, such was the beauty of the sound and the warmth he felt. And then he saw it, the light, both brilliant and terrible, blinding and rendering him unable to move or talk, other than to shield his eyes. It was both terrifying and majestic but with it came a renewed strength and the voice called to him, as clearly as a bell. "Gerard-Maurice Poré," it commanded, "you still have so much to do. And upon you the fate of all will one day rest."

Almost as soon as the light had come it vanished, and the kneeling man was cast once more into cold and darkness, save for the meagre pale light of dawn at his back.

He lifted his head to the horizon, discerning a line of red dawn across it. Then he slowly gathered himself to his feet and walked on, knowing every step took him closer towards it, to redemption and to sacrifice.

PART FOUR

"For it is not an enemy who reproaches me, then I could bear it; Nor is it one who hates me who has exalted himself against me, then I could hide myself from him. But it is you, a man my equal, my companion and my familiar friend; We who had sweet fellowship together walked in the house of God in the throng."

Psalm 55:12-14

FIFTY FIVE

"Which way?" called Isabella, confused by the layout of the corridors. It was years since she'd been to this part of the Vatican, her work rarely taking her to the areas of the city afforded to the Sodalitium Pianum. Only the most resolute and austere of men resided here.

"Left," replied Tacit, feeling Henry stir on his shoulder, leaving him relieved that he hadn't wasted his energy dragging a corpse halfway across the central offices of the Vatican. "Go left." He indicated with the thrust of his head and turned to look back down the way they had come. "Keep going!" he called. "Keep going. Don't stop!" He could hear footsteps coming, heavy booted steps, and he knew to whom they belonged.

Isabella followed his directions, her feet tracing lightly over the wooden floorboards and through an arch of grey stone which led into a long broad corridor. Portraits of Priests adorned the walls, a carpet of faded lime lining the passageway, making their footsteps sound hollow and dull as they ran.

They reached the far end and Tacit told Isabella to go right, which she did without hesitation, reaching a flight of steps taking them down into blackness beyond.

"At the far end," called Tacit, using his right hand to help steady himself on the narrow steps, his left still grasped around Henry's middle, "go left."

From the maze of corridors behind, inquisitional voices barked orders and teams of Inquisitors peeled away, taking other routes through the building, hoping to head Tacit off.

At once Isabella spun to look round upon reaching the relative safety of the bottom of the stairs.

"Keep going!" Tacit replied, pushing her on and into a dashing run along the wood-panelled passageway. They could all now hear many pairs of hobnailed boots coming down the stairs behind them. They landed with a weighty thud at the bottom, twenty paces behind, as Tacit veered right and then instantly left, the corridors taking on the feel of a labyrinth, dark and claustrophobic.

"Whatever they want," called Sandrine, "let me fight them!"

But Tacit scowled and bundled into her to keep her moving along. "They want us. But in your condition, I don't think you'll be fighting anyone!"

"I'm a wolf!" resisted Sandrine.

"Who was floored by a single punch," Tacit reminded her. "Shut the hell up and keep going." All the time Tacit ran he was rooting in a pocket with his hand. A cloth bag came to his fingers and he tore it open, scattering the flowery contents on the floor beneath his feet. With his right hand, he delved deep in another pocket and took out his lantern. He admired it briefly, as if saying goodbye to the item, before clicking it twice into life and then throwing it over his shoulder. It bounced on the wooden floor and shattered open. Instantly the corridor was rocked by a series of explosions, everything behind them bursting into flame.

"What the hell was that?" cried Isabella, dropping low as she was turned left by the Inquisitor's guiding hand.

"Something to keep a bit of distance between them and us."

"Why don't you shoot them?" spat Sandrine, blinking the sweat out of her eyes.

"Why don't you keep your ideas to yourself?" replied Tacit. He stopped at the next fork in the corridor and looked back into the clouds of smoke which trailed in their wake. The shadows of figures seemed to loom within the swirling mists and Tacit cursed, pushing the pair of women with him back into a run.

"Ahead," he shouted, looking briefly over his shoulder and hearing what sounded like laughter and the stomp of heavy feet still following, "there's a flight of stairs and corridor. Go around them!"

Within twenty feet, Isabella reached the stairs, veering right and running along the landing above them as they had been told. There was light coming up from the floor below, while only the darkness of a cramped corridor lay ahead.

Tacit stopped at the stairs and snapped a nail into the left hand wall, dragging a fine wire across the full width of the corridor to the right hand wall into which he drove a second nail. The metal wire reverberated in the clinging smoke as Tacit tested its strength.

"Choke on that, you bastards," he muttered, before waving Isabella and Sandrine on into the darkness and crouching down after them. The passageway was narrow, like a secret tunnel, ferreted away, and Tacit dropped Henry to the ground, dragging him by the feet so that he could manoeuvre himself between the constraining walls.

Ten seconds later, many cries roared out and heavy bodies thudded down the stairs. Tacit allowed himself a wry smile and squeezed himself on.

Ahead was only black and nothing else, and Isabella, trusting Tacit, thrust herself into it, her hands raised. Her palms struck a solid wall, which held for a brief moment, before the panel snapped open and she fell out into a broad well-lit corridor, Sandrine tumbling after her. Tacit loomed large through the secret door.

"Where is Henry!" cried Sandrine, aghast, before seeing him follow in Tacit's wake, dragged like a slaughtered prize from a hunt. At once she batted Tacit's hands away and took Henry into her arms, her hands on the back of his head, looking into his slowly opening eyes.

"You carry him then," growled Tacit, looking up from the pair of them to Isabella. He took her hand and helped her to her feet from where she had fallen through the door. "Are you all right?" She nodded and tightened her grip on his hands in gratitude.

He stepped away purposefully, looking left and then right down the passageway with alarm.

"Which way do we go?" asked Isabella.

But Tacit had other thoughts on his mind.

"Get behind me!" he roared, taking out his revolver. "Quickly. Quickly!" He positioned himself in front of the three of them and levelled his gun towards the far end of the corridor.

"What is it?" cried Isabella, but she now heard the heavy thump of boots, many more pairs of running feet. "Tacit! Let's go!"

"No," he replied, his face etched with anger. He closed one eye to aim. "No more running. Now we fight."

Three, and then a fourth Inquisitor suddenly appeared around the corner of the passageway, their weapons drawn. Tacit's finger whitened against the curve of the trigger.

"Stop!" shouted Sandrine, bundling forward.

At once Tacit paused, and opened his eye a fraction.

"Flint!" she called.

"Sandrine!" replied the Inquisitor, stepping towards her, his hands held open in a surprised and relieved greeting.

"Accosi! Santoro! Kell!"

"What is this, Prideux?" growled Tacit, letting the revolver drop a fraction from his eye line.

But Sandrine said nothing, as she shook the Inquisitors' hands.

"Goodness, it's good to see you again! I thought you were dead!"

"After we heard about Cincenzo, we feared the worst of you too!" replied the one called Kell.

Smiling with joy and relief, Sandrine turned to face Tacit.

"These are our friends," she said, "the Inquisitors we thought were lost."

FIFTY SIX

The Vatican. Vatican City.

Cardinal Bishop Korek had been drawn from his office by the sound of an explosion long before he smelt the smoke. Instantly he knew that Tacit must have been found. In a lower corridor of the Borgia Apartments he discovered a large group of Inquisitors and Priests fanning through clouds of smoke, attempting to seal exits.

"What on earth is going on?" he asked, spotting Bishop Basquez among the throng.

"Tacit," replied Basquez, and Korek saw that the thin smile the Bishop so often wore was missing. "He was here. Within the building. And Monsignor Benigni."

"What about him?" asked the Cardinal, feigning a cough and wafting at the acrid smoke.

"Murdered. They found him in a passageway not far from the inquisitional hall. A broken neck. Appears Tacit came back for his stuff and the Monsignor got in his way. The inquisitional storekeeper, Gaulterio, has admitted to seeing him, just a short time before."

"So it would seem it is true that your subject *has* slipped free of his chains? I trust you were able to discover enough about the man before his prison escape?"

"Don't blame me that he's escaped. I did what was requested of me by the Holy See, to test the rumours of who, or what, Tacit is, of what he possesses, or what possesses him, not that he was securely held."

"Well, something possessed him enough to do the impossible, to break free of Toulouse Inquisitional Prison and then break into the Vatican! What doesn't make sense is why kill Benigni?"

"Does anything with Tacit make sense?" Basquez scowled.

"I don't know," replied Korek. "He was your subject."

But Basquez shook his head. "He was your subject too, Cardinal. We have an interest in the man, especially if the rumours are true."

Korek frowned. "Where was he discovered?"

"The Monsignor's office."

Korek's watery eyes narrowed. "Benigni was investigating the murder of Inquisitor Cincenzo. The two must be connected. Hopefully answers will be found once Tacit is recaptured."

"Grand Inquisitor Düül sent only one unit of Inquisitors to hunt Tacit down, and he didn't accompany them. I wonder if our Grand Inquisitor underestimates him, or perhaps there is another reason why he doesn't wish to face him?" Basquez was aware that Korek's own face had grown suddenly paler than usual. He felt a presence behind him. Turning, he looked up into the torn, ravaged face of the Grand Inquisitor looming over him, the wound across his dead eye glistening with sweat.

"Grand Inquisitor Düül," he said in nervous greeting, regretting his words. "You're here?"

Düül ignored the Bishop, lifting his nose to the smoke.

"Get the dogs," he growled. "Tacit's scent is still strong, even in this smoke. We'll follow him, we'll find him and kill him. Him, and all those foolish enough to have accompanied him."

FIFTY SEVEN

The Vatican. Vatican City.

They worked their way back to the secret shelter the Inquisitors had been using, close to the Via della Cava Aurelia, a cellar beneath a town house, fifteen minutes' walk from Vatican City.

"How long have you spent down here?" scowled Isabella, holding her nose, as the eight of them crowded into the main room. It smelt of sweat and piss. Inquisitor Kell sought out a lantern and lit it, while the other two lowered the blinds. "I thought you said they'd gone missing only a few days ago?" she asked Sandrine. "Smells like months."

"Where did you go?" asked Sandrine, ignoring Isabella's question. "We thought you were dead."

"We found ourselves a little tied up," replied Kell, pulling off his robe and chain mail with a sigh and setting it on the table. There were tears in the links of his armour, as if something had gored him from behind.

"Demons," added Inquisitor Santoro.

"You got anything to drink?" asked Tacit, shifting his weight onto his left leg as he surveyed the stinking lodgings. He had long fallen sober with all that had happened and his ribs ached. Only alcohol could soothe him.

"What do you think?" replied Kell. "We're Inquisitors." He indicated the packing crate to the side of the barn and Tacit lifted the lid, producing an oval frosted bottle of brandy from inside. He broke the seal and lifted it to his lips, swallowing several times.

"What do you mean, 'demons'?" asked Henry, who had found a chair and set himself gingerly down, his head nursed in his hands. Whoever had hit him had hit him harder than he'd ever been struck before.

"What's your description of a demon, Englishman?" spat Kell, his broken mouth puckering up with distain.

"Something out of hell," said Henry.

"Then you know. You don't need to ask." The Inquisitor turned to look at Tacit. "So how did you get to be among our prestigious company, Inquisitor Tacit?" he enquired, the corner of his mouth turning up with the hint of a smile. "I thought you were chained to a wall in Toulouse?"

"I was. Something encouraged me to break out," replied Tacit, his eyes turning to Isabella, before drinking down half the bottle straight. He felt restored thanks to the surge of strong liquor within him, feeling his ribs gingerly. "What happened to you?" he asked, looking at the four Inquisitors. "How did demons waylay you? First-year acolytes are weaned on them. Shouldn't be a problem for experienced Inquisitors." He took another glug from the bottle and assured himself he would finish it before the hour was out.

"Maybe," replied Kell, stepping towards a column in the room and leaning his weight against it, crossing his arms as he did so. "But you didn't see them."

"Don't need to," retorted Tacit. "Seen all manner of demons."

"Not like this."

"What does that mean?"

"These were powerful, from one of the lower levels of hell. There were nine of them."

"Nine possessions?" he pondered. Isabella cursed, but Tacit kept his drunken eyes on Kell. "In one place?"

Kell nodded. "Entire dormitory possessed. They fought hard, trapped us for days within the place."

"Which college?"

"Vittoria Colonna."

Tacit nodded. He'd visited the place several times to deal with possessions in the past, but nine in one place was new even to him. "What did they have to say for themselves?"

"What do you mean?" exclaimed Sandrine, mocking the comment. "This wasn't a social visit! They were demons! Not Priests!"

But Kell came forward and calmed her with a hand on her shoulder. "It's all right, Sandrine, I know what Tacit means. Demons, they cannot resist mockery and arrogance, trying to prove their mastery and might over anyone who might listen, especially anyone who comes to attempt to defeat them."

"And were they forthcoming?" Tacit asked, sitting back on the lid of the crate and folding his arms, the bottle nestled within them.

Kell nodded. "They were. They confirmed that something is coming."

"The Antichrist?" asked Isabella urgently, looking at Tacit and then back to the Inquisitor. Kell considered the comment for a while.

"Perhaps, but they referred to whoever was coming as their 'lieutenant'. Whoever that might be?"

"A person?" Henry suggested.

"Maybe. Whoever they are, whatever they are, apparently they are waiting, waiting for the right moment to arrive."

Accosi dragged a gloved hand through his hair. "Resurrection. They kept talking about 'resurrection' and 'a chamber of bones'."

"Does that mean anything to you?" Henry asked Tacit. Tacit made a face and took another mouthful of brandy, hoping that after it things might begin to make a little more sense. Everything at the moment seemed a confused blur. In fact, everything had been confused ever since he had broken out of Toulouse.

Inquisitor Santoro, who had said nothing but had drunk heavily from a tankard of ale, spoke for the first time. "Baptised in blood."

"I wonder what's meant by that?" asked Tacit, feeling drunk and relishing the sensation.

"It was what one of the demons I exorcised said. Admitted it right at the end of the third day, before I finally hounded the evil from the child it had possessed. That is how he described the lands where this lieutenant would return. Baptised with blood."

"The war?" suggested Isabella.

"They have a war," Tacit nodded. "A war across most countries in Europe, on many fronts. But baptised with blood? It sounds like some sort of ritual."

"A ritual to create a chamber of bones?" suggested Isabella.

"Perhaps they are gathering an army," said Henry, "baptising them with blood to get them to fight."

"Well, they already have an army," answered Tacit, scowling. "Six of them in fact. Six nations committing crimes across all of Europe. Perhaps this baptism is something to do with the letting of blood upon the ground?"

"Demons," growled Sandrine. "Can we trust them?"

"No," said all five Inquisitors at once.

"No," repeated Tacit, "they cannot be trusted, but from out of their lies, truths do come out."

"And names," said Kell.

"Sister Malpighi?" asked Tacit, dropping the brandy bottle from his lips. "How did you know about her?"

"You sent message of a word ahead of you. 'Seer'."

Kell nodded. "That was the word we strangled from one of the demons. Over and over he said it, particularly as the end drew near, as if it was a taunt. Seer. Seer. Over and over. Immediately we too thought of Sister Malpighi. The Seer of secrets."

"It's a start," nodded Tacit. "Let's go." He drained the remains of the brandy from the bottle and stood, Henry catching hold of his elbow as he pushed past.

"Tacit, the Inquisition, they'll be watching for you everywhere. You know that, don't you? They'll be waiting for you. They won't let you get away next time."

"Let them try," Tacit replied, a drunken leer coming to his face. "If what we've heard is true, that something is coming, some evil, this is not the time to be skulking in the shadows. It's time to step into the light and face it. And destroy it, if we can."

FIFTY EIGHT

THE VATICAN. VATICAN CITY.

Bishop Basquez stood with his hands flat to the sill of the arched stone window, staring out over St Peter's Square, watching as the crows flocked across the terracotta and beige rooftops in their thousands. Something had drawn them to the city. Something was festering within the holy city. Something foul had been awoken.

The young Bishop sighed loudly and looked across to his desk and the file lying upon it. The final manuscript of Salamanca's ill-fated attempt to unlock the darkness that many believed drove Tacit, at least until Salamanca was parted from his tongue and with it his mind. Basquez knew something lay buried within the Inquisitor. They all did, all those involved with his capture, his incarceration and his torture. That's why they had asked Salamanca to record every subtle revelation, every clue released through the agony of torture to help reveal what power it was that lay within Tacit, waiting to be unlocked.

What had started as rumour and suspicion, supported only by the speculation of prophecy, had grown into something manifest, something real before their eyes. A world in flames. The Antichrist's return. The theft of the dagger of Gath from its secure keeping in Paris.

Thirty-eight years ago, the dagger with its twin had been used to attempt to forge a crossing between the two worlds and bring damnation to the earth. Those who had witnessed the event claimed to have heard the High Priest at the time announce that something had come through.

Now, after all that had been seen and heard, Bishop Basquez was not alone in believing that what had come through was in fact Poldek Tacit.

They had only to unlock the secrets within the man in order to be able to step closer to the Abyss, to peer into its fiery depths and witness first-hand its terror and power.

But the man, the subject of their experiments, the one born out of the satanic ritual and sulphur, had escaped and now Grand Inquisitor Düül had involved himself personally. This would not end well. Basquez knew it would almost certainly end with Tacit's demise and with it the secrets and the potential untapped power stored deep within him.

FIFTY NINE

ROME. ITALY.

Tacit had wanted to take only Inquisitor Kell up to Sister Malpighi's residence, leaving the others in the entrance below, safe from any dangers they might encounter there, but he'd lost the argument. Partly through the determined spirit of his party and partly due to the clumsiness of inebriation which had embraced him. He had relented, leaving just the three Inquisitors behind to fend off the enquiring Sisters in the main hall.

They stood in the dark of the convent corridor, Tacit beside Kell, the rest of the party behind him, shoulders almost touching, not talking, their breath barely audible in the quiet of the place. There was a smell of polish and teak oil in the still air, incense too, but above it all was the putrescence of rot, seeping like a creeping thing from the closed room beyond. Flies bothered about their faces. Tacit knew exactly what had made them so active.

"Perhaps we weren't the only ones told about Sister Malpighi?" he muttered, fumbling in a pocket for another drink to help face the nightmare he knew lay beyond.

Sandrine scowled, puckering up her nose. "Surely no one would murder here?" she replied. "Not here, in a monastery?"

"Sister Maltese said Malpighi had a visitor, two days ago," Kell revealed, his voice shallow. "Apparently he had come from the Vatican."

"Who had come?" asked Tacit.

"A Priest. Sister Maltese said she didn't know him. But he was a big man. Muscular."

"An Inquisitor," nodded Tacit, and he instantly knew to which organisation he belonged. The Darkest Hand.

"Whoever it was, it obviously wasn't someone she was expecting," said Henry.

"Don't forget this is Sister Mapighi we're talking about," replied Tacit. "She must have known they were coming for her."

Henry removed his revolver from its holster and snapped the cylinder open, studying the brass rounds inside. Against the metal barrel they sparkled like coins of gold. Sandrine peered at him from the corner of her eye, an eyebrow raised.

"Think you'll be needing that thing?"

"Nowhere seems safe anymore," replied Henry.

Sandrine raised the back of her hand gently to Henry's and their fingers intertwined.

"You all right back there?" asked Tacit, an indignant look on his face. "You can always go back down to the lobby, wait with the Inquisitors for us."

"No," said Henry firmly, pulling his hand away and snapping the cylinder of the revolver shut. He thrust it back in his holster and prepared himself for action, clearing his throat and rolling his shoulders loose. There were tears in his eyes, anger in his face at how fate had catapulted him into this seemingly doomed world. "Shall we go in?" he asked.

"Good idea," replied Tacit and he raised his boot, kicking the door open off its hinges. A fetid wave washed over them; it was a stench so bad that even the horrors Sandrine had seen and smelt in the lairs beneath the killing fields of the western front paled into insignificance compared to this reek of almost indescribable abhorrence.

"Oh my God!" cried Isabella, her hand tight to her nose and mouth. The smell flooded the corridor, engulfing them in its stink, a depraved malingering thing that seemed to embalm them in its putrescence. "The smell!"

"Do you think that's –"

"Sister Malpighi?" answered Tacit. "Who else could it be?" Tacit peered into the darkness of the little residential chamber. Blackness entombed everything. There was a malevolence to the place, something everyone could feel, something ungodly which had settled within the room. It prickled skin, raised hairs on backs of hands and necks. Sandrine's hand dropped to the nape of her neck.

"Something came to this place," she said coldly. "Some evil." There was a pressure in her chest and she was aware she was shaking. Henry reached out and took her hand to steady her.

"Kell," muttered Tacit, "come with me. The rest of you, stay where you are." In the fetid darkness, the two Inquisitors stepped over the threshold and waited for their eyes to adjust.

The soft hue of moonlight seeped through the thin blind of the window at the far end of the room. But there was something else as well as the stench, thick, like a soup, the repugnant reek of rot. A chill, an ungodly cold.

Flies buzzed excitedly around them. At first Tacit couldn't see the source of the appalling smell, but as he looked up he recognised the shape of a decomposing figure hanging from the rafters of the room. Haloed silver from moonlight, the body hung in the middle of the chamber, suspended in the air as if floating, like an angel hovering within the room.

He swallowed and scowled, his eyes never leaving the body, barely recognisable as the Sister. He stared directly into the bored out sockets of the victim's eyes and felt something shift inside him, revulsion and something resembling sorrow. From the look on her face, the eyes had been burnt clean out of her skull, eyeballs, eyelids, optic nerve, everything, all the way down to the socket bone behind. This was not the work of men.

Kell, hands wrapped about himself like an embrace, noticed that even the silence seemed to have grown into an almost overwhelming presence in the room. He looked aside, snatching a brief breath, before lifting his eyes to look at Tacit.

Tacit, however, did not look back at him. His focus was solely on the naked figure in front of him.

Hanging upside down, the woman's arms and legs were tied tightly to the walls and rafters by what looked like ropes. On closer inspection Tacit saw that the Sister had been strung up by her own entrails, each limb wrapped in such a way that it tensed white against the strain of her own organs. At her belly was a wide and deep cut, her drying bloodied innards, crimson and blue, slumping down over her withered breasts to the bony line of her chin. Holes had been drilled into her wrists and ankles through which entrails had been threaded and pulled. Tacit had witnessed crucifixions before, when he was younger, but never anything like this, never a victim crucified by their own intestines. No human heart could ever conceive such a horrific desecration.

He turned towards the side of the room, as if intuition called him that way. A chill seemed to emanate from nearby and he could see vomit on the floor. Something caught his attention in the far corner of the room: three coins, piled on top of each other. He stepped over the pools of sick and reached down to pick the money up. Round golden Austro-Hungarian Krone coins.

"What have you got there?" asked Kell.

"A payment for the Ferryman in the east," he said, weighing the coins in the palm of his closed hand.

SIXTY

ROME. ITALY.

The first suggestion of amber dawn light was feeling its way through the city. One of the three dark-gowned Priests coughed to clear his throat and announce their arrival but there had been no need to do so. In the quiet of the capital at that hour of the morning, Georgi had heard the men's footsteps from the moment they had stepped onto the Trevi Fountain's long flagstone approach.

"The first ritual is complete." Georgi said, brushing the surface of the water with his fingers. "Did you not feel the change? Did you not sense the gathering powers? Now the second of the three can be performed."

"What did you do?" asked the Priest, playing awkwardly with his hands at the front of his robe, the other two standing silent either side of him, their heads bowed as if in awe of the man.

"Why do you ask?"

"We have been sent to ask."

"I see. Does our master in the Holy See wish to know all the sordid little details?"

The lead Inquisitor nodded and Georgi smiled, producing a small soft brown pouch marked with patches of discoloured fabric, tossing it to the member of the Darkest Hand. "I took her eyes, among other things."

"What am I supposed to do with these?" asked the Priest, holding the damp mottled bag away from him by the tie.

"Whatever you wish. Their value has been spent. They can give no more."

Georgi smiled and looked up into the tall heights of the Vatican, seeing the dawn brighten behind it.

"They are concerned," the Priest to his left said, following Georgi's eye to St Peter's Basilica.

"What have they to be concerned about?" Georgi asked. "All is going according to plan. The war in the Carso proceeds as hoped. Word has returned that they have found the one who will be sacrificed, as was foreseen."

"Tacit," the leading Priest spoke.

"What about him?"

"We hear that he was seen in the Vatican. In Benigni's office. That Inquisitors cornered him. That they fought."

Georgi laughed and nodded. "Something to warm Tacit up after his long incarceration, no doubt?"

"Our master doesn't see the funny side of it," the Priest said, his face grave. "We need to be careful, especially now we know Tacit is back and the Sodalitium Pianum are sniffing around."

"The Sodalitium Pianum are finished," Georgi replied, striking with a voice like iron. He turned back to the Trevi Fountain and once more absently brushed the surface of the water, watching the long ripples with something approaching wonder in his eyes. "Benigni is dead. With him gone, the Sodalitium Pianum will collapse."

"And the file he was gathering on you? On us and our plans?"

"Removed."

The Priest nodded, relieved to hear this.

"But what of Tacit?" he asked.

"What about him?"

"Does it not worry you that he is back? He might ruin everything?"

But Georgi shook his head. "Have you listened to nothing? Tacit cannot ruin anything, for he is bound up with everything. The prophecy. Without him, we cannot hope to achieve our vision. I promise you, I would be more concerned if Tacit was still rotting in that Inquisitional Prison." Georgi cracked his knuckles and worked the tension from them. "He must be present, to play his part. Although I doubt he realises yet that he is central to the plan."

"It just wasn't expected for Tacit to have been drawn to events quite so soon," said the Priest. "The prophecy, of course, predicts his involvement. We were expecting him to eventually escape from Toulouse, but ..."

"Isabella. He loves her," said Georgi, almost fancifully. He peered into the dark waters of the fountain, staring into its depths for a long time, before continuing to speak. "Even I was surprised by the speed by which he returned to the Vatican and found their safe house. He cares for her very much. I suspected he loved her, but I never realised to what extent." And then he laughed and shook his head. "Love! What has love ever brought Poldek Tacit other than pain and anguish?" The laughter evaporated on his lips. "You would have thought he would have learnt to control his emotions by now? But that was always his weakness." Georgi looked back to the surface of the water, his face pink from his outburst.

"Grand Inquisitor Düül," the lead Priest said, at length.

"What about him?"

"He has taken personal control of the situation. He is using dogs to track Tacit and those he has fallen in with, enemies against us. They have tracked them to Trastevere Monastery."

Georgi pondered the news carefully. "Nothing can be done. And nor should it. Our hand must not be revealed, not yet."

"But what of Tacit, of his safety?"

"Like I said, Tacit is tied up within the prophecy. It was destined to be that he found this path and walks upon it. He will not come to any harm, not until his part is played. But this soldier, the half-wolf, and these other Inquisitors who have joined with them, they are of no consequence. We need to tighten the cordon around the prophecy and remove anyone unnecessary. We cannot risk anything interfering with its true course.

"Make sure our followers fight, and fight hard, but target the soldier and his bitch especially. Kill them, but let Tacit and Sister Isabella live. Let them both go. Let them discover what they must. The prophecy is well advanced. They cannot stop what has begun and they will not know that their role is caught up within it until it is too late." He looked again at the water's surface, as if it held a fascination, and smiled, watching the sun shatter into a thousand shards across the ripples. "And by then Tacit will be as irretrievably tied to the darkness that is coming as the rest of us. In the meantime, I will carry out the second ritual." Georgi looked up and smiled, his eyes flashing eagerly. "By doing so, we will not only be a step closer to their returning, but will also have rid ourselves of one of the problems which so concerns you."

SIXTY ONE

ROME. ITALY.

"They're here!" Tacit cried, his voice like a bark in the silence of the dreadful room. "Inquisitors!"

Trouble had found them, the eruption of brief gunfire confirming his fears. He knew that the three Inquisitors left waiting for them downstairs were now dead.

Kell pushed past him to look himself. From the window he could see a figure holding a lantern cross the cobbles at speed. Tacit strode past the grim discovery of the hanging Sister, checking the corridor beyond for movement. "Do you know if there's another way out of here?" he called to Kell.

"I don't," replied Kell urgently, taking out his own gun and stepping alongside. "Only one way to find out. You go right, I go left?"

Sandrine stood between them, her face determined. "Then let us waste no time!" she said, and Henry at once knew what she meant to do.

"No, Sandrine! No!" he cried, stepping to block her path. "You can't fight them. There's too many of them." Noises came from the depths of the convent, the sound of many boots climbing long creaking wooden staircases, armies of men scouting down dark corridors, all of them drawing nearer to their targets. "They'll be prepared this time. They know what you are, after what happened before at the last safe house." Tacit was peering both ways down the corridor. He vanished right, Kell going left, both trying to detect the sounds of the coming Inquisitors and the direction from which they were approaching. Sandrine tried to push past Henry, but he caught hold of her arm. "I'm not letting you do this."

But Sandrine laughed, a short cruel laugh of defiance, and followed it with a cold smile. "Stay here, with her," she said, looking back at Isabella. "If they break through, take the window and climb to the roof."

She pulled herself free of Henry's grip and prowled to the door, Henry trailing in her wake, trying to draw her back. She spun on him, a wild terrible look about her. At once his hand gripped unconsciously at the pendant at his neck.

"Get out of here!" she half shouted, half growled at him, before turning back to the door and dropping to her knees. And then Henry did step back, no longer attempting to reason with her, knowing it was too late for negotiation, his heart dredged with fear and angst. His right shoulder hit the wall behind him and he grabbed hold of Isabella, navigating their way through the open door into the bathroom beyond, looking back desperately one final time to see Sandrine's head lolling uncontrollably on her shoulders.

He closed the door and stood against it.

"Do you have it?" he asked Isabella urgently. She looked at him confused before she realised what he meant, dragging the pendant of Francis of Assisi out from under her top. "Good. Keep it on display at all times." He rose his finger to his lips. "And keep quiet, for God's sake, at least until she's gone."

Gunfire and cries rattled the corridor outside the residence. A howl, horrible and vengeful, came from the chamber. Something rocked the corridor outside Malpighi's room, and the cries and gunfire smashed together, a mangled and terrible cacophony.

Inside the bathroom, Henry and Isabella held onto each other, their eyes, wide with fear and loss, filled with tears and focused on the door.

SIXTY TWO

ROME. ITALY.

For a team of Inquisitors attempting to stalk an enemy on the upper floors of a monastery, they were making a hell of a racket. Tacit would have lamented their lack of procedure if it wasn't for the fact they were now his enemy.

He heard the first two Inquisitors long before they appeared on the stairs of the right-hand corridor down which he had run. He took their heads off with two clean shots from his revolver before they had even caught sight of him. The empty casings hadn't even spun from the cylinder and hit the ground before he was down on one knee and fishing in a pocket for replacements.

He threw a grenade two heartbeats later and immediately reloaded his six-shooter. Determined voices from the bottom of the stairs ordered a charge, before the bodies of the dead Inquisitors tumbled out of the black towards them, and promptly turned to panic the moment the grenade fell among them. The passageway rocked and filled with sound and smoke. Tacit rose and powered towards it, his revolver raised.

Kell could feel his pulse in his throat as he reached the end of the left-hand corridor and flashed a look around its blind corner. It was empty, but below him he could hear sounds of inquisitional voices and boots, and he knew his kin were on the floor directly beneath him.

He went forward, stooping down, both hands on the grip of his revolver for comfort and control, an explosion somewhere behind him seeming to rock the foundations of the building. A grenade had been thrown and instantly Kell knew Tacit had just raised the odds.

Every third step, he paused and looked back over his shoulder to check he wasn't being followed. The howling, which had begun in the room where Sister Malpighi hung, was growing louder and more protracted. He'd seen Sandrine change just once, and once was enough to last a lifetime. He'd killed a mountain of Hombre Lobo in his time without ever questioning his actions. But to see the beautiful Sandrine turn into one of those beasts, it turned his stomach to think of it.

He pulled his own pendant of Assisi from out of his shirt and pressed on, more urgently now, looking to put some distance between himself and the half-wolf in case she choose to come his way. He'd pull the trigger and gun her down without a moment's hesitation, but he knew it would wound him as much as it would her.

A door in the right-hand side of the corridor burst open and two Inquisitors fell out of it. Kell fired and they hit the deck, seconds before two more rolled from the opening, their guns blazing. They too went down, clean shots through the heart.

Kell opened the cylinder to his revolver and dragged the empty smoking rounds clear.

It always hurt when she changed, the wrenching agony of her limbs as they popped, the screaming from her bones as they elongated and hardened, the eruption of hair from her skin, as if her body was being flayed by a thousand whips. But once a wolf, the pain instantly abated and was replaced with a renewed energy and dominance, a carnal desire to feed, to seek out enemies and feast upon their flesh.

Sandrine smashed the door to Sister Malpighi's room aside and sprang forward, the baleful howls from her lungs echoing like hell's legion in the tiny corridor. She dashed right and flew down the stairs, catching the scent of stale alcohol and sweat and the compulsion to follow it, and the man she knew she detested the most.

There were body parts covering the floor at the bottom of the stairs. Something resisted inside her, a desire to stay and feast, to try to sate her hunger. But an anger raged stronger inside of her, to pursue and kill, and she sniffed at the air and bounded with a withering cry along the right-hand corridor where the air smelt staler, shattering through the closed door at the end of it. A shout of alarm was thrown up the moment she powered out in an explosion of shattered flying wood, and the Inquisitors waiting there unloaded their arsenal of weapons on her.

She tore into them, decapitating and disembowelling with ease, snapping and devouring in three dreadful mouthfuls any caught within her slavering bloody jaws.

"Fall back!" cried the commander, and at once the Inquisitors tried to retreat. "And get silver!" But Sandrine came after them, her wrath made even more terrible by the taste of hot blood in her mouth and her belly.

SIXTY THREE

The Italian Front. The Soča River. Northwest Slovenia.

The stars had come out and it was bitterly cold. This merely confirmed what Pablo already knew about the Carso. That it was an ungodly place. Unbearably hot during the day, so much so that beneath every seam of clothing skin was rubbed raw with the sweat. Fiendishly bitter at night so that the cold sunk into the very marrow of your bones.

But despite the cold Pablo had to shit. He had felt the need for the last hour of walking. He'd eaten so little of the barren tasteless food since he had arrived at the foot of the mountain days ago. He was amazed there was anything in his system to push out.

"Where are you off to?" asked Corporal Abelli, his green eyes glistening like jade in the firelight around which some of his unit were sitting and singing and drinking coffee.

"To shit," replied Pablo.

"Take care. There was a sniper's nest around here. That was what the forward contingent were saying."

Pablo swallowed, trying not to pay much notice to the warning. It was dark, too dark for a sniper he supposed, and he was not intending to go far. Just far enough away for a little privacy. He stepped to the edge of the light of the camp and circled around a boulder, behind which stretched the inky black nothingness of the sky and void of the western heavens. He stood for a moment watching and listening, thinking then that if a sniper did shoot him it would be a good place to die. And for that instant, with the pleasing mutter of fellow soldiers' voices behind him and the crackle of fire, he felt something approaching peace, for the first time since he had crossed the Soča river.

He unbuckled his trousers, bearing his cheeks to the biting cold, and sunk to his haunches, squatting close to the limestone rock. He could feel the heat of the stones touch his bare buttocks, scorched from the long day. He pushed in his guts, absently looking about the circle of rocks he had found. Down the mountainside he could hear the dull clamour of army camps along the valley, muttering voices, occasional flutters of laughter, the bang of metal and bray of mules. Beyond, the night was punctuated by rifle-fire, frequent cracks, like sharp hammers on stone, shooting blindly into the black, shooting at an enemy they could not see, warning them not to try and attack, for they were ready, with their worryingly low stocks of ammunition and abject morale.

But there was something vaguely comforting about the miasma of sounds, a familiarity, a homeliness. A haven.

Pablo finished and stood up, buckling his trousers as he peered out into the far dark edge of the clearing. He suddenly realised that he was being watched. He thought it strange, both that he hadn't seen the figure watching him before, and that the person would choose to stand where he had, out in the open, unmoving, staring. There was vague outline of a gown around the bearded man who observed him at the very edge of where the light reached. At once, the young soldier thought him peculiar, and made to call out to him, but something made him falter, perhaps the way in which the man was watching him, saying nothing, just staring with his large dark eyes, almost red in the light from the camp behind Pablo.

Regardless, Pablo went forward, just a step, and could no longer resist calling to him.

"Hey there!" he shouted, taking another step into the dark towards the figure. But with every step, it seemed as if the figure was growing more faint. "Hey! What is the matter with you?" he said, striding quicker now in order to catch the man up. But Pablo realised that he had reached the sheer edge of the mountain, the ground before him giving way to the cool night air, and there was no one there, and nowhere for anyone to have gone.

SIXTY FOUR

ROME. ITALY.

Inquisitor Kell kicked open the door to the chamber and scanned the room for movement. Nothing stirred and he stepped inside, his gun tight to his eye line. Something moved from his right and he fired before he had time to think, the Sister standing there going down with only the slightest of sounds, her hands clutched to her bleeding belly.

Kell swore and rushed towards her, bundling her into his arms, moments before three Inquisitors poured from a swinging door onto him. His knife was in his hand, its point plunging deep under the ribcage of the leading Inquisitor before he had a chance to draw breath.

Something struck Kell hard on the side of the head and the room swam, his vision blurring, as he wrestled his right hand free and fired twice, the Inquisitor on top of him tightening before toppling off.

The third stabbed something into his guts and Kell kicked out, feeling his groin moisten and his left side go numb. The Inquisitor tumbled away and Kell found purchase enough to stand, firing twice more. The Inquisitor lay still in an expanding pool of blood on the floor around him.

With that, an almighty bang sounded and something struck Kell in the stomach. He cursed and dropped a fist into the wound, the pain from it bending him double. His hand came away red.

"Damn," he muttered, slumping onto his knees before everything turned mottled and dark.

Grand Inquisitor Düül stepped forward and took off Kell's head with a single swing of his scimitar.

"Find the others," he hissed to the Inquisitors around him. He lifted his ear to the wild sounds from the monastery. "There's a wolf loose in the building." His eyes narrowed with surprise and disgust. "Load up with silver. Find the wolf and kill it. And find Tacit and bring him to me broken. But don't kill him. That pleasure will reside with me alone."

SIXTY FIVE

Rome. Italy.

Tacit's revolver was smoking hot by the time he opened the cylinder yet again and ejected the spent rounds. He rooted in his pocket for new ones and found nothing but metal tubes of powdered acid. Three more Inquisitors ran at him and he popped the corks from the vials and threw the contents at his attackers with a wide arching arm, dropping as he did so, their fired rounds passing harmlessly overhead.

He heard their screams as the powerful acid burned their eyes and ate through skin into bone in a matter of seconds, springing to his feet, his knife clenched firm in his hand. It was an act of mercy to silence their pained cries.

Two Inquisitors appeared from an open door and Tacit threw the knife, sending one thudding back from where he had come, only the handle of the blade protruding from his ribs. The other Inquisitor leapt forward and quickly Tacit raised his hefty right, battering the Inquisitor's lower jaw which shattered from the blow.

Tacit paused, breathing hard, and turned his ear to the dreadful sounds of Sandrine somewhere in the building above him.

Sandrine sensed that her hide was drenched in blood, hanging warm and heavy against her skin, matted in thickly clotted clumps. She spun on the pile of slaughtered bodies about her, searching for any more victims. Through the windows which ran along the side of the hall she could see that the moon was climbing.

She bounded towards it, drawn irresistibly, the window bursting in a halo of glinting glass fragments, as she leapt through onto a wall outside. She stared straight up into the round pale face in the night sky, her eyes growing wide, filled with yellow luminescence. A madness festered in her mind, spreading like a cancer, polluting and infecting every avenue of her thoughts. She arched her back and howled. Within moments, the cry was answered and then answered again, more and more howls sounding all across the city, carrying the message of hate and rage and desire. Wolves rose out of the sewers and dark places of Rome and bounded into the streets and courtyards to seek out their hated enemy and to feast upon him.

SIXTY SIX

ROME. ITALY.

Inside the monastery, Tacit had cleared the building of Inquisitors, as far as he could tell, and had gone back up into the upper floors. He kicked the bathroom door within Sister Malpighi's residence off its hinges and immediately deflected the aimed rifle-butt with his right forearm. He wrenched it free and pointed a finger at its wielder.

"It's me," he growled, handing the weapon back to Henry.

"Thank God. Is it –"

"Over?" Tacit shook his head. "No, but the fighting has moved away from the monastery." Isabella ran into his arms and he embraced her, pulling her close to him for a moment.

"Kell?" asked Henry.

Tacit grimaced and shook his head.

"Sandrine?" he asked, even more urgently.

"Not seen her. Come on," Tacit said, stepping back out through the door of the bathroom and past the hanging body of the Sister for the final time. "Let's get out of here."

"How did they know we were here?" asked Isabella.

"We were ambushed." Tacit pressed his fingers hard into his exhausted eyes. His head throbbed with noise and the early tightening screws of a hangover.

"The Inquisition, they ambushed us," said Henry, his words simmering with rage. "They knew we'd be here."

"Grand Inquisitor Düül," muttered Tacit.

"Who the hell is he?"

"Someone to avoid. That's who he is. They tracked us, with dogs."

"Are they still here?" asked Isabella, her hand to her neck.

"No, they've moved off. Sounds like they've got more pressing problems to deal with."

"Such as?"

At that moment howls tore across the skyline of Rome and Isabella had her answer.

They ran down the corridor, following Tacit without hesitation or question. Henry looked back to the Sister's room for a final time.

"I have never witnessed such a thing before," he thrust with his thumb over his shoulder.

"It's a vision," replied Tacit.

"A vision? Of what?" asked Isabella.

"Hell," Tacit replied. "The manner of the wounds, the way the Sister was crucified upside down. It was a satanic ritual, although for what end, I don't know." He rubbed his hand against the sides of his temple, as if grinding some memory from his mind.

"Perhaps this killing is a single event?" Henry suggested, ducking through the doorway where bodies of Inquisitors were piled.

"No, this is just the beginning," replied Tacit, a knowing look in his eye.

"How do you know that?"

"This ritual. It is the first. Others will follow. The coins, left behind. They're a sign, a payment to greater forces to unleash something into the world."

"The coins? They were Austro-Hungarian Krone?"

"That's where the culmination of the ritual will take place. Something is telling me this was the first act. The lust of the eyes."

"The lust of the eyes?" asked Henry, his own growing large. "What is that?"

"One of the three sins." Tacit knew where the ritual was leading. There would be bloodshed, there would be carnage, the loss of many, many lives. And his mind turned to the war, to Italy's recent entry, the rumours of battles on the border, of new battles which were coming, of Italian and Austro-Hungarian forces meeting on the border between Italy and Slovenia.

"I don't understand," said Isabella, accepting Tacit's hand and being lead through an open door into the cool of the Italian night. After the fog and stench of the Sister's apartment, the fresh air was like a tonic, washing them clean. "What do you mean 'it is the first'."

"The first of three rituals."

"And what are they?" asked Henry.

"The beginning."

"Of what?"

"The end."

SIXTY SEVEN

The Vatican. Vatican City.

There was uproar in the Holy See that evening. Shouts reverberated around the inquisitional hall, cries of panic and alarm from all who had flooded into the chamber to listen and make their fears known about what was occurring in Rome. Cardinal Berberino was at the head of the outburst, laying out the facts like charges.

"I do wish you would calm down, Cardinal Berberino!" said Cardinal Secretary of State Casado, shaking his head, trying to give the appearance of stability and control.

"Calm down?" the thick-set Cardinal retorted, the wide neck of his collar stained yellow with sweat. "There are wolves running wild in the streets of Rome, Casado!"

"And we have Inquisitors dealing with them," Casado tried to reason with him.

"Are you hearing me correctly, Secretary of State? There are wolves, in Rome! There has never been such a thing before! Are we to think we have lost control of the city?"

"Far from it," Casado assured him.

"And what of Sister Malpighi!" shouted Cardinal Bishop Korek. "Murdered!"

"Cut apart, I heard!" someone else exclaimed, burying his head in his handkerchief.

"Whatever will become of us and our faith?" lamented another Priest.

"Gunfights within Rome's streets! Wolves running amok! I thought it bad enough when it was Inquisitors, but wolves?"

"The Devil has already planted one cloven foot within our land!" warned Cardinal Bishop Korek, waving with his finger.

"And chaos runs free in the streets!" added Berberino, sinking his head into his right palm and swiping the sweat from his tightly wound hair. "End times!" He raised a pointed finger to the ceiling, the noise rising to a crescendo so that no one could be heard against the clash of voices. "We were wrong. End times are not coming! They have arrived!"

Suddenly, a single gunshot thundered in the hall, instantly silencing the raging masses and sending some members of the Holy See cowering beneath their desks. Papers fell from their grasp and knocked glasses rolled off tables to smash on the flagstones of the hall. Grand Inquisitor Düül stepped forward into the middle of the auditorium, pushing his smoking revolver back into his white holster, his hob-nailed boots crunching hard on the polished wooden floor.

"I think everyone needs to calm down a little," he announced, looking around the circle of Cardinals and making no effort to hide his disgust. "These pitiful lamentations, your childlike hysterics, they are not becoming of our great faith. It was not built upon fear and weakness, but proud valour and strength, attributes we still retain, particularly in the Inquisition. You all know my methods. For too long you, the Holy See, have debated and considered, safe within your halls and chambers, while people, our people, are dying and a darkness is growing within the Vatican and beyond. No more." He shook his head slowly, before turning to the Secretary of State. "From this moment, I'm taking control. I'm deciding policy within the Holy See."

"Is this some sort of coup, Grand Inquisitor?" asked Korek.

"Let's call it a temporary seizure of power, shall we, until this latest incursion is brought under control?"

"Very good," nodded Casado, bowing his head and linking his fingers together to stop them trembling. "What do you propose?"

"To take the fight to the enemy. They have dared to enter our capital city and they will pay the ultimate price for such a sacrilege. At this very moment the wolves are being hunted and killed in the streets. I've received assurances that they'll be brought under control within the hour."

Something resembling a ripple of applause responded to this assured announcement. Düül ignored it.

"Meanwhile, I'm going to bring the dog Tacit to heel. Personally. He's still here, within Rome. We've got a lead on him. He slipped out of Trastevere Monastery a short time ago. The rumours you've heard are true. He's murdered Sister Malpighi. He's gone rabid but will be put down before the night is over. My men are in pursuit right at this moment. Once we have him contained, I'll drag him in front of you to explain himself. You can all get your answers from him then, about this so-called ritual, about who else, if anyone, is involved. About what it all means. And once you're done with him, he'll never trouble the Holy See or our faith again. That is my assurance to the house. No one makes a mockery of the Inquisition and lives."

"Of course," nodded Casado. "But what exactly will you do with him, Grand Inquisitor Düül?"

Düül threw back his white gown to reveal the array of weaponry at his belt. "Like I said, nobody steps out of line in my Inquisition. Tacit killed a lot of good men in Toulouse Inquisitional Prison, and now he's killed a lot in the Vatican and Travestere Monastery, not to mention Sister Malpighi. When I finally get to work on him, he'll wish he never set foot within Rome, let alone the Inquisition. Salamanca's methods will seem like therapy to him in comparison. I'll take the skin from his back and hang it as a warning to all others in the inquisitional hall."

SIXTY EIGHT

CONSTANTINOPLE. TURKEY. OTTOMAN EMPIRE.

A blood moon had climbed above the Constantinople skyline, dusk the colour of slaughter. Ragged columns of civilians, Armenian men, women and children, were leaving the city, long snaking lines shepherded by armed guards heading north while behind them calls to prayer rang out from minarets across the city. The excited shriek of Turkish children playing in the streets of their newly emptied capital rose up from the myriad of twisted thoroughfares and squares to meet the exotic smells of evening feasts being prepared in the houses above.

"Sounds like they have starting deporting Armenians," announced a fat Turkish man as he worked a date into his mouth from the plate in front of him. He stared down over the balcony which overlooked the Galata neighbourhood.

"Finally," replied Mahmut Sadik. The trader had made his fortune shipping exotic spices and silks into the west through his privately owned caravan lines, but was always generous in sharing his wealth and hospitality and his home with his closest friends. He sat up on one arm and admired the rings on his fingers.

"Never been an advocate of our Armenian neighbours, have you, Mahmut?" asked a dark-skinned man sitting alongside his host.

"Impudent and feckless," replied Sadik, shaking his head so his ample chin wobbled. "Let's just say I've never trusted them enough to use their kind as workers on any of my operations. And I know of few other traders who have found them satisfactory employees. If Armenians are unwilling to contribute to our society, then they are deserving of no place within our city."

"Or elsewhere within the empire," added his friend opposite, and the ebony-skinned man motioned in agreement. "I hear we're building them their own city?"

"A necropolis," nodded Sadik, "out in the sands."

"And they dare to call us oppressors? Ungrateful wretches!"

A line of women bearing trays laden with plates of delicacies filed onto the balcony and towards the table where the three businessmen sat waiting.

"At last!" cheered the fat Turk, smacking his meaty lips. "I feared I might die of hunger!"

Choice dishes of vibrant colours and enticing smells were arranged on the low table and goblets filled with cool water.

"Please," announced Sadik, waving his hands over the food. "Enjoy!"

He waited for this friends to help themselves before spooning a generous serving of fragrant rice onto his own dish and promptly into his mouth.

He didn't gag, not at first, but he hesitated, thinking it strange how the rice teased against his tongue, as if the individual grains were alive. Moving. He chewed, working the mouthful around, tasting a bitterness he'd not experienced from one of his favourite dishes before. For he only ever procured the best ingredients and employed only the finest chefs to prepare them. But there was no doubt that something was awry in the taste of the dish.

At once he spat his mouthful into his hand and his eyes grew large. Maggots, foul engorged red maggots, writhed and twisted in the half-chewed remains in his open palm. Sadik leapt up, cursing, fighting against the urge to vomit, sending plates flying and alarming his fellow diners. He stared with growing horror across the table. For all the dishes were now moving, pulsating and throbbing, every dish was heaving with maggots, rotten, fouled.

And, at the very same time, all across the city, at every dining table, restaurant and café, citizens spat their food from their mouths in revulsion and shock as the plague descended.

SIXTY NINE

"Clearly I missed something while I was away?" said Strettavario, remarking on the frenzied activity within the Vatican. He stepped into the Apostolic Palace and took a moment to observe.

"Where have you been?" demanded a voice Strettavario recognised at once. Casado looked more exhausted than ever, his skin flaccid and grey like that of a dying man.

"Here and there," replied the Priest, watching as a troop of Inquisitors marched the entire breadth of the palace before slipping from view behind pillars. "I see the Inquisition is no longer trying to hide their existence?"

"I don't need to remind you, Father Strettavario, that you are still under the employ of the Holy See," replied Casado, ignoring the comment. "It is not your place to go here and there as you choose."

"I had no assignments."

"So you made your own." Casado seized Strettavario's sleeve, his hand like a claw. "You ensured Tacit's escape!"

"I gave him the tools to escape."

"Whatever were you thinking?" Casado hissed the words so as not to draw attention to them. "It was not your place to do so!"

"They would have killed him had he not been released. I am sure you would not have wanted that, Cardinal Bishop Casado. At least not until your questions had answers." There was a searching tone in the pale-eyed Priest's voice.

"Do you know the problems you've caused?"

"I suspect the problems were caused when someone decided to chain what cannot be chained. If you wanted Tacit removed, you should have killed him when you had the chance, not tortured him with idle fascination."

"They're going to kill him anyway. Grand Inquisitor Düül has taken personal responsibility for his apprehension and punishment."

"Then Grand Inquisitor Düül is going to be deeply disappointed. This is Tacit we're talking about."

"This is a murderer we're talking about!" He drew close to the Priest, an aroma of incense and garlic clinging to him. "Don't put him on any pedestal, Father Strettavario. He is a criminal."

Strettavario smiled, a sly cold smile. "Yes, Tacit is many things. A killer?

A murderer?" Strettavario weighed the charges on his lips and found himself in agreement with the senior Cardinal. "Perhaps. But he is not a criminal, not unless the tasks we give him are criminal in themselves and so make him one."

"He killed Sister Malpighi."

Strettavario laughed, making no attempt to subdue his reaction. At once Casado took him more firmly still, guiding him to the shadows at the side of the hall. "We both know he did not kill Sister Malpighi," Strettavario said.

"So who did then?"

And at once Strettavario's pale eyes seemed to darken. "Do you really need to ask?"

"Which is why Tacit must be stopped."

"So that is what you think, is it? That he is one aligned with the Lord of Darkness?" He looked away across the hall, disgusted. "Is that what you have been trying to prove, with these acts of torture Inquisitor Salamanca was requested to perform? An attempt to draw the Devil out of him? Reveal his secrets to you?"

"We prefer to think of them as experiments and observations."

Strettavario was impressed that the Cardinal had at least made no attempt to lie or feign ignorance over what they had done to the man in that prison cell. "From the very beginning you've wondered, haven't you, Cardinal? About him. About who he is. What guides him. What empowers him. How that power could be harnessed, understood. Channelled."

"It is our role within the Holy See to observe and act in order to benefit the brotherhood and our faith."

"Then you should have observed that Tacit cannot be controlled. He answers to no man. He goes wherever his path demands he goes. For so long you have shackled him, bound him by faith and blinded him with rhetoric from the Holy law, turning him to your needs and your gain. But the bonds have broken loose, the blind has slipped. The beast has broken free. And who knows where or when he will stop in his rampaging?"

Strettavario stepped out from the shadows, but almost immediately Casado called after him.

"Is there really nothing which can be done?"

"Yes, there is something," said Strettavario. "Pray."

SEVENTY

The Vatican. Vatican City.

Antonio Fellacuti was eighty-seven and almost blind. Crippled with arthritis and twisted like a gnarled tree root, for the last seventy-two years he'd been a presence within the Vatican, as constant as the hymns and psalms resonating through the great halls and churches of the city. Still today he walked the corridors of the Vatican, his bucket of lukewarm water gripped tight in his right hand. Perhaps his passage through the city was slower these days, maybe the water sloshed a little more frequently from the bucket's rim as he walked, but he still cleaned every statue, washed every floor, burnished every handle in the Vatican as he had done as a young man over seventy years ago. He knew of nothing else, certainly nothing which could bring him such joy.

He'd long dreamt of entering the Church as a servant of God, a deacon, a Priest or even, should God show him good fortune, perhaps a Bishop? Every night, as he retired to his bed, prayers were always on his tongue, God within his thoughts, his dreams never tarnished by impropriety or sin. Even in sleep he believed himself pure.

He never did find service within the Church in his lifetime, not as one of the cloth, his ability with words and people considered inappropriate for one to lead congregations. But he had since realised that, by cleaning the Vatican, he was in many ways more than doing his service to God and his faith. After all, cleanliness was godliness.

Every cranny and surface of every statue he knew by touch alone. Every turn of every chin, every bridge of every nose, he could detect and name by his fingers. His eyes might not be able to see the dirt nearly so well as when he was young, but what he had lost in sight, he made up for in his ability to feel. Seven decades on, people still commented on how spotless the Vatican was when Antonio had been at work.

Antonio was pleased to be working this evening in St Peter's Basilica. It was his favourite part of Vatican City, and while the great halls were vast and cold, particularly with the city seemingly caught in the grip of a strange chill this evening, the majesty of the building couldn't help but warm Antonio's heart and fire his emotions.

He'd set his small ladder to the lip of the marble column on which Michelangelo's Pietà was placed and climbed it slowly, one rung at a time, setting his feet next to each other to ensure he was balanced before tackling the rung above, the bucket set in the crook of his right arm, his grey dull eyes staring blindly straight ahead. The statue of Mary with the crucified body of Jesus laid across her lap appeared more a worked lump of incandescent marble to Antonio's eyes than the exquisite piece of sculpture it was, but when the old man's hands began to feel the daring contours and delicate mastery of the marble, at once it came alive, a work of wonder and divine glory beyond comprehension. As he always did with this statue, he took out his finest of cloths, silk with just a little water to more easily remove any dust from the stone.

How it glistened in front of him, the water shimmering off the perfectly smooth marble to dazzle even his dull failing eyes. Something which sounded like thunder reached his ears. He shrugged and thought it strange for summer storms to have set in so early in the year. And then something which sounded like a wolf's howl. Most bizarre, wolves in Rome? He chuckled, and knew he must be tired. It would be his final sculpture this evening, he said to himself.

Suddenly something caught in his cloth, something tacky, globulous. He rubbed harder, confused and surprised that such a stain should have found its way onto the statue. Perhaps it had fallen from the ceiling above? But the liquid was slick, and the more he polished, the more it seemed to flow, as if he was working at an open wound. The cloth had become dark, and his hands too were now slick and dark, as if he were bleeding. He stopped and held the cloth close to his eyes, crimson and drenched.

And then he realised what the liquid was. The bucket dropped from his arm, falling to the floor, splashing its discoloured contents far across the tiles of St Peter's Basilica. Antonio felt himself topple backwards after it. He cried out and lunged for the ladder, just managing to snag his crooked fingers to the nearest rung and pull himself to safety before he fell too.

Blood!

The statue of Jesus was bleeding, bleeding from every inch of his skin, as if the marble had been stripped away to reveal haemorrhaging flesh inside.

PART FIVE

"Their tongue is a deadly arrow; It speaks deceit; With his mouth one speaks peace to his neighbour, but inwardly he sets an ambush for him."

Jeremiah 9:18

SEVENTY ONE

Poré watched the flames of his camp fire dance, tendrils of amber and red weaving like an enchantment in front of his eyes, drawing him nearer to sleep with every rhythmic sway. He had walked for days, every part of him ached, particularly his wounded leg, which now seemed to groan with every step, his limp more pronounced than ever before. He was sick and broken but he knew he could not give up. Not now. His eyes closed and he shook his head. He still had more miles to put between himself and where he had now chosen to rest before he finally succumbed to exhaustion. After all, he knew that every minute was precious, a race against time and great forces which, if unleashed, might well control time itself.

His eroded thoughts drifted to another time and place, exploring the dark recesses of his mind and his past, a young boy waiting anxiously at his classroom desk, a boy who never had any aspirations or dreams, only to be happy and to bring happiness to the world. And Poré was a happy child, until the man who entered the room, looking like an apparition of death himself, came into his life. Even now, thirty years later, Poré's guts hardened, just as they had then on seeing the man.

Up until that moment, Poré had never seen a man like him before, his life being always so full of light and colour, not dark like the savage who had visited, dressed in black from head to toe, a hood of felt covering the crown of his heavy square head. He had stood statuesque at the far end of the chamber, his large fists on his hips, staring at each child in turn, eyes boring, deciphering what he could from the young boys' appearance and manner, his mouth locked in a perpetual sneer, after which he had shifted his weight from his left to his right foot, stepping forward between the rows of desks, his long strides pacing the length of the room in an instant. The large shadow he had thrown seemed to shrivel and chill anyone caught beneath it, like a curse. Poré could still recall the sound of metal clanking dully beneath his tattered black robe with every heavy step he took, as if the bones under his shirt were exposed and made of iron.

Poré hung his head and clutched his hands, trying to choke the memories from his mind. But they refused to leave, growing clearer and even more real.

Although at the time Poré feared he knew who the man was, he had never dared to guess that the Inquisitor had come to call him away to join the acolytes for the Inquisition. When all that remained of the class was a ragtag collection of slight and brittle-looking children, only bloodless strained faces staring back, Poré had allowed himself a fleeting surge of hope that he would not be one of those called. But all too quickly his name was called, and afterwards nothing was ever the same again.

"What's the matter, boy?" the Inquisitor had hissed, as Poré had approached him that first time from his desk. "Where's your pride at being chosen for the Inquisition?"

Poré had tried to speak, but words had failed him and he'd hung his head lower and shuddered with tears.

"Is there some mistake?" the Inquisitor had spat, looking across to the man leaning with his elbows upon the heavy leather tome of names. "Can this whelp surely be one of the chosen?" He'd looked at the boy as if he were a piece of discarded filth. "He weeps like a child and has the arms of a girl."

"He is wise," the man at the book countered, holding his fingers to the point in the register he had reached. "It is said he has a great mind."

Young Poré lasted just two months within the Inquisition. The Inquisitor who had greeted him in the class had also decided to take personal responsibility for him, and subjected the boy to the very worst abuse. Daily beatings, verbal assaults, cruel interrogations and hostility shown to him at every opportunity, all exacerbating the true horrors he was supposed to face and fight as an Inquisitor. From this tortured life he could never find peace, for when the demonic cries of a possessed child or the phantom wails of a spectre had fallen silent, Poré was subjected to the taunts and violence of his master when they returned to their residence.

When he decided he could stand no more and resolved to leave, his pitiful pleading turning him prostrate before the local Cardinal, his eyes full of tears, he was granted his wish. But at a terrible cost. His mother and father were placed into inquisitional hands.

Root and branch. It was the Inquisition's way.

He'd beseeched the Cardinal to leave his family alone, to take him, but to no avail. He never saw his family again. It was then that the seed of hate was planted and proof, if ever Poré needed it, that at the heart of the faith was a blackness which could only have been forged in hell by the Devil.

Poré returned from his memory back to the wilderness of the Slovenian-Italian border and his current predicament, his cheek pressed into an open palm. His eyes were full of tears and he wept in pain at his loss and isolation. He was alone, so alone, as he had always been. And at once doubt seized him. How could he, one man, hope to do what had been decreed to him when the word of God had been revealed and assured him and told him to be strong?

The howl of a wolf thrust his senses back into the forefront of his mind. The crack of a branch sounded, followed by another howl, this one closer and directly ahead of him. Slowly he moved his hand towards the pelt lying at his feet. Another howl came, this time to his left, just beyond the light of the camp fire.

And now there was movement, a large hulking body running towards him from out of the trees, a vast terrible creature. Without any hesitation, Poré pulled on the pelt and spun to howl down on the approaching wolf with his talons splayed wide and his blood-red jaws open to receive him.

SEVENTY TWO

ROME. ITALY.

"They're still after us!" said Isabella breathlessly, the moment they had run inside the house Tacit had found for them and locked the door. She leant back against it and swept the hair from her face. "I can hear dogs."

"I can hear a lot more than just dogs," replied Tacit, pacing through the rooms to the rear of the house to check all was clear throughout. All across the city, wolf howls haunted courtyards and narrow side-streets.

"Sandrine," muttered Henry, looking to the window.

"She'll be fine," said Isabella, going to his side.

"Unlikely," replied Tacit, returning to the room to snatch a bottle from the sideboard and slump into a chair at the table. "But she and her kind are keeping the Inquisition busy." He twisted the cork off the bottle and set it eagerly to his lips. "That's all that matters. For now. We need a little time to think."

"I just hope Strettavario got away all right from the last place we stayed. Everywhere seems cursed!"

"Don't worry about him," replied Tacit, setting down the bottle and vanishing back into the depths of the house. "They're not looking for him. And anyway, I've known Strettavario long enough to know he can handle himself."

"Strettavario, he reminds me a little bit of you."

Tacit came back with a large roll of paper under his arm, scowling, and shook his head, but there was the suggestion of humour in his face. He set the paper on the table and rolled it out, setting the dead weight of his revolver in the centre of it. Isabella and Henry came forward, seeing that Tacit had found a map of Europe.

Isabella sat back on the edge of a table and crossed her arms. She flicked her hands to loosen her wrists and tousled her hair, forcing it into some sort of shape.

The giant of a man gathered an oil lamp from the room opposite, groping in his pocket for matches.

"Thank goodness," she said brightly, when he produced a packet of them. "Light! It feels like we've been encased in the dark ever since you came back."

Tacit lit the wick and replaced the glass cover, adjusting the flame so that its thin light eked miserably through the darkness. Any light was enough for Isabella. Tacit set the lantern down on the table and spread out the map, softening the edges and creases with his hands so that it lay flat.

"There are some more chairs through there," the Inquisitor announced, pointing with his thumb through the doorway from which he had gathered the map, as he leaned over the table, "if anyone wants to sit."

"What is this place?" asked Isabella.

"A very old inquisitional safe house. Known only to a few of us. Most of those who used it are long dead. I'm hoping no one thinks to look for us here."

"It sounds like the whole of the Inquisition is against us out there," Isabella said, as Henry reappeared with two chairs and offered one to her. He set his own across the table from Tacit and dropped into it, exhausted.

"The whole Inquisition isn't against us. We know that," replied Tacit. "But we need to work quickly. I'm hoping we'll be safe here, for a little while at least. For long enough."

"Long enough for what?" asked Henry

"Those numbers we found in Benigni's office."

Isabella nodded. "I have them here." She took the paper onto which she had copied them from her pocket and pushed it across the map towards Tacit.

"I've been thinking," he said, turning the sheet in front of him. "These aren't library record numbers at all."

"They're longitude and latitude," announced Henry suddenly, leaning forward and catching sight of the numbers from where he sat.

Tacit nodded, impressed.

"When did you get these?" asked Henry.

"When you were flat out on Benigni's floor. But I think you're right. They're coordinates on a map."

"Northern Italy?" asked Henry, watching Tacit's finger come to rest over the border with Slovenia.

"The Carso," said Tacit. He tapped the spot on the map with the end of his index finger. He looked up at Isabella and then across to Henry. "That's where the coordinates point. There's something there. At the Karst Plateau. Something that Cincenzo found there, or believes to be happening there." He looked at the pair of them. "That's where we need to go."

"Tacit," said Isabella, her voice wavering. "All this! The murders. The Inquisition. The map." She closed her eyes for a moment, as if letting the momentum of everything catch up with her. "I'm scared."

"Only just now?" he replied, a light coming to his own eyes.

"This thing we're getting into, is there no one we can call upon to help? Surely there is someone else you can trust? Someone in the Holy See?"

"No."

"Cardinal Bishop Adansoni?" she suggested. "You speak so highly of him, like he was your father?"

Tacit's eyes grew very large and dark. "No."

"He's a good man. He cares for you." She clutched his hand tighter so that her knuckles whitened. "I know he cares for you very much, from the times I have spoken with him previously. We should try and find him. Maybe he can help explain the map?" she suggested, waving towards the table.

"No," Tacit replied firmly, the darkness within him almost instantly crushing any softening of emotion he had shown. "It's too dangerous to involve an old man like him." He stood and returned his attention to the table. "This is for us and us alone," he announced, tapping on the area marked on the map. He looked from Henry to Isabella, and then back at the point on the map he was indicating. In the thin light of the single lantern, Tacit looked more determined than ever, his face butchered and broken from all he had endured.

"The Karst," he announced, his finger set to the place on the map where the Italian and Austro-Hungarian borders met. He looked again at the pair of them. "That's where the coordinates point. There's something in the Karst. That's where we need to go." He saw that the soldier looked troubled. "What is it?" Tacit spat. "Getting cold feet?"

But Henry ignored him and buried his chin in his hand, his eyes searching the recesses of the room's far corner.

"Resurrection," said Henry. "The Chamber of Bones." Now both sets of eyes were on the soldier and he dropped both hands to the table. "What Accosi mentioned before. I've been thinking. I know of it," he said. "I've heard of it."

"What do you mean?" growled Tacit. "You mean it's a place?" And then it seemed as if the realisation struck him.

"Nostra Signora della Concezione," they said together, and Isabella's eyes widened.

"Of course!" she said, her hand to her hairline. "The church of Santa Maria della Concezione of the Capuchins, in Rome!"

"Beneath which is the Crypt of the Resurrection."

"The Chamber of Bones," confirmed Henry, nodding.

Tacit's eyes narrowed. "I wonder how it's connected? Maybe it's a location for one of the rituals? If we can get there first—"

The sound of glass breaking and wood snapping disrupted them, and as one they leapt up from the table and the map.

"We have company!" hissed Henry, gathering his revolver from his holster. "I thought you said this place was safe?!"

"Followed!" spat Tacit, taking his own revolver from his thigh. "We must have been followed."

SEVENTY THREE

Rome. Italy.

The wild-eyed Inquisitor battered the wolf to one side with the butt of his rifle and vaulted the wall, dashing down the cobbled passageway as fast as his booted feet would carry him.

He sprinted into the small courtyard where Düül had set up his position of command within the city to direct his men. Three alleyways fed the darkened yard, buildings encircling all sides, making the central location perfect for directing tactics.

"There's Hombre Lobo all across Rome, Grand Inquisitor!" the Inquisitor cried, his hands on his knees gasping for breath, the side of his face raked by claws. "They're everywhere, but we are winning on the southern and western sides. From the east, their numbers are greater than we expected. And we are being slowed by having to burn bodies and hide evidence from the citizens of the city."

A howl came from the street out of which the Inquisitor had appeared and moments later a vast wolf bounded in. Instantly Grand Inquisitor Düül's revolver was in his hand and the barrel flashed. The beast vaulted forward and turned over, coming to a dead stop at their feet.

"One less," muttered Düül. "What are you doing here anyway?" he demanded of the Inquisitor, peering down on him with a scowl. "Not just to report to me, surely? Have you found Tacit?"

The Inquisitor nodded, stepping away from the prostrate wolf to put a little distance between him and creature. "Apparently someone matching his description has been spotted."

"Where?"

"The church of Santa Maria della Concezione. He told me to come and find you."

Düül's scimitar flashed from his hilt and he held the bloodstained blade up to the light. "It ends tonight," he said. "It ends by my hand."

SEVENTY FOUR

Rome. Italy.

One side of the room exploded in fire and debris and noise. Everything shook and seemed to move very far away. It appeared to Tacit as if he had fallen into the earth, the air becoming heavy and hot. The table had been turned on its side, the map ripped and torn, half covering Isabella who lay close by, while Henry sat upright next to her, pointing at his boot which had been blasted to a burnt, bloody mess. He was saying something, but Tacit couldn't understand the words. Another explosion rocked the room.

"Find them," Tacit heard a voice command within the maddening confusion as Inquisitors flooded into the room. He was on his feet and bounding over the table, landing among the attackers in a matter of seconds, his great arms battering and pummelling all within reach. Gunfire erupted, but he paid it no mind, ploughing into the middle of the shocked Inquisitors, breaking jaws and splitting skulls with his hammer-like fists.

A grenade was tossed and the room flashed with light, filling moments later with smoke and the choking smell of cordite. Tacit began searching for Isabella and Henry, trying to regain his bearings. A figure swam into view and Tacit grappled him around the neck, breaking it easily and letting him fall, snatching the Inquisitor's rifle as he did so.

"Isabella!" he cried, stumbling blindly through the fog, knowing the overturned table was nearby. More gunfire sounded and something bit into his thigh. He roared in pain and turned to unleash two returning rounds from his rifle. Someone cried out ahead of him and fell to the ground. Isabella appeared through the haze, coughing, and he clutched hold of her, drawing her close. Her head was cut, blood streaking down one side of her face, but otherwise she looked unharmed. There was a wild look about her and at first Tacit thought she had been driven mad from the assault, until her hand slipped to his holster and she took out his revolver. Their eyes met and Isabella's flashed.

"Like I said," she said, raising the revolver, "you never leave me behind again!"

She peeled away from him and fired at the first shape she saw wandering out of the smoke. The Inquisitor was thrown backwards, going down with a cry.

"Where's Henry?" asked Tacit, taking the rifle from his shoulder and ejecting the spent cartridge.

"Here!" Henry called, hobbling through the slowly dissipating smoke, before turning and battering an Inquisitor full in the face with the butt of his rifle. "It's no use!", he shouted, stooping low as gunfire buffeted the walls behind them, his weight set on his right foot to protect his blasted boot. "There's too many of them!" At that moment, three Inquisitors swam into view and Tacit shot two through the head with the rifle, Henry wrestling the third by his collar onto the floor. Isabella's gun flashed and another Inquisitor collapsed as he ran towards them through the swirling mist. Henry dragged himself slowly to his feet, shaking the pain out of his bleeding knuckles. "We can't win this!"

"Rubbish!" cried Tacit, taking the smoking barrel of the rifle in his hands and wielding it like a club. "Just more bodies for the crypts! Follow me and stay close!" He waded deeper into the smoke, Henry and Isabella in his wake. He took an Inquisitor, who saw Tacit too late, in the throat with a round, and then another in the eye, blowing the rear of his skull out. "The door!" Tacit called, spotting its dark outline. "Let's make for the door!" He battled his way towards it, any Inquisitors in his path bludgeoned down, Henry and Isabella picking off any who stepped close enough to be spotted through the smoke. They broke out into the street, eyes stinging, rasping breaths straining at the clean air outside. Dawn was a vague pink smudge on the horizon. A line of Inquisitors faced them from the buildings and streets opposite, each one with his gun trained on them.

"Drop your weapons!" one of them cried, as Tacit pushed Henry and Isabella back into the smoked-out ruin.

"No way through!" he warned, dropping to his haunches, "We're trapped!"

The night was suddenly filled with the sound of howls, a tumultuous noise that shredded nerves and bowed bodies, spreading fear deep within everyone who heard it. Inquisitors looked at each other, confused and alarmed, fingering their weapons clumsily in their hands. They'd been assured that the wolves had been cleared from this part of the city, disposed of.

And then the vast feral creatures came, tearing like a grey black wave into the road, enveloping the Inquisitors in their stinking monstrous tide. Gunfire erupted, but screams and the tearing of flesh soon overwhelmed the sound. From everywhere, it seemed, huge wolves appeared, from side-streets, from rooftops, from out of the sewers. And everything turned grey and crimson and black.

"Hombre Lobo!" wept the cries, as Tacit shouted "Go!" from the doorway in which they crouched, watching the carnage unfold. He pushed them back into the clearing fog of the building behind them. "Go! Go! Get out of here!"

They sprinted blindly through the house, Inquisitors now running with them, out into the back-street beyond, not daring for a moment to pause, not daring to look back at the carnage and destruction left behind by Sandrine and the wolves she had brought with her.

SEVENTY FIVE

The Italian Front. The Soča River. Northwest Slovenia.

There was a long line of mules to the left of Pablo, twelve of them linked together by a rope, being guided by soldiers positioned at the shoulder of every other animal. Not that they need guiding, it seemed to Pablo. Like him, like all the soldiers of the Italian Third Army, there seemed only one way they could go: up, towards the noise and smoke and violence.

They were laden down with goods of all kinds, boxes of food, ammunition, picks and tools, cooking pots and utensils precariously strapped to their backs as they sure-footedly followed the vague path in the mountainside, all clanking and knocking about, the sound reminding him of goat herds in the hills of Riano.

Pablo had fallen in with a ragged unit of infantrymen going up the mountain. They'd not seen any action in hours, although ahead of them he heard rifle-fire, and behind him the Staff Sergeant bawled in his ear when he suspected that the unit was slouching and not making progress fast enough. The Sergeant seemed to have picked Pablo out for special treatment and struck him every now and then across the shoulders and back, making him turn around constantly to see when the next blow was coming.

On an almost vertical shard of rock Pablo saw a field gun teetering, one wheel having vanished over the side of the mountain completely, the drop a thousand feet to the twisting valley below. All around, tall muscular men, stripped to the waist, battled to heave the precious small-calibre artillery piece out of danger. The Italian army had too few of these guns and to lose one this way would be a tragedy, far more than the loss of a man, or even a unit of men. Watching them try to save the gun, shouting and straining, gesticulating and rushing this way and that to tie ropes and set themselves against the wheels, Pablo realised that a man's place had been reduced to less than a piece of hardware. Or perhaps each one of them was nothing more than a piece of hardware for the war effort, something to move and lug and shoot and kill? And die.

The gun faltered and slipped back. Someone gave a cry and instinctively every man trying to drag the gun to safety sprang clear. The rope tied to the mule at the head went tight. The beast dug in its hooves, but it was battling against a half-ton gun and gravity. The gun slipped back further, the mule tumbled after it and then both gun and animal vanished over the edge. Everyone who had tried to save the artillery piece rushed to the edge in time to see it crash and break apart on the rocks below.

"Fuck it to hell!" someone shouted, and the bare-chested artillerymen circled the ground for a little while, inspecting the spot where they had lost their piece, appearing unsure what to do now they didn't have a weapon to drag to the summit.

One mile behind the front line, a small assembly of black figures stepped to the side of the mangled remains of a cannon and its mule and continued up the mountain path.

SEVENTY SIX

ROME. ITALY.

Grand Inquisitor Düül pushed the broad wooden door to the church of Santa Maria della Concezione dei Cappuccini open and stood back, his gun tight to his side, his eyes glued to the darkness beyond. From the palisade he had climbed to reach the door, he could hear the dwindling sounds of gunfire and howls across the city, but in front of him all was quiet within the church.

He stood at the doorway listening, watching, waiting for his eyes to adjust to the light from the flickering candles and the silver moonlight streaming through the high windows above.

"Tacit?" the white-robed man called, lifting his head to hear, sniffing at the air like a dog. "Tacit? I know you're here."

There was no reply, nothing but the echo of his voice. For a moment he thought about backing out of the church and returning to his command within the city. But his curiosity overwhelmed him and he stepped forward, his hobnailed boots grating on the marble floor.

He would have smiled, if he had any humour in him, at the arrogance of the man in coming here, to this church. To think he could hide from him here. Düül knew Tacit was good, but so was he, and Tacit had spent nine months chained to a prison wall. That would have slowed him, made him dull, cautious. Even so, the prospect of facing the feared Inquisitor alone teased Düül, and he swallowed and felt his gut twist.

He walked down the main aisle, past the narrow plain wooden pews on either side, over the white and grey marble towards the altar, bathed in moonlight and flame, the expensive glint of gold across it and inlaid into the murals and antiquities all around, shining like rich treasure. Five strides from it, Düül heard the sound of movement from the far right corner of the auditorium and went towards it slowly.

"Tacit?"

He knew where the sounds had come from, from below, from something down in the crypt. There were six of them, the crypts of bones, small chambers lined with the mouldering skeletal remains of four thousand friars, nailed, hung and piled high around the walls, a macabre place of haunting power and mystery.

"I know you're hiding down there, Tacit! Hoping to pass the night away, were you?" The Grand Inquisitor turned his ear to the dark beyond and heard a boot scrape against the stone, someone inching themselves into the shadows. "It's over. Someone saw you come here. Come out where I can see you. It'll be easier for you that way."

Düül took a lantern from the table beside the stairs and stepped down into the darkness, lifting the light high as he went, his hand gripped firm to his revolver. The stairs ended in a long narrow corridor which ran back along the length of the church. Düül swallowed and tested the weight of his revolver in his hand. He was a big man, tough, yet to be bested by anything, man or beast. But Tacit, he knew the man well, and the stories too. He swore silently under his breath, reminding himself who he was, the feared Grand Inquisitor, chasing away any suspicions of doubt and finally taking a first step along the corridor.

At each narrow archway to a chamber, he stopped and peered inside, each one of them proving empty save for the remains of the long dead friars. After a cursory glance into the dark shadows of each small room, Grand Inquisitor Düül moved on to the following one, the crypt of leg bones, the crypt of pelvises, the crypt of skulls, all of them silent, empty, save for the racks and piles of bones lining the walls. At the ossuary chapel, the next chamber, Düül lifted the lantern high and stopped to study The Souls in Purgatory, surrounded by hundreds of skulls and bones, the altarpiece of the room featuring Francis of Assisi. Empty. He recalled the wolves across his capital and allowed the anger to grow within him. He'd need it, if he was to face Tacit.

One crypt now remained unchecked, the Crypt of the Resurrection. Düül stepped into it, knowing what he expected to find, and raised his lantern and his revolver. There was a figure standing in the corner of the room, his back turned, as if he were studying the depiction of Christ raising Lazarus from the dead, inserted into the wall, at close quarters.

"How apt, Tacit," Düül growled. "To have picked this chamber. I never realised you liked your theatrics?"

The figure in the corner rocked from foot to foot, and turned to face the Grand Inquisitor.

"Who the hell are you?" Düül asked.

"Don't you remember me, Grand Inquisitor Düül?" asked Georgi. "Admittedly I did leave your service a long time ago." His voice seemed to hold Düül in a spell, for the Grand Inquisitor didn't move or say a word as Georgi stepped towards him, his senses focused entirely on the stranger. "You took me in as a young man, and you trained me to kill, to feel nothing for my actions. Now I have a different master." Georgi smiled and raised a knife hidden inside the folds of his sleeve, drawing it up close to his face so that its blade shone. "But enough talking," he said, his eyes flashing, "let me show you one of the skills he imparted. This will hurt, Grand Inquisitor Düül, but the pain you suffer is nothing compared to the pain the Seven Princes have suffered for so long, chained within the Abyss. Princes should not be chained in the darkness. They should be set upon thrones and given kingdoms to rule. And they will, for through your release from this world by my hand, they will take one more step closer to finding theirs."

SEVENTY SEVEN

SLOVENIA. NEAR THE ITALIAN BORDER.

Poré had not killed the wolf which had attacked him, even though he knew he could have, had he wished to. Frederick Prideux was powerful, even when his pelt had been divided down to a single cut of fur. Poré shivered to think how monstrous he must have been in wolf form when he had lived, if existing as Hombre Lobo, cursed forever under the ground, could be called living. He needed them, the wolf clan who had found him, and supposed letting one wolf live rather than killing it might prove more advantageous.

After the short fight, Poré had receded back into the night, watching the wounded wolf limp back to its lair from a distance, waiting until dawn before he had dared to enter.

The wretched stench from inside the lair assaulted his senses, offending them in every way. The horror of the smell was matched by the sight of the desolation of the wolves' existence, the passageway littered with the pathetic detritus of their lives, bones of victims, clothing and items of the deceased, but also flowers gathered, as if by an earlier memory, and then discarded at the entrance, ground into the dirt by the coming and going of many feet each dusk and dawn. Poré felt repugnance and shame in equal measure at what he witnessed, swallowing back his nausea and walking on, deeper into the lair complex.

The floor of the cave, littered with spoil, began to descend and Poré inched down it slowly, his hand to the wall to stop himself tumbling forward. Ahead he could make out the feral sounds of the clan, the weeping lamentations at their plight, the ceaseless moans of the bereft and broken.

Poré stopped and looked back. He was standing in almost complete darkness and at once felt vulnerable to anyone or anything lying in wait for him. Behind him, far off, he could see the pale light of dawn filter through the small hole through which he had wriggled to enter. Ahead, there was only darkness and a dark amber light.

He gathered the last of his resolve and pressed on, stepping down into the cavern from where the faint red light emanated. At once the entire cavern erupted into shouts and cries of disbelief, some of the clan shrieking and weeping, but all of them gathering into a group in the centre of the cavern, all of them bowed low on their haunches, their blind pink eyes on the unexpected visitor.

"What are you doing here?" spat one of the larger and most corrupt looking of the pallid creatures. "This is no place for a man who walks the world above."

But Poré held up his hand in a sign of amity and acknowledgement.

"I do not come here as a man who walks the world above," he said, pulling out the pelt and holding it aloft. "I come here as one of you, to tell you that your time for skulking in caves is at an end."

SEVENTY EIGHT

ROME, ITALY.

"Seems like we're late," said Tacit, looking at the open door to the church of Santa Maria della Concezione dei Cappuccini.

"Anyone home?" asked Henry, his firearm in his hand, peering over Tacit's shoulder.

"All quiet," Tacit said, before stepping inside. He paused, his eyes drawn to the far corner of the building. Without another word he stepped that way, taking a lantern from the table and descending into the cold shadows of the crypts below. Quickly he worked his way methodically from one crypt to the next, as if he knew precisely what he was looking for, until he reached the Crypt of the Resurrection. He then stopped and looked in, Henry and Isabella by his side.

Slowly an image began to appear out of the black and, staring hard, the three of them tried to comprehend what it was they were seeing. A skinned figure of a large man hung upside-down from the ceiling of the room attached by what looked like strings.

"Not again," said Henry, his voice choked by the gravity of the scene. "Who the hell is it this time?"

"Grand Inquisitor Düül," replied Tacit, looking from the body to the hook from which it was strung. "Or what's left of him." Düül hung contorted and suspended from green-black twisted cords and Tacit knew right away they were intestines, drawn out from a cut in his belly and then looped around his ankles. His skinned arms hung by his head, thick blackened blood running in trails down to his stripped fingers, dripping like bloody stalactites.

"Good God!" said Isabella, from behind them. "Like Sister Malpighi. What have they done to him?" She looked up at the suspended body with growing horror.

Tacit didn't reply. There was no need to give voice to what his eyes were telling him, another ritualistic killing, the second of three, the injuries made to gain favour with the Devil.

Henry shook his head, his eyes glazed. Something seemed to harden within him, a fierce resolve, a cold vengeful anger crystallising like a sharp frost. "Whoever did this to him, they've not just murdered him. The bastards. The fucking bastards. They've defiled him!" Isabella thought she could hear Henry sob. "They've fucking … they've fucking tortured and humiliated him, the bastards!"

"The Darkest Hand," hissed Isabella, venom infecting her features. "They know no limits."

"But this?" cried Henry incredulously, his hands and fingers wide, wrenching his eyes away, while Tacit held the light up to the hanging butchered figure.

"I wouldn't get too upset for him," cautioned Tacit. "He was a mean bastard while he was alive. Probably deserved this death ten times over. Be more concerned for where this is leading." The light revealed the full extent of the wounds to the Grand Inquisitor. Even Tacit found his face hardening to see them. "My other concern is whoever did this is tough. Strong. Beating Düül in combat is hard enough, but skinning him alive as well?" He thought back to all his old opponents and creatures he'd faced who were still alive, still existed, but doubted any of them were capable of this crime.

"Why've they done this?" asked Isabella, close to weeping.

"Lust of the flesh," said Tacit, scrutinising every inch of the Inquisitor's carcass. "Freshly killed, by the look and smell of him. Must have just missed the killer."

Henry swore again, reaching out for a stone ledge into which to collapse, nursing his face in a hand as if he could no longer bring himself to look at the body.

"They've taken his skin," Tacit revealed, steel in his voice, "whoever did this. They were proficient with the blade, whoever went to work on him."

"Maybe an Inquisitor?" Isabella suggested.

He looked at the floor directly beneath the body and dropped to a crouch. The blood had collected in deep curdling puddles on the cold flagstones. Isabella stepped around the body, the soles of her boots sticking to the floor. Every inch of the corpse had been cleaned of skin with immaculate attention to detail. The cuts, the precision by which they had been made to the flesh, suggested there was no damage to the muscle or fat, the Inquisitor's skin having been removed in a single perfect cutting motion from head to toe. Whoever had committed the crime had a skill with a knife unlike anything any of them had seen before.

Something suddenly occurred to Tacit and he turned his attention to the sides of the chamber. On the far wall, opposite the archway through which they had entered and partially obscured by the hanging body of Düül, a wide stone altar stood, flanked by hundreds of skulls. A robed skeleton stood at end of the altar, and Tacit knew his instinct had been correct. "What is it?" asked Isabella, stepping next to him to see, as Tacit raised the lantern to shine a light on his new grisly find.

Grand Inquisitor Düül's skin, bloodied and raw, had been draped around the skeleton, hanging limp on its bones. With fascination Tacit realised it had not been placed haphazardly; it had been stitched, tailored carefully into a suit.

But this was no suit for any human. This was made for a unique and terrible figure. The elongated crooked shape of the limbs and back. The tail. The cloven feet.

SEVENTY NINE

ROME. ITALY.

Georgi wiped Düül's blood from his hands with a cloth the Inquisitor had given to him as he walked to the automobile. He handed it back to the Darkest Hand member and bowed his head to enter the back of the car.

There were two Inquisitors waiting for him in the front compartment of the Sedan, and they both turned to look as he settled himself in the seat.

"It's done," growled Georgi, looking with heavy eyes out of the partially opened window to the moonlit streets of Rome. "Drive. Let's get out of this city."

The driver released the handbrake and the car jolted forward, one of his comrades asking, "Everything is complete?"

"Yes, the second ritual is done. Another layer has been peeled back. Just one more remains."

"And Sister Isabella will play her part?"

"Tacit will play *his* part," replied Georgi, scratching at his nose and smelling blood. "Sister Isabella will have no say in events, in what happens to her. And Tacit will not give her up easily. He has already proved that once. All will be fine."

"She has spirit. She will not go willingly," warned the driver, turning the black wheel slowly in his hands and guiding the car onto the main route north out of Rome.

"And that is why she is perfect. She always was perfect."

EIGHTY

The Italian Front. The Soča River. Northwest Slovenia.

Clouds of sulphur billowed over the butchered mountainside, a sickly grey in colour. It stung eyes and caught in throats, making lungs tighten and shriek against the chemical stench. At every point there were junior officers willing their men on, boys, not men, with wild staring eyes, horrified at what they were witnessing, at what they had been sent to do. To kill or be killed. It came down to that.

The sun had now climbed over the rim of the eastern mountainside to shine on Pablo and Corporal Abelli, and from points all along the summit machineguns and rifles opened up, bristling the lower slopes, tearing the advancing Italians to bits.

Pablo no longer conceived any thoughts. He just did. He no longer fired his rifle. He had no more rounds to fire anyway, even if he had the desire to do so or the initiative to replenish his stocks by stealing from the dead who covered every inch of the mountainside. He kept moving, as he was told to by his Staff Sergeant, always two paces behind him, as he had been commanded to do from the very beginning, days ago. Or was it weeks? Pablo no longer remembered.

He reached the circle of wire which separated the Italians from the Carso summit and, almost on cue, machineguns swept the ground around them. Engineers crumpled and fell, snagging on the mesh of razor wire, their bodies dancing under the torrent of bullets, limbs frayed, chests and stomachs sprayed open, uniforms sagging and oozing blood, as the hard rain tore them apart.

Panic started to catch hold at the wire. The soldiers were wedged in. They could go neither forward nor back. The front row crumpled and fell, followed by the second and then the third wave falling on top of them, crushed by the hail of bullets and the charging ranks of Italian infantry. Wire-cutters were snatched from the gore-churned ground and desperately worked against the wire to cut a way through. The air was filled with bullets and cries and explosions from every angle. A fine drizzle of blood drenched everyone. Men wept and pissed their trousers. Holes were finally made in the defences and the soldiers streamed through, climbing over the mound of bodies.

In the wave behind, Pablo slipped and fell, his right hand sinking up to his elbow in the blasted stomach wound of a dead soldier. The smell and sight made him gag, but nothing came up. He'd not eaten for forty-eight hours. He'd not been able to eat, not since the assault had begun.

Hours passed, perhaps longer. Time had stopped on that mountainside. All he knew was that he was in hell. He swore that should he survive, he would live a good life. Two soldiers to his left were raked with machinegun-fire and without thinking he fell onto his front, the bullets passing over his head and buffeting the men charging behind. He sunk his head into the dirt thinking it was a good time to die, the sun on his back, among all his fallen colleagues.

And then a hand touched him and it seemed that a warmth shimmered through his body.

"Go on," Corporal Abelli said to him. "Go on. It's not safe here." There was a light in his green eyes, both reverential and urgent.

"But the gunfire!" cried Pablo, and the Corporal shook his head.

"We will protect you."

EIGHTY ONE

The Vatican. Vatican City.

Cardinal Berberino caught sight of the messenger the instant he appeared at the entrance to St Peter's Basilica and headed him off at the doors leading down into the bowels of the building.

"You have something for us?" he enquired of the young messenger, caked with dust from his hard ride south into the city. He smelt of grass and horses.

"I was instructed to take it to the Holy See directly, Cardinal Berberino," the messenger replied swiftly, "not linger in the outer chambers." He clutched a letter tight to his chest in clamped white fingers. Berberino appeared flushed to him, troubled, his skin waxy, his eyes wild and unfocused. "Is everything quite all right, Cardinal Berberino?" the messenger asked.

"No," replied Berberino honestly. He hung his head and rested gently against the young man's shoulder, shuddering gently as if weeping. "Chaos is erupting. Rome is enflamed. Wolves are running wild. I had hoped for news. Some news. Any news. Anything to give a little hope."

"I am not sure if it is good news," the messenger replied, "but I was told to bring it to the addressee within the Holy See with utmost speed. However, considering your anxiety, and as you are a senior member of the Holy See, I see no reason why ..."

The messenger tentatively proffered the letter, Berberino snatching it urgently from him. He marched away towards the inquisitional chamber, tearing open the envelope as he walked and reading the contents silently, his darting eyes growing wide and his paunchy face slackening at the news it contained.

EIGHTY TWO

THE ITALIAN FRONT. THE SOČA RIVER. NORTHWEST SLOVENIA.

They had taken the Austro-Hungarian post, but at a terrible cost. All across the mountainside behind the new Italian front line, thousands of corpses lay strewn among the rubble and shattered rocks of the Carso, the night too dark, the open too dangerous, to clear them away. So instead they lay there, a generation crushed and torn, strewn over and beneath rocks, like seaweed deserted on the shore.

Now all Pablo wanted to do was sleep, hoping he might find a little solace and peace from the roar and seething torment of war.

He dreamt he was in a ward full of other soldiers, all lying prostrate on beds, all bound up in bloody, tight bandages. There was a smelt of disinfectant and the mutter of quiet serious voices, the clack of hard heels on the wood floor, the clatter of surgical instruments as they were placed into metal dishes, the moaning, the constant moaning. While the other noises rose and receded as patients were inspected and doctors swept out into other wards, the moaning remained always, a maddening constant, like the itch beneath the bandages which could never be scratched.

Pablo rose and left his bed, immediately thinking it strange that when his feet touched the floor, his eyes were level with the mattress upon which he had been lying. He looked down and swooned, horrified to see that his legs had been blasted to bloodied stumps, maggot-riddled beneath the greying cloth, just like so many limbs he had witnessed on the climb to the summit.

And then his horror changed to surprise that he was able to walk upon his stumps without discomfort or pain. All thoughts of shock where chased away and he left his bed and walked around it in an awkward waddle, like the dwarf he had become. He stepped down the aisle which ran between the rows of beds and out of the ward, following where the nurses had gone. Something told him he had to go and look, a nagging doubt as to who they really were and what exactly they were doing beyond the confines of the ward. He didn't trust them, not any of them, the way they looked at him, the way they tended his wounds, spoke to him with soothing words.

He reached the exit to the ward and looked out, seeing a corridor stretching off into the far distance. There were no doors leading from it, only a single point of light at the very end. He made for it, noticing that with every stride closer to the light his stumps seemed to stick more firmly to the floor, as if he were walking through deepening mud. Every stride grew more difficult but also with every stride the light grew nearer and larger.

In the light there was a battlefield similar to the one on which he had fought, and a circle of Priests, a line of ragged trees behind them. A black-bearded Priest stood in the centre, before him a man on his knees, two daggers held to his throat.

"I don't want to go to hell!" the man screamed. "I don't want to go to hell!"

"Then don't," counselled the bearded Priest, moments before the blades retracted across the man's neck and blood flowed over the ground in front of him.

"What are you doing?" a nurse asked Pablo, one among the circle of Priests who had gathered to watch the murderous ceremony. Her voice was gentle but firm.

Pablo tried to talk, but she shooed him into silence and escorted him back to bed, her arm linked around his.

"I can't go to sleep again," Pablo pleaded.

"Of course you can," the nurse told him. "You're ever so tired, Pablo." She rolled him under the sheets. "Ever so tired. And you have such an important job still to do. You must get your strength back. After all, everything depends on you."

EIGHTY THREE

ROME. ITALY.

Henry reached out for the stone wall outside the front door to Santa Maria della Concezione dei Cappuccini and tried to make sense of the nightmare in which he seemed to be living. A world at war. A city in flames. Tortured and murdered figures strung from churches. Sandrine gone, maybe dead.

"Come on!" Tacit called, bounding down the church steps to the avenue below them. The second of the rituals had been performed. They had to move if they were to have any chance of stopping the Darkest Hand and the final act. Without a word, Henry and Isabella flew after him.

Terraced buildings, blood-red in the grubby first light of day, flashed by as the three of them ran, guided by Tacit's barked commands. Every now and then he allowed himself a glance over his shoulder towards the sounds of conflict behind him, the shrieking cries of dying Inquisitors, the terrifying howl of wolves on the rampage. And as he ran he saw the brightening sky turn powder blue, and was aware that dawn, and salvation of a kind, was at hand.

"Over the road!" he roared, as they reached a junction where the narrow street was bisected by another broader one, lined with saplings rich with a new harvest on their branches.

"Where are we going?" called Isabella.

But Tacit did not reply. His eyes scoured the shadows for any movement, any sign of the enemy, whatever guise that enemy might take.

He did see the thing come at him, but too late.

The huge wolf sprang from the street on the right, bundling the giant man over the cobbles, its claws and slavering jaws shimmering in the final rays of moonlight.

"Tacit!" cried Isabella, as the wolf and the Inquisitor rolled and tumbled across the road, smashing into railings on the far side, buckling the blackened, weathered metal bars. Isabella pulled out her revolver and took aim.

"Don't shoot!" warned Henry, pushing the gun to the side. "You might hit him!"

The wolf climbed over Tacit and raked his chest with its terrible talons, slicing at the chainmail armour beneath his shirt. Tacit kicked the beast clear with the metal toes of his boots and sprang to his feet.

"And that thing might be Sandrine," Henry added, his eyes glowering with fear.

Isabella batted him aside and prepared to take aim again, but before she could do so Tacit had tumbled away, entwined with the creature, into the shadows of the street.

"If it's her," called Tacit, finding his feet and landing a plum punch to the wolf's midriff, "prepare to be widowed." He battered the wolf once, twice, in the side of the head, sending it stumbling backwards. There was a flash of silver in his hand. The wolf came back at him without a moment's pause, but Tacit was now armed, the knife flashing no more, instead dripping red with blood.

The wolf howled feebly, a pathetic attempt to summon up a cry, and went down onto its hindquarters, a cruel wound to its neck. It struck out with a paw to slice at Tacit a final time, but he reared back and then thrust again, catching the beast under the chin and sinking all eight inches of blade into its flesh. The wolf's yellow eyes glazed and closed and it slammed forward onto the cobbled pavement between the trees. Tacit stepped back, drenched in his own blood and that of the creature.

"Tacit!" cried Isabella, dashing to his side.

He held up his hand to restrain her, his free hand on his knee, bent over to help draw the air into his lungs. He gulped four deep breaths and skewered Henry with a glare.

"You figure out whose side you're on, Henry," he spat, his lips snatched tight to his teeth, "and you figure it out quick. If you're not on my side then you're my enemy. And if you're my enemy, you die like everyone else."

He slammed the bloodied blade hard into its sheath at his waist, the hilt connecting with a dull ring, before ushering Isabella's searching hand away from his wounds.

"I'm fine," he growled, snatching a bottle from his pocket and drinking three gulps from it, as if it were an elixir to heal his wounds. "Come on." He broke back into a run, "let's keep going. Let's get out of this city." And he shook his head, his hand to his wounds. "Wolves in Rome!" he exclaimed. "I've never known of wolves in Rome before."

Isabella jogged beside him. "Sandrine, she said they had gathered beneath the capital. Beneath the Vatican, in underground lairs, tunnelled by their own hands."

Tacit nodded. "It seems there is no holding their masses back. For decades they gathered in small groups. They seem now to be banding together in larger and larger clans, as if they sense a change. Perhaps one day they will envelop the entire world. But for now, dawn is coming. And with it, they'll return to their lairs." He froze, his eyes snagged by something across the road, half hidden in the dirty light of a side-street.

"So you came back, did you?" he called. Sandrine slunk forward towards them into the street, a long coat she had purloined from somewhere covering her naked flesh beneath, her face vibrant with blood.

"Sandrine!" cried Henry, coming forward. Sandrine accepted his embrace, but her eyes remained fixed on Tacit.

"As I always suspected, you're a beast," he growled. "A monster. A half-wolf." He took three steps towards her and stopped in the middle of the road, his hand resting on the handle of his gun. "I'd be doing you a favour if I killed you now."

Instantly she dropped from Henry's arms and sunk lower, her face etched with anger, her eyes wide. "You're just a man," she hissed.

"And you're a half-wolf who's just recovered." Something malign moved inside him, urging his hand to pull his revolver free from the holster. Tacit ignored it.

"Faced a few of us in your time, have you?"

"No," muttered Tacit, power bristling within him, "Not half-wolves. But I know enough about your kind. That you'll be drained. That you can't change again. Not till you've recovered. Even if you could, I would kill you before you even moved." His hand clenched tighter to the silver revolver strapped to his left thigh. "So, it seems to me, I have the advantage over you. Seems to me, I can rid myself of something I've been hunting all my life in a single moment."

Then his palm dropped from the handle and instead he held out his hand for Sandrine to take it. "But it seems to me that I also owe you a debt of thanks."

"What do you mean?" hissed Sandrine, rising a little from the protective pose she had adopted, but her eyes still distrusting.

"Back in the monastery, here in the city, you fought like one of us and you fought well. You and your Hombre Lobo. You helped save us."

He turned his eyes down to his hand as a prompt for Sandrine to take it, and she did so, slipping her fingers over Tacit's huge palm.

"The wolves," he said, "they're still my enemy. What you tried to do in Paris, I will never agree with it or forget. But all that is over now. It's in the past. Everything now is about the future and what we can do to stop it."

"And what can we do?" asked Henry, admiration gritted in his face. He played his rifle from his left to his right hand.

"What we always do. We fight. We try and stop them, whoever is trying to complete the rituals. Isabella, you asked me where we're going? We're going north, to the Karst Plateau in the Carso. We stop the third ritual from happening and whatever they are trying to summon from coming through."

The final ritual. Pride of life. Tacit knew it came down to this. The thought of it, of what it represented and what it might achieve if it was allowed to happen, was as terrifying as it was tantalising. He did not know exactly how the ritual would manifest itself, how it would be realised, but he had begun to have an inkling – and with it a sickening lingering fear of just what it would mean for him, and for the person he loved.

"We take a train," he revealed, cracking his knuckles. "Time is of the essence and therefore the train is the only way. Termini Station." He waved roughly in the station's direction. "It's not far from here. We'll take the first train for the northern border. Do you have any money?" he asked, looking at each of them.

"A little," Isabella replied. "Enough."

"I have some," nodded Henry.

Sandrine dug deep in the pockets of her coat, finding them empty. "The Inquisitor to whom this belonged, he obviously was not one to pay his bills."

Tacit smiled grimly. "Looks like the Inquisitor settled up," he said, looking at the dried blood on her face. "We'll need to try to get on board as inconspicuously as possible. The Inquisition will be watching for us. I suggest you find some clothes and get washed," he said to Sandrine, dark humour gracing his features. "I suspect no eye will look the other way with you walking around like that."

EIGHTY FOUR

The Vatican. Vatican City.

The Holy See had been called to session, just three hours since the last. The atmosphere was more charged than ever.

"Grand Inquisitor Düül," said Casado, clutching his skullcap tight to his head. "He is dead." He exhaled loudly, defeated by this latest news.

"Where?" asked a Cardinal opposite, horrified. "How?"

"In the Church of Santa Maria della Concezione. His body was found in the Crypt of the Resurrection by the resident Father, Father Fesetti, when he came to open up the church for morning Mass."

"The wolves?" someone asked. But Casado shook his head.

"We believe him to be the second victim of these rituals."

"The lust of flesh," muttered Korek, and many in the congregation who heard him nodded in feared agreement.

"But how did this happen?" asked Bishop Basquez. "The head of the Inquisition? Slain?"

"There are grave adversaries in the world, Bishop Basquez," replied Casado.

"But to have killed Düül? What exactly did they do to him?"

"I don't think we need to go into details," said Korek, raising a hand of restraint.

"Indeed," agreed Casado. "Needless to say, how he was discovered aroused our suspicions immediately. The second of the three rituals has been performed. *He* is a step closer to achieving his plans."

"And so Tacit has killed another," said Basquez.

Cardinal Bishop Adansoni played with the loose threads on the sleeve of his gown. It seemed to him that his entire life was now spent in meetings, either private closed affairs, shared between just a few in claustrophobic chambers, or within the main inquisitional chamber, as the Cardinals currently found themselves, deep within the bowels of the Vatican. An exhausting treadmill of discussions and lamentations, an attempt for the assembled great minds to find wisdom and a way forward.

"We don't know that," he said, but Basquez rounded on him, laughing.

"Your attempts to protect that murderer grow more pathetic with every passing crime. If not Tacit, then who? It stands to reason it was him. If he killed Sister Malpighi, he killed Düül. The man's crazed, possessed. He knows no boundaries."

"I agree," nodded Korek, before catching Casado's eye.

"With Düül gone," muttered a hirsute Cardinal, long greying hair like a mane, "what hope is there? Who can protect us?"

"With Düül dead, we can take back control and responsibility for the Holy See. Let us be strong. Dawn is almost upon us," Adansoni said, iron in his voice. "And with it, the Hombre Lobo will retreat back to their lairs."

"Those who are left," added Korek. "The Inquisition, they have killed a great many. The bodies of dead wolves are being burned as we speak."

"And tomorrow night?" the hairy Cardinal continued. "What then?" He cleared his throat. "To think of it. A clan of wolves? Within the city? When has such a thing ever happened before?"

"But what of Tacit?" asked Basquez, leaning forward serpent-like, his arms wrapped about his body. "It is clear he is more dangerous than a clan of Hombre Lobo. The order was also to stop Tacit. Where is he now? And the others who travel with him. "Sister Isabella? The soldier? The woman they are suggesting is a wolf herself?"

"We have neither the manpower nor the time to look for Tacit now, I suspect," growled Casado.

"Check the railway stations," announced Korek, and all heads turned in the old Cardinal's direction.

"You expect them to leave by train?" replied Adansoni doubtfully.

Korek nodded. "After all this mayhem, I am sure Tacit will look to get out of the city. He may have brought murder and the wolves with him, but I doubt he finds their company to his liking. Not yet."

"So you think him guilty of bringing the wolves as well, do you?" asked Adansoni, feigning incredulity.

The old Cardinal smiled, the grey of his eyes catching the pale light hanging from the orbs above. "I suspect him of many things. From what I have learnt, there is little which is beneath the man."

Casado nodded. "Double the inquisitional guard on all stations," he said, looking at the Inquisitor posted on the door. "Check all trains heading out of the city."

But at that moment the door was pushed open and Cardinal Berberino rushed into the chamber. "Tacit is gone!" he called. "Left Rome!"

"How do you know?" someone asked.

Berberino held up the letter he had taken from the messenger. "Someone is trailing him," he replied. "Someone has been watching him, watching him from the very beginning, from the moment he escaped from Toulouse Prison, to when he first boarded a train to come here, throughout all his bloody deeds he committed since he arrived within the city. Even from when he was first imprisoned! They are watching him now, on his journey north from here."

"Cardinal Berberino, what exactly are you saying?" asked Adansoni, standing himself.

"I mean," said the heavy-set Cardinal, lowering his eyes on his counterpart opposite, "that while we were trying to discover where Tacit was and what his plans were, all the time someone knew exactly what he was doing. Someone within the Holy See for whom this letter was bound. The messenger would not give me a name but revealed enough to confirm its recipient was someone among us."

He waved the letter above his head. "This letter explains everything of Tacit's movements, where he has been and where he is going now. In other words, all the time we were searching for answers, there is someone in here who has known Tacit's intentions from the start. In answer to your question, Cardinal Bishop Adansoni," said Berberino addressing him directly, "I am saying that we have a traitor within the Holy See!"

EIGHTY FIVE

Rome. Italy.

The noise of crowds and steam and the smell of coal smoke rising from the platform of Termini Station whirled about them as Tacit, Isabella, Sandrine and Henry ran along the boulevard, just down from the platform approach. They'd found clothes and a solid pair of boots for Sandrine from a shop near the station, stolen when the shopkeeper's attention had been drawn elsewhere. Tacit's pocket clinked with other items to sustain him for the journey ahead.

Countless units of soldiers stood in long lines, shuffling their way step by step slowly onto the platform and the train beyond, the open black iron gates of the station like the entrance to a conveyor belt processing each soldier as they were drawn inside.

Everything appeared monochrome, as if a vast grey-black sea had flooded the station, punctuated by the occasional ruffle of a black feathered hat among the crowds, sported by one of the Bersaglieri, the elite sharpshooters of the Italian army, weaving their bicycles between the thick crowds of infantry soldiers.

"No way through," muttered Tacit, sinking behind a wall to watch the progression of soldiers inside. Officers studied the rank and file of the men going in from various vantage points around the approach. There would be no chance of following the soldiers in and boarding the hissing and groaning troop train at the platform. Among the officers Tacit could spot Inquisitors watching all thoroughfares.

"Let's go on around the station," suggested Henry, craning his neck to follow the curve of the road. "There's a bridge over the railway tracks, under which the train will pass. Perhaps we can jump?"

Tacit nodded and the four of them scuttled away, running up the incline of the road towards the iron bridge, its painted girders like blackened bones spanning the width of the four-lane track. There were women on the bridge, dressed in pretty dresses and coats, umbrellas shadowing them from the dawn sun, handkerchiefs clutched to noses. They were staring down at the procession of soldiers, weeping and cheering, every now and then raising a hand and waving towards a loved one on the platform before the son or husband vanished inside the train.

"Now what?" called Isabella, as they slowed to a walk to avoid drawing attention to themselves.

"First we need to get rid of those women," whispered Sandrine before stepping forward to address them. "I wouldn't stand there if I were you," she called, indicating a circle around where the women were stood.

"But why ever not?" replied one of the assembled ladies tearfully.

"You wouldn't want your beautiful dresses to be ruined by the soot from the train, would you?" Sandrine asked, indicating the smoking chimney of the train's engine, already billowing blackened plumes from its funnel. "When it comes through here, the smoke will be terrible. Go down to the front. The guards will let you onto the platform to say your goodbyes."

Without hesitation the women clicked away, back down the bridge towards the platform entrance.

"I never knew lies came so easily to you," said Henry to Sandrine, a half-smile on his face.

"They do, when needs must."

From up here they could see that the train consisted of wooden pens and carriages, stretched to the end of the platform and beyond. The platform was a bustling chaotic scrum of soldiers, porters, horses, crates of munitions and covered carts, all wedged in between the train and the wall of the platform. Sergeants, elevated on boxes above the writhing masses, barked incoherent commands and orders as the war effort surged and churned slowly towards the open doors of the train.

"Madness," they heard Tacit say, and Henry nodded.

"That is this war, yes."

"Sandrine's bought us a little time," said Tacit, "but the women will be back, once they're turned away from the front gates."

"And bring with them soldiers maybe," added Isabella.

"It's not the soldiers I'm worried about," replied Tacit. "It's the Inquisitors I spotted among the crowds. They're watching the routes into the station. They suspect we'll be heading out of the city by train."

With that, a shrill whistle blew and the straining of the crowd of soldiers intensified as they battled to board the train before it departed. Slowly the platform cleared, the last door slamming with the finality of a gunshot, and the stationmaster's whistle blew again. Groaning and toiling against its burden, the steam train slowly drew itself forward towards the bridge where the four of them stood, clouds of choking grey smoke filling the skies above the station. With every chug of its pistons, the train gathered speed, reaching them more swiftly than any of them had expected. Tacit climbed the handrail and balanced himself precariously on the thin edge of the bridge, looking down onto the carriage roofs flying past fifteen feet below. The others followed his lead, balancing next to him, arms held wide.

"When I say jump," he called, his hair full of smoke and ashes from the locomotive's chimney, "jump."

They didn't wait for Tacit's call. The moment the train drew beneath them Henry and Sandrine jumped, followed by Isabella, aware that the women were coming back up the path towards them, and with them soldiers. Tacit cursed and leapt after his friends. He struck the wooden roof of the carriage and it shattered under him, the Inquisitor vanishing through the broken buckled hole like a skater through ice.

Immediately Henry, Sandrine and Isabella were at its edge, peering down into the darkness below, Tacit lying on his back on the floor of the carriage, staring up at them.

"You weakened it," he muttered, seeing their laughter.

The train jolted and buckled as it powered north through the Italian landscape. The carriage near the front of the train, onto which they had dropped, had been set aside for livestock. There was hay on the floor of the wooden pen, deep in places. Only one sliding door granted entrance to the carriage.

"Couldn't you have chosen a different wagon?" asked Henry, looking about himself disdainfully.

"If you felt so strongly, you should have found us a carriage yourself," replied Tacit. "We're on board. That's all that matters. And no one saw us enter."

"What do we do now?" asked Sandrine, her eyes passing from Henry to Tacit.

The train rolled on a broken part of the track and they rocked together as if caught in a swirl.

"We stay in here, and we wait," said Tacit. He effortlessly threw open the vast heavy door, running on rusted uneven runners, revealing the Italian countryside cantering past. Tacit rested against its frame and searched for a bottle buried in a pocket of his coat. He uncorked it and set it to his lips, gulping down the amber liquid, scowling and shutting his eyes, allowing the movement of the train to rock him like a boat on a gentle eddy.

"So next stop the border?" asked Isabella, stepping over to the open door to join him and snatching the bottle from his grip. He nodded. "That's good," she said and she toasted him, setting the lip of the bottle to her lips, watching the sun-seared fields roll by. "Rome was getting claustrophobic. It felt like we were always being chased. It's good to feel safe, at least for a little while."

In a corner of the carriage opposite, Henry set himself down gingerly on the straw, his hand nursing the sprains and pulled muscles in his neck from their recent exploits, Sandrine next to him. She stared at Tacit.

"Some comfort!" she said, pushing the straw around distastefully.

"It's an animal cart," spat Tacit, taking back the bottle from Isabella. "You should be right at home." He took another swig.

"The Karst Plateau," said Isabella, crossing her arms and peering out over the slowly undulating terrain. "Have you ever been there? To the Carso?"

Tacit nodded. "The Devil's land."

"How so?" asked Isabella, her hand creeping unconsciously to her neck.

"It's a place forfeited by God. Nothing dwells there save evil rumour and malice. There is a legend that an angel of God was sent to the lands of the Carso to take away all the stones in order for the people living there to grow their crops, farm their animals and raise their families. The Devil came there shortly afterwards and saw this beautiful land, with its fertile meadows and fast-flowing clear rivers and the angel flying away with a huge sack thrown over its shoulder. And the Devil thought at once that there were riches and sweet produce within it. So he slit the bag open from behind, but instead of treasure, stones and debris poured out of the sack and covered the beautiful lands below. And so it became a kingdom of stone, and a domain of the Devil."

"What do you think we'll find there, Poldek?" asked Isabella.

"I don't know," replied the Inquisitor, hanging his head, exhaustion finally appearing to win over him. "I just hope we get there in time. And that between us, we can handle it."

He turned back to the carriage door and slammed it firmly shut.

EIGHTY SIX

PRAGUE. AUSTRO-HUNGARY.

The bell tower of the Church of Mother of God before Týn signalled six o'clock, chiming across the Old Town. An angry crowd, gathered in the square before the church's twin towers, moved away into the city, their flaming torches and cudgels held aloft, curses and recriminations on their tongues.

"It's another child," said the young aide standing next to Father Mészáros on the steps of his church, watching the mob leave. "Gone. For two days now. The ninth child in Prague this summer. They say there is a wickedness come to the city, an evil spirit who steals away children in the middle of the night. What has become of the world, Father?" he asked, bowing his head. "As if this war was not bad enough, now we must contend with phantoms in our beds!"

"Suffer little children," muttered Father Mészáros, and the young man thought he heard the Priest chuckle to himself before turning his back on the now empty square.

"Let us hope not, Father!" he called after his master, shutting the great black door with a bang and following him. They padded up the slate-grey aisle towards the ornate altar at the far end in silence, the arched cream ceiling soaring a hundred feet above them.

"There is no need for you to stay late tonight, Kristián," said Father Mészáros. "There will be nothing this evening for which I need your help."

"But what of this evening's mass?" asked Kristián. "The people ..."

"The people will come," nodded the grey-haired Priest, "when they have searched in vain for their missing children, returning here to look for answers from their God which will never be given."

Kristián thought the Priest's prediction strange. "Then should I not stay here and help you to prepare to receive them?"

"No," replied the Father, and a sullen light came into his eyes.

The young man looked at his master, troubled. "Are you quite well, sir?"

"It depends what you mean by well, Kristián," Father Mészáros answered.

A deep rumble suddenly came from the shadows to the left of where they stood. Nervously Kristián turned his head towards it.

"That noise!" he exclaimed, "It came from the vault! It might be the missing child! Perhaps he sought refuge here and became lost or trapped in the darkness?"

"Kristián!" Father Mészáros called, suddenly animated, but the young man had already plunged into the shadows and begun to descend the stairs to the vault.

It was pitch-dark within the crypt beneath the church and at once Kristián thought about going back and finding himself a lantern. His breath rose in clouds in the chilled air and he paused and waited for his eyes to adjust to the dark. And then he heard it. A voice! A child's voice, pleading from somewhere in the black of that place.

"Father Mészáros!" cried the young man. "Father Mészáros! Come quickly! I think I have found the child. Bring light!" and he saw that the Priest had done exactly that, holding a lantern in his hand as he descended the stairs with careful, deliberate steps. "Father Mészáros! I heard a voice, that of a child. In the far corner of the vault!"

He spoke so urgently that the words caught in his throat and he bounded forward in the direction of the voice, stopping every ten feet or so to allow the slow pace of the Priest to catch up.

There were coffins in the vault, rows of them, set side by side, and Kristián went about them, cocking his ear to each in turn to try and find from where the sound had emanated. Eventually he stopped and paused, lowering his ear to one coffin set in the very corner of the room.

"Here!" he cried, setting his fingers to the lip of the lid and looking back to the Priest. "Here! Here! I have found him! I have found the child! Help me, Father!" he cried, heaving the heavy coffin lid an inch to the side from where it had been set.

Father Mészáros watched him impassively at the very edge of the lantern's light, moving closer only when Kristián had shifted the lid enough to enable him to peer inside. The young man shrieked and drew back.

"The child!" he cried, half weeping, wild with confusion. "The child is inside! Bound by ropes and cord! Help me free him!" He moved forward to heave the lid completely from the coffin, but stopped and pulled away as Father Mészáros stepped close to him. "What is it?" he asked, the look in the Priest's face contorted and unholy.

"Suffer little children," muttered Father Mészáros, as he turned off the lantern's light.

EIGHTY SEVEN

The Vatican. Vatican City.

The windows to the chamber had been thrown open and the dawn sun flooded in, drenching the white marble stone, turning it to radiant quicksilver. Great swarms of crows flocked and circled around the squares and over rooftops, a cacophony of noisy squawks and fighting black bodies.

Cardinal Secretary of State Casado crossed the sun-kissed stone and collected the decanter of wine, pouring a stream into glasses for each of the four Cardinals gathered within the room.

"I took the liberty of ordering a little wine," he said. "Perhaps a little wine might calm our nerves, assist with our private discussions, particularly with this most recent and terrible of news?" Cardinal Adansoni joined him at his side and distributed the four wine glasses among them. "I trust you gentlemen approve?"

"A little drink, to lighten the mood? I entirely approve," announced Berberino with a quick nervous smile, peering about himself urgently, his sagging chin wobbling with anticipation of the drink.

"To think, a traitor in the Holy See! Have you ever heard of such a thing, Cardinal Secretary of State?" he asked of Casado.

The white-haired Cardinal shook his head, distributing the last full wine goblet.

"Father Berberino, may I see the letter again?" Adansoni asked. Berberino handed it over without question. Slowly and deliberately Adansoni pored over the words, sipping from his glass.

"It explains everything of Tacit's next movements, where he has been and where he is going to. In other words, all the time we were searching for answers, there is someone within the Holy See who has known exactly what Tacit's movements were, what his plans are."

Casado nodded grimly. "Father Strettavario, will you not join us for a drink?" he asked, extending his hand over the tray of glasses.

"Excuse me, but I will not," Strettavario replied, burying his hands into his sleeves. "I find at such times it is wiser to keep a clear head. I have heard it suggested that Poldek Tacit was seen at Termini Station. A group of ladies saw him jump from the bridge onto a passing train. If he has left that way, it might be prudent for me to keep my wits about me, should any more information become available and I am called upon to act."

"As you wish, Father Strettavario," said Berberino, nearly draining his glass in a hurried swallow. "For me, the merits of the grape outweigh any disadvantages it might have, especially after such a shock." He nodded excitedly when Adansoni offered to refill his glass. "Whoever could the traitor be?" he asked, emphasising the point with a heavy hang of his head. "I suppose it must be a young upstart, one of the junior Cardinals, one recently promoted to the Holy See? One looking to gain advantage by having news of Tacit's movements relayed solely to himself? I swear, it's enough to send one to the bottle."

He drank half of his glass and looked about himself, as if momentarily lost, blinking twice, a confused look upon his face. The wine seemed a little more bitter than he was used to and his collar a little tighter than usual. He cleared his throat and pulled roughly at the top button of his cassock to allow a little air to his neck. It seemed to him that the room was swaying, as if he was on a boat in a strong tide. He tried to focus on the other Cardinals, but they seemed distant, out of focus. Erased. He shivered and reached out for a nearby chair to steady himself.

"Cardinal Berberino?" asked Adansoni, putting down his glass and rising to his feet, taking a step towards the large faltering man. "Are you all right?" He hurried forward as fast as he was able, and half caught the Cardinal as he toppled to one side, his left leg and hip seeming to crumple as one. With great effort, and help from Strettavario, they eased him into a chair.

"Cardinal Berberino?" called Strettavario, looking hard into the Cardinal's glazed eyes. His breathing was snatched and hurried, and each gasp was shortened and clipped. "Cardinal Berberino?" the old Priest called again, slapping his cheek so that it reddened against the otherwise pallid sweating veneer that was his skin. "Can you hear me?"

The voice sounded far away to Berberino. He felt as if his very being was aflame, his limbs and body consumed by a fiery hell. He looked about himself and realised that he was floating in a sea of darkness and fire. He shivered, frozen, despite the heat all around him, causing him to cry out in agony.

"He's convulsing!" cried Casado, gathering a towel and drenching it with wine in an attempt to try and cool Berberino's roasting forehead. The wine pooled in his eye sockets, giving the impression that his eyeballs were bleeding.

He mouthed breathless words.

"He's trying to say something!"

Something was coming, out of the flames. Berberino could see it. The horror! The horror of it! He tried to claw his way from it, but every hand-hold he gathered collapsed beneath him, every foothold gave way, slipping him further towards the demonic thing advancing towards him.

The beast gathered over him, ancient and eternally wicked, sucking in stale air. Then everything went black and Berberino felt no more.

EIGHTY EIGHT

Approaching the Italian Front. The Italian-Slovenian border.

"Tacit?" Isabella murmured quietly in the dark. He cleared his throat.

"Yes."

"Are you awake?"

"What do you think?" came the growled reply.

She smiled and shook her head gently in the quiet of the carriage, gently rocking over the tracks, as the train climbed ever higher into the mountains.

"You know, it's the first time we've been alone."

"We're not alone," Tacit muttered, his eyes flickering open and over to the sleeping pair by the door.

Isabella blinked and shook her head. "Tell me something. Have you ever been happy, Tacit?" She said it in jest, but Tacit replied almost at once with utter sincerity.

"Once," he said, staring into the dead space before him. "I was happy once."

"Poldek," soothed Isabella, reaching across and taking his arm. "I was only joking," but he ignored her, or never heard her, lost in his memories.

"It was long ago. I … I was in love. And she loved me."

Isabella swallowed and her eyes grew wide and moist. "What happened?" she asked, a weight growing in her stomach, rising to clutch her throat. She drew her knees up to her chest and gathered her arms around them, the straw knotting around the heels of her shoes.

"She died." He said the words as if they meant nothing to him, as if the memory had gone cold. He looked across at her, his eyes empty, dark pits. Unreadable.

Isabella lowered her head and shook it. "Look, Poldek," she said, shuffling a little closer and burrowing her hand deeper into the crook of his arm. "I'm sorry. I shouldn't have joked." The honesty with which he had spoken astounded her. It also unnerved her to see him so human, so damaged, so vulnerable.

"Do you believe in curses?" he asked quite suddenly, and the question hardened the pain within her, leaving her breathless.

"Tacit, look, I don't know what you mean or why you're saying this, but –"

"I do." And he looked away as if he couldn't bear her to see into his empty eyes, dark pits of grief. "I believe I am cursed." He growled the words, like a charge set against him. "I believe that anything I love, the curse will pursue. That my love will condemn them. They will perish, to be slain for the love I have shown. My mother. My first love." He lifted his eyes to her from where they had fallen away. "You."

Isabella shuddered and felt the tears well in her eyes. She dragged a hand to her mouth.

"You remember I spoke of the lights, of the voices which accompany them?"

"Yes. What do they say?"

"Terrible things." Tacit drew a hand across his eyes and held it there for a moment, as if nursing the pain within them. "They taunt me, compel me on to do terrible things. Their bidding. They empower me."

"These lights you talk about? What are they?"

"I can't explain it, Isabella. All my life I have pursued those who are possessed, or attempt to possess, and yet all along I myself feel ..." The words faded from his lips.

"What do you feel?"

"That I too am possessed." He shook his head, defeated. "Someone told me once," he continued, breathing deeply, "told me that I wasn't as big as I thought I was." He shook his head, recalling the memory of the witch on the shores of the Black Sea, weighing the sentiment in his mind. "I think that she was right."

"Tell me about her."

"Who?" he replied.

"Your first love."

Tacit stirred in the straw and for a moment Isabella thought her impetuousness might have been too premature, too swift, thinking that Tacit might be rising from the bedding to turn away from her, closed once more. But instead he said, quite softly, "What do you want to know?"

"Whatever you want to tell me. It is clear that you loved her very much, and she you."

"How do you know?" asked Tacit.

"The warmth of your smile when you think of her. The light within your eyes. A sadness captured within the lines of your face." She rolled gently onto one side so that she was lying opposite him. "What was her name?"

Tacit hesitated. He uncorked the bottle and swilled the liquid within it before snatching a brief drink. And then he said tenderly, "Mila. That was her name."

In the darkness, the name seemed to echo within the small carriage. Isabella closed her eyes and imagined her, a beauty no doubt, forthright, strong, an independent woman. She imagined that she was all these things, and a lover too. And then Tacit began to speak and she didn't need to imagine anymore. "She was beautiful, like a warm sunrise after a cold hard frost, like the calm after a storm. You know when you lie under cover and hear the rain rattling on the roof above you, when you feel warm and safe and secure, knowing outside the elements are raging but inside you're safe and you're warm? That was how she made me feel. She took away my pain. She taught me what it was to love, to live without shackles, to forget a past filled with too many troubles and bad memories and to live with hope for the future. She was my hope. She was my future."

"What happened?" asked Isabella.

Tacit didn't answer for a long time. But then he said, in a voice which sounded distant and fragile, as if any moment it might break. "She was murdered."

"I'm sorry."

Tacit swilled the bottle again and drank, longer and deeper this time.

"Does her passing still hurt? Does it still hurt to remember her?"

"No," Tacit lied. "I've learnt to forget. Like I do with everything I experience, as I do with every wound I take. It's easier to bear the pain than it is to try to heal it."

Isabella rolled onto her back, a tangle of hair splaying like an explosion of red across the straw, her hand on her stomach.

"You should never forget, Tacit," said Isabella, very quietly. "Not the beautiful things in life, the things which touch you. But also you should never hold back. Life is not about being constantly in pain or in sorrow. I don't think God would want you to be sad."

And Tacit, who was looking down at her, surprised her by smiling sadly.

"What is it?" she asked.

"I know someone else who said something similar once."

Isabella smiled back, and slowly, with utmost caution, she moved her hand to the straw between them, wishing he would reach out and grasp it. And he did, his giant hand enveloping her long delicate fingers in a warm, gentle embrace. He watched her fingers entwined with his, his thumbs nursing the tops of them, his eyes gentle and thoughtful on them as he did so. After a moment he looked up and found that he was looking directly into Isabella's eyes.

She smiled, feeling the urge to leave where she lay and join him. She moved a fraction to do so, allowing the weight of their passion to narrow the gap between them.

Without warning there came a sound alongside the carriage, heavy hands searching, heavy doors being heaved back on rusted runners.

The door to their carriage was thrown open and dark figures powered in. Henry and Sandrine, closest to the door, jumped awake but not quickly enough to avoid being grappled and thrown from the rolling train. They fell out in the black of night, tumbling and spinning away from the train and the track, turning over and out in the wilds of the foothills of the Carso.

At once Tacit was on his feet, his fists like giant hammers, setting himself between the Inquisitors and Isabella, just the pair of them left to face the intruders.

"Isn't this just beautiful?" growled Georgi.

EIGHTY NINE

APPROACHING THE ITALIAN FRONT. THE ITALIAN-SLOVENIAN BORDER.

The three figures fell upon Tacit as he ran across the wagon. The Inquisitors were armed with cudgels which they wielded like whips. If Tacit felt their weapons strike him, he gave no sign that he did, battering one Inquisitor full in the face. As the struck man reeled away Isabella could see that the blow had splintered his jaw, his mouth a hanging bloodied maw clutched in his shaking hands.

A cudgel struck Tacit hard across the back of the head and this blow he did feel, turning on his attacker and snatching the weapon away, bringing it back down so hard on the Inquisitor's own head that it shattered his skull and buried itself inside his brain, lodged deep. The third Inquisitor wrestled Tacit around the middle, half dragging him to the ground, before an explosion rocked the carriage and the Inquisitor slumped off him, his back torn open by the revolver fired by Isabella, crouched in a corner.

Georgi leapt the carriage in an instant and dashed the weapon aside, striking her hard on the side of the head, spinning her down into the straw with a grunt, reopening the wound on her head, blood streaming from her ear.

"Bastard!" roared Tacit, pummelling hard into him, partially shattering the wall of the wagon, planks of wood breaking free and splintering away down the track and into the night as the train rolled on. They wrestled, the battle brutal and fast, both men fighting like dogs, whipped by the wind and the rain rushing through the smashed panel.

They rolled away into the middle of the carriage, jabbing and striking whenever they could. Georgi's cudgel was caught and thrown wide, spinning through the open door of the carriage, tumbling and cartwheeling away. The cold whip of rain dashed the room. Straw and hair was flying as Tacit feigned a blow and kicked out with his boot, catching Georgi hard on the shoulder.

"You don't recognise me, do you, Poldek?" shouted Georgi, as he caught hold of Tacit's boot and spun him away.

Something in the voice, coupled with the question, made Tacit hesitate. He stared hard at the man facing him, trying to place him. And then, like little pieces of a puzzle falling into place, the realisation of who he was fighting hit him. Like a steam train.

"Georgi?" he asked incredulously.

Georgi bowed, smiling, before hammering his fist hard through Tacit's open defences and into his nose. The blow seemed to drive sense back into the man and he knocked the following punch aside, putting some distance between himself and his old friend.

"I ... I thought you were dead?"

"I was dead, yes," said Georgi. "Dead to that way of life, that faith. Let's just say I found myself reborn, with a new Lord. One who appreciated my talents." He launched himself at the shocked Inquisitor, battering him left and right with his fists. "I understand if you're surprised. It's been a while, Poldek. Many years. A lot of water under many bridges." He brought up a boot, bringing Tacit down onto it, and then clattered him onto his back with a right hook.

Georgi shook the pain of the blow from his knuckles and circled the winded Inquisitor. "Take your time," he offered cynically. "I know it's a lot to take in. Your old friend returned. The one who murdered your first love."

At once something flared within Tacit and he scrambled to his feet.

"She died badly," Georgi growled, fending off a following blow and returning Tacit's feint with interest in the form of a shattering undercut that rocked the big man on his heels.

"I don't know who you mean!" Tacit cursed, lunging for Georgi and getting hold of his neck. He pulled hard and twisted, feeling something give in his lower back, but a blow to his old friend's midriff caused him to loosen his grip and draw back, his hand to his bruised ribs.

"Yes you do!" smiled Georgi through bloodied teeth. "The only person who ever meant anything to you. The only person you've ever cared for. Other than her," he added, looking at Isabella unconscious in the corner.

Tacit paused, enough for Georgi to catch him off guard with a glancing blow, which shuddered Tacit's vision to a blur.

"Mila." Georgi spoke the word like a triumph.

Tacit hesitated, his eyes wide.

"They told you it was Orthodox, didn't they?" Georgi laughed, and struck Tacit without any resistance twice in the face. Tacit's nose exploded and blood flooded his mouth. "That was the official line you were told. The one to get you back on side. To get you back doing what you do best." He worked his way through Tacit's fumbling defences, battering his right eye so hard that it instantly it closed with blood and he thought Tacit might be close to breaking. "You're too valuable to lose, you see, Tacit, especially to some Italian farm whore." Georgi caught him in the ribs, following with a blow to the chin. Tacit rocked over onto his backside, instantly trying to find his feet. "It was a test for me. My first real test for my new master. To see if I had what it took to follow their every order, their every command." Tacit came at him, but he was too blinded by pain and the words he was hearing to attack with any purpose or focus. Georgi stepped aside and slammed his boot into Tacit's knee, causing it to crumple and sending Tacit down. As he was scraping blindly in the straw of the carriage to collect his bearings, Georgi took Tacit's hair and pulled so he was looking down into his face. "Seems I keep coming between you and the women you love?"

Tacit roared and lashed out, but his anger had blinded any hope of striking his foe. Georgi caught him and threw him against the right-hand side of the open door. Tacit's wild clumsy hand reached out to grasp it, locking firm to the lintel, stopping him from falling out into the rolling blackness of the mountain plains. He looked with bloody tear-drenched eyes across the carriage to Isabella. Georgi followed Tacit's gaze to her and smiled.

"Oh, don't worry, Poldek," he said, searching in a holster for his revolver. "I'll take good care of her. She has important work to do. But I suspect you knew that all along. That it's always been you and her. Ever since the start. Since Arras."

There was a flash of metal and Tacit knew instantly what he was about to do. He powered desperately towards Georgi, but too slow to stop the gun from going off like a cannon. Tacit crunched down, holding his shoulder, his hand over the wound dashed with vivid crimson.

"Georgi!" cried Tacit, his wide eyes pleading.

"Pathetic!" replied Georgi, any smile now polluted by the sheer venom staining his face. He raised the pistol again at Tacit.

"No!" was all Tacit could say before he was hit for a second time in the shoulder, sending him backwards out of the open door and somersaulting out into the blackness.

PART SIX

"No one can serve two masters. Either you will hate the one and love the other, or you will be devoted to the one and despise the other."

Matthew 6:24

NINETY

The barrage started, as it always started, with the dull clunk of shells, sounding so far away that Pablo thought they couldn't be firing at him or the crowd of broken Italian soldiers of his unit. But the whine in the sky above grew louder and the grey dawn became too bright to see anything. The air was sucked out of the lungs of the Italian soldiers, their ears ruined by the torment of the falling shells, their eyes blinded. Pablo sank down in the trench on the very edge of the Karst Plateau, opposite the Corporal.

"I'm going to die here," he shouted through the noise. In all that death and terror, he knew the end had almost certainly come. He supposed that perhaps it would be the last thing he would ever acknowledge, before a shell landed and tore him to pieces. And his memories and spirit would be blasted and caked about the rocks along with his flesh and blood.

But the Corporal shook his head. "Not you. Not here. Not yet."

And for the first time since they had climbed the mountain together, the Corporal's eyes grew severe and his lips puckered in defiance. "The Devil, he has told me. He told me everything. And the Devil told me where to come, and what I was to do. It is why I joined the Italian army, knowing it would bring me to this place, at this moment in time to protect you. And I will reach the top of this mountain, the top of the Karst Plateau, and there I will do my duty to him and them."

"What do you mean?" cried Pablo, over the whine of more shells and the pleading cries of those caught in their blast.

The Corporal smiled. "The Devil, he is a powerful ally! He told me! He spoke to me! He said that it would be here that he would return and that our enemy, he would come here too!"

"They are coming!" a voice shouted in alarm, and Pablo became aware that the shells had stopped falling. "The enemy, they are coming!" the voice called again, and thousands of Italian soldiers set themselves at the front lip of the trench and counted out their last remaining rounds.

"Here, in the Carso, you will offer yourself to him," chuckled Corporal

Abelli, falling in alongside Pablo, his rifle clenched in blackened, scarred hands.

But Pablo hadn't heard him. He peered over the trench, knowing that something strange was happening. For now just occasional firing could be heard and beyond there was nothing but an ocean of grey growing closer and closer.

"It's a sea!" cried Pablo, his rifle trembling in his hands. "It's a giant wave of grey water, flooding towards us! A great flood!"

But Abelli laughed and shook his head.

"No, Pablo," he said. "It is a wave of grey, but no flood ever carried so many men with rifles and bayonets. Now we will find out who are the real men, the ones who deserve to stand on the Karst Plateau as victors, and who shall be trodden into the rock. Now we baptise the lands in blood, a sacrifice to him and his returning lieutenants."

"Get up off your arses!" bawled the Staff Sergeant from behind the front line. "Get up and get going!" and he struck out with his boot and caught Pablo in the thigh, turning him over.

Pablo sprang back to his feet and spun to face the Sergeant. The dull flash of gunmetal was in the Sergeant's hand and the barrel of his service revolver pointed at Pablo's head.

"Don't be having thoughts above your station, young man!" he warned, a glimmer of pleasure lifting the corner of his lip. "The enemy is that way," he said, gesticulating with the gun.

But Pablo shook his head. "From where I am standing, it seems the enemy is all around."

The Sergeant suddenly straightened up and his eyes widened, full of surprise and pain. He slumped with a groan to the ground and didn't move anymore.

"I told you," said Abelli, his eyes on the grey wave of the enemy coming towards them across the plateau. He pulled his knife out of the Sergeant and put it back into his sheath. "I told you I would protect you. All the way, up until the end."

NINETY ONE

The Vatican. Vatican City.

Cardinal Korek was not at all happy to be leaving his quarters at such an hour of the evening, especially after the events earlier in the day. It had not been possible to save Cardinal Bishop Berberino. He had died on the chamber floor within minutes of his first convulsion.

"A heart attack," the doctor concluded, who had been called and had arrived minutes after the Cardinal had stopped breathing.

"Rubbish," Korek had muttered under his breath, while the doctor gathered his belongings together. He had long recognised the signs of poisoning, the discolouration around his lips, the pallid drawn skin. But he said nothing openly, knowing it prudent not to advertise his knowledge to those gathered around the prostrate body. For if Berberino had been murdered, he surmised that the murderer would still be at large and alert to any who might doubt the doctor's diagnosis.

So when the request was made to meet in the Sala Del Cartone chamber, he went to it with reluctance. He wished for nothing more than a quiet night to mourn his friend and ponder just who might have been responsible for his murder. Recent events within the Vatican, the recent signs of the Antichrist's returning, the ritual killings, the wolves, now joined with the murder of one of the Holy See, had done little to daunt the shrewd Cardinal Bishop's mind. Wickedness it seemed now stalked the Vatican's corridors, as well as the streets of Rome. He assured himself he would seek the Devil out, one way or other.

The door to the chamber was just ahead and he pulled his sleeves up to his elbows as if about to do battle, reaching forward to open it. Before he could grasp the handle, the door flew open and a figure beyond stared out at him from the darkness inside.

"Goodness!" Korek cried, in shock and surprise. "I didn't think there was anyone here yet?"

"Only me," the figure beyond replied, dark eyes watching behind hooded eyelids, his skin sallow and sweating.

"What are you trying to do?" Korek asked, his hand clutched to his chest. "Are you not satisfied that there has already been one death within the Holy See? And why have you called me here? Do you have news about Berberino's death?" Korek said the word, 'death' with delicacy. "I'll be honest, I had wished for nothing more than to sit and ponder and remember our fallen friend this evening. Not be dragged out into the depths of the Vatican to converse. May I come in?" he asked, pushing his way inside before he received an answer and wandering towards the middle of the chamber, his thin hands knotted at his middle.

"Why should Cardinal Berberino be remembered?" the figure asked, watching the Cardinal stop and turn to look back in surprise. "I mean, what did he ever do to make his memory worthy of recall?"

"Are you quite well?" asked Korek.

"Quite," the figure replied from the shadows, stepping past the old Cardinal to stand at the window, peering out into the dark over Vatican City. The sky was full of crows. "What a sight!" he muttered, and Korek tutted and joined him at the window.

"Indeed! All these blasted crows. The doves, their numbers will be decimated. They might never recover. I assure you!"

"Yes, you assure me," the figure next to him said, still rapt, but his voice seeming to grow in authority and corruption. "But can you also assure me that what you have done in your service to the faith will be remembered for all time as well?"

"What is the matter with you?" asked Korek, wrinkling his long nose and looking down it. "Don't tell me you have taken ill from the wine too?"

"Not in the slightest," the hunched man replied, a smile coming to his face. "In fact I've never been better. Everything is progressing exactly as planned. Perhaps I should have taken the path upon which I am now walking years ago."

"And what do you mean by that?" asked Korek, turning on the man as he stepped from the window to the table to fill a single goblet from a decanter of crystal. "How can things never have been better? We have lost a dear colleague of the Holy See. War has come to the borders of Italy. A world war has developed across all of the Europe, Asia, and much of Africa. Crows have made the Vatican their home!"

"I know, things are progressing just as planned."

"You are clearly unwell!" Korek called, marching from the window, but he found his path blocked by the man. A blast of cold evening air flowed into the room, gripping the back of his neck. "Out of the way!" he roared. "I demand to leave right now!"

"Of course, Cardinal Bishop Korek. I can think of nothing better."

Korek felt heavy hands on his throat and he was half lifted, half thrust towards the window, as if he were no more than an ungainly weight. "Stop!"

he cried, "what are you doing, you fool?" But then he felt his thigh strike the base of the window and he went over it, teetering one moment on the ledge, and then falling. He grasped out with his hands, but they clawed only the cool night air as the ground of Vatican City rushed up to meet him.

The hunched figure peered briefly over the edge of the window to the bloodied husk of flesh and bone below, before slipping back into the shadows like a reptile before the chill of autumn's bite. Something ancient and terrible snaked its way from the crushed remains, like a wraith lifting from a deceased body.

NINETY TWO

Approaching the Italian Front. The Italian-Slovenian border.

Tacit had fallen for what seemed like an age, spinning over and around, jarring into rocks and tree roots.

He came to a stop with a grunt, slamming hard into the dirt by the side of the railway track, feeling the cold of the rain on his back, his clothes, his hair. His shoulder moaned with furious pain from his wounds, his head felt light and broken. He tasted nothing but earth and blood. He lay there supposing he was dying, but then he still felt the air come in and out of him in short pained breaths and he moved, just a little, a momentary shudder, enough to prove to himself that he was still alive.

Something spun and twisted in front of his eyes, bright lights too intense for Tacit to see. He groaned and dragged his hand to his face, chasing the burning pinpricks of colour away. Voices screamed and compelled. Energy surged within him. And then slowly, oh so slowly, he moved his giant frame, closing his arms on the gravel of the trackside, using it to give him the traction and support he needed to push himself up. He staggered blindly to his feet and looked up at the smudge of disappearing lights that was the rear of the train cranking away into the darkness, climbing ever higher into the mountains, towards the Carso and the Karst Plateau with Isabella inside.

Something within beseeched him to rise, to gather the last of his strength and go after her.

He grunted and closed his eyes, fighting back any pain he felt, burying it, as he buried everything. And then he thrust one foot in front of the other and slowly plodded after the vanishing lights in the distance, led like the dog on a lead that he knew he had become. That he had always been.

NINETY THREE

Slovenia. Nearing the Italian border.

The abject pallid figures crept towards Poré on their hands and knees, their heads low to the ground like pale fleshy insects, through the dark of the cavern. They seethed and hissed both their interest and displeasure.

But Poré stood firm, unmoving, his back to the cavern exit, and the clan gathered in a half-circle in front of him, confused as to his bold manner, the fact he did not find them dreadful to look upon. And they watched and waited for him to make the next move.

"I am not here as your enemy," Poré announced. At once the clan cackled in unison with mischievous cruel laughter, and took a step closer towards him. "I am not here to bring trial or retribution to you."

"Then what are you here for, earth-walker?" snarled one of the clan, whom Poré supposed was their self-appointed leader. "Have you come here to mock us, to view us for entertainment? You have made a terrible mistake, even if you bear the pelt of one of our kind. For you are not welcome within our domain, and now you have entered it we will never allow you to leave."

The sound of scurrying feet came from behind Poré and he turned to see that the passageway down which he had entered was blocked by more of the clan, hunkered low, rocking on their gnarled joints.

Poré looked back at the loathsome man who had addressed him. He was aged and bowed by time, broken by a terrible weight no one but the wolves could understand.

"I am not here to mock or shame. Nor am I here to die among you." His voice rang like a hammer on an anvil and all the wolves save the one who had addressed to him drew back. "I am here to offer you an opportunity to rise and fight back. To fight back against those who have too long left you within these ungodly caves."

"So that is it!" spat the man. "You have come for our pelts to add to your own?"

But Poré shook his head. "No! I have come to give you hope and a chance to strike back. For too long you have stayed entrapped within your lairs. For too long you have been commanded only by the moon. The Catholic faith, its power and reach is waning. Its Inquisitors are overwhelmed, the Holy See bowed."

Barbed laughter followed this announcement.

"Why should we care?" asked the man. "Yes, we delight in their downfall. May it be as long and protracted as is our torment. But what other reason should there be for us to believe this changes anything for us or our predicament? What is it you are proposing?" He took another step forward. "That you take the moon from the sky? That you lift our curse?"

"Eventually, yes," replied Poré, and there was uproar and cursing at his perceived lie. "But first, that you come with me. That you fight with me, because of what is coming." He set his hand flat to the limestone rock of the cavern. "At the very end of these seams of rock, in the mountain they call the Carso, something terrible is about to be summoned."

More laughter and shrieking filled the cavern, the wolves slapping and beating themselves in torment and confusion.

"And, again," spoke the lead wolf, "I ask you, why should we care? Our lair is already corrupted. Our lives condemned. If by something 'terrible' you mean the Devil, perhaps he will prove himself to be a more sympathetic Lord to us? Heavens knows the one who sent us down here was not."

"Blame not the Lord on high for what you became!" spat Poré in sudden anger.

"And so you show your true colours, follower of God!" And the Hombre Lobo prepared to leap at the intruder.

But Poré threw a hand across him in defiance.

"No!" he called. "It was not the Lord's doing which cast you down here. It was those who constructed and performed the rituals of excommunication, those well versed in the corrupted arts of life and death."

"And one day we will take our revenge," growled the man.

And Poré nodded. "Yes, you will, if you follow me."

"How so?"

"Because the architect of the summoning within the Carso, he was the one who performed the very final excommunication upon your kind."

NINETY FOUR

Approaching the Italian Front. The Italian-Slovenian border.

It was dawn.

At least Tacit supposed the dirty grey light which rose from the crest of the mountain edge ahead was the dawn. The air was full of dust and smoke from the munitions, forming a creeping mass that slunk down the mountainside, searching out new places to pollute and choke.

Tacit's right eye was still closed from where Georgi had struck him, his left full of dirt from where he'd fallen from the train among the stones and the earth beside the track. Every step was slow and tortured and required him to summon every ounce of resolve. But he was no longer alone as he half walked, half stumbled towards the Carso and where he knew Georgi had taken Isabella. Because the voice accompanied him, shrieking within him, urging him ever onwards, imploring him to make haste, for the time of their coming was nigh.

He stopped and felt in a pocket, his heart lifting a little when he found an emergency flask of spirit buried deep, enough perhaps to silence the demons and dull his pain for a little time. He took it out and spun off the cap, lifting the bottle to his lips, surveying the long winding path up the Carso ahead of him.

Georgi? Alive?

He could barely believe it. But he knew it was true. Though aged and corrupted by whatever dark power now possessed him, there was no doubt the man Tacit had fought on the train was him.

Tacit took another drink, a longer one this time, and ruminated on Georgi's words, his admission of Mila's death. Hate and wrath congealed within him like a poison. He felt ready to erupt with an outburst of fury as strong as any he could remember his entire life.

Georgi.

His oldest friend. His only friend. The murderer of Mila.

The crunch of stones behind him immediately drew his attention and he snapped his hand to his revolver, spinning in a flash, the weapon trained on whoever it was coming up behind him.

"Thank God you're alive!" croaked Henry, reaching forward to grasp at the Inquisitor. "We thought you and Isabella were dead." Tacit allowed his torn clothes to be touched briefly by the Englishman before pushing him away. "What did they do to you?" Henry asked, aghast.

Tacit scowled and unlocked the hammer of the gun, setting the firearm back in its holster.

"Much the same as you," he growled, lifting the flask back to his mouth and guzzling the whiskey inside. "Just gave me a hiding before they threw me off the train."

"Where's Isabella?" asked Sandrine. Her right arm was in a makeshift sling, the right side of her clothing torn from where she'd landed among the stones and rolled. Tacit said nothing, instead turning back to the Carso where he knew Isabella had been taken. "You're joking?" said Sandrine, reading Tacit's silence and the direction of his eyes.

Henry traced the railway track along which they were walking up the mountainside to the smudge of buildings in the distance, which he supposed was the end of the line. "Why've they taken her up there?"

"You know why," replied Tacit, looking around at them briefly before turning back. "The third ritual. Pride of life. I'm going on," he said over his shoulder, stowing the partially empty flask and walking on. There was a fire now in his belly. "Come if you want. Or go back. It's up to you. My advice? Go back. Don't follow. There's only death and darkness where this path leads." He heard both Henry and Sandrine follow and felt something warm shift inside him, a vague sense of appreciation stirring. For the first time in as long as he could remember, Tacit was glad not to be alone.

"Where are we going, then?" asked Sandrine.

"All the way," replied Tacit, setting one large boot slowly in front of the other. "All the way to the top."

NINETY FIVE

THE VATICAN. VATICAN CITY.

The hunched figure at the table was slicing through the cuts of raw beef on his plate, his eyes fiercely intent on the dish in front of him. He fed the bloody chunks into his mouth with the speed and repetition of a machine. In the half-light of the room, the Priest approaching him could see the man's cutlery had been turned crimson by the dripping flesh, his jaws chewing briefly at each meaty morsel before swallowing it and forcing another into his slavering mouth. He didn't pause from eating when the Priest stepped up, instead turning briefly to acknowledge him before setting his attention back to the meal and last few strips of beef.

"We have received word," said the Priest.

"And?" replied the man flatly.

"The woman, Sister Isabella, she has been taken."

"And Tacit?"

"He lives. He follows."

"Of course he follows!" exclaimed the figure at the table, his face flashing with sudden rage. "It was prophesied that he would. He cannot help himself. He is drawn to her, as he is drawn by the prophecy. A moth to a flame." The figure forced the last of the meat into his mouth before pushing the plate away. Standing with some effort, he made his way to the window and peered down onto St Peter's Square. "Make sure all is made easy for him. I know Tacit and his impatient ways. He'll not want to be idle. He'll be keen to pursue so make sure he can. Make sure nothing stops him."

"Of course," replied the Priest, bowing.

"Things have proceeded just as intended. Berberino and Korek's intrusions were dealt with, just like Monsignor Benigni." The man turned his back to the window and raised his hands. "Was this moment not prophesied by Pope Leo XIII? Did he not then receive a vision from the Devil himself telling him that he would return and that his return would be heralded by terrible war, covering much of the lands? And that from the Devil's flesh would crawl his seven lieutenants?" He looked up into the heavens, wonderment in his face. "Already the first two rituals have been completed, lust of the eyes, lust of the flesh," he spoke as if a prayer, and lowered his eyes onto his acolyte. "Pride of life. The one destined to complete the final ritual comes. Everything converges. Everything reaches its climax, and on the pinnacle of the Carso, the act shall be done."

He paused, and glanced absently out of the window, following the path of a large black crow as it circled around the square, cawing fiercely.

"Tacit," he continued, weighing the name in his mind. "For years too many to count I have watched him, contrived to bring him and Sister Isabella together, ensured that their union was secured. They now are all that matters. Make sure Georgi is ready. Make sure nothing affects the plan."

The crow flew across the window before coming to land close to where the hunched figure stood. It croaked, as if forming words in its beak. The figure smiled and nodded his head. Nothing could stop them now.

NINETY SIX

The Italian Front. The Soča River. Northwest Slovenia.

The men stank, of shit and piss and sweat and dirt, as they waited for the vast wave of grey Austro-Hungarian soldiers to rush onto them for a second time. Their uniforms, so pristine when they first boarded the trains in the foothills of Italy, where flags were unfurled and their loved ones bore brave faces and waved lace gloves of farewell, not goodbye, at them from the platforms and bridges, were now torn and bloodied. Their boots had broken open through the heat and the exertion. Caps and hats, once firmly and precisely drawn across heads, were now shoved to the backs of skulls to cover burnt necks. There was no more pride in how one appeared. There was only survival.

Pablo stood cowed beside Abelli on the crest of the Karst Plateau, resting on his rife, using it as a staff with which to hold himself up. He looked down the mountain up which he had walked and crawled and fought, every yard of which had cost a hundred lives. It felt to him that he was standing on top of the world, elevated to the mightiest of positions. Though corrupted by coal smoke and the pungent stink of cordite, the air seemed somehow thinner and fresher, above only blue skies across the entire horizon. Below them, clouds huddled against the sides of the mountain and Pablo felt that despite being on top of the world near the heavens, he was perhaps nearer to the lowest, darkest voids of hell.

"Does anyone care about us?" he asked, looking down through the clouds to the valleys far below. "Does anyone even know we're here? We have no ammo. We have no shells. We have little food. It seems as if everything we have done and achieved to reach here has been for nothing. It seems as if our sacrifice has been in vain. Why have we taken this place? For what purpose? Does anyone care?"

Corporal Abelli chuckled and took his pipe from the side of his mouth, knocking it empty against his thigh.

"No," he said, setting the bowl of the pipe in the heart of his palm and filling it with the last of his tobacco from the pouch at his belt. His face was blackened with dirt and dried blood, the filth of four days' battle. "No one cares about us. No one save the Devil. For no one else resides here but him. No God will listen to you here. Only the Devil can come to your aid, can hear your pleas."

He was aware that Pablo had begun to weep, his whole body shaking with grief, the young man's face racked with sorrow, tears pouring down his face and falling onto the parched rock beneath him. He was bent double, his hand clutched to his mouth, a voiceless cry from his lungs.

"I don't want to call for the Devil," he wept, pleading like a child. "I don't want to ask him for help."

But the Corporal laughed. "Neither did I," he said, lighting his pipe and sending clouds of cherry-scented smoke into the air about him. "But sometimes he is the only one who listens and hears. Look about you, boy. Listen out for him." The Corporal's eyes grew wide and serious. "Watch for him. He is coming. He is coming here soon." He tapped the side of his nose and lifted Pablo's rifle so that the young soldier held it firmly into his chest. "His time is nigh. Stay close so that I may keep you safe and lead you to him."

"Who?" cried Pablo. "Who do you mean to lead me to?"

But Corporal Abelli turned away and joined the other Italian soldiers at the front face of the shallow trench they had built across the long width of one side of the Karst Plateau. On this plateau, a flat circle of rock a mile wide, ringed by jutting conical peaks of green and grey, Pablo knew everything would end. He breathed deep, chasing his tears away. A chill wind picked up and tugged at his hair and his uniform, as if some invisible force was trying to wrench him away.

A shrill whistle cut through the monotonous rumble of troops preparing their defences.

"They are coming!" came the cry. "The enemy! They are coming again! Get to your defences! Prepare your arms! They are coming! They are coming again for another assault!"

Without thinking, Pablo padded to the trench and threw himself down into it. He watched the horizon fill and grow with the gathering of Austro-Hungarian soldiers charging towards them and he knew now the end truly was nigh. For there was nowhere else to go, neither forward nor back. They had gone as far as they were able and he had no more bullets left. And what was more, he knew that most of the men either side of him didn't have any either.

NINETY SEVEN

Slovenia. Nearing the Italian border.

Poré was aware of a shadow falling across him and roused himself from sleep to face whoever it was who had sought him out.

"What is it?" he asked, sitting up on the spot.

The clan leader dropped to his haunches, so that he was level with Poré, and stared hard into the gaunt Cardinal's eyes. The stench of the wolf surrounded him like a mantle, catching Poré hard in the back of his throat and making him gag.

"Why?" the man asked, ignoring Poré's reaction. "Tell me, why are you driven to fight these Priests you say are summoning the seven Princes of Hell? Why should it you care? They hunt you, like they hunt us, if what you have told us is true. Why should you wish to do the duty of the Catholic faith, when they have long turned you from their flock?"

Poré didn't speak immediately. Instead he turned his eyes to the earth and cast his mind back to when he was a young man, beating hard against the church door, as hard as his broken arm would allow.

"I was an Inquisitor," he revealed, and the wretched man hissed and showed blackened rotten teeth, rearing back, his long gnarled fingers splayed wide like talons about to strike. "For two months and only ever an acolyte." The words seemed to momentarily quell the Hombre Lobo's anger. "I was forced to commit to their cause and, when I refused, they beat me, mercilessly, until one day they beat me too hard."

Poré recalled the day he went to the Church to ask to be excused from the organisation, the memory still bitter. Still raw. "Cardinal Gílbert," said Poré, and the pallid filthy man could tell at once it was a name loathed by the gaunt figure in front of him. "He wore a robe of gold to greet me that day, the day of hearing, but a cloak of black suited his soul better."

Poré remembered the way the opulent Cardinal's glowering eyes had darkened and the scowl on his face deepened as he'd approached the dais, how Cardinal Gílbert had run his hand down his long black beard as he watched the broken man labour down the aisle towards him, while figures in the shadows inched into the light for a better vantage point. "I told them my wishes, that I wanted no part of the Inquisition, that I wished to return to the mainstream faith, to open worship. To lead services. To offer hope to the needy. To provide solace for the weak and afflicted within my local church. 'Weak and afflicted like yourself?' the Cardinal spat, and the flanking Bishops made no effort to mask their laughter."

The crouched man before Poré sneered and felt the rage of deception seize him. "So this desire for revenge, it's solely because of how you were made to feel, ridiculed when you asked to leave their employment?"

But Poré hardened. "No. It's because of what they took from me afterwards."

"And what was that?"

"My family." In the dark of the cavern, Poré's face blackened to match the shadows around him. "They took my parents, my brother, for what purpose I cannot, or do not dare to think, only that they assured me that my failings would be branded onto my family for eternity."

"And so you plotted your revenge?"

Poré nodded.

"And yet still I do not understand. If you wished revenge upon the Inquisition, upon this Cardinal Gílbert, why does this summoning fascinate you? How is it that it drives you and compels you to act? Why do you not seek out Cardinal Gílbert yourself?"

"Who says I have not?"

"I don't understand," growled the wolf.

"The one who committed the final excommunication upon your kind and Cardinal Gílbert are the same person, the High Priest who is to perform the final ritual on the topmost pinnacle of the Carso."

NINETY EIGHT

THE ITALIAN FRONT. THE SOČA RIVER. NORTHWEST SLOVENIA.

All the fighting that had gone before, every barrage, every charge, paled into insignificance ahead of the horror which filled the Karst Plateau now. Pablo clutched his rifle as a club, no longer as a firearm. It seemed that few in the Third Army in fact had any ammo left, and those that did used their allocation sparingly. Instead soldiers fabricated themselves weapons from whatever they could lay their lands on, barbed wire wrapped about clubs, nails driven hard through sticks, the handles of axes finished to a sharp stabbing point, brutal barbarous things for an army long brutalised by the torturous climb, reduced to animals in every sense.

And it also proved true that the Austro-Hungarians had very little ammunition either, two armies starved on that mountaintop, that bowl of blood, save for their fists and whatever weapons they could fashion themselves. So the battle of these two great seas of men, fifty thousand strong on both sides, crashed into each other, fists, feet, blades, maces, the butts of rifles being their tools of war, only the occasional crack of a bullet punctuating the terrible clamour. They were marooned on the plateau with only their anger and their hate and their brawn.

Knuckledusters and knives, anything which could be wielded quickly and still be delivered with force, proved the most efficient. Very occasionally an explosion rocked one corner of the plateau, a bomb thrown, annihilating several soldiers on both sides. The butt of a rifle or the blade of a spade was often enough to take an enemy down. There was no need to hit such an enemy twice. If the blow was good, it would do for him, and if he only went over onto his knees or side, the ground and the relentless feet would pound him slowly to death. There was no need to waste time and energy on one mortally wounded. Pablo soon learnt all this, that it was more important to worry about those who weren't being slowly crushed on the floor of the plateau.

Soon it was impossible to tell who was who, everyone so drenched in blood that soldiers paused, looking for a sign to tell friend from foe, so that they didn't kill an ally. Fighting became more a game of wits and luck than skill. Everything turned red, a slick, stinking convulsing mess in the mounting heat of the day.

And all the time Pablo fought surrounded by a slowly dwindling shield of Italian soldiers, as if they were his own bodyguards, his protectors.

NINETY NINE

The Italian Front. The Soča River. Northwest Slovenia.

It felt to Isabella that they had been walking in infernal darkness for days. After leaving the train, clapped in handcuffs and led like a prisoner by Georgi, he had commandeered a truck which had taken them the last few miles to the foot of mountain she supposed was the Carso, the place Tacit had spoken about so often. They'd been met by others there, awkward wicked-faced people, with a hurried excited look about them. They'd watched her as if she was some great prize that had been obtained for their pleasure.

Georgi had taken a pack from them and a lantern, and had headed off into the foothills of the mountain with Isabella, now holding her by the arm. At least the handcuffs had been removed once they had begun to walk again. She needed her hands, for the climb was treacherous and steep in places.

He'd found the entrance to the cave quickly and had pushed her inside, checking for a last time that they had not been spotted, before following and guiding her along the sandy path which climbed inside the heart of the mountain.

She'd asked him on many occasions where they were headed, but he never replied and she knew anyway, from the fact that the path climbed all the time, that they were heading for the summit of the mountain, the Karst Plateau, as Tacit had predicted. She suspected she knew the devilish conclusion which lay there for her and fought to keep her fears from overwhelming her.

At times they stopped and ate, the unappetising food seeming all the more bland through the pallid light of the lantern.

"What are these caves?" she asked him, trying to win his trust and perhaps the chance to flee should his attention drop for long enough.

"They run through the Carso, forged by underground rivers running through the limestone long ago. The mountain is riddled with them, like honeycomb."

That was all she got from him. Georgi never rested for long, only enough for them to stave off hunger and then continue, as if time was of the essence. Isabella snatched brief moments of sleep whenever they stopped, for she was deathly tired, all the time aware of Georgi's cold unyielding eyes on her.

Finally the path levelled out and the tunnel up which they were walking opened to reveal a broad chamber, thirty feet high and thirty wide, a silty fine dust covering the floor. From within it she could hear the sounds of battle hammering out of the darkness beyond and she supposed they were now close to the summit. Another passageway, a yawning tunnel twisting up and away to their left, curved into pale light that Isabella guessed was daylight.

Georgi dragged her to the wall of the cavern and threw her onto the ground. There was a ring hammered into the rock close to where she landed and he looped the handcuffs around it and locked them about her wrists.

"What are you doing?" asked Isabella, watching as he stepped into the very centre of the cavern. He set the lantern down and walked away from it, a set number of strides, silently counting as he went. He set the toe of his shoe into the silty floor and began to drag it over the surface, walking towards her, making a line. He stopped, his foot still dug into the earth, and turned back on himself, walking once more, making another straight line, the same length as the previous one.

"He's coming for you," Georgi said, turning again and creating a third line, this one running over the first one he had made. "Tacit. He's coming for you." He stopped and turned for a fourth time, dragging his toe to make yet another line, this one crossing the second he had made. Isabella recognised the symbol he was creating. She had seen it in many dark places of the world and she knew its function. He turned for a final time at the fifth point of the star and dragged his foot back to the tip of the very first point. "Can you hear that?" he asked Isabella, raising his palm to his ear. "The battle? The carnage which is unfurling just beyond this chamber? Ninety thousand soldiers will come together on that plateau. Sixty thousand of them will perish, broken to bloody pulp under the blunt edge of man's combined hate. Their bodies will make a carpet of the dead, their dead fluids will run into the rocks of this mountain. Their deaths, their life blood is his welcoming toast. The blood to stir his arrival and the coming of his lieutenants."

"Lieutenants?" hissed Isabella. "What do you mean?"

"Come, come, Sister Isabella," smiled Georgi. "You can't have a Lord without lieutenants to protect him. The time is right for their returning. The time long prophesied has come. The world is ready for them, the ground fertile with the dead. Together they shall complete the work and make a world truly ready for the Antichrist." He looked at the pentagram he drawn in the dirt. "Through this gateway they will come. For so long they have been desperate to be free of their chains and return once more to our world above. Every night I have heard them crying out to be freed. Trying to get across. It is nearly time."

"Lust of eyes. Lust of the flesh!" muttered Isabella. "The ritual."

Georgi nodded. "Correct. The first two rituals have been completed. It is now the third, Pride of life, which is all that remains before the gateway shall be opened and they will come through. Pride of life. The arrogance to defeat the powers of life, the very fabric of existence and draw life back from the dead." He studied Isabella as he spoke. "Don't cry," he said, as she dropped her head. "Don't be scared. After all, you're the starring role. And Tacit is your lead. He will never leave you, you know? He loves you. He loved Mila. But she wasn't the one. He knew that. Or he would have saved her. He's always been able to save those he's loved. He's always had the power. The lights, the power they imbue. And the voices which drive him on. He has been prophesied for so very long. And he knows you're the one. And he will save you." Georgi grew angry that Isabella was still not looking at him, her head hanging, and he shouted at her. "Listen to me! Stop crying! He will come and he will save you. And by doing so, you and he will be together. But at such a price for mankind!"

ONE HUNDRED

St Petersburg. Russia.

Cool dawn light flooded through the windows of the Church of the Saviour of the Spilled Blood, charging the gold-haloed saints adorning the walls with a dazzling raiment almost too beautiful to behold, their gowns of flame orange and iris blue appearing like lush fabrics around their shoulders. The maniacal cries from the antechamber of the church had died instantly, like an extinguished flame. Where barked curses and roars had polluted the sanctity of the place moments before, quiet sobs and whimpers of benediction from the rescued victim were all that could now be heard.

The door to the antechamber opened and a haggard-looking Priest appeared, dropping his head and taking a moment to gather his breath. Exhaustion washed over him and he swayed woozily on his legs, drunk with fatigue from the night's trials. The exorcism had been long and difficult, dangerous too at times. Recently they had been getting harder to complete, demonic possessions far stronger, the toll on the Priest this time even more costly. This was his third exorcism this month, and without doubt the most testing yet. Exorcism had been the domain of Inquisitors, but Father Svyatoslav had not seen an Inquisitor in the city for the last two weeks and lately the duty had fallen to him.

He waited for his breathing to recover and looked back over his shoulder at the sleeping woman. She had been brought in last night, but now slept, at peace again, free of the demon who had possessed her. He smiled wearily, satisfied at this latest victory over the Devil. *He* would never triumph, not here in Father Svyatoslav's church, or in his city. People had been talking of bad omens, of ill signs being seen within the lands predicting End Times. But Svyatoslav would never give up. He would give every ounce of his body and his soul to the fight. He would be victorious no matter how long the journey, how hard the sacrifice. He would overcome, just as he had this morning.

He surveyed the grandeur of the church with its intricate mosaics, every wall alive with colour and shimmering light. In that moment, in the quiet of the ornate building, he felt peace and satisfaction. A little gift from heaven.

Svyatoslav closed the door behind him to allow the woman to sleep and began crossing the marbled floor to his offices on the opposite side of the church. He would change out of his clothes, fouled by the demon, and wash with the water brought to him last night, still untouched due to his being called to perform the exorcism. He reached the central point of the church and looked up, as he always did whenever he crossed it, to acknowledge Jesus Christ captured in the vivid coloured mosaic in the dome directly above. Christ looked down upon him, his head adorned with a silver and gold halo, a host of angels enshrining him with their wings, the colours of ochre and laurel.

The Priest muttered a silent prayer of thanks and continued to cross the floor. A noise like a clap made him stop and turn. At first he couldn't see anything, but Svyatoslav's interest was caught and he went back, looking over the floor for the thing which made the sound. A small coloured stone was lying on the black marble circle in the centre of the church. The Priest bent down and picked it up, holding it in his fingers to examine it. It was a mosaic tile and Svyatoslav looked up at the ceiling from where he supposed it must have fallen.

"Loose mortar," he muttered to himself, searching the dome's image to see if he could spot from where the piece had dropped.

The clack of a second falling tile sounded nearby and focused his eyes on where it had landed. He stepped over to the spot and picked it up, rattling the square of stone in his palm next to the other piece.

Where one goes, often another will follow, he thought, before a third fell onto the marble in front of him, joined by a fourth. He bent down to pick them both up, but before he could do so a fifth tile fell and then a sixth, this one striking him on his shoulder. He looked up squinting through the pale light, peering hard at the domed ceiling. Perhaps there was a hole in the roof and rainwater had worked its way into the mortar, weakening it? He frowned and made a private agreement with himself to ensure it was looked at straight away.

He bowed his head to leave the moment a seventh piece fell, after which a cascade of tiles flew down, thundering like hard rain onto the marble all around him. Almost at once he was aware that the air had grown cold, his breath billowing, his chest tight. He spoke a rushed panicked prayer and made to step away, but now a great shower of mosaic was flung down forcibly in front of him, blocking his route, ripped from the ceiling and thrown by enraged invisible forces. He jumped back and tried to step around it, but still more tiles fell, barring any way through. He shrieked and turned around. Coloured mosaics had begun to fall from the opposite side of the dome, preventing any chance of escape that way too. There was dust in the air and in his throat, his eyes now blinded. The noise was like thunder. His senses were overwhelmed, not knowing which way he should, or could, go. He tried to push his way through the torrent of stones but the force of the hurled masonry was too strong, ripping his clothes and flesh, his hands and arms cut open.

"Please!" he wailed pathetically, moments before the tiles began to be hurled directly onto him, slicing the skin from his skull with their razor-sharp edges.

Father Svyatoslav stumbled through the growing downpour of coloured stones, drenched in his blood, hanging ribbons of flesh stripped from his face. He fell onto his knees, the mosaics falling even harder still, battering him over onto his side, his skinned hands clasped tight to the bloodied hunk of flesh his head had become. He wept, pleading for the onslaught to stop, but there was no remission. In seconds he was covered in debris, his cries, and then soon after his lungs, crushed by rubble and the dust of the once beautiful mosaic of Christ.

ONE HUNDRED AND ONE

The Vatican. Vatican City.

It had been Cardinal Bishop Casado's idea that the casket be left open to allow people to look upon the deathly pale figure of Cardinal Korek for a last time as they paid their final respects to him. He'd been a constant presence, in wisdom as well as body, at the Vatican for over sixty years. His death had shocked and touched everyone, both within the small circle of the Holy See and in the wider community of the Vatican. The golden rays of sun burst through the stained glass window at the back of the church, drenching the casket in a gentle glow. A long stream of well-wishers and mourners shuffled slowly by, a general murmuring and praying rising up from the snaking line.

Casado leaned across to Adansoni as they stood watching from the rear of the ambulatory, their faces drawn tight, their hands clenched. "It was a shock," said Casado, nodding to himself. "A shock to us all." He looked across at Adansoni. "For him to have died this way."

"He fell on his back," replied Adansoni. "His face was almost entirely undamaged."

"God's grace. God's way of preserving his body. It is a shame God could not have preserved his life for a few years more. Goodness!" he exclaimed, "I am amazed I am saying this!"

"He was old," countered Adansoni gently, reaching with his hands and patting Casado's in a show of kindness and care. "He must have slipped and tumbled out of the room. Probably chasing crows. You know how he hated those crows!"

Casado chuckled sadly, a solitary tear rolling down his face. He let it run down the length of his cheek to his chin where it welled and hung from the coarse white hairs missed from his morning's shave. "He could be a difficult man sometimes," Casado said, turning his head a little so that only Adansoni would hear. Casado nodded his head. "But he'll be missed. He was loved."

A cry rang out, high pitched, from the line of mourners and both Casado and Adansoni frowned. The line jostled and then withdrew, hurriedly. People were shouting, some were screaming but everyone was running, fleeing from the casket, trying to get away from it as quickly as possible. Both Cardinals stepped forward, watching as people scrambled to get away. A woman went down and people ran over her in their urge to flee.

"What is it?" called Casado as a member of the Swiss Guard, posted to oversee proceedings, rushed forward in an attempt to bring calm. Something was stirring within the coffin. Casado and Adansoni saw it as they stood behind the casket, saw the pallid grey of Korek's scalp rise to reveal the butchered crushed wound at the back of his head, caved in and blackened with congealed blood. Both of them fell back, their hands to their mouths.

"Lord preserve us!" Adansoni cried, his heels catching on the ground and causing him to lose his balance. He flailed out and Casado caught him, just managing to hold him upright.

"What is that thing?" Casado cried, his eyes firm on the hideous ghoul, as it began to sit up in the casket, bony hands gripping the edges of the box.

"When the dead rise …" Casado heard Adansoni say, above the clamour and roar of the disintegrating line. The Cardinal Secretary of State turned to look at his fellow Cardinal and friend. "The third ritual! The pride of life!"

At the far end of the church, doors were thrown open and Inquisitors surged in, sprinting up the aisle to where Korek was now attempting to stand in the casket. Words were on his rotting lips, indiscernible sounds, but baleful and cruel. A revolver was raised and trained at the creature. As a shot sounded, Korek's blackened mouth twisted into a smile before he was thrown backwards. He somersaulted off the back of the casket and flipped over onto the white marble of the apse. Korek's corpse twitched and stirred for just a moment and then fell back onto the marbled floor. Black blood seeped out from the wound in his chest. But this blood seemed strange. It didn't flow. It looked as if it was crawling, as if it was made up of individual little elements, each moving, writhing out from beneath the body of the Cardinal. And then they realised the blood wasn't blood at all but a host of tiny insects, biting and stinging creatures burrowing out of his chest and out of hell's depths.

PART SEVEN

"Bless the Lord, O my soul, and forget not all his benefits, who forgives all your iniquity, who heals all your diseases, who redeems your life from the pit."

Psalm 103:3–4

ONE HUNDRED AND TWO

Pablo realised that there was no one left to fight, just a carpet of dead, three bodies thick, all around him. Already corpses had started to bloat and expand in the heat of the day. Around him he saw other Italian soldiers, bloodied and bowed from the scourge of battle, clutching their battered makeshift weapons, all dripping with the remains of the enemy. There was nothing else, only bodies and ash and smoke and stone, all punctuated with the mournful cries of the dying, for whom Pablo could do nothing, and had no compulsion to help either. Not anymore.

Pablo felt sticky and hot and sick. His whole body shook and he dropped the short bloodied pick he had armed himself with mid-way through the battle. It fell with a dull thud onto the bodies beneath him and he looked east to the haze of the plateau's horizon, the smudge of grey growing more faint as the last of the Austro-Hungarian army fled the field.

He wanted to cry, to roar out his passion to the heavens, but he had no energy to do so. And so instead he just stood and stared, stared into the eastern haze, mind empty.

And then he stopped and he blinked the filth from his eyes. Corporal Abelli.

Desperation grasped him like a noose. Now the tears came and he sobbed, weeping for his loss, weeping for fear he was the last one alive from his unit on that mountainside. A cloud passed in front of the sun and he shivered.

He dropped his head and slumped his shoulders with it, falling to his knees, the blood of the fallen seeping into his trousers. The limestone ground was soft, like a sponge, a carpet of pulverised flesh, skin and blood. Kneeling there Pablo felt he could stay slumped on that field of murder for an eternity, caught within the pall of death, neither able nor willing to leave it.

"Pablo!" called a voice, and at once his heart stirred, for he recognised it.

He gathered himself to his feet and staggered towards the sound, his vision blurred by exhaustion and the clouds of smoke rolling over the battlefield.

"Corporal Abelli?" he cried. "Is that you?"

Figures swam into view and Pablo hurried towards them at the edge of the battlefield. At their head stood Abelli, battered, blood covering his uniform and the side of his head, his hair matted with the stuff.

"I am pleased to see you're still alive!" Pablo cheered, reaching out to him as a friend might to another.

Pablo thought it strange that Abelli did not reply. Instead the tallest of the figures, dressed in a gown of black and sewn jewels, took Pablo by the shoulder and turned the young soldier so he might look at him more closely. And Pablo shivered, as if remembering a terrible dream.

"Prepare the defences!" a Sergeant called from a little way off. "Strengthen our line. Come on, you bastards! You might have won the scrap but you've not won the battle. They'll be coming back to have another go! You!" he barked at Pablo, and Pablo instantly turned and drew roughly to attention to answer his commanding officer. "Where's your fucking rifle?"

"Not this one," commanded the bearded figure, his face partially burnt away, waving gently with his hand. Pablo noticed that the man's fingers were very long and his left hand encased a ram's head cane.

Without question, the Sergeant nodded and turned to leave.

"There will be another," the bearded man called after him, drawing the Sergeant to a halt. "A large tall man. He goes by the name of Tacit." The Sergeant nodded, mute, his face expressionless. "Let him pass. I have need of him, on that pinnacle." And he unfurled his fingers to revealed the blackened stone monolith behind, as if up to that point it had been invisible.

The High Priest turned to look at Pablo again and smiled slowly. "Come on, Pablo," said Abelli, putting a hand to his shoulder and leading him on, "it is time."

ONE HUNDRED AND THREE

The Italian Front. The Soča River. Northwest Slovenia.

If it surprised Henry and Sandrine that the climb to the summit of the Carso went unchallenged, it didn't Tacit. He knew why they let them pass, why he had been summoned. He knew the Darkest Hand was here.

They climbed the final few steps to the edge of the Karst Plateau and each of them took a moment to try to take in what they saw. Bodies covered every inch of the field, bodies on top of each other, intertwined, smashed together so it was impossible to see where one ended and another began. None of them had ever seen such a thing before, not even Henry in his short time on the western front.

No trees stood across the entire vista, no colour gave life or hope to the scene. The world beyond was nothing but an undulating mess of grey and brown uniforms, drenched scarlet with blood.

The smell, like that of a slaughterhouse, engulfed everything. Underneath the rancid veneer of roasting flesh one could smell fear, sweat, shit, all festering beneath the unerring sun above.

"What are you three up to?" called a voice, a soldier walking over from where he had been organising the disposal of bodies.

"No, it's okay Lance Corporal," said a Sergeant, waving a hand and stepping into his path. He put the hand around the man's shoulders and led him away. "They've been allowed through. Special dispensation."

Tacit nodded and walked on, Henry and Sandrine following. A bleak solemnity had descended upon them. They looked no longer to the right, over the battlefield

The path they followed was raised along the lip of the summit, away from where the majority of the fighting had taken place. Only occasionally now did they come across strewn corpses of soldiers, often in pairs, as if they had died at each other's throats.

The pinnacle of black rock, reaching for the pure blue of the heavens above, was just ahead now. A cave mouth stood its base, partially concealed by numerous thrusting shards of limestone stalagmites. Here the battle had been severe. Bodies were strewn in deep piles about the fingers of rock as if the cave were some sewer into which the detritus of the war had flowed.

"I suppose this is the place," said Tacit.

"Part of me feels it'll be a relief to get inside," replied Henry. "Away from all this." He waved his hand over the butchered landscape of the battlefield behind him.

But Tacit growled and peered into the darkness beyond. "I wouldn't be so sure about that."

ONE HUNDRED AND FOUR

The Italian Front. The Soča River. Northwest Slovenia.

The cave mouth soon narrowed to a dark claustrophobic passageway. Tacit searched inside a pocket for his lantern, before remembering back to the corridor in the Vatican when he had thrown it in an attempt to delay those pursuing him. He cursed.

"Does anyone have a light?" he asked, turning to look at them. Henry and Sandrine shook their heads, and Tacit cursed again. "It looks like we're going in blind." He shrugged and took a swig from his bottle, the last of the bottles he'd picked up from a shop as he left Rome. "At least they won't see us coming."

They went forward slowly and carefully, feeling their way into the black. The tunnel was dry and smelt of earth, sharp jutting faces of rock lurching out from the walls as the path deviated left and then right. Uneasily, Tacit had to blindly squeeze his muscular frame around each corner. He was aware that the path was slowly descending and eventually it ran true, down towards what appeared to be a wider cavern, out of which crept faint orange light from a lantern.

The light came as both a relief and a burden. Tacit stopped and took what he supposed might be the final drop of brandy he ever tasted. He ran the stinging sharp drink around his mouth, savouring every aroma, every allure of the spirit. Throughout his life, brandy had been his one constant. The one thing he could always rely on. He had deviated of course, when geographies and cultures had forced him to, the local spirit sometimes having to suffice. But nothing had rewarded him quite as much as brandy. Uncomplicated. Uncompromising. Rewarding.

He drank deeply, nursing his wounded shoulder as he did so, turning it in its joint to ensure that it still had movement. He'd have need of it. Of that he was sure. The chain mail had taken most of the sting out of the rounds fired by Georgi on the train, but his shoulder was still bruised and hurt to move.

The hot Italian sun had roasted his sunburnt neck through the high thin atmosphere of the Karst and it pulled when he stretched at it to work any stiffness away. He took another long final swig from the bottle and, as if suddenly remembering that he was not alone, offered it to Henry. The soldier took it graciously and toasted him.

"Once more unto the breach?" Henry suggested quietly, raising the bottle to his lips. He handed it to Sandrine, who took two large gulps before handing it back to Tacit. He put it back in his coat, reaching down and checking his revolver in his holster, and the pack of ammo in a separate pocket. He'd lost a lot of kit back on the train, but he had enough for whatever lay ahead. He was sure of that. And he had his anger. He supposed with it he'd have enough for whatever he came up against. He'd have to.

The Karst Plateau. The place of the third and final part of the ritual. Tacit grimaced and promised himself it would end here.

"Pride of life," he growled at Henry and Sandrine. "Let's try and kill it," and he thought of Georgi and a hatred pulled within him.

He stepped forward and the anger began to burgeon at once. He let it. He could feel the darkness and the power almost overwhelm him as he stepped down into the cavern.

And then Tacit stopped dead in his tracks.

There was his old friend, dressed in black, standing above a woman who had been pushed down onto her knees, her hands tied by chains to a hook in the ground. Isabella!

She cried out to him and pulled hard at her bonds.

Tacit felt wrath build up inside him as he took another step forward, his eyes surveying the cavern for anything else, for any traps, for any other adversaries. It seemed that only Georgi faced him. He saw that he held a gun, thrust tight to the side of Isabella's head. There was no way he could get close enough to save her, not with a forward charge. "I'm here," said Tacit, his face etched with hate.

"I was expecting you to come," retorted Georgi, looking down momentarily at Isabella before stepping towards his old friend, a cold smile coming to his lip. There was a shrewd look in his eye. "After all, I knew you'd never leave this," he said, lifting his hand to indicate Isabella.

"Get out of here, Tacit!" she cried. "Leave!"

But Georgi shook his head and chuckled. "He won't," he said. "He can't."

Tacit noticed that a pattern had been drawn into the floor of the cavern, a pentagram in the very centre, and immediately it confirmed all of Tacit's fears. After all the rituals, it was here that they concluded. To summon something wicked from hell.

"Lost your way badly, Georgi," said Tacit, turning back to him. "What changed you?"

"Let's just say that death was the making of me," replied Georgi, the smile hardening, the revolver waved in Tacit's direction. Tacit considered his chances of wrestling it from the Inquisitor. He was ten feet away now. Close enough, but he knew Georgi was good. Perhaps too good. Tacit's old friend had proved that already on the train.

"Perhaps you should have stayed dead?" he said. "Seems to me you've caused no end of trouble since. Grand Inquisitor Düül? I suppose that was your handiwork?"

Georgi smiled and bowed in recognition, holding his hands wide. "My master commands and I must do."

"It seems there's no limit to the depths you're willing to go to for your master?"

"Let's just say that he has been generous in what he has given to me. What skills he has taught me, what powers he has provided to me. Mind you, you're a fine one to talk, Poldek," replied Georgi, laughing. "Unyielding in your commitment to your own faith, aren't you, misguided though it is. Almost to the point of obsession. I must admit you have surprised me. I thought you would have wavered in your faith long ago. You were always a mean bastard, weren't you, Poldek? But we always said you, of all of us, would be the first to break."

"How so?" asked Tacit, his fierce eyes on the man with the gun.

"Because you were the hardest of us, and the hardest blade is often the easiest to shatter. But it turned out that you were the one who never questioned anything he was told. The one who never doubted. Although …" He stopped and looked at his friend, his head tilted at an angle. "I heard you failed once when you were younger? When you thought you were in love?" He laughed, a short, spitting laugh like a wound. "What was it that made you leave the Church, Poldek? Love? True love? Did you prefer to lie in the arms of your lover than the arms of the Lord?"

"I know what you're suggesting, Georgi. Keep Mila out of it," warned Tacit, his eyes flashing. He could feel the blood pumping behind his ears, could feel his heart rage. "Let's finish this," he growled.

But the black-clad man laughed. "Finish this? No, my friend. It's only just begun. It's only just beginning. The lights. The voices. Is it true they talk to you? Is it true they empower you, empower you to take life, and give it? You understand now don't you, Tacit? You understand why you're here, why Isabella is here? What we're going to do?"

Tacit did. He had known from the moment they had taken Isabella. Perhaps he had always known. He nodded. His heart raged, but if there was any emotion, he didn't show it.

"You are the final piece, just like you were with the Mass for Peace. We needed a world upon which our lord could return, one fitting for him. And only through completion of the ritual will that happen. Pride of life!" He spat the words, spittle flying from his mouth, and Tacit knew at once that madness had entrapped him totally. "The desire to break that bond between life and death. The final act. The ultimate sin. To break God's will and ensure that they who he captured and enslaved are claimed back to earth."

And without another word, he raised his revolver and levelled it at Isabella's body.

"Georgi!" hissed Tacit, his hand raised to urge him back, but Georgi's finger whitened against the trigger and the gun instantly exploded in his hand. Isabella let out a short cry and was thrown back with a grunt, lifeless in the dirt of the cavern, blood streaming from her chest.

"No!" roared Tacit, running forward and taking her into his arms, Henry and Sandrine standing in horrified silence at the entrance to the cavern. "No!" he cried, rocking her to and fro, as he had Mila all those years ago. "What have you done?" Looking up at Georgi, his eyes were full of tears and anger. Georgi smiled and pointed the revolver to the sky.

"My bidding for the Lord, beginning the final part of the ritual, Poldek. You know what to do," he said, his face darkening. "Do it!"

Georgi backed away as Tacit turned back to Isabella, hanging limp in his arms. He held her tightly to his body, tears flowing down his cheeks, still rocking her gently.

ONE HUNDRED AND FIVE

THE ITALIAN FRONT. THE SOČA RIVER. NORTHWEST SLOVENIA.

Figures, all dressed in black robes, gathered around Pablo and ushered him forward through the complex of caves. He resisted and felt hands take hold of his arms and push him in the back, forcing him on.

"Come, come, Private Gilda," said Corporal Abelli, leering at him closely. "This is your moment to become the great warrior you've always wanted to be, to justify the blood which runs in your veins."

He was bundled on, half pushed, half pulled, resisting the best he could against the army of hands and whatever ritual it was they were dragging him towards. But the strength had all but run out of him after the exhausting battle, and fear had taken the rest.

The archway of the cave ahead opened out onto a broad exposed circle of rock, thirty feet wide, at the far end of which were gathered an assembly of Priests, all watching Pablo intently, hoods pulled high up over their faces. At their head stood the High Priest, tall, bearded, in his hands two long pale daggers. Forty feet below them on the plains of the Carso, the battlefield of the Karst Plateau festered in the dying heat of daylight's final hour.

Now Pablo fought harder to flee, but the hands just gripped him more firmly and pushed him ahead. At once the Priests scurried forward and laid out the elaborate relics they had brought with them with well-trained efficiency and speed. Above them, a full pale moon had begun to rise over the eastern horizon, a scatter of stars appearing above. Crows circled the pinnacle in vast flocks, gathering on rocky outcrops and the single needle of stone which climbed yet higher into the heavens, squawking and croaking loudly.

Moonlight felt its way across the vast plateau, its silvery fingers creeping over the blackened stone of the pinnacle and onto the jet-black robes of the Priests. The wind had fallen away and from the depths of the battlefield below, the smell of churned bodies and blood began to climb, assaulting the senses.

A large silken black cloth had been set out on the dark rock, on which white ribbon had been laid out in the shape of a five-pronged star. Black candles had been set at its points.

Pablo was pushed towards it and onto his knees. Lightning flashed and sparked above and thunder rumbled in from the east. The Priest threw his arms wide, both daggers held in his hands, moonlight glinting off their blades.

"Deadened eyes. Torn bloodied skin. Branded tongues burnt from toothless mouths. These are signs pleasing to our Lord."

The growing dusk was torn open with shards of electric white lightning.

"They who would sacrifice all and nothing for their master, they who would fight and die and yet can never be destroyed for his majesty and his safe returning and reign, for they are as old as the foundations of time itself and created in the very fires of when time too was made.

"He has seen the sacrifices we have made for him here in this plain, ensuring the nourishing life blood of the fallen has seeped down into the bowels of his domain. For too long this world has been full of light and life. The new age has arrived, foretold by many and by just a few, an age of apocalypse and ruin for those who choose not to believe, not to follow, to give themselves entirely to his darkness and might."

He let his arms drop to his side and stared at Pablo. "Bring the final sacrifice!"

ONE HUNDRED AND SIX

The Italian Front. The Soča River. Northwest Slovenia.

Again. It was happening again. Everything he loved, everyone for whom he cared, who touched his life, died or fell away from him. His mother. Mila. Now Isabella.

"What can we do?" asked Henry, as he and Sandrine fell alongside Tacit.

But if Tacit heard the question, he did not acknowledge it. Instead he cried out, louder than ever, shaking his head, his eyes tightly shut, muttering "No" under his breath over and over again. Her deathly pale, beautiful face was void of any life, a death mask. He crushed her lifeless, chilling body to his, feeling the cooling of her blood against him.

"Isabella!" he cried and anger rippled through him, anger at Georgi, anger at himself, anger at his curse, for he knew then that it was a curse which he carried.

The lights and the voices, they had always been there, his constant companion. He couldn't remember when they had first come to him as a young boy, but always they came whenever he was tested, whenever things were most bleak, the spirits filling him with their might and their majesty and their horror.

At first, when they came to him as a boy, he had thought it was a madness which had struck him down, when the voices spoke to him, whispering wicked enticements in his ear, the lights dazzling his eyes. But when the voices and lights subsequently returned, and each time they returned after that, they brought with them power and speed and foresight. It was then that Tacit knew them not to be an affliction but a gift, a strength in dark times. And while the words spoken to him were cruel and the lights blinding, they empowered him to achieve things beyond the measure of his years. To become more than a man. To become a god.

Always he had feared where the voices and lights were leading, down which path they were drawing him. But Tacit always followed without question. For after all, they gave him only strength, and could such a force be a terrible thing?

The lights and the voices were with him now and he knew what he had to do. All his life he knew he had been waiting for this moment, that everything which had gone before had merely been passages of time down which he had travelled to be here now. He looked down at Isabella and his love for her surged like a wave he could not hold back. He kissed her on the forehead as the lights spun and shone and sparkled and took hold of him, filling him with their corrupt power, emboldening him with the mastery of life over death.

An energy wrenched its way out of him and he felt himself begin to rise from where they sat, elevated on invisible hands. The chain which held Isabella to the stone snapped free and fell away, and the wound in her chest, which throbbed with blood, dried in an instant and sealed. And suddenly Isabella coughed, a short choking cough, colour once again returned to her face, and there was movement behind her eyelids. Tacit ripped her clothing to reveal the place where she had been shot. But the wound had vanished, and with it the lights began to vanish and fade too.

He held her, weeping, refusing to let go, as if fearing she might slip from his grasp and return once more to the world of darkness beyond his reach.

"Tacit?" she muttered weakly, feeling she had returned to a safe place after a long, cold and terrible sleep. She was aware of strong arms holding her.

"You're all right," he wept, kissing her forehead and clutching her tightly. "You're all right."

"What have you done?" she whispered, "What have you done, Tacit?" For she knew the place from where she had come and she knew that she should never have returned, that some force, some power too great and terrible to comprehend had drawn her back.

"I told you," he said, wiping the blood and tears from her eyes, his chest shuddering as he swallowed. "I promised you, I would never leave you behind again." And he smiled and held her close to him, kissing her hairline.

ONE HUNDRED AND SEVEN

THE ITALIAN FRONT. THE SOČA RIVER. NORTHWEST SLOVENIA.

The storm hit the Carso with unnerving speed. All across the Karst Plateau, soldiers tried to seek shelter from the torrential rain and lashing lightning that had unleashed itself upon the world. Water flooded trenches and soaked anyone not able to find cover, turning the limestone mountain red with blood from the massacre on the plateau above.

On the pinnacle rock, Priests hunched beneath their drenched cloaks in wonderment at the powers being unleashed around them, each rejoicing at the forces being invoked and trusting that this time the offering, the baptism of blood, would be enough. All eyes were on the bearded High Priest and the kneeling six-fingered man in front of him, not able to tear their eyes away, not even for a moment to wipe the rain from their eyes.

"We have soaked the lands with the pure blood of the innocents," the High Priest began. "Into this let us spill Satan's blood that courses within his descendant's veins before me."

He turned the knives in his hands, the cold steel catching the rising moonlight and shards of white lightning clashing above.

"Abaddon, Prince of Darkness, Lord of the Abyss, I summon thee and thy princes forth from your chains of Hell! Cross over the Abyss! Ascend, and make manifest yourselves within our mortal world and with our mortal semblance. For he is returning and he must be protected. We are willing servants but unable to provide him the succour and protection he requires as he prepares to ascend once more to his throne. Only you, and your lieutenants, can offer him the solace of the shield and the mace. Share with us thy thoughts and make known to me thy will, for thou art our guardians, and we are thy foot soldiers."

The candles, which had remained lit despite the howling wind and the lashing rain, suddenly went out, plunging the pinnacle into darkness, the only faint light being that of the rising moon climbing ever higher.

But lights now began to appear in front of Pablo, swirling fiery balls, almost too bright to look at.

"With these blades I commit this final sacrifice." He looked down at Pablo and presented the knives to him. "Take them, and decide now if you wish a quick death from which all pain will be removed, or if you will have your hand forced and submit your soul to the endless torments of hell for the remainder of all time."

Pablo hesitated, unsure what was being asked of him. Abelli crouched and spoke into his ear. As if held in a trance, Pablo reached forward and took the daggers into his hands. He saw there were holds down the edges of both grips for the six fingers and thumbs of his hands. Now he understood. Now he knew why. Tears and rain mixed on his cheeks. He shuddered, his face racked with pain.

"It is time," growled the High Priest. He looked up and addressed the congregation in a loud clear voice. "Let his blood merge with that of the others fallen in this place, given to you as a sacrifice, and be as a lifeblood to their returning. We have praised you in the three sins, we have given you this mass sacrifice to provide succour for your thirsty tongues. Now we ask you to come across the great divide and be among us, to act as his defenders, his lieutenants and guide us all for when he returns!"

Lightning struck the pinnacle of rock and many of the Priests leapt in shock at the power which had gathered.

"So much majesty!" someone called. "They are coming! They are coming through! You can feel them!"

"My head!" another cried, his hands clutched to the side of it. "You can feel them! So much pressure! Too much!"

"Do it!" the High Priest commanded to Pablo. "Do it now!" And, as if in a trance, Pablo pulled the knives to his throat, and pressed the blades into his skin.

ONE HUNDRED AND EIGHT

The Italian Front. The Soča River. Northwest Slovenia.

Gathered around Isabella in the cavern below, transfixed by the miracle which had happened in front of their eyes, the first they knew that something was happening on the pinnacle above them was when the storm struck the broad shard of rock and the air turned electric. Tacit turned, his vision blurred with emotion and tears.

"They're coming," he growled, his face twisted with anger and revulsion. "They're coming through. Nothing can stop them now. Look after her." Tacit lifted Isabella gently from the ground and turned to place her in Henry's waiting arms. In the skies above the Karst, the dark storm shook the pinnacle. Tacit turned to look at the pentagram. The lines had begun to shimmer and smoke, as if an energy was forcing up between the interconnecting lines. "You all need to leave," he commanded, running his hand down Isabella's face. "Both of you, you cannot fight this. Get away. Get as far away as you can!" He stood and pointed with his finger to the passageway down which they had entered. "Quickly! Go!"

"Where are you going, Tacit?" Sandrine asked.

"Where am I am destined to go," said Tacit gravely.

"Tacit," said Henry, "what do you mean?"

"Inquisitor Cincenzo. He spoke my name, at the end, when he died."

"Yes," said Sandrine, tears in her own eyes. "He spoke it to Isabella."

Tacit nodded. "He knew. He knew it was me, the one who would complete the ritual. To close the circle. To bring them back. He wasn't telling you to find me. He was warning you that I would be the one to blame. I would be the one to bring them back."

"Where are you going now?" cried Henry after Tacit.

"To finish something I should have finished last time."

Tacit ran up the cavern slope, the toes of his boots biting into the limestone floor. Ahead he could see the opening to the pinnacle beyond, the wind and rain lashing down on the black rock and the figures gathered upon it. Lightning flashed and thunder shuddered, as if the forces of hell were finally being unleashed upon the place.

Tacit bounded up the slope, his teeth clenched, his fists tight white. He knew certain death lay ahead for him. He just hoped he could take as many of the Darkest Hand with him before his time was up.

In the mouth of the cave he could make out the outline of Georgi. He narrowed his eyes on his old friend and sped towards him.

A terrible noise erupted from behind him, the thundering pad of heavy feet on stone, the animalistic growl of a pack, chilling howls reverberating. At once Tacit stopped and turned wide-eyed to see a great clan of wolves appear out of the cavern, pouring from holes and side passageways and tearing up the passage towards him, wide blood-red jaws, glinting black talons, the odious stink of matted fur. Instinct kicked in and instantly he reached for this gun but it was too late, the wolves were upon him, swallowing him in their howling mass.

Rolling over and clawing his way to his feet, Tacit watched in shock and surprise as the wolves passed over him, leaving him unharmed. They charged onto the pinnacle and threw themselves into a killing frenzy on the Priests gathered for the ritual.

ONE HUNDRED AND NINE

The Italian Front. The Soča River. Northwest Slovenia.

At the very moment they attacked, Pablo snapped out of his trance and withdrew the knives from his throat.

"What are you doing?" shouted Corporal Abelli above the screams of the dying. "Cut your throat or reside forever in hell."

But Pablo shook his head, as all around them bodies were ripped down and devoured by slavering jaws and talons, the feel of the blows reverberating through the rock.

"Do it!" Abelli screamed, stretching towards him to force the blades back to his throat. But Pablo was too quick for him. He forced the tip of the right knife through Abelli's uniform and between his ribs, finishing hilt-deep in his chest. Abelli croaked and sank to his knees, the breath straining from his lungs, staring disbelievingly at Pablo before he toppled forward to lie still on the black rock. The heavens crashed with thunder and lightning and with it the pressure seemed to burst.

And the rain dashed down on Tacit, who had now run after the wolves onto the pinnacle, his murderous eyes on his old friend.

ONE HUNDRED AND TEN

THE ITALIAN FRONT. THE SOČA RIVER. NORTHWEST SLOVENIA.

Georgi caught sight of Tacit and smiled. He opened his hands, his right holding his blade dripping with wolf blood, as a sign for Tacit to come at him. Behind Georgi a narrow flight of stairs climbed above the pinnacle, running up and around a further needle of high stone. Georgi turned and ran up them, taking the steps two at a time. Instantly Tacit bounded after him.

The pinnacle shook and raged with the howls of wolves and dying Priests, smoke of the faltering ceremony drifting across the scene, flashing sparks of lightning punching through the clouds. Tacit charged up the winding stair, leaving the noise and chaos below, in and out of the lashing rain and wind, as he wound around the needle of rock. Forty stairs, cut by the elements, led to the narrow roof of the shard of black rock, appearing slick from the storm raging all about them.

At its edge stood Georgi, drenched in lashing rain, his head bowed, his dark eyes fierce on Tacit, his hands drawn into fists.

"Poldek!" he shouted in greeting through the storm.

"Georgi," replied Tacit. He was already soaked, his dark hair slick to his face, his overcoat stuck to his body by the torrential downpour. "It's over. I could gun you down right now," he said, pulling back his coat to reveal his revolver in its holster.

"You could," replied Georgi calmly, puckering his face in agreement, weighing the announcement in his mind, "but you won't. Because then you'd never know if you could beat me."

"I've beaten you already," growled Tacit.

"Have you?" replied Georgi, surprised. "I think not. I've beaten you, Poldek. Twice. You've done exactly what was required of you. You've opened the doors to hell. They are coming through." He turned his eyes skywards, rejoicing in the storm raging above them. "We've been waiting all our lifetimes for this moment. And now your work is complete."

"You're wrong," replied Tacit. "The wolves. They've killed everyone."

"Well then. I'm going to kill you, Poldek. You know that, don't you?"

"You'll try."

"Oh, I will try. And I will succeed. I'm going to kill you, slowly, so you can feel the shame at what you have done, what you have unleashed upon the world, for the petty emotion of love."

He came at Tacit wildly. He was strong, stronger than Tacit ever remembered, as if the opening of the doorway to hell had empowered him. But there was something not quite right, as if he was carrying a burden. As if the might of hell's curse weighed him down. Tacit swivelled to face him, his own fists raised. Georgi smiled.

"What is it, Tacit? Think you have the drop on me?"

"No," replied Tacit. "It's just that I feel no shame for saving Isabella. Putting love before hate."

He launched himself at Georgi, feigning a blow and catching his old friend on the side of the head as he tried to duck. Georgi rolled away, turning over onto his hands and knees and then springing to his feet, shaking the punch clear.

"What you have done?" Georgi cried, flinging himself forward, kicking out with his boots. Tacit parried the blows and pummelled him hard in the chest, putting Georgi onto his back. He rolled clear and sprang to his feet, breathing hard. "Are you not aware of what you have done to the world?"

"I have saved my love," replied Tacit, and he caught Georgi's leading fist and snapped hard at his wrist, battering him twice in the face and flinging him to the ground. He followed with a boot in the rib cage, turning Georgi over so that he rolled to the edge of the plateau, putting a little distance between himself and any more blows for the moment. "Tell me, Georgi, have you ever loved?"

Tacit moved towards him fast, hunkered low like a boxer, and swung with a strong right. Georgi ducked but Tacit caught him firm with a quick left followed by a devastating uppercut.

Georgi stumbled back, his hand to his chin, grimacing in admiration. He nodded and laughed coldly.

"Love?" he spat, so that bloody spittle splashed Tacit's face. "Pah! You talk of love. You cannot understand the true value of love till you have been touched by the Devil's care."

"The Devil has no care!" growled Tacit, stalking closer.

Georgi laughed louder, and seemed to grow more powerful as he did so.

"No care?! I think you'll find the Devil cares very much for those who serve him. Very much indeed." He charged Tacit and ducked at the last moment, battering him hard in the stomach and then bringing up his knee which he powered into Tacit's face. Tacit somersaulted backwards and landed hard on the ground. "I've unleashed hell!" cried Georgi, his eyes wild. "I'm stronger than I've ever been."

He leaped forward and Tacit tried to spring clear, but Georgi's speed was ferocious. He knocked Tacit back to the ground and kicked him hard in the head, skidding him across the shimmering wet stones. The plunging cliff face of the pinnacle grew near, and Tacit scratched hard with his fingertips to find grip and avoid going over the edge. "We're not here to love, Poldek! We're here to play our part. You? Me? We're mere cogs in a giant machine." Tacit came at him and Georgi spun forward in a cartwheel, knocking Tacit to his knees and then striking him in the temple with a downward punch.

Tacit lay on his back, staring up, his coat thrown open, rain pouring on his face. Georgi stood over him, smiling. "Tell me," he asked, swinging a boot hard into Tacit's side and making the giant man curl up. "Tell me, don't you ever feel that life is just one long cruel joke?"

He swung again, but Tacit caught his boot and spun him away, dragging his revolver from its holster. Immediately Georgi knocked it clear, spinning it out of his hand.

"No, my friend," he said, wagging a finger, "we do this the hard way. You and me. With fists. We never fought like this. Not when we were younger. I wanted to. Many times. To beat you. I envied you. I hated you."

He swung a fist and Tacit ducked under it, rolling away, his fingers splayed to the ground, watching every move his friend made. They circled each other, neither daring to make the next approach.

"That's why I loved cutting Mila open," said Georgi, his eyes flashing with dark pleasure.

Tacit snarled. "What are you talking about?"

But Georgi laughed and began to pace back around the other way, watching Tacit for any sign, any weakness to prove that his words had struck home. "She begged me, like a whore. Begged me to stop. Swore she'd come away with me, leave you, if only to save your child, but that wasn't in the plan. Me? I couldn't have cared less whether you did or not. But it was always you in their plans, you and the damned lights!"

Tacit surged forward, his aim and balance wild, shattered by his confusion and hatred. Georgi batted him aside with his fist, drawing yet more blood from his nose.

"Your child," he said. "It was a boy, you know?"

Tacit roared and launched himself, but Georgi ducked under his trailing arms and threw him over onto his back.

"It fought for life when I cut it from Mila's womb, though she clawed at me to stop, pleaded me not to kill it, or her. She would have made you proud, the way she fought, to save your son. He died in my arms. Slowly. Perished because of the cold and the blood in his lungs."

Scalding fury tore out of Tacit and he threw himself at Georgi, snatching out at him, looking to drag him with him to the edge of the pinnacle and throw him over. But Georgi spun aside and kicked Tacit away, toppling him instead over the edge.

Georgi ran to the side, laughing to see Tacit clinging by his fingertips to a rocky outcrop ten feet below.

He leaned over, hands on his hips, and shook his head.

"Yes, it was always the damned lights. For years you ignored them, scorned them. Never used them. Tried to follow the faithful, honourable path, without their wickedness influencing your life. Me? I was sent to do the Devil's bidding."

Tacit felt his fingers slip on the wet rock and found a new hold.

"I would offer you a hand but I'm otherwise engaged. I'll return to the cavern below. I'll find Isabella. I'll throttle the life out of her. And then I'll wait for the Dark Lord to call for me."

The aquamarine river swam up from below. Tacit swung across to try to find another hold but there were none to be found, his cold wet fingers beginning to ache.

"Come on, Poldek!" laughed Georgi, "don't keep us hanging around all day! There are a great many things I need to do. A certain person to kill, demons to meet."

A howl came from the stairs and Georgi turned just in time to see a huge feral creature leap from the stairs and cross the needle's tip. It landed squarely on his chest, bucking him backwards towards the edge. Georgi fought against gravity, his arms flapping wildly, his eyes manic. And then he slipped and fell. Shooting past Tacit, he managed to grasp Tacit's right boot and wrenched him from the pinnacle. Together they tumbled and fell in an embrace.

The wolf sat at the edge of the cliff face looking down and watched as the two figures fought and tussled all the way to the valley bottom before they hit the surface of the blue Soča River far, far below with an enormous splash.

ONE HUNDRED AND ELEVEN

THE ITALIAN FRONT. THE SOČA RIVER. NORTHWEST SLOVENIA.

On the summit of rock, the High Priest turned and surveyed the carnage all around him, his plans lying in bloodied, tattered ruins. Pablo was crouched on the floor still cradling the knives in his hands, one slick with Abelli's blood.

"You!" he cried, and it seemed as if the heavens thundered above him as he spoke. "Why could you not have done what was commanded of you? Forever now you are condemned to lie open to the torments of hell!"

He strode towards the terrified young man, who held his hands across his face in readiness for the killing blow. A shadow swept over him, something large, smelling of blood and rot, and instantly his eyes snapped open.

An enormous wolf stood between Pablo and the High Priest, standing on its hind legs but hunched over so that its giant front talons were almost scraping the surface of the rock floor. Even bowed, the wolf still towered above the tall bearded Priest, monstrous in size.

But if there was any fear in the Priest's mind, he showed none. He stared hard at the beast and spat at the ground in front of it.

"You dare to come and face me, condemned and cast down off-cut of man?" the Priest seethed, his eyes like flaming orbs, the burn on his face glistening in the rain. He took a step forward and pointed at the creature. "You do not have the authority to threaten me, if you cannot face me as a man! And you were stripped of that title long ago. Get out of here! Go back to your lair and your cursed existence!"

With that, the wolf reached up with one of its taloned hands and grappled at its neck, pulling the ragged pelt from its head. Instantly the wolf withered and shrank to the naked, gaunt figure of Poré.

"But I do face you as a man!" shouted Poré, and the High Priest glowered and sank back, his hand to his heart.

"What is this witchcraft?" he hissed.

"Do you not remember me, Cardinal Gílbert?" Poré asked, his pallid skin splashed with dirt and blood. The great bearded Priest hesitated, confused. "Many years ago you placed a curse upon me, but of a different kind, the condemnation to a life of full of bitterness, of longing, of questions. My family taken from me, sent to the rack and the torturer's chair of the Inquisition. Sent there by your hand!

"By the time I had regained enough of myself and my senses to seek you out, you had vanished from the Catholic Church, slipped into the black hole and onto this corrupt path you have followed ever since. I have sought you much of my life, and now I have found you. Now I shall have my revenge!"

But Cardinal Gílbert laughed. "Pathetic!" he spat. "That you should have carried such a burden of resentment and spite towards me for so long, and yet I have no memory of who you are, or your family. I suppose I should feel pride that you think of me with such passion, but then, I sent so many to the inquisitional chambers. And still so many are weak and in need of correction and grinding out, under the guidance of my Lord."

Poré shook his head. "No," he said. "It's over. It's finished."

But the Priest scowled, rage gathering in his face. "It's never finished!" he roared. "This is only the beginning! Now I see you, skin and bone!" His eyes grew wide. "All the easier to kill!" He reached for a knife at his belt and sprang forward, wrestling Poré to the ground and rolling with him over the prostrate figure of Pablo. His hand gripped tightly around Poré's gaunt throat, as he fumbled with his blade in the other. But as Poré struggled, he managed to snatch one of Pablo's knives and, turning over, raised it above his shoulder and plunged it deep into the High Priest's chest.

The six-fingered blade slipped effortlessly between his ribs. The air gushed out from Cardinal Gílbert's choked lips, as if his spirit was trying to flee his dying mortal remains before it was trapped within.

Poré fell away, lying with his back to the cold wet stone, and closed his eyes, the last of the power crackling and dying around him before everything went dark.

ONE HUNDRED AND TWELVE

The Italian Front. The Soča River. Northwest Slovenia.

In the moment the High Priest was slain, a noise and heat rose from the pentagram in the inner chamber below, a sound as if all the hordes in hell had been set free and a thousand thunderstorms were tearing open the heavens.

The broken vanquished powers came screaming from the claustrophobic chains of hell where they had been caged for so long, the cool air dissolving their ruptured, fractured shadows. Cursing and shrieking, the spectres of the princes of hell fought and clawed over each other to be the first to taste the air of earth, knowing that it would be for but a fleeting moment, a harrowing taunt of what they could have tasted, before their chains pulled them once more back into the fiery abyss. They took to the skies, spinning and evaporating in the moonlight like shadows before the sun, until only their frightful cries hung on the wind like a dark memory.

Sandrine sunk to her knees at the edge of the needle of stone, high above the pinnacle, the last of the rain washing the filth from her body. She lay there panting for breath, the low sun now breaking from between the clouds on the western horizon, capturing her in its final warming rays.

There was a noise from the steps behind her and, exhausted, she turned her head to look, as Henry and Isabella appeared. Henry set Isabella down and rushed forward, taking Sandrine into his arms, removing his coat and setting it about her, pressing the hair away from her face.

"Sandrine!" he cried. "Sandrine! My darling! Are you all right?"

She nodded, slumping in his arms. He looked around the empty circle of rock.

"Tacit!" cried Isabella, weeping and holding her hand to her mouth. "Where is he?"

"Gone," replied Sandrine, tears of remorse and pain in her eyes. "He fell." She looked over the edge of the cliff and cried long into Henry's chest as he pulled her close to him. "They came through," she sobbed. "The demons. They came through. I heard them! I heard them come!"

But Henry shook his head. "No. They were only shadows of what might have been. The summoning was stopped. It is over."

Isabella got to her feet and shakily staggered to the edge, peering over it. She screamed out to the valley far below, sinking to her knees, sobbing uncontrollably. She felt hands around her shoulders and let Sandrine embrace her.

Dusk fell. The three of them huddled close on the pinnacle of rock, chilled and sodden. The storm had stopped in an instant. They clutched onto each other, both weeping and cursing, sometimes animated and enraged, at other times quiet and withdrawn.

A gentle wind tugged at Isabella as she closed her wet eyes to the breeze and tried to make sense of everything. Tacit, the man they had followed, the man she had loved, was gone. Dead. He couldn't have survived such a fall, a mile drop into a surging river far below. A noise drew them all to look towards the steps up to the stone circle. Pablo approached cautiously, hands gripped in front of him as if in prayer, his head bowed like a subservient slave to a master.

"He's gone!" he cried. "Poré, the one who came as a wolf. He killed the High Priest, the one he called Cardinal Gilbert. I saw it, with my own eyes. Stabbed him clean through the heart with one of the daggers." The words came like a cascade, a rush of noise.

"Poré!" muttered Sandrine, shaking her head so her damp lank hair tickled the edge of her shoulders. There was the hint of a smile on her lips, amazement twinned with admiration. "So he followed us, all this way! I thought he'd died at the Mass for Peace."

"How did he know?" asked Isabella. "How did he know to come here? Is he still on the summit?"

"He was," replied Pablo. "But he left. He took the wolves with him."

"Small mercies," Isabella added, looking across at Henry and Sandrine.

"What do we do now?" asked Sandrine.

"We get off this mountain," said Henry. "We get far away from here. The Austro-Hungarians," he said, looking away to the east, "they're gathering for another assault."

"Take me with you!" pleaded Pablo, his hands bound together in a white knot. "I have nothing left here."

"How can you say that?" asked Sandrine. "What about your war?"

But he shook his head. "It is not my war. It never was. They groomed me for this moment, those Priests dressed in black. I cannot follow that same path, not now, not after all I have seen and heard and done."

ONE HUNDRED AND THIRTEEN

Two weeks later.
The Vatican. Vatican City.

The sun scorched the cobbled street, the flagstones so hot that to walk barefoot would burn one's feet within a few steps. Children squealed and splashed in the pools and fountains, their shimmering skin roasting under the endless glare of the sun. Their shrieks of delight sounded like a festival after recent dismal days, everyone seemingly buoyed by the return of the warming sun which had lifted the gloom that had engulfed the city for so long.

Father Strettavario stood looking down into the clear waters.

"And the third angel poured out his vial upon the rivers and fountains of waters. And they became blood."

Strettavario looked up at the figure who had stepped close to him unnoticed and quoted from the bible.

"Cardinal Bishop Adansoni," said Strettavario, smiling weakly.

Adansoni smiled. "All along I suspected it was an algae infestation which turned the waters red. Not the Devil at all." He looked long into the waters, his lips pursed in thought, before turning back at the old hunched Priest. "Why've you come here, Father Strettavario? Usually only tourists come here to the Trevi Fountain hoping for a miracle? Do you not have sermons to read, Priests to admonish, Inquisitors to scrutinise?"

Crowds of people drifted about them, chattering and gesticulating. Ladies dressed in pretty white dresses, cooling themselves with matching fans, threw coins into the waters. Men, moustached and elegant in their open-collared shirts and waistcoats, tutted and laughed, before guiding their wives away to the shade of Roman side-streets. Strettavario could hear that the main topic of the conversation was the war and Italy's checked expansions into the east.

"What is the point, Cardinal Bishop Adansoni, of anything?" shrugged Strettavario. "Tacit is dead. Perhaps it is a miracle I'm hoping for as well?" he said, before throwing three coins from his own pocket into the waters and walking away.

ONE HUNDRED AND FOURTEEN

A dust devil blew across Orange County, a spiralling column of stinging sand that made the two figures walking up South Raitt Street turn their faces away.

"Why ever did I agree to an afternoon walk?" asked the man in the light cotton plaid suit, knocking his hat against his hand once the whirlwind had passed. "A lie down after today's matinee would have suited me far better, Noah."

"Nonsense, Ethan!" exclaimed the man next to him, smoothing down his hair and running his fingertips down the lengths of his moustache. "What better way is there to spend an hour than in the great outdoors?"

"There's dust in my eyes," Ethan replied, looking down McFadden Avenue dismally. "We really shouldn't have ventured out. I have quite a headache."

"And I must say, Ethan, that you have become quite a headache yourself. All day. Your performance this lunchtime at Clunes Theatre was barely passable. The critics will have a field day. If you're going to commune with the dead, or at least give the impression that you are, you really need to do so with a little more passion. As your agent it's my duty to speak truthfully and the truth is you sounded as morose on stage as those you were trying to raise."

Noah searched in a pocket for his cigarette case and drew it out, offering one to the clairvoyant. Ethan shook his head and took a deep breath, letting it out in a long exhalation. "We have a reputation to uphold," continued his agent, lighting a cigarette for himself. He picked a strand of tobacco from the tip of his tongue before blowing smoke out of his nose. "People come from all over to witness the miracle of you speaking with the dead. Don't let them down, dear fellow, and, more to the point, don't let us down." He pressed a finger into Ethan's breast, before flattening his hair with a palm and taking another puff on his cigarette. He looked back and studied his colleague closely. "That said, you do look a bit peaky. Perhaps you're ailing with something after all?"

"I think I am."

"I suggest a strong drink and a little sleep before this evening's performance."

A black saloon car drove slowly past, the driver, a Priest, watching them intently.

"And the meek shall inherit the earth," Noah muttered under his breath, watching the expensive car vanish down another avenue. "More like the bloody wealthy shall inherit it." He turned his attention back to his charge and slapped him gently across the shoulder, as if to shock the despondency from him. "Rest and a strong drink. What do you do say?"

But the clairvoyant shook his head. "I don't need rest, or a strong drink, Noah. I just need to get this ... this malaise off my mind."

"And what exactly is this malaise?"

"A most ghastly feeling. About the world."

"For Christ's sake, Ethan!" muttered Noah, taking a drag on his cigarette and slipping a hand into his suit pocket. "Can you not save the apocalyptic visions for your performances? These emotional outbursts are exactly what your act has been missing recently. What our paying public are wanting. Terror! Revelation! Excitement!" He scrunched his chin into the neck of his shirt. "Try not to use up all your energy when there's no one around to witness it, dear fellow!"

"But this feeling, it's been nagging at me for days."

"Probably the chicken salad you had in the Lancaster. I warned you at the time to eat only beef in those places. You never risk poultry at a steakhouse."

"There's something coming, Noah," said Ethan, growing ever more serious.

"Yes, so you said," replied Noah.

"A war."

"A war?" said the agent, and he frowned, as if the word unsettled him. "Whatever do you mean? Surely you don't mean this damned war in Europe?"

"I do. I mean exactly that."

"And how exactly does a war on the other side of the world concern America?"

"Because America's going to join it," said Ethan, deathly pale. "I just know it. America's going to join Britain and France in the war and things will turn far worse than anything that has gone before."

EPILOGUE

The Priest knocked twice and entered only when he received the invitation to do so. It seemed to him that the chamber beyond had grown even colder since he had visited it earlier that day. A single candle, black, burned on the central table, weak flickering light seeping into the corners of the room. A solitary figure stood in one corner, his back turned to the door.

"Well?" the figure asked.

"It … it failed," said the Priest.

At once the figure spun on the messenger, skewering him with a piercing stare. "What do you mean 'it failed'?"

"Wolves," the Priest replied, his own voice appearing to disbelieve what it was he was saying, before he cleared his throat and said the word again, more clearly this time and with it a name. "Poré."

The hunched figure's eyes narrowed, the light in them ice-cold. "What about him?"

"He was there. He arrived. With wolves. They killed everyone before the ceremony could be completed."

The figure in the shadows slowly shut his eyes as if he could not stand to look at the world any longer, turning his head away. "And Tacit?" he asked. "What about him?"

"Dead," replied the Priest. "He fell, with Georgi, into the gorge. They were swept away by the Soča River. We have dredged it but found no trace of either of them. It's over. It's finished."

The figure rocked gently where he stood and, for a moment the Priest thought his master was weeping silently. "No," he said solemnly, grit in his words. "It is only just beginning." He turned and stepped away towards the window. "His returning is nigh. Born upon a battlefield too terrible to conceive, he will come and tear down all that has gone before. Nothing can stop this from unfurling. We must be ready, and protect him the best we can, even if we are without his lieutenants. Gather around him powerful people and forces of the world. Summon all demons to be his protectors. Make sure witches prepare their most potent incantations."

He watched the birds through the open window. "His lieutenants' return has been thwarted. It falls then to mortal men alone to protect him and see that he grows into a position of power from where his plans may finally be realised."

And it seemed to him that there were fewer crows within the square and that there were doves now returning in the dusky sky.

ACKNOWLEDGEMENTS

A huge thank you to all my friends and family who have supported and encouraged me throughout the writing of *The Fallen*. The demands of writing a novel, and the sacrifices you and those close to you have to make, are considerable. I would have struggled to achieve what I have without their unwavering belief and motivation.

I have been so touched by how many people have got behind both me and the books of The Darkest Hand trilogy. Heartfelt thanks to Claire Eastham, everyone in Farley (particularly the Thursday night drinkers), Waterstones Salisbury (especially Jo and Leonie), the Salisbury Writing Circle, Tom Bromley, Russell Mardell, Dave Key, Paul Malone, Joy and Andrew Bailey for the use of their 'cliff top writing cell' and fellow Duckworth housemate Ed Davey.

Once again, my agent Ben Clark at LAW has supported and guided me with endless wisdom and grace. If you knew just a little of what I put him through, you'd be in awe of him. I am lucky to have him and LAW on my side.

Big thanks goes to my fantastic, and ever patient, editor at Duckworth, Nikki Griffiths. Inquisitor Poldek Tacit has never been the easiest of individuals to keep under control and yet she seems to have expertly and effortlessly found a way. The whole team at Duckworth Overlook deserve a mention for the support and encouragement they've given me from the start. They, and Overlook Press, my American publisher, are wonderful publishing houses and I'm proud to be part of them.

Finally, many thanks to both Jon Phillips at Muen and Paul Clifton Photography for proving a sow's ear can make a silk purse.

NOTES

There has been woefully little written about the Italian Front during the First World War. This third, seemingly forgotten, front of the conflict, fought in some of the most extreme of conditions and costing almost one and a half million men, has always stood in the shadow of the desperate horrors of the Western Front and the inconceivable destruction of the Eastern Front. For Italian soldiers to have wished for nothing more than to be transported to the flooded killing fields of the Somme rather than face an enemy on a brittle inhospitable shard of rock gives you some idea of what those poor men must have experienced.

Thank goodness for Mark Thompson's *The White War*, both eloquently written and passionate in its details. It was the bedrock upon which I began my research for this novel. H.P. Willmott's *World War I* proved an invaluable and accessible book regarding maps and visual references for weapons and uniforms. Also, Peter Hart's *The Great War* was, once again, a reliable and solid reference tome for the war as a whole.

ALSO BY TARN RICHARDSON

THE HUNTED

Discover the free eBook prequel to THE DAMNED

In the bustling streets of Sarajevo in June 1914, the dead body of a priest lies, head shattered by the impact of a fall from a building high above. As the city prepares for the arrival of Archduke Franz Ferdinand, grim-faced inquisitor Poldek Tacit is faced not only with the challenge of discovering why the priest has been killed but also confronting other menaces: the demon rumoured to be at large in the city and the conspirators of the Black Hand organisation who plan to assassinate the Archduke.

With terrible danger only ever one step away and his private demons silenced only by strong drink, *The Hunted* introduces us to the damaged soul that is the unorthodox Catholic inquisitor Poldek Tacit. It is a world both like and unlike our own, where evil assumes many horrific forms, from werewolves to the slaughter of the trenches and where the threat to humanity–and to love–is ever constant.

NOW AVAILABLE AS A FREE EBOOK

ALSO BY TARN RICHARDSON

THE DAMNED

1914. The outbreak of war.

In the French city of Arras, a priest is brutally murdered. The Catholic Inquisition sends its most determined and unhinged of Inquisitors, Poldek Tacit, to investigate.

On the French battlefield, armed forces, led by Britain and Germany, must confront each other. But a mutual foe more terrible than any solider can imagine lies waiting beneath the killing fields; waiting for the light of the moon for the slaughter to begin.

Faced with impossible odds and his own demons, Tacit must confront the forces of evil, and a church determined at all costs to achieve its aims, to reach the heart of a dark conspiracy that seeks to engulf the world and plunge it ever deeper into conflict.

Set in an alternative twentieth century, in a world overwhelmed by total war and mysterious dark forces, *The Damned* is the first gripping instalment in *The Darkest Hand* series.

'A kind of three-way mash-up of horror fiction, war novel and ecclesiastical thriller…. it works surprisingly well.' ***Daily Mail***

'A sublime work of dark fiction meets mystery, meets horror… It is fast paced, atmospheric, it blends genres with ease and it keeps you hooked throughout.' *Intravenous Magazine*

OUT NOW

ABOUT THE AUTHOR

Tarn Richardson was brought up a fan of Tolkien, in a remote house, rumoured to be haunted, near Taunton, Somerset. He has worked as a copywriter, written mystery murder dinner party games and worked in digital media for nearly twenty years. He is the author of *The Darkest Hand* series, comprised of *The Damned*, *The Fallen*, *The Risen*, and free eBook prequel *The Hunted*. He lives near Salisbury with his wife and two sons.

COMMUNITY HELPERS

Mail Carriers

by Christina Leaf

BLASTOFF! READERS

BELLWETHER MEDIA • MINNEAPOLIS, MN

Note to Librarians, Teachers, and Parents:

Blastoff! Readers are carefully developed by literacy experts and combine standards-based content with developmentally appropriate text.

Level 1 provides the most support through repetition of high-frequency words, light text, predictable sentence patterns, and strong visual support.

Level 2 offers early readers a bit more challenge through varied simple sentences, increased text load, and less repetition of high-frequency words.

Level 3 advances early-fluent readers toward fluency through increased text and concept load, less reliance on visuals, longer sentences, and more literary language.

Level 4 builds reading stamina by providing more text per page, increased use of punctuation, greater variation in sentence patterns, and increasingly challenging vocabulary.

Level 5 encourages children to move from "learning to read" to "reading to learn" by providing even more text, varied writing styles, and less familiar topics.

Whichever book is right for your reader, Blastoff! Readers are the perfect books to build confidence and encourage a love of reading that will last a lifetime!

This edition first published in 2018 by Bellwether Media, Inc.

No part of this publication may be reproduced in whole or in part without written permission of the publisher. For information regarding permission, write to Bellwether Media, Inc., Attention: Permissions Department, 5357 Penn Avenue South, Minneapolis, MN 55419.

Library of Congress Cataloging-in-Publication Data

Names: Leaf, Christina, author.
Title: Mail Carriers / by Christina Leaf.
Description: Minneapolis, MN : Bellwether Media, Inc., [2018] | Series: Blastoff! Readers: Community Helpers | Includes bibliographical references and index.
Identifiers: LCCN 2017032150 (print) | LCCN 2017041182 (ebook) | ISBN 9781626177475 (hardcover : alk. paper) | ISBN 9781681034485 (ebook) | ISBN 9781618913081 (pbk. : alk. paper)
Subjects: LCSH: Letter carriers–Juvenile literature.
Classification: LCC HE6241 (ebook) | LCC HE6241 .L43 2018 (print) | DDC 383/.145–dc23
LC record available at https://lccn.loc.gov/2017032150

Text copyright © 2018 by Bellwether Media, Inc. BLASTOFF! READERS and associated logos are trademarks and/or registered trademarks of Bellwether Media, Inc. SCHOLASTIC, CHILDREN'S PRESS, and associated logos are trademarks and/or registered trademarks of Scholastic Inc., 557 Broadway, New York, NY 10012.

Editor: Nathan Sommer   Designer: Brittany McIntosh

Printed in the United States of America, North Mankato, MN.

Table of Contents

Chilly Delivery

The mail carrier climbs out of his truck. Icy wind stings his face.

The mail carrier puts letters in the mailbox. Cold weather does not stop him!

What Are Mail Carriers?

Mail carriers pick up and **deliver** mail. They work for **post offices**.

Mail carriers serve towns, cities, and the **countryside**. Their delivery **routes** visit homes and businesses.

What Do Mail Carriers Do?

Mail carriers sort mail at the post office. Then they put it into mailbags or trucks.

13

Many mail carriers drive. Their trucks carry **packages** and letters.

Other mail
carriers walk.
They carry mail
in their bags.

Mail Carrier Gear

mail truck   mailbag   hat   mail tray

17

What Makes a Good Mail Carrier?

Mail carriers are strong. Many walk miles with heavy mailbags.

Mail Carrier Skills

✓ active   ✓ friendly

✓ strong   ✓ orderly

Mail carriers are friendly, too. **Customers** ask questions. What mail is there today?

Glossary

countryside

land outside of cities or towns

packages

boxes and other packs filled with things to be mailed

customers

people who pay for goods or services

post offices

places where mail is received, sorted, and sent

deliver

to take something and bring it to someone else

routes

paths that are commonly traveled

To Learn More

AT THE LIBRARY

Kenan, Tessa. *Hooray for Mail Carriers!*
Minneapolis, Minn.: Lerner Publications,
2018.

Murray, Julie. *Mail Carriers.* Minneapolis,
Minn.: Abdo Kids, 2016.

Shepherd, Jodie. *A Day with Mail Carriers.*
New York, N.Y.: Children's Press, 2013.

ON THE WEB

Learning more about
mail carriers is as easy
as 1, 2, 3.

1. Go to www.factsurfer.com.

2. Enter "mail carriers" into the search box.

3. Click the "Surf" button and you will see a
   list of related web sites.

With factsurfer.com, finding more information
is just a click away.

Index

The images in this book are reproduced through the courtesy of: fotog/ Tetra Images/ SuperStock, front cover; karamysh, pp. 2-3; kdow, pp. 4-5; Bloomberg/ Getty Images, pp. 6-7; Jim West/ Alamy, pp. 8-9; Zoran Milich/ Getty Images, pp. 10-11; 400tmax, pp. 12-13, 17 (mail tray); Peter Titmuss, pp. 14-15; Justin Sullivan/ Getty Images, pp. 16-17; Leonard Zhukovsky, p. 17 (mail truck); Keith Homan, p. 17 (mailbag, hat); rappensuncle, pp. 18-19; United States Postal Service, pp. 20-21; Thomas Dekiere, p. 22 (top left); Syda Productions, p. 22 (center left); MikeDotta, p. 22 (bottom left); Kaesler Media, p. 22 (top right); Kumar Sriskandan/ Alamy, p. 22 (center right); pio3, p. 22 (bottom right).